They Called Me

The Cat

Margaret Routcliffe

Order this book online at www.trafford.com/08-0650
or email orders@trafford.com

Most Trafford titles are also available at major online book retailers.

© Copyright 2008 Margaret Routcliffe.

All rights reserved. No part of this publication may be reproduced, stored in a retrieval system, or transmitted, in any form or by any means, electronic, mechanical, photocopying, recording, or otherwise, without the written prior permission of the author.

Note for Librarians: A cataloguing record for this book is available from Library and Archives Canada at www.collectionscanada.ca/amicus/index-e.html

Printed in Victoria, BC, Canada.

Cover Design/Artwork by Margaret Routcliffe.
Designed by Margaret Routcliffe.

ISBN: 978-1-4251-7893-2

We at Trafford believe that it is the responsibility of us all, as both individuals and corporations, to make choices that are environmentally and socially sound. You, in turn, are supporting this responsible conduct each time you purchase a Trafford book, or make use of our publishing services. To find out how you are helping, please visit www.trafford.com/responsiblepublishing.html

Our mission is to efficiently provide the world's finest, most comprehensive book publishing service, enabling every author to experience success. To find out how to publish your book, your way, and have it available worldwide, visit us online at www.trafford.com/10510

www.trafford.com

North America & international
toll-free: 1 888 232 4444 (USA & Canada)
phone: 250 383 6864 ♦ fax: 250 383 6804
email: info@trafford.com

The United Kingdom & Europe
phone: +44 (0)1865 487 395 ♦ local rate: 0845 230 9601
facsimile: +44 (0)1865 481 507 ♦ email: info.uk@trafford.com

10 9 8 7 6 5 4 3 2

This book is dedicated to my friends and family that believed in me and taught me to believe in myself. They taught me that if you believe in yourself than all your dreams can come true.

Chapter One

Sitting on the porch looking out over the bay, it now seems so long ago, and yet at times it seems like only yesterday. So many years have passed since this old woman was that lonely child, who was out on her own at such a very early age. We have come very far since those days of affairs and murders, but we did survive them. Now, when I look back on those days, I know why my friends called me "The Cat". It wasn't because of the pitch black hair that I was born with, or the mysterious eyes that no-one knew what went on behind them, but it was more for the number of lives that I had lived. Now that I am in my ninth life, I know that there won't be any more after this one.

They told me that when I was born on that cold, wet Friday the thirteenth, that I was special, although I never quite understood why. They said that anyone who was born on Friday the thirteenth was lucky. However, on the night that I was born there was the brightest full moon that they had ever seen, especially in March.

From day one, I fought for what was rightfully mine. The dynasty that was mine from the day I was born, and there wasn't anyone who would do me out of it. They say the strong shall survive and the meek shall inherit the earth, but I was determined to prove I could accomplish both, and proceeded to do just that.

Before being nicknamed "The Cat", I learned to use the talents of that animal to my benefit. Although, I was named Stephanie McConnell, I suited "The Cat" better. Cats, if you watch them, will suck up to people with sweetness and charm so that no-one can ever refuse them. You must however, always be on guard with them, as their claws will come out in a blink of an eye if you ever cross them.

I was able to learn about these fascinating creatures first hand when I toured Africa with my family. I never understood at that time, why we were there but I later found out that my father was doing a study for the University he worked for. Being young, I cared only about having fun and learning about the animals; this was both fun and fascinating. The lion and tiger cubs were so cute and playful, that it was hard to believe that these were creatures that could do us harm. I learned to observe them at a distance. I watched how gentle they would be toward their young, and how they would then turn into ferocious animals when other creatures approached their young even if they were just children.

The monkeys were quite different and so carefree that they would eventually come up and make friends with you. You wouldn't want to trust these friends though. If you didn't watch them they would go into the tents and pull everything out and then run off. It was we the kids who were at fault when our parents discovered the mess and not the monkeys. When I look at my mother's pictures of the campsites where we stayed, I must say they didn't do justice to these places. It was impossible to capture by camera or on canvas the serenity found there. The waterfall pouring into a small lake with hardly a ripple in it, the sounds of water meeting water at the falls and birds calling to one another were just a few of the things that couldn't be captured by the camera.

Looking back at the pictures brought back memories of what life was like back then. If I looked at them long enough I could feel the dry heat, the large ferns slapping us (the kids) in the face when we walked along the trails. In trees and vines overhead, we heard the chattering monkeys that were climbing or jumping. The trails were full of adventure. There were interesting sights to see with every step. There might have been a small lizard or a snake crawling on the ground or in the trees. There could be a flower that you had never seen before. At night, we usually set up camp by water of some kind, a lake or a river, with the tents in a clearing area. No matter where you were the insects followed. The only time that you seemed to find relief from those pesky things was when it would rain. It was times like these that Mother would hand us a cake of soap and tell us to take advantage of the shower that the Lord had sent us. During one of these times, a monkey who had become somewhat of a pet of ours, decided to join in. Picking up a cake of soap, he tried to imitate our actions. He thought that this was great fun until he got some soap in his mouth. With foam in his mouth, he began jumping up and down. What a sight! You would have thought that we had tried to kill him!

    They say that because of my two months stay in Africa's heat, I can stand the heat so much now. The time over there seemed to fly by and then it was time for us to return home. Who was to know that when we returned to the United States our lives would change so drastically?

Chapter Two

We arrived back home to our little white cottage in the small town of Shellscliff, Maine. We lived right on the edge of the water. That suited us, the kids, just fine, since there was always something to do, but it drove our poor Mother crazy. She never knew if we were up the coast or down the coast, if we were in the water or in the caves on the shoreline.

Having been home for two months now, the twins and I were right at home getting into all kinds of mischief. My brother Ben (one of the twins), had suggested that we play a game of hide-and-seek. This was usually a great game since there were always so many great places to hide, especially on the beach. We told Bridgette (the other twin) that she could be it. Though the twins were the oldest among the three of us, Bridgette should have been a blonde instead of a redhead, because she never really seemed to have much on the ball. Ben, on the other hand was blonde with blue eyes and brains.

Even at our ages, which at this time were nine for the twins and seven for me, we seemed to have our minds made up as to what we would do in life. Ben, because he was such a whiz at anything that he touched, thought that he would like to follow in the mathematical field. Bridgette, because she only cared about looking great and having people like her, thought that she would like to be an actor. Unlike my brother and sister, I wanted to be not only rich, powerful and known to the entire, but I wanted to be able to run my own dynasty.

Back to our friendly game of hide-and-seek. While Bridgette started to count, Ben and I took off to hide. We knew that we would have more than enough time to hide as she was so slow in counting. Ben took off to the caves up the coast, since hiding there was so easy unless the tide was coming in. I decided to go in the opposite direction and hide in the bushes, just up from the beach. This was my favourite hiding spot, since you could see anybody going up or down the beach. We stayed in our hiding places for what seemed to be about an hour and still there was no Bridgette. I started to think this was odd, but decided I would enjoy the sunshine.

Where I was hiding, there was a little opening in the bushes, where you could lay down and get a nice sun tan without anyone disturbing you. I must have dozed off into a nice sleep because when I woke up, the sun had drifted away. I could see that it was late afternoon, but where was Bridgette or for that matter where was Ben? I decided that I would go looking for Ben since if he was in his normal hiding spot, the tide would soon be coming in to meet him. I went up to his normal cave and yelled to him, "Hey Ben have you seen Bridgette yet?" There was no response. I thought that this was strange, surely they wouldn't have called off the game and not come looking for me. I kept calling out to him, as I slowly went into the cave. You could hear the tide slowly getting closer and closer. If he didn't come out soon or answer, then I would have to leave or get stranded in the cave. I kept on going until I tripped over something. As I picked myself up, I yelled at the top of my lungs. "Ben, if you thought that was funny, you better start to run now, because you won't like what I'm going to do to you." Again there was no answer. So I started to look around to see what I had tripped on and then I saw that it was Ben. I hit him in the face and yelled at him to wake up, but he didn't seem to hear me. So I started to drag him. They always kidded me that I was rough and tough, but I wasn't that strong. Still I had to get him away from the cave before the tide came in. It seemed like forever, but finally I got him to safety. I knew that I couldn't drag him any farther so I left him while I ran up to the house. I yelled all the way there but no one seemed to hear me. As I went into the house there was Mother tending to Bridgette, who apparently had taken ill shortly after we had left her. Quickly, I told Mother about Ben and where I had left him.

"You stay with Bridgette while I go and get Ben, just keep watching her." Mother told me as she ran out the door to get Ben.

Mother came back with Ben in her arms, placing him on the bed next to Bridgette. Neither one of them was moving. I got the terrible feeling that they were dead. I stood at the doorway just looking at the two of them. All of a sudden I felt a hand on my forehead.

"Stephanie, you feel fine, so why don't you go outside and play for a while. Let me take care of the twins." Mother was saying to me as she headed back into the room with another cloth for Ben's head.

When Father arrived home from the University that night, the twin's fever still had not broken, so he called the doctor over. When the doctor arrived it seemed like that they were in the room checking the twins for hours, but still the twins were not awake. The doctor came into the living room and took blood from the rest of us. From the point of view of a seven year old this was scary stuff; people coming and taking your blood.

After a long night, where our parents took turns watching the twins, placing cold compresses on their heads, the doctor returned with news that would change my life. They had run tests on the blood that they had taken from all of us and found that the twins were the only ones that had contracted the disease. They had no idea what the disease was and could only advise that we take the twins to Boston General Hospital to have more thorough tests done. The only possibility that they could come up with was that the twins might have caught the virus in Africa. So in the morning I found myself on a train to someplace in Ontario, Canada, to an Aunt and Uncle that I never even knew that I had. My mother and the twins went off on another train to Boston.

Chapter Three

It seemed like I was on the train forever, although the stewards kept me amused by playing games with me. There were games like I Spy, Xes and Ohs and of course I couldn't forget the odd game of Hide and Seek in the baggage car. Although I got to do these things, I was very much alone. You see I had never travelled by myself before, I had always travelled with my family and this trip seemed very scary for a little girl to make by herself. I would go to sleep every night hearing the clicking of the tracks under the train's wheels. Just before drifting off, I would hear the voice of my father. "Don't worry you will be fine. You're my strong little girl; besides it won't be long and you'll be back with us."
I wish I knew than what I would later find out, but at that time these things comforted me enough to put me to sleep. I hoped that the morning would bring the day that I could go back home. Some days I would look out the windows and think what a pretty countryside and how lucky I was to own it all. After all, what else would a child think. This seemed be my new home as the days went slowly by. Then one day, the steward by the name of Tom came and said, "Hey, little one it's time to get yourself ready. The next stop will be yours and we want you pretty for your Aunt and Uncle now, don't we." I was so happy at the thought of finally getting off this train. I was trying to help put my clothes in my suitcase, but instead I just kept tripping over things and making things worse for Tom. So finally, he put me up beside the window and said, "Now you just sit and look out the window until we get to the station and let me continue getting your stuff together, okay." We both agreed that I would just sit

there taking in the sights, until we got to the station.

I got scared then; everything was so large that I thought for sure I would get lost. I started to cry at the thought of never seeing my family again. Tom seemed to realize what had happened and quickly comforted me by saying, "Hey, what's the matter with you? Did you think that I was going to leave you out here all by yourself to find your Aunt and Uncle? Well I have news for you, I'm staying right at your side until they come, what do you think of that?"

I replied, "I am so happy that you are staying with me, but how are we going to locate my Aunt and Uncle? I don't know what they look like and they have never met me?"

"Well, you see we will just have them paged. It's as simple as that," he said.

"What does it mean to have somebody paged?" I replied. I was just a child, and to me that meant that we had to put them in a book.

"When we have somebody paged we have their names called out on a loud speaker." Just as he was explaining a voice called out above us; "Train on Track Nine now leaving for Montreal in five minutes."

So off we went to the information desk to have my Aunt and Uncle paged. The next thing we heard was, "Now paging Mr. and Mrs. Pat McConnell, would you please come to the information desk at the north entrance of the station?" We waited and waited, and then Tom asked the person at the desk to make the call again. I sat and listened to the girl page my Uncle and Aunt again, "Would Mr. or Mrs. Pat McConnell please come to the information desk at the north entrance of the station, thank you." I started to get worried that maybe my Aunt and Uncle had forgotten that they were to meet me. Maybe something happened to them and I would have no place to go. Then what would happen to me? I sat and waited for what I considered to be a long time, but Tom said it was maybe fifteen minutes. Still I thought that it was a long time before a young and good looking lad came up to the information desk.

"I am answering the page for Mr. Pat McConnell." Now looking at the person I knew that he couldn't possibly be my Uncle, yet here he was saying, "I am here to pick up Stephanie McConnell."

Tom stepped forward and said, "Let me introduce you to Miss Stephanie McConnell, sir. And who might you be?"

"I am Master Stuart McConnell, my parents sent me to pick up my little cousin Stephanie." He sounded so upper class that I was wondering where I was going to be living.

"These are the bags that she brought with her," Tom said as he gave him the bags. Then he turned to me and said, "Now you go with your cousin Stuart and have a nice visit and maybe we will see you when you are going back home, okay?" I wished him good-bye and left with Stuart to go to the car. Now Stuart was a young lad as I said before, but he wasn't of driving age yet. So how were we getting home?

"Stuart, how are we getting home? Is Aunt Elizabeth or Uncle Pat waiting for us in the car?" I decided to ask. After all, how else do you get answers.

"No, they will be waiting at home; Charles will be taking us there." Now he got me going again. "Who's Charles?" I asked.

"Well he is our chauffeur," was his reply.

I might have been only seven, but I did know that we didn't have a chauffeur and only people who had money had them. We got to the car and Charles met us there.

"May I take the bags Master Stuart?" He put the bags in the trunk. Then as he came around and opened the door, he said,

"May I help you in Lady Stephanie?" I accepted his outstretched hand. A cute little smile crossed my face because no one had ever called me Lady Stephanie before. Later when I met my Aunt, no-one in the house would ever call me that again except when she gave her approval. I got seated in the car and Stuart climbed in after me. "I hope you had lots of rest on the train, because we have approximately another hour by car to the house."

I said, "Another hour!" He could tell right off the bat that I was not happy about sitting for another hour. "Hey, don't worry I'll show you the sights as we go." And that is just what he did.

First he lifted me up on his knee so that I could see out the window. He then started to show me the sights, from the tiniest detail to the largest item. By the time we reached the long driveway I felt as though I had lived there all my life. I knew I had found at least one friend in Stuart, if not two including Charles.

When I first saw the driveway I was glad that we were driving and not walking for I couldn't see the end of it. When we finally got to the end, there was a huge mansion of a house there. At first I thought that it was a palace. Finally Charles stopped the car and helped me out of the car. He proceeded to remove my bags from the trunk and handed them to a girl that had just come out of the house. She took them into the house without a word. Stuart said, "Come on Stephanie, I'll take you to meet the rest of the family before dinner." He took me into the house and started to go through room after room.

"Stuart, whatever you do, please don't leave me alone in one of these rooms, because I'll get lost," I called to him. He just laughed as we proceeded through the maze of rooms. We finally came to a room with large comfy looking chairs in it.

"Father, are you in here?" Stuart called out.

"Yes, I'm over here," came the reply from a large chair by the window. "Did you manage to find Stephanie?"

"Yes, I'm just bringing her around to meet everybody before dinner."

As we got close to the chair where we heard the voice coming from I began to see the outline of my Uncle. Uncle Pat had black hair that was slowly going grey a bit on the top and at the sides. He had a mustache that also had tinges of grey with a cleft in his chin. As he looked up from his newspaper to greet me he had a smile on his face that was so gentle. His soft brown eyes seemed so warm that they took away the fear that I had. "Did you have a nice trip Stephanie?" he asked with such a gentle voice.

"It was very nice Uncle Pat, but it was awfully long. Have my parents called for me to go back home yet?" I asked.

Uncle Pat replied, "No, but don't you want to visit with us for a while? I'm sure that it won't be long before they will call for you."

"It's not that; I just wish my family was here too. I'm worried about the twins."

"Well don't worry, just enjoy yourself and let us be your family for a while. Now Stuart take Stephanie to meet her Aunt Elizabeth and show her the rest of the house. Stephanie, you go with Stuart now, and I will see you at dinner."

"Come on Stephanie. I'll take you to meet Mother now, but you will have to wait until the school semester is out to meet your cousin Deborah-Anne." I followed Stuart back out into the hallway and up the huge staircase of the house. After we got to the top of the stairs, we went to our left and Stuart knocked on a set of doors. "Mother, are you in there?" Stuart called out and then patiently waited for an answer.

All of a sudden the doors opened and there stood the most attractive woman I had ever seen. She looked like she should have been a movie star.

"Yes Stuart, what do you want?" The woman responded to Stuart..

"Mother I wanted to introduce Stephanie to you before dinner."

"So you are James and Valerie's girl. Please make yourself at home while you are here. Stuart will show you around and let you know where everything is. If you have any questions please ask. Stuart, take your cousin to her room so that she can rest for a while before dinner." Although Aunt Elizabeth seemed quite nice there was something in her green eyes that sent a cold chill down my spine.

Stuart and I left my Aunt's room and went to the opposite end of the hall, where there were three bedrooms. "The first one here is Deborah-Anne's. When she gets home she will show you the inside of it. This one is mine, and last but not least this is your room." He opened the door to what was to be my room. The room was decorated in shades of pink. The windows had pretty lace curtains on them. The bed was one that had a canopy over it, the kind that I saw in all my story books. There in the corner was a toy box with dolls in it, and just beside that was a bench that when you sat on it you could look out to the flower garden.

"Well how do you like it?" Stuart questioned.

"Is this just for me?" I asked, with astonishment written all over my face.

Stuart started to laugh. "Of course it's just for you. Don't you have a room like this back home?"

"No," I replied. "At home I share my room with Bridgette, and it isn't this big."

"Well I guess you can consider yourself a princess

for the time that you are here. In the meantime, try to get some rest and I will come and get you for dinner so that you won't get lost."

"Thanks Stuart." I was tired, so I kicked off my shoes and climbed up on my bed for a short afternoon nap. I went right off to sleep and the next thing I knew Stuart was calling at my door, "Stephanie, are you awake? It's time for dinner."

I quickly got out of bed and put on my shoes not wanting to miss my dinner. I opened the door and Stuart said, "Did you have a good sleep?"

"Yes, I did."

When we got downstairs to the dining room, everybody else was at this large table. Uncle Pat was at the head of the table and Aunt Elizabeth was off to his right. Stuart showed me to my seat and quickly took his own. When we sat down at the table Uncle Pat said grace (something we did not do in my house). "Thank you Lord for the food that we are about to eat. Thank you for delivering to us our niece Stephanie from her long trip, and please help to make her brother and sister well again. Amen."

Uncle Pat sure had a way to make you feel at home. After dinner, when the housekeeper had taken the dishes away, we were each allowed to take our final drink into the room where I had first met Uncle Pat. We went into the family room as they called it and sat there until we finished our drinks. I sat there looking around the room. In the room there were large paintings, nice chairs and a fire place made out of stone, and above the mantle piece there was a plaque or something.

"Stuart what is that thing?" I asked as I pointed to the object.

"Haven't you seen that before, surely you must have? That's the family's coat of arms. I'm sure that your father has a copy of it in your home somewhere. We got ours when Grandfather McConnell died."

"No, I have never seen it before," I replied. Later on I would find out that this coat of arms had a lot to do with my destiny, and was the reason why my Aunt was cold toward me.

"Now that we have finished our drinks, do you want to watch TV or see the rest of the grounds?" Stuart asked.

"TV!" I exclaimed. We got up and went into another room and watched TV. We stayed there until I started to fall asleep. Stuart said I had better head off to bed since his mother did not approve of people falling asleep watching TV. So he helped me get up to my bedroom and showed me where the bathroom was from my room and then he said good night to me. I got changed and I looked out my bedroom window and made a wish. "I wish tonight, please let Ben and Bridgette get better." Then I climbed into bed and dreamt that I was a princess.

I awoke in the morning and went downstairs after I got washed and dressed. In the room off the kitchen were Stuart and his mother sitting having their breakfast.

"Well good morning Lady Stephanie. Did we sleep well?" Stuart called. I didn't even have my mouth open to answer when Aunt Elizabeth told Stuart

"Her name is Stephanie and she has no title. Please refrain from calling her Lady Stephanie."

I didn't know what to make of it. I thought that Stuart was just joking around but Aunt Elizabeth was not. I said to him, "Yes I did, thank you. Could you tell me where I can get some cereal, Stuart?" Stuart called out to the girl in the kitchen, "Anna, could you please get Stephanie her breakfast, thank you." The girl in the kitchen brought me a glass of orange juice, a bowl of cereal, a slice of toast, and a glass of milk.

"Now Stephanie if there is anything else you want

just ask, okay?" Anna said to me. I found this all very strange since at home Mother got us our food but for things that we could reach, we got them ourselves.

"Stephanie when you're through, we will go out and I'll show you the rest of the place," Stuart said to me as I ate my breakfast.

"Stuart, please tell Stephanie about the rules around here at the same time," said Aunt Elizabeth. "I am going into town for a while."

Aunt Elizabeth got up and left the table. When I finished my breakfast, Anna came and took my plates away and Stuart and I left to see the sights.

"First, we will go out and around the grounds," he said. "Do you like horses?"

"I like all kinds of animals, but I have never seen a horse up close before. I've seen lions, tigers, and monkeys but not horses. Why?"

"Oh yes! Your family went to Africa, didn't they? Well, now you have a chance to see horses because we have some here. In fact, there is one here that I know that you will like."

So we walked over to the barn. As we were walking, the smell of the hay became stronger and we could hear the horses neighing in the distance. We walked into the barn where there were ten stalls. On each one of the stalls there was a name. The first stall had the name Elizabeth's Spirit. The next stalls were named Pat's Hurricane, Stuart's Command, and Deborah-Anne's Comet. There was a stall with no name on it, but inside was a tiny colt.

"Hey Stuart how come there is no plaque on this stall even though there is a horse in there?"

"Well, you see, Father thought that we would wait until you got here to put the name on the stall. We want you to feel like part of the family. If you notice all the other horses have one of our names in front of theirs. So we waited till you came so we could hang the plaque up. So, are you ready?"

"Sure, but what did you name it?"

"Here it is. We named it Stephanie's Fury. What do you think?"

"Does this mean that this is my horse?"

"For as long as you stay with us. When it gets a little bit bigger and you get a little bit bigger we will teach you how to ride, or do you already know how to ride a horse?" Stuart asked as he laughed.

"Boy, I can hardly wait until I can tell Ben and Bridgette about this," I exclaimed with joy.

"Would you like to feed Stephanie's Fury?" Stuart asked.

"Boy would I ever."

Stuart gave me a carrot and the colt took the carrot slowly from me until the softness of his nose was up against my hand. We groomed the horses and then we took off to see the rest of the grounds. We walked from the barn to a wooded area where I could hear water falling as we got closer. I could see a pond.

"This is where we usually ride the horses back to and let them cool off while we go for a swim in the pond. Do you know how to swim yet?"

"Yes, living on the coast we learned to swim early. Can we go for a swim later?"

"Maybe after I get through showing you the rest of the grounds and the house," Stuart said, as he was looked at his watch.

We continued the tour, and just before Uncle Pat was due to return from work, we finished touring the house. I wanted to thank Uncle Pat for Stephanie's Fury, so I went out and waited on the front stairs until Charles brought him home. When the car pulled up and Charles opened Uncle Pat's door, I ran up to him and gave him a hug.

"What's that for?" Uncle Pat asked.

"That's my way of thanking you for Stephanie's Fury. She is so nice. I love her so much," I exclaimed.

"Maybe we should have called her Stephanie's Sunshine because you are just beaming," he laughed.

We went inside and Uncle Pat sat down to read the newspaper. I learned that was the first thing that Uncle Pat liked to do when he got home from work, and no one was to disturb him. So while Uncle Pat did that I went to the other room and watched TV until dinner was ready.

Soon Anna came and called us into dinner and we went to eat. That was one of the other rules. You were never to be late for dinner.

Chapter Four

I guess I had been there for about two weeks when Aunt Elizabeth said that Deborah-Anne was coming home from school. There still had been no word from my parents saying that I could go home yet. Stuart had been home for three weeks from his school because it was nearby, but Deborah-Anne's school was far away and she had to board there. This seemed strange to me, as anybody that I knew who went to school always came home at night-time, even my father did.

I was curious as to what this cousin was like. I hoped that she would be like Stuart and Uncle Pat, but when she arrived I found out that she thought she was better than everybody, even better than Aunt Elizabeth. She sure was pretty though. She was sixteen, tall and slender with a body that had all the right curves. Her hair was long, dirty blonde but with every strand in the right place, and she had eyes that could see right through you.

Stuart came and got me to introduce to his sister, "Come on Stephanie. I'll introduce you to Deborah-Anne, and then we will go and see the horses and take a swim."

"Deborah-Anne, this is your little cousin Stephanie. She is staying with us for a while," Stuart said to his sister. She looked at me as though I was a peasant with dirt all over me, and made me feel as if I had no reason for being there. She didn't seem to want to even speak to me, so I thought I would speak first. "Hi Deborah-Anne."

"I see that Stuart has not taught you all the rules around here. Children such as you do not speak unless spoken to. Other rules are that you stay out of my room and basically keep out of my hair. Do you understand?"

"Deborah-Anne, don't you think you are being a little hard on her? After all, she is just a child and she is having a hard enough time adjusting to our way of life," Stuart reprimanded his sister.

"No, I do not Stuart. And just remember who is the oldest here. And as for you," she turned to me now, "do we understand each other?"

"Yes I understand," I replied, but I didn't really. After all, what did I do to her?

"Come on Stephanie, lets go see the horses now," Stuart called to me as he turned his back to his sister. I ran to catch up with him. All I wanted to do was to get away from Deborah-Anne. We left her in the flower garden that was just off the back door.

Going down to the horses had become a special part of the day for me. I always took Stephanie's Fury a nice carrot from the kitchen, and as each day went by I got the feeling that she knew who I was. We would just get to the doorway and she would put her head around the corner of her stall and neigh as if to say, "Hi Stephanie, have you got my carrot today?" Stuart had already started to teach me how to groom my colt. By the time we got through that part of the day we needed our swim to get us cooled down, and get rid of the horse smell that we had picked up.

I swam at the shallow end of the pond. Stuart usually chose between diving from the diving board at the far end or the old willow tree that stood over one bank. The old willow tree had one limb that hung over the pond that was wide enough for one to get a good foothold to dive from. Since Stuart and I had been at the pond every day since I had arrived there, I had started to think it was only our pond. I had forgotten he had a sister. Although up to this moment, I thought it would be great when she got back from school so she could join us.

Now I hoped she didn't like to swim.

My dreams were soon to be shattered, because Stuart and I had no sooner cooled off from a quick dip in the pond when Deborah-Anne showed up. I thought, just maybe we could enjoy swimming at the pond together, but I was wrong.

"I thought you were going to be with the horses? If I had known that you were going to be here I wouldn't have come for my swim," she said.

"We finished with the horses and we always have a swim afterwards. We would be more than happy to have you join us, if you'd like," Stuart explained to her, while I just sat back wondering if I would be allowed to stay.

She proceeded to the end of the pond where the diving board was and placed her towel on the ground near it. She had on a bikini that emphasized her gorgeous body in the sunlight. As she dove off the diving board, her body turned into a knife as it cut into the calm water of the pond.

Stuart and I stayed at the pond for another half hour, which was more than I could stand, with her eyes watching every move that I made. When we left she was sunning herself on her towel. Stuart called to her before we left, "We are going up to the house. We will see you at dinner."

When we got up to the house I decided to take a nap before dinner and asked Stuart to call me, so that I wouldn't be late for dinner. I lay down on my bed not because I was tired, but because I had had enough Deborah-Anne for one day.

During dinner it was little bit better, as one of the house rules was that there was to be no talking at the table unless it was to have something passed to you. The fact that Uncle Pat was there made me feel more comfortable. After dinner, we took our drinks into the other room where the family coat of arms was hanging. That strange plaque was becoming a fixation with me. Every night I would stare at it trying to figure out what each part meant.

Once we finally went to bed, I looked out my bedroom window making my usual wish with an added touch. This time, I also wished that Deborah-Anne would like me. As I walked down the stairs in the morning I found that not to be the case. I didn't mean to appear to be spying but it just appeared to be that way. I came down the stairs so quietly that nobody heard me, but I heard them as I was just about to come around the corner.

"I know I have just returned from school, but it appears Stephanie seems to be spending too much time with Stuart. Whenever you see Stuart, there is Stephanie right at his heels. I know Stuart is quite a handsome young man at fourteen, and he must be like an idol to her. Now I think she should be doing things on her own and let him do the things he likes. By the way, how long is she going to be here with us anyway?" Deborah-Anne was in great form for first thing in the morning. She wasn't going to let anybody forget she was home.

"I had a call from her parents last night after she went to bed. Apparently the twins aren't any better. It looks like she will be here at least till the fall or maybe even longer. Maybe it is time to let her do some chores around here, so that she knows it isn't a free ride. That way she will be out of your way and you could spend some of your time with Stuart like you usually do when you are on vacation," replied Aunt Elizabeth. Why it was just the two of them at the table I don't know, but I did know I didn't have anybody to back me up.

I was sitting there trying to be brave enough to go in and have my breakfast, when Stuart came up behind me. "You better get in there before they close up the kitchen for breakfast. Hurry up now and I'll see you later."

I went in to get my breakfast. Anna came over and gave me my orange juice, and asked what I would like to have for breakfast. I gave her my order and greeted both my Aunt and Deborah-Anne. My Aunt said to me as I was eating my breakfast that to help keep me amused and out of mischief I could help Anna with her chores. When I completed these chores then I could go and see my horse and then go swimming. My Aunt summoned Anna into the room to inform her of the change in plans. Deborah-Anne sure knew what she was doing. I was so exhausted after the first day of my routine that I went to bed almost as soon as dinner was over. The next day things went a little bit better and I went to see Stephanie's Fury after dinner. She was so happy to see me, that I knew I must make it to see her every day no matter what. After all, she was my sunshine on a cloudy day.

I got through doing the dusting and asked Anna if I could go down to the barn and give my colt a carrot. She didn't see any reason why I could not do that as long as I came back and completed the rest of my chores. So off I ran. I got a carrot for my horse and went down to see her. I would come back to groom her later. I was walking out of the barn when I heard laughter, so I thought I would go and look. As I neared the pond I thought that I had better not be seen by Deborah-Anne, so I was very quiet and hid behind the bushes and watched Stuart and Deborah-Anne swimming in the pond. I shouldn't have been there in the first place, and I shouldn't have stayed as long as I did. I was watching them having so much fun; I didn't notice that Stuart was missing from the picture. All of a sudden he was over top of me saying, "You're getting pretty good at creeping around so quietly that nobody even notices you. You're just like a cat ready to pounce on a poor bird. What are you doing here anyway?"

"Please Stuart don't tell Deborah-Anne that I'm here, but I heard laughter and just wanted to see what you were doing," I stammered.

"I won't tell her. I'll walk back to the house with you, since I'm going that way anyway." He put his arm around me and we walked back to the house.

When I got back, Anna gave me the rest of my chores and there was nothing more said. This went on for the rest of the summer. I thought that when Deborah-Anne went back to school things would get back to the way they were before, but they didn't. There was still no call saying that I could go back home. Stuart was going back to school and Uncle Pat thought that I should too. So they enrolled me in the public school in the area. Whereas Charles drove Stuart to his school, I went with them only to the end of the driveway, where I would catch the school bus. Everyday, Charles would drive me to the end of the driveway at 8:00AM and he would pick me up at the end of the driveway at 4:00PM. When I got home I had my chores and Stuart had his homework. It seemed we would never spend time together except on weekends. These were the times that we looked forward to, with Deborah-Anne now back at school.

Chapter Five

Our lives continued this way for the next few years with phone calls from my parents, with updates on how the twins were. They told me they preferred that I stay where I was. During these years I started to believe that this was my real family, regardless of how Deborah-Anne and my Aunt Elizabeth treated me. I knew that I was loved and considered to be one of the family by Stuart and Uncle Pat. I had learned how to get my chores done quickly, so I had time to spend with Stephanie's Fury, Stuart and Uncle Pat.

I had learned that Uncle Pat read the financial section of the newspaper when he came home, particularly the stock market page. When I showed interest in it, he started to explain to me how to read the information. Even though I was still young, I showed that I could grasp things quickly, so my Uncle decided to let me try the stock market purely in a pretend way of course. I would pick the stock that I thought would do well and we would place it on a chart; at the end of every week we would mark down how well the stock performed.

Stuart taught me to ride Stephanie's Fury and was teaching me to jump on the tiny circuit they had behind the stables. I thought this was marvelous and the praise they bestowed on me made me feel like I was the best in the world. Funny thing was Stuart also felt that way, and one day without telling me he asked his father to observe and give his opinion. Stuart started the time clock and I was off. I was making every jump, sitting erect in the saddle when I wasn't jumping. I crouched close to Stephanie's Fury when she was in the air jumping, making it seem as though we became one for the jump. At the end of my ride I saw Uncle Pat come out from his hiding spot. "You know Stuart you might have something there. She didn't have one fault and by the looks of her timing, she was on her mark there too."

We continued practicing and on my birthday the following year when I went down to have breakfast, there were Stuart and Uncle Pat with several large gift boxes in front of them.

"We thought the birthday girl was going to sleep forever and we would have to return these packages," laughed Uncle Pat. "Now when are you going to open them up?"

I opened the first box. In it was a helmet and riding boots. Then, I opened the next box and found a riding outfit. I was so happy I ran over and gave them big hugs.

"Well, what do you think? Are they going to be okay or not?" Stuart questioned. "After all, we did not want you competing this season without the proper attire."

"Competing? You have to be kidding me!" I exclaimed.

"No, we are not kidding! Your first competition is on April 15. You better be ready for it or else! See this riding crop that goes along with your outfit? Well it might just find its way to your bottom," said Uncle Pat with a smile on his face.

I could see that all this fuss over me was not going over too well with Aunt Elizabeth, but nothing could ruin today, not even Deborah-Anne.

After the first competition in which I came in fifth place, there just seemed to be one competition after another. I soon did prove that my cousin and Uncle were right, and I finally took first place. We came home after the competition and celebrated for a while and I found out how nice it felt to be number one.

By the time that Deborah-Anne returned from school for the summer, things had changed a bit. In order to fit in some training time with Stuart, I completed my chores in the early afternoon so we wouldn't be training in the hot afternoons. And because of the training, Stuart was spending more time with me. After all, he had a percentage at stake with me. You see, every time I won a trophy there was prize money that went along with it. We had decided a three way split would be the best way to divide it. One third of the prize money went to Uncle Pat because he actually owned the horse, a third to Stuart because he trained me, and of course one third to me because I was the rider.

Well of course, this didn't sit well with Deborah-Anne or even Aunt Elizabeth but there was nothing that they could do since Uncle Pat was the one who started all the fuss. For the first few years that we started doing the circuit, we thought there was nothing that they could do about it. At least, we thought that way until the week after I had just won the cup. Uncle Pat thought that it would be nice to have a celebration for the championship. He decided to combine it with Stuart's birthday which was two weeks after the championship. Everything was just going fine, Stuart and I were still doing some practicing with the horses and everybody else was taking care of the party arrangements. The party would consist mainly of Stuart's friends and friends of the family which suited me fine. I knew most of Stuart's friends since they were always over visiting and I wasn't allowed to have any of my friends from school over.

This one day, Stuart and I had finished the workout and decided to go for a swim. While we were there, Deborah-Anne came for a swim. "Are you going to join us today, sister?" Stuart yelled to her.

"Yes, I suppose it would not hurt for a change,"

she said with this look on her face that got those cat instincts up in me. I was in too good of a mood and things had not been going too badly up to this point, so I put those feelings to rest. "What is the water like today?" she asked.

"It's not bad, warm in some spots," I replied, deciding that if she is going to be nice then so could I.

We all played around together for about half an hour or so, when Stuart remembered that his friend Dave Thompson was coming over. "Look I have to go. Dave is on his way over. Are you coming up with me Stephanie?" He asked knowing that Deborah-Anne and I didn't agree all the time.

"No, I think I will stay just a little bit longer. I will catch you later," I answered. Anyway, Deborah-Anne was older now and more mature, and I didn't think that she would try anything. If only I had caught the glint in her eye when Stuart said that he was leaving, I would have left too. So Stuart left the two of us sunning on our towels. Deborah-Anne was showing off her body in her nice little bikini. I was in a two piece bathing suit that I pretended was a bikini showing off what was developing into a body that would someday compete against Deborah-Anne's. We lay there for a while and then Deborah-Anne started to speak. "How about if we have a little race to the other end of the pond and back?"

"Okay," I said knowing that swimming was one of my better sports.

"Incidentally, what do you think of the party coming up?" She asked me as we got up to go to the pond.

"I think that it's great, Stuart has been teaching me how to dance so that I will fit in," I replied, thinking that it felt so nice not to be fighting with her. We dove into the pond and that was the last time I remembered seeing her in the pond. She came up from behind me under the water and dunked me, not once but at least seven times. Every time that I went under I swallowed more water. I started to think that she was going to kill me. Instead, in the process of this drowning maneuver she managed to yank off my swimming gear. She got out of the water and away from the pond before I surfaced for the last time. When I surfaced I was spurting water out and choking at the same time when all of a sudden I felt water all over my body and I knew that something was missing. I looked up in the old willow tree and there hanging from it was my bathing suit. Now what was I going to do? If I got out of the pond to get my suit I might be seen in the nude. I was now starting to feel sick from that dunking. It wasn't too long before I had something else to worry about, there coming through the bushes was Dave, Stuart's friend. "Stephanie is Stuart here? I seemed to have missed him." He called out to me as he was looking around at the same time. It was while he was looking that his eyes caught sight of my bathing suit hanging in the tree. "Now you know that if you were older, I might take advantage of the situation that you are in," he said as he started to climb up the willow tree. "I thought that you and Stuart had your swims together, but by the looks of this I would say that Deborah-Anne was here. Here catch, you can put it back on in the water," he called out as he threw my suit down from the tree. When I got dressed, I swam over to the shore and got my towel. Dave watched intently, "You know someday you are going to give that girl a run for her money. That is who did this to you isn't it?"

"I'm not saying, but someday she is going to get hers," I replied with revenge in my voice.

"Now I can see what Stuart means when he says that you are like a cat. That look in your eyes, I wonder what you are thinking?" He laughed as he made that last remark.

"Look, don't say anything about what happened down here. It will be our little secret. I just want to go up to the house and get changed. If Deborah-Anne sees us coming from the pond together she will absolutely flip, okay?"

"Okay Cat, you don't mind me calling you that do you?"

"Not as long as it isn't in public. It might give away my secrets. Agreed?" I looked at him with those cat eyes.

"Okay," he replied as we started to walk up the path to the house. As we got close to the house, there she was sitting in the flower gardens looking so innocent, but when she saw us laughing and joking, her face almost dropped.

"Are you coming to the party next week?" she asked Dave as we approached her.

"I wouldn't miss it for anything in the world. Incidentally do you know where Stuart is?" he asked.

"He is in the family room waiting for you," she answered with a look on her face. She must have been wondering why her plan backfired.

"Come on Dave. I will walk in with you, while I am going to get changed." As we left her sitting there looking puzzled, we started to snicker. Stuart was waiting for Dave as we walked in laughing.

"Hey you two, what is so funny?" he questioned.

"Private joke, Stuart. Just a private joke." Dave laughed.

"I shall see you guys later, I am going to change," I called to them as I left the room. I went to my room and changed into some warmer clothes and went to do my chores before dinner.

I was determined to go to the party even though I had developed a cold from my stay in the water. Deborah-Anne was crossing her fingers hoping that I wouldn't be able to make it. The night of the party I got all dressed up to go to the party even though I still didn't feel well. The cold had started to settle in my chest, but I was determined that nothing would keep me from this party. Deborah-Anne came down to the party dressed in a very attractive dress and she looked as though she was dressed to kill. Aunt Elizabeth looked like a movie star as usual. Uncle Pat and Stuart just looked like the most attractive men around. The party began at about eight o'clock and everybody was having an exceptional time dancing and just having plain fun. The heat in the place seemed to be rising, so I kept going in and out. I figured that I would be okay, but then my stomach started to get that upset feeling again, so I went to tell Uncle Pat that I was leaving the party.

I approached him and started to say, "Uncle Pat, I don't..." I never finished the line. I passed out on the floor. Uncle Pat picked me up and carried me upstairs to my room. "Elizabeth call the doctor now," he commanded my Aunt.

The doctor arrived and examined me.

"You will have to keep an eye on her for the next twenty-four hours. If the fever doesn't break then we might lose her. What she has is a very bad case of pneumonia, the cold that she had has gone straight to her chest. Call me tomorrow and we will go from there," the doctor told Uncle Pat as he was leaving.

Well, Deborah-Anne's plot had worked but not as she planned. Yes, she did a good job on me, but the party was canceled when I collapsed. Now both her parents were spending all their time at my bedside.

"I am phoning her parents to tell them. I will be back up afterwards," Pat told Elizabeth as she applied cold compresses to my hot head.

The next day the doctor was back at the house and after checking me, ordered an ambulance to take me to the hospital. The fever instead of dropping started to rise. They needed to do something fast. Once I arrived at the hospital, they put me on an intravenous drip with hopes that they could lower the fever.

They notified my parents, but they were unable to make it up to see me because the twins still required so much of their attention. Uncle Pat would make a call to them every night giving them a progress report on me.

Every day a group of people would make their way to my room, all at different times, of course.

"Cat, do you know how many days I have been here telling you to wake up? Don't you know that cats have nine lives? So what if you have wasted one? Wake up and land back on your feet." Dave was calling to me, but I still didn't wake up.

"Stephanie, come on now wake up. This isn't like you to lie down and quit. Would you call on all your cat like strengths and rebound, since we have next years circuit to concentrate on." Stuart was giving me all his best pep talk, like he always did before competition.

"Cat, I do not believe you are quitting. I know that you are not letting Deborah-Anne off that easy, although you have her worried, that maybe she just might have gone too far. Now I want you to show me that you have not given up the fight and that you are not a pussy cat, but more like a wild cat that she should be afraid of. Hey Cat what do you say?" Dave was calling the shots the way they were and with that I opened one eye and then the other.

"I have her worried, have I?" I whispered.

"Hey, I knew that you were a wild cat the minute I met you. I knew that you would use each one of your lives, but the next time, do you think that you could do it with a little less drama." Dave was chuckling.

"Didn't I tell you that she would get what was coming to her?"

"Yes, but you almost had yours in the process. I am going to tell the doctor that you are awake now, and then I will tell the family. Is there anything that you want brought back?" he asked.

"You could ask the doctor for a glass of milk, and just seeing the family will be enough, thanks Dave," I answered in a whisper.

"Hey, you gave us a good scare young lady," the doctor said as he was checking me over. "Now what was the big idea of going to sleep for four days?"

"Well doc you see I needed the rest. I'm a growing girl you know." Being sick sure didn't hurt my sense of humor.

Uncle Pat came into the room and turned to the doctor, "Well, how is she? Is she going to be all right? When can we take her home?"

"You can put your mind at ease; she is going to be just fine. And as for taking her home, how does two days sound? I want to run some tests to confirm that the chest is clear so we don't have a relapse, but after that she should be as good as new."

"You know young lady; you gave us quite a fright. Why didn't you just tell us that you weren't feeling well?"

"I thought it was just a cold, Uncle Pat."

"Well you get some rest and I will phone your parents and let them know that you are all right. Now get some rest and we will see you tomorrow."

Chapter Six

Several months had passed since my stay in the hospital when Uncle Pat came into my bedroom.

"Stephanie, that was your father on the phone, he wanted to know whether or not you were strong enough to go back home. It seems that your mother has become ill from looking after the twins and they need you back home. I have already told them that you were and we would send you back by plane so that you can arrive there faster. Your flight will be leaving in the morning; Charles will be driving you to the airport. Now you can get packed and then go off to bed."

The next morning after breakfast I went to say good-bye to Stephanie's Fury. As I was giving her a carrot the tears started to run down my face. I knew more than anything that I would miss riding her most of all. I was so busy with Stephanie's Fury that I didn't hear the footsteps behind me.

"Hey Cat, don't worry. Stuart will take care of her, and if you like I will come over and ride her for you." Dave had snuck up behind me, I quickly tried to wipe the tears from my face, but it didn't seem to work, they still continued coming.

"You know Dave I believe you would do that too. It's too bad that you are much older because I really like you. You know me better than even Stuart. If I give you my address, would you write and tell me how Stephanie's Fury is doing?"

"No problem Cat. I would be happy to do that. When you come back to visit, you will be able to ride her.

Hey, but right now they are waiting to take you to the airport."

We went around to the front of the house and Charles had already put my bags in the car. I thanked Uncle Pat and Aunt Elizabeth for having me and letting me be part of the family.

"Uncle Pat, before I go could you do me a favour? I have saved some money up from last year's circuit and I would like to put some of it on the stock market. I left my chart up in my room so you may place it on as many stocks and companies that you see fit."

"Stephanie are you sure about this? Do you not want to take the money with you to spend?"

"Yes, Uncle Pat I am sure. I want it to grow a bit if I can," I replied. I understood my Uncle's concern since the stock market wasn't the safest place to put your money. Finally my Uncle agreed and took the envelope with the money in it.

"Stuart and Dave are taking you to the airport and your father will meet you at the airport in Boston. Have a good flight. Keep in touch and maybe someday you will come back for a visit. It's been a pleasure having you here," my Uncle said as he gave me a kiss good-bye.

I got into the car with Stuart and Dave. In about half an hour we were at the airport. Charles got the bags out of the car and then helped me out of the car. "It was nice having you around Lady Stephanie."

"Bye Charles. I am sure that I will see you again."

"Come on Stephanie. Let's get you checked in," Stuart said. With that Stuart and Dave took me by the arm, one on each side.

"Now you have nothing to worry about, the plane is going to take off and land with no problem. It won't be too long till you will be back here riding Stephanie's Fury."

"The trouble is guys this feels more like my home

than where I am going. I have been away from them for so long now, that Stuart seems more of a brother then Ben does. I know that between the two of you Stephanie's Fury will be taken care of, and I guess it is time to go home now." I no sooner said that than the announcement came over the loudspeaker, "Gate eight now boarding for Boston."

"Well I guess this is it! Wish me luck," I said as I gave Stuart a kiss on the cheek.

I turned to say good-bye to Dave; but as always he beat me to the punch. "Good-luck Cat, but you won't need it. Just let your instincts lead you," he whispered and then gave me a little kiss.

"Now don't forget to write." They both called out to me as I went through the gate.

Chapter Seven

At the Boston's airport I wondered if I would be able to recognize my father, or he would know me since I had been gone for so long. I decided to take no chances and proceeded to the information desk and asked for Mr. James McConnell to come to the information desk. In no time a man who looked somewhat like my father did when I left but with grey hair and a worn out looking face answered the page.

"Father is that you?" I called to the man.

"Stephanie. My little girl is all grown up. How are you feeling now? Are you better? The rest of the family won't recognize you."

"Father, how are the twins now?" I knew that I would find out how they really were very soon.

"Well Stephanie, when we were in Africa the twins apparently picked up a bug. They never did find out what it was, but they finally broke the fever. When the fever broke they ran all kinds of tests on them." We walked to the car as he continued to tell his tale. "The strange thing was it hit them in different areas of the body. Ben was struck first in his muscles and his ability to move, whereas it struck Bridgette in her ability to swallow. We no sooner got these things under control when something else would be affected. They are slowly recuperating and the doctors seem hopeful that in another year or two they should be back to normal. Right now, what we are dealing with is Ben's inability to hear all of the time and he still cannot walk by himself. Bridgette on the other hand cannot talk and has a bladder problem. The doctors feel all these things will take time to correct, and that is why we left you at Pat's and Elizabeth's for so long, and why we couldn't come when you were sick."

"How is Mother then, what happened to her?"

"With her running back and forth to the hospital and looking after the twins, she ran herself down and pneumonia set in similar to what you had. However, because she let herself become run down, they are not hopeful as they were with you." We drove in silence for a while.

"I'm sorry that you had to come back to this. I know that you wanted everything to be the same as when you left," he said in an apologetic way.

"Don't worry Father, I'm back now and things will just have to get better, right." Dave had said to follow my instincts; well I just hoped that they were telling me the right things to do.

We drove for a while and things slowly started to look vaguely familiar. Then we drove into the driveway. My little white cottage was now dreary grey, with the flower beds left untended. Nothing seemed remotely the way I remembered it. I started to dread the thought of going through the doorway into the house. I wanted to say that I didn't know the people that lived inside; but I knew that wasn't possible. Maybe Deborah-Anne could do that but I couldn't. I wasn't a snob and besides these people were my family.

I went into the house; it was so dark that I wondered how anybody could feel well in this place. When I walked in someone grabbed me by the arm. I could tell by how weak the grab was that it must be Bridgette. She opened her arms and gave me a great big hug, and then pulled me to the other side of the room. There in a wheelchair was Ben.

"Hi Stephanie. Boy is it good to see you. How are you feeling? You sure gave us a scare."

I thought that I would see if he could hear now so I replied to both of them, "I'm okay now, but I thought that when I got back you guys would be doing somersaults. I guess we can't take you guys traveling anymore. You seem to pick up all the bugs that they have going. By the way, where is Mother?"

Ben answered, "I can hear some of the time but not always. When I can't, I try to read lips. Mom is in the bedroom."

I went into the bedroom and there she lay sleeping. "Why haven't they put her in the hospital like they did with me? I mean she is as bad as I was if not worse. She should be in a hospital."

"They thought that she would be better off at home. That way she could know how we were doing and not worry; but I don't know how they thought that she wouldn't worry knowing that she couldn't do anything for us." Ben was telling me with tears in his eyes. "You know it just isn't fair. She had to do almost everything for us and then she becomes sick and could die."

"Hey, we will have no more talk like that; I'm back now to take care of you and her. So now she doesn't have anything to worry about." I was trying to be the strong one that everyone made me out to be, but who was I trying to kid. Mother was very sick and I could see why I had given Uncle Pat and the rest of the family a scare.

"Ben, could you or Bridgette show me where all the medicine is kept? I need to know, so I know who gets what and when?" Bridgette took me by the hand and led me to the cupboard. There she pointed to the first shelf on it was about twelve bottles of medicine. I looked at them and then at Bridgette and asked myself, why me Lord? Why couldn't you have let me come home to the family I left before they all became ill? Why couldn't you let me keep the fantasy I had about my family. How do I to cope with this?

Chapter Eight

Well, I got through the first night that I thought seemed a little long; but now it was morning. The only way I figured to make a headway was to get a routine going in order to fit everything in. First thing on the agenda was breakfast. No more Anna to fix it or to wait on me hand and foot. It was now up to me to fix it for the rest of the family, and to ensure that they either had their medicine before or after the meal, depending on what the medication called for.

Next, would be to organize the house and the house work. The way this house looked, so dark and dingy, I couldn't see how anybody living in it could feel better. Maybe, I had just got used to having a nice bright bedroom. All I knew was that this place was starting to get me down.

I took Ben and Bridgette outside for a while as I cleaned inside the house. They looked like they could use some fresh air. After doing the cleaning and looking after Mother, I made lunch and took it outside for the twins, like a picnic but not on the ground.

Both Ben and Bridgette had learned to use sign language, which was good because they could communicate with each other, something that I would have to learn if their illness was to continue. I watched them both signing to one another with fascination.

Ben turned to me, "Bridgette wants to know what you did at Uncle Pat's?"

"Uncle Pat and our cousin Stuart are very nice. They live in a mansion with Aunt Elizabeth and our cousin Deborah-Anne. They have a chauffeur by the name of Charles who drives them everywhere. He was nice, nicer than Aunt Elizabeth and Deborah-Anne. They didn't like me for some reason or other, but Aunt Elizabeth was nice to me when I was in the hospital. They gave me my own horse while I was at their place, and they had a pond that we went swimming in."

"Sounds like you had a great time out there, Stephanie." Ben looked at Bridgette who was signing to him again. "She wants to know if you actually went riding or if you just fed the horse?"

"The horse's name was Stephanie's Fury and Stuart taught me to ride and jump with the horse. He taught me so well that I went to competitions and won trophies for my jumping and riding skills."

"Stephanie you sound like you had such a great time there. How are you going to like being back here? We don't have a horse for you to ride, and now you are going to have to look after us?" Ben was looking so worried at the thought that I would hate it back here. The truth of the matter was that the thought had crossed my mind too.

"Hey Ben I'm back at the coast, and I'm with my family who I've always wanted to be with. What else could I want?" I laughed as I said that hoping to cheer Ben up. "Incidentally, do you two go to school now? I need to know that so that I can arrange to go back to school myself."

"Yeah, we go to a special school. They come and pick us up and then return us at night-time. Hopefully we will be able to go to regular school soon."

"Well, Father should soon be coming home from work, so I'm going in to make supper. You may stay outside for a while longer, or you may come into the house while I'm working."

"I think that we will stay out for a little bit longer.

It's nice to be out here. We haven't been out like this in a while except to go to the doctors," he said after signing to Bridgette.

So I went into the house, checked on Mother and started to prepare supper. I had no sooner set the table than Father was home from work. "How did it go today, did you manage okay?" He asked as he came through the doorway.

"I managed well. I got a little cleaning done and things went from there," I replied. "How was work today?"

"It didn't go too badly. It was slow since it is summer vacation." As he was answering me something must have clicked. "We will have to register you for school out here for the fall, what grade did you get to anyway?"

"I was just going into the first grade of High school. I was top in my class. I guess having a teacher for a father rubbed off a bit."

"Well, that is my girl, isn't it? Look if you want after supper I will mind everybody while you check out the beach; I know that you didn't have time yesterday when you came back."

"Thanks Father. I would like that. It was always my favourite spot."

So I went down to the beach and walked about for a while until the sun started to set. And oh, what a beautiful sunset it was. The sound of the tide coming in along the beach was so peaceful that I felt totally restful. I walked back to the house. It had been such a long day, so I told them that I was turning in early.

A few months had passed by, when one day in the mail there came a letter addressed to Miss Stephanie McConnell. Its postmark was from Ontario, Canada. I quickly opened it and read it while I was having a coffee break from my daily chores. It read.

"Dear Cat:
I promised you that I would look after Stephanie's Fury for you, and that I would let you know how she was doing. Well, the first few days she moped around as if she knew that you were gone. Every day, I would see her and tell her that you only went away for a little time and you would be back in no time. When she heard that she would perk up her ears and give a little neigh, as though she knew just what I was saying. I ride her every day and we do the jumps at least twice a week competing against Stuart, and winning every time.

How are things going for you down there? Is it just as you remembered it? Has your family recovered now that you are there? Do you still go for your afternoon swims? I still get a chuckle when I think about that day I found you down at the pond.

I am enclosing a picture of Stephanie's Fury. I thought that maybe you would like to be able to look at her and maybe show her to your brother and sister. Well, that is all the news for now. Don't forget to write back. I miss having you around.

             Love Dave

When I read "Dear Cat" I knew that it was from Dave, since who else would call me cat. I looked at the picture of Stephanie's Fury and a tear rolled down my face. Ben came into the room, catching a glimpse of my face as I tried to dry my face.

"What is wrong, Stephanie?" he asked. "Is it bad news?"

"No, it's not bad news, it's just happy memories. Dave, Stuart's friend who is looking after Stephanie's Fury for me, sent me a picture of her, so that I wouldn't miss her so much. Look at the picture." I held out the picture so that he could see it.

"That was your horse? No wonder you have a tear in your eye. She is a gorgeous animal, isn't she?" He went out of the house in his wheelchair to show Bridgette the picture. In a few minutes he came back with the picture. "Bridgette wants to know if you have any pictures of you riding the horse."

"I will have to go through my things later and see if I brought back any. There were some that were taken when I was in competition. I know that if I didn't bring them with me I am sure that Stuart or Uncle Pat would send me one or two." The two of them were fascinated with the fact that they had a championship rider for a sister that they made me proud of myself. As for writing back to Dave, well I guess that would have to wait until another day as my schedule didn't allow that today.

I checked for pictures of me and Stephanie's Fury and found that I only brought back one. It was the one from the championship with the judge presenting me with the trophy for first place. Once again the tears found their way to my eyes. How could I really and truly adjust to this way of life? Was I always to be a nursemaid and the person to take care of everybody instead of the lady of the house? I know that I loved my family very much, but I was determined to get ahead and be the lady of the house. I had this feeling that I would get through this and everybody would recover and fend for themselves.

The special school that Ben and Bridgette went to opened for the school year two weeks prior to when mine would. So during that time I would have more time to spend on the beach and do things that I liked to do, provided that I kept going back to the house to check on Mother. Seeing whether or not she needed anything and how she was doing. She still hadn't recovered and mainly slept during the day.

I admit that I seemed to be growing up very quickly since arriving back home. I now took over all the work that my mother did in the house. I also started to make adult decisions right off the bat when I arrived home. I needed to know who did what and if it was safe for them or not, since Father wasn't always there to help. Here I had no Anna to rely on for help. Sometimes I wondered if Deborah-Anne was hiding somewhere watching, happy that I had been shoved back to the life I was born into, and that I was no longer in her world.

Chapter Nine

School had now started and I had to make friends all over again. It wouldn't have been so bad had I gone to public school here, then at least I would have known at least one or two people, but I knew no-one. My days were now busier than ever. They started with cooking breakfast for everyone, handing out medications and seeing that the twins got on the special bus that took them to school. Next, I made sure that Father got his lunch for work, and then finally I checked on Mother before I left for school. My school was only five minutes down the road so I could come home for lunch and check on Mother at the same time. At three thirty, I would come straight home and be there when the twins came home. This meant that Mother wasn't left alone for too long, and the twins would have someone at home in case they needed help when they arrived home.

Upon arriving home it was time to make supper and do the housework, things that I used to do in the morning. After supper, it was time for the dishes and my homework. Now it really seemed like there was no time for doing things that I wanted to do.

On the weekends, I would fit in my swimming by taking the twins down to the beach area. I had made some new friends at school, and they would come over to go for swims with us and help me get Ben down to the beach. He was getting a little bit better and could now use a new form of crutches. In order for him to use these he would put his arms in a clip at the top of the crutch, but they weren't very useful in the sand.

Sandy MacGregor, who I met through school, lived only two houses down the street from us, and we started to go back and forth from school together. She would come over to go swimming since the coast behind her place was mainly rocky. Since she had grown up in the area, she knew all the kids around which helped me out since I knew no-one.

When Sandy came over, you never knew who would be with her. She always seemed to have somebody different with her. Today would be no different.

"Hey Stephanie, are you guys ready to go to the beach?" A voice called through the screen door.

"Just give me a few minutes, would ya?" I yelled back.

Finally, I had everything ready. The twins were outside with Sandy already. "Gee I thought that we were going to have to go to the beach without you. By the way these are Tom, Jenny, Cathy and my brother Bill." Sandy was standing with hands on her hips as I came through the door and then quickly pointed to each one of the people that she brought with her.

"Hi everybody! You know me Sandy, I just had to get a few things ready to take down with us. I take it you already introduced Ben and Bridgette, huh?"

"I introduced them and I explained earlier to the other guys about Ben and Bridgette's disabilities. I had forgotten that Tom knew sign language from one of his cousins, so he and Ben will get along great."

"I don't know how you do it, but whenever you seem to touch things they just seem to get better," I laughed. Through this girl I not only made new friends but so did Ben and Bridgette.

We got down to the beach and we put down the large beach blankets that we brought to lie on. Then we set forth to have a great day in the sun. Jenny was a blonde with short hair almost in what we called a boy's bob, but wore a bikini that showed off her nicely shaped body. Cathy was the shortest one of the whole group. Since she was a little bit on the chubby side, she had on a one piece bathing suit to make her look a little bit more on the slender side. Tom was tall with a very muscular and tanned body that made it look as though he worked out on the beach every day. Sandy's brother Bill was much like his sister, both had dirty blonde hair and nicely tanned shapely bodies, but not like Tom's. Bill wasn't as muscular as Tom was.

When the group was at the house, I hadn't noticed the gear that they had brought with them. I normally brought enough refreshments for as many people that I thought Sandy would be bringing. We were all sitting there after coming in from swimming, when Tom finally mentioned the gear that they brought with them. "I hear that you're quite the sports person, Stephanie. Have you ever tried scuba diving before?"

"No Tom. That's something that I haven't tried. I used to do horseback riding and jumping. As far as water sports, I've only continued my swimming. Why do you ask?"

"Well, had you grown up here, you more than likely would have learned how to scuba dive by now. We all do it and you having the beach, have the perfect spot to learn, if you want to."

"If you want Stephanie, you may use my gear to try it out to see if you like it or not," Jenny called out to me.

"You don't have to worry the rest of us will keep an eye on Ben and Bridgette," Bill yelled out. He had Ben in the shallow water.

"Well, the underwater has always intrigued me, but do you really think that you can teach me, Tom?" Everything about the sea had always seemed to be calling out to me to come and investigate it. Now Tom was giving me the opportunity to do just that.

"I can teach anybody to scuba-dive, I learned from my Uncle. He used to teach classes in it, and when I got to the age that I could help him around the shop, I used to do it for spending money. I haven't lost a student yet, have I gang?" Tom turned and looked at everybody for their moral support.

Sandy said, "Go for it Stephanie, what have you got to lose? Besides, he's right. He hasn't lost a student yet, but there is always the first time." She was laughing so hard that had she been sitting on anything of any height she would have fallen off.

"Okay Tom, you have a student. Anything that seems the slightest bit dangerous seems to be up my alley," I said to him as I got up off the blanket. Tom picked up the two scuba tanks and some weights to put on so that we wouldn't float to the surface of the water. When we got down to the shoreline, Tom helped me put on the tank. Then he firmly did the straps up in the front. As he was tightening the straps under my bust, I could feel my face getting warmer as I started to blush. I had never had a guy touch me. I felt strange, even though I knew that he was only tightening the straps for my own safety. I looked up from watching his hands doing up the straps. As my head rose, a smile came over my face as my eyes caught his. I saw that he was smiling back at me. "There, that should keep that on tight. It doesn't hurt you the way I have it now, does it?"

"No, not at all," I replied. He then put his tank on.

"Okay then, the next step is to learn how to breathe with the breathing apparatus. First try it without the mask on, put this into your mouth and you're going to take air in your mouth and exhale it through your nose. Got it? Now try it." I did exactly what he said, and when I took the mouthpiece back out of my mouth you could hear the air coming out of the tanks. "The next thing is put on your flippers, put your mouthpiece back in your mouth, wet down your mask, then put it on and then we will go into the water. Just remember that when we are under the water you follow all my instructions and don't panic whatever you do. Now let's go." I followed all of his instructions and soon we were under the water. At first I was scared, but after the first few breaths of air I got the hang of it and felt more at ease. Tom would signal to me where to swim, keeping an eye on me to make sure that I was all right and not having any problems. The world under the water was different from what I was used to. Down there, you could see all types of plants that were of different shapes and colours. There were different types of fish and instead of being a blah greenish colour that you would expect them to be, they were different colours and shapes. Along the ocean floor you could see little crabs crawling around the rocks and tiny caves. Tom looked at his watch and signalled that we would have to head back to the surface. Taking me by the hand, he held me back so that I would not surface too quickly. When we hit the surface he took his mouthpiece out and said, "Well how did you like it? Have I convinced you to take up the sport?"

"Tom, it's so fascinating down there! I just love it." I responded after removing my mouthpiece.

"Put your mouthpiece back in and we will swim close to the surface till we get to the shore. We have enough air to get us there." We put our mouthpiece back in and headed toward the shore. We came out of the water by the caves. Tom took off his gear and then turning around saw me struggling with the straps. Although I watched him do them up, I didn't quite see how the safety catches were done. "I guess it will take a couple of lessons for you to get the hang of all the gadgets involved. Here let me give you a hand." He came over and undid the straps, once again I watched every move that he made, and once again I felt my temperature rise. When he finished, he just looked up at me and smiled. There was something that attracted me to him, but right now I didn't know what it was.

"Part of scuba-diving is carrying your own gear, so you can carry Jenny's. Well do you think that you will join me again in scuba-diving? You did like it, didn't you? I can see it your face," he asked as we walked back along the beach to where we had left the others.

"I would like to, but I'm guessing that it costs money for the gear, doesn't it? And that is something that I don't have."

"Well, we will have to see what we can do in that regards," he said as he smiled down at me.

We reached the others a few minutes later. "Well, how did you like it?" they called out, as we laid our tanks on the sand.

"It was great; it's so interesting down there. I would like to go there someday with a camera and take pictures," I replied with a smile on my face.

Sandy came over and sat down besides me. She bent over close to me and whispering said to me, "You know Tom likes you. It was his idea to come over here today."

"What do you mean?"

"He has seen you at school, and knew that you and I were friends; so when he was over last night visiting Bill, he asked if there was some way that he could meet you informally. I told him that Jenny and I were coming over to go swimming, so he asked if he and Bill could come as well."

By this time I was blushing again, but at the same time I was trying to locate where Tom had gone. "I'll admit he is a nice guy." Tom was down talking and signing to Ben; he sure had a way of getting a girl's attention. The fact that he was good looking, had a nice personality and was great with my brother had my attention.

Ben and Tom were on their way back up the beach. "Tom says that maybe the next time he might take me down, providing the doctors and therapist says that it is okay. What do you think of that, Stephanie?"

"I say that is great, but how about if we get you walking first, heh?" I replied trying not to dash his hopes. It was now time to head back to the house. When we reached the house, we said our good-byes and we all agreed to do it again. "Bridgette says that Tom seems to like you, what do you think?" Ben said to me as he stopped me before going into the house.

"I think that the two of you had too much sun. He's a nice guy and that's all. Got it?"

"Got it," Ben said and turned to go into the house.

We managed to spend a few more weekends together. Sometimes it was the same group of people, and on other days it would be different group, but Tom and Bill were always a part of the group. I got some more scuba-diving lessons in before we all called it quits for the winter. We managed to find other things to keep ourselves amused with as long as the weather held out.

I used the days on which it rained to catch up on my letter writing. After all, I couldn't forget my other family or Dave. I thought that I should write to Dave first since my letter to him was long overdue. I picked up my pen and started.

"Dear Dave:

I'm sorry that it has taken me so long to write you back, but things were not as I had remembered them. The house that I remembered has now turned into a grey dilapidated looking place; with nothing having been done to it in years. My brother Ben can hear part of the time, the other times he reads lips. He either gets around by using a wheelchair or by using special crutches. My sister Bridgette doesn't talk and has a bladder problem. My mother has pneumonia worse than what I had, and now I can understand why I scared you guys so much. I look after the three of them during the day along with taking care of the housework and doing my schoolwork.

I've met some new friends out here through school. Tom, one of my new friends, has taught me how to scuba-dive. It seems like any sport that has danger in it, is the kind that I like. How is Stephanie's Fury doing? I hope that someday I will be able to come back to Uncle Pat's, so that I can see her and you too of course. You know that if you are ever are down this way, that you can drop in too. I might not have a mansion down here, but it's the best that I have right now. If you come down here, we can go for a swim in the ocean. Well, that is all my news for now. Please keep writing, I love hearing from you.

Love

Stephanie (The Cat)

PS Thanks for the pictures of Stephanie's Fury. I love it."

Then it was time for Stuart's letter.

"Dear Stuart:

How have you been keeping? Was Deborah-Anne happy when she found out I was gone? I bet it just made her day. I hear that Dave has been working out Stephanie's Fury for me. I'm glad to hear that she is doing well.

When I got back here, I found out that Ben can hear only part of time and he gets around in a wheelchair or on crutches. Bridgette has a bladder problem and doesn't talk. Mother has pneumonia worse than I did; in fact she is still quite bad with it. When I saw all of this, I looked around to see if I could see Deborah-Anne standing there laughing.

I have looked around and can't find a picture of the coat-of-arms around here. Do you think that you could send me a picture of yours? Well, that is about all the news for now since I don't have much spare time anymore. Please give my love to your parents. I will write to you again soon.

Love

Stephanie"

When I finished writing my letters, I grabbed an umbrella and took the letters to the post box to mail them. In order to get to the post box, I had to go by Sandy's house. She was at the window so I waved to her as I went on my way. On the way back she called out to me to come in for a while. With nothing else to do I decided to go in for a short visit. When I got in the house, there was Tom visiting with Bill. They were playing cards at the kitchen table, so I said "Hi" as I passed by them. Sandy suggested that we go into her bedroom and listen to records.   "Well come on now, tell me what do you think of Tom?" she asked when she closed the door behind us.

"Sandy, I don't know. He's a nice guy, but right now that is all that he is. Anyway, I don't really have time for anybody in my life who wants to be more than a friend. You understand that, don't you?"

"But if you did, wouldn't you like him?" She just wouldn't give up on this one.

"Yes. If I had more time to be a normal girl like you, then yes, I would like him to be the one in my life."

"I knew it. I just knew that the two of you would make a nice couple, but now we are going to have to do something about getting the two of you together." She got the look on her face that seemed to say, watch out Sandy is on the warpath of match making.

"Look, you can scheme all you want, but I just

don't have any time for it. During the day I look after the house, Ben, Bridgette and Mother. Now that Christmas is coming up I'm going to get a job on Saturdays, so that I can have some spending money for gifts. That leaves Sunday for my homework," I said, pleading for her to back off the subject, although I knew that it was almost pointless. Once Sandy gets something in her mind, it's hard to get her to change it.

"Look Stephanie, we could arrange something at school."

"Thanks Sandy, but would you please leave well enough alone. If we are to get together, we will. Until then, please leave well enough alone okay?" We listened to several records and then it was time for me to leave.

"I have to go now, so remember, don't try anything right?"

"Right," she replied as we started out the doorway. As we went by the guys, I said good-bye to them. "You're not going already are you?" Tom asked.

"Yes, I have to go home now. I have work to do," I replied.

"Well, if you wait for just one minute, I'll walk along with you, if you don't mind, of course?" He stood up and got his coat, saying good-bye to Bill as he rose up from the chair.

"You know that I only live two doors down. You could have stayed at Bill's," I said to him when we got outside.

"I know that. I just wanted to walk you home. I don't get to see you since the weather started to grow colder."

"Hate to say it, but you're going to see less of me. I'm looking for a job for Saturdays to earn money for Christmas, and there goes my free time."

"Well since you are working because you want to earn money for Christmas, I don't feel so bad. I thought that you were trying to get rid of me. I might be able to help you. You're still too young to work in stores. The only jobs that you can get are a paper route or to help someone around their house on Saturdays. Now I know that you can do that. I also know that my Grandmother is looking for someone to clean her house one day a week, why couldn't that person be you?"

"It sounds great, but wouldn't your Grandmother be looking for someone that is older than me?"

"Yeah, but I could talk to her for you if you would like?"

"Where does your Grandmother live anyway?" I had just remembered one thing. I had to work close to home because I would have to walk there and back.

"That is what is so good. She just lives on the next block from here. So do you want me to ask her?"

"Yes, you go and ask her and I will think a bit more about it." By this time we were at my house, so I said good-bye as I left him at the end of the driveway.

Chapter Ten

Stuart and Dave were out working the horses on the weekend as they usually did and had done since I had left to go back home. The sun was bright and it was a nice fall day with the leaves falling slowly off the trees.

"I received a letter from Stephanie yesterday." Stuart said to Dave, watching at the same time to see what his reaction would be.

Very coolly Dave replied, "How is she doing, anyway?"

"You mean that you don't know? She tells me that you sent her pictures of Stephanie's Fury. I didn't know that you two were that close. It seems that she had a bit of a rough time when she got back."

"We became close when she was here and I really got to like her. I told her before she left that I would work out Stephanie's Fury for her, and that I would keep her posted as to how she was doing. She mentioned in my letter how hard it was for her when she went back. Nothing was the way she remembered it, but knowing her I know that she will make things better. It might be a hard fight, but then she was made to fight. Remember when she was sick and everybody was about to cut her out? She brought all her strengths together and came back as if nothing happened. I wish I could give her a hand, but I know she wouldn't accept the help and I have to respect her for that."

"You know Dave, if I didn't know better I would say that you were in love with her." With that Stuart gave Dave a shove and laughed at the thought that Dave could be in love with his cousin.

"You never know, but with her down there we will never know, will we? Anyway, what so strange about me caring for your cousin in more than a friendship manner? She is pretty good looking, you know. So what if she's just a bit younger?"

"Well, what are you going to do about it? The fact of the matter is that you are up here and she is down there. Are you going to stop seeing other girls up here?"

"No. After all, she is making new friends down there. In fact one of her new friends, a guy by the name of Tom has taught her how to scuba-dive. Did you know about that?"

"No, she had not mentioned that in my letter. How does that go over with you?"

"Hey, I'm happy for her. Anyway, she needs something in her life to give her some enjoyment. I just hope that she doesn't get hurt." Dave had a worried look on his face almost as though he didn't think the Cat could land on her feet a second time.

"Hey don't worry. We both know Stephanie has something about her that seems to protect her. She may experience rough times but she will always get through them." Stuart tried to reassure Dave, but he knew that it would take more than words to convince him.

They continued to groom the horses, when Stuart thought of a way to take his friend's mind off his cousin. "How about if we go to a movie after we are through here? It will take your mind off things?"

"Okay, maybe that will work." So off they went to the movies.

Chapter Eleven

I started to work for Tom's Grandmother on Saturdays and received ten dollars a day for the work that I did. Mrs. Webster told me that I not only did my job well, but she got to see her grandson more often. Tom would come over and have lunch with his Grandmother and then would spend the afternoon with her. He did this so that he could walk me home. So he had an ulterior motive for getting me the job with his Grandmother. I got the job and he got to see me every week.

The week before Christmas, we received some good news about the twins. Bridgette's medication was lowered to almost nil, and they said that within about two to three weeks her bladder condition should be cleared up. Her voice they said would take time, but if she kept trying that maybe shortly she should be able to talk too. Ben on the other hand, had taken his first steps without the crutches. It finally looks as though things were starting to look up. Now if Mother would recover, we would have a great Christmas. I started to prepare for Christmas, baking Christmas cakes and cookies, and making decorations for us to hang. I did these on Sundays, my only day off from working. I was determined to make this a Christmas that we would enjoy. At school, just before we were to break for Christmas we had a school dance. The group that I hung out with was going to the dance together. There was a great turnout at the dance when we arrived there. There was a group to provide entertainment and they provided great dancing music. I was up on almost every dance with somebody different. I was just about to take my seat when Tom came over to me.

"You know that when I got you the job at my Grandmother's I thought that I had it all figured out. I thought that I would be seeing you as much as I could. I also thought that at this dance I wouldn't have to compete with every guy in this place to have a dance with you. So if you aren't too tired may I have this dance?" He stretched out his hand toward me as he asked me to dance.

"Yes of course you can have this dance. You know that if I didn't know you better I would say that you were jealous, are you?"

Since this was a slow dance we were dancing close to one another so he whispered to me. "If I am do you blame me since you are the most attractive girl here? Just tell me, do you have to dance with everybody that is here. Couldn't you say no to some of them?" As he asked the last question he looked down at me, waiting for me to say no.

"Tom you know that we are just friends. Although I know that we both want something more, you know I can't. If you want I will put you on my priority list, but I love to dance. I don't get to do it too often, so I take advantage of the time that I can. Please understand."

"Okay, I guess I was coming on a little bit strong, but I thought that you and I were more of an item. I guess that I jumped the gun just a little bit, huh? Do me a favour though, the last dance of the night, save that one for me okay? he said looking me directly in the eye.

"That's a promise. I may dance with other guys, but when that one comes up I will find you." We finished our dance and managed to dance some other dances together. I was on the dance floor with somebody else when they announced that this was the last dance. Quickly I looked around and spotted Tom. I walked over to him. "I believe that this dance is yours," I said as I offered my hand to him.

Although we had danced other dances, this one seemed different. As we danced, we seemed to know what the other one was doing with every step. I suddenly had the same feeling that I had when he had been teaching me to scuba-dive. Suddenly, it was as though we were the only couple dancing. When we left the dance Tom and I walked a step or two behind the group. I turned to Tom and said, "Did you feel something during that last dance?"

"Yeah, but I wasn't going to say anything until you did. Stephanie don't you realize that I think that you are special. I want you to be my girlfriend.

"I guess then it was hard on you when I was dancing with everybody tonight, heh?" Tom had slipped his hand in mine.

"Now what is it going to be? Are you or are you not going to be my girlfriend?"

"Tom, don't you think that we should catch up to the others?" I replied, trying to avoid the question. I knew the answer that we both wanted to hear, but something inside me was trying to avoid it.

"Stephanie they can go on. Why are you trying to avoid the question? We both know that we want to be with each other."

"I know that Tom, maybe I don't want my family to know. Maybe I'm scared. All I know is that I do want to be your girlfriend."

"Then it's settled you are now my girlfriend. We will just keep it our secret until you decide that you want them to know, okay." He pulled me closer to him and slowly gave me a kiss. "There it is now official." He put his arm around my shoulder and walked me to my house.

"See you tomorrow at my Grandmother's?"

"Yes, I'll see you there, good-night." I was floating on cloud nine as I walked through the doorway. My father was sitting in the living room waiting up for me.

"Did you have a good time Stephanie?" he asked as I came in.

"I had the best time of my life. I danced every dance there was. I'm going to bed now, I have to go to work tomorrow."

So off to bed I went but sleep was the furthest thing from my mind. I kept tossing and turning as I kept replaying the last dance over and over in my mind.

Chapter Twelve

The week before Christmas, Tom and I exchanged our gifts at his Grandmother's, since we would not be seeing each other over Christmas. On Monday morning, I received two packages in the mail, both of them from Ontario, Canada.

I opened the first one which was from Stuart. Inside there was a small version of the family's coat-of-arms and a letter with a Christmas card. The letter read.

"Dear Stephanie:

Merry Christmas, hope it is a good one for you. I had a small version of the family's coat-of-arms made for you, so that you can hang it on your walls. How is life going now? I was talking to Dave about you; I hadn't realized that you two were so close. He more than likely has written to you himself, since you seem to have captured his heart. He says that you are seeing other people there, so I am trying to get him out in the world to meet someone new.

Father said to wish you a Merry Christmas and has sent you a listing of how your stocks are doing. Are you sure that you came from that family? The way that your stocks are doing well, you can invest my money anytime. He has been re-investing your dividends back into the market just the way you instructed. Out of curiosity what are you going through for in life, anyway?

We have the stalls all decorated as usual for Christmas. Dave is still taking care of Stephanie's Fury. Do you think that you will ever be back up here? Dave and Stephanie's Fury miss you and so do I. Well, have a Merry Christmas and a Happy New Year.

                                                  Love
Stuart"

I took the plaque out of the box and looked at it, wondering where the best place was to hang it. Then I decided to open the other package which came from Dave. It was larger than Stuart's. I started to feel lousy as I opened it, since all I sent the two of them was a Christmas Card. Inside there were two framed pictures. One was of me jumping Stephanie's Fury over the final jump. Blended in with it was the picture of the judge placing the ribbon on Stephanie's Fury. The other picture was Dave and Stephanie's Fury at her stall with all the Christmas decorations on it. In the picture was a sign on the stall saying, "Merry Christmas Stephanie." Attached to the picture was a note that said, "We both miss you, please say that you will be coming home soon." Along with the pictures was a letter.

"Dear Cat:

Merry Christmas, I hope that all your dreams come true and that you have a good Christmas. I hope that you will enjoy the Christmas gifts that I sent you. I'm glad to hear that you are seeing other people, just be careful, please. I know I have no right to worry or to show you that I care for you. I hope by saying this that you will know that you will always have a friend here that you can count on. Just so that you know that if you need me I will be here. I guess that will have to satisfy me.

Stuart has been trying to match me with other girls, but none have the mystery that you have. I suppose that is what I like in you. Hope your family recovers soon, so that you can enjoy life the way that I know that you would like to. Please continue to write. At least, we can be pen pals and I will know that you are all right, so I can tell Stephanie's Fury.

Merry Christmas Cat, have a very Happy New Year and I hope to see you in the future.

Love always Dave"

I sat and had a little cry for a while. Then I took the plaque and the picture of me jumping Stephanie's Fury over the jump to find a place to hang them. The one with Dave in it I would keep in my room, for my eyes only.

We made it through Christmas with everybody enjoying a very nice meal and opening the gifts that we all got for each other. I sat Mother up for a while as we opened the gifts and then again at supper. She seemed to have improved slightly in the last month, but we didn't know for how long that would last.

She claimed her best gift was having me back home with the family for Christmas, and she was glad to think things were slowly coming around. The twins seemed to be finally on their way to recovery.

We told her that she would be up and about in no time, doing the things that she loved best with the rest of the family. I got her camera out of storage to capture this moment on film. She started to give a few pointers as to how to work the camera, since hers was a 35mm and you had to focus the camera with each shot that you took.

"See Mother, soon you will be up and about, showing me how to use the camera to its full potential. Maybe, even how to do underwater photography," I said to her as she was showing me how to adjust the dials on the camera.

"I have been missing quite a lot around here, it appears. Why would you want to do underwater photography anyway?" she asked with a tired voice.

"I went scuba-diving this year and found it very interesting under the water," I replied.

"Then Stephanie I would advise you to take as many photography courses at school that you can, but I'll warn you right now that photography is expensive."

We took a few pictures of everybody opening their gifts and then Mother said, "If you don't mind I think that I want to go back to bed now. I'm getting tired again." So Father and I helped her back into the bedroom.

"Now rest and maybe we can get you out of bed for a few hours again if you feel up to it," I told her.

This seemed to be the best Christmas gift that any of us could have asked for. It was because of the fact that we were all together and able to spend the time together. How were we to know that it would be the last one that we would have together.

Chapter Thirteen

Time went by and my birthday was coming up. I was still working for Tom's Grandmother, since I liked having the money at hand in case there was something that I wanted. Ben has now been walking under his own steam for the last month. They were now trying different medications for his hearing disability. Bridgette's bladder problem has finally cleared up, and we are now working on her speech. The doctors felt that since she could speak before the illness, she should be able to do so again. For the first time in two months, Mother showed much improvement, but then last week she had a set back and once again had to be kept in bed.

Tom and I had finally made it official that we were going out with each other and everybody seemed to accept it. We still didn't have much time together though, but for my birthday we decided that he could come over to our place for supper.

Two days before my birthday without fail I received my birthday cards from Ontario, Canada. One card from Stuart and one from Dave. This time Dave just left it as a regular birthday card. There was no note in it this time asking me to hurry back home. I figured that Stuart had finally set him up with a girl that he liked, or at least he was now able to keep me in the back of his mind.

I put them up on the counter where all my other cards were. As Tom was waiting for me to come out of the kitchen on the day of my birthday, he started to look at all the cards. He picked up the one from Dave.

"Stephanie why does this guy Dave call you Cat on your card?"

"That was his nickname for me because he felt I had the ways of a cat."

"Is he somebody special? Do I have to worry about competition from him?"

I laughed at him. "No he is a very good friend and he is looking after Stephanie's Fury for me. Besides, he is in Ontario. Now, don't be so silly."

He started to look around the room and he saw the picture that Dave had sent me. "Is this Stephanie's Fury here in this picture?"

"Yes, that was shot when I took the championship. Dave put the two pictures together for me for Christmas."

Ben coming into the room now commented to Tom. "Don't the two Stephanies look great in that picture?"

"Stephanie always looks great but in this picture she looks different. She looks as though she is on top of the world."

As I came into the room he stopped me. "Do you miss riding Stephanie?"

"I do, but someday when I have enough money saved up I'll go back and ride Stephanie's Fury." I couldn't help the distant look that I had on my face as I said this.

"You know that you could go riding out here if you wanted to. Some of my friends have horses. I know that it wouldn't be the same, but if you wanted I'm sure that I could arrange it."

"That would be nice," I replied. There was still this distant look on my face. I knew that Tom thought that he had to compete against Stephanie's Fury and Dave, but really he didn't have to.

"Do you think that Bridgette and I could go and

watch you ride if you decided to go?" Ben asked.

"Sure Ben, I will borrow a car and we can all go together," Tom answered Ben before I could open my mouth. Tom could drive now since he got his license on his sixteenth birthday.

"Enough of this talk. It's my birthday and I want to open my gifts," I said with a look of impatience on my face.

Tom had given me a lovely necklace with a little heart on it. Ben and Bridgette had gone together and bought me a small miniature china horse. My parent's gift was a strange one, a ticket for a plane ride to Ontario. The ticket said that I would leave on Monday. I turned to my father and asked, "What is this for?"

He replied that because I had grown up most of my life there, it was only fair to let me go back to my other family occasionally. "Your mother and I thought that it would be nice to let you go back and see Stephanie's Fury, but you only have a week."

"But Father, can you manage without me?"

"I think we can manage for a week. Ben is walking now and Bridgette is nearly fully recovered. I am on March break from school so we should be able to look after your mother. Your cousin will meet you at the airport."

I then opened my last gift from my mother it was a fair size package. I wondered what else she could give me. When I opened the package, in it was her camera gear. I excused myself and went into Mother's room to thank her for the gifts.

"Mother, the trip was more then enough. You didn't have to give me your camera too."

"Just enjoy yourself at your cousins, and then when you return I will start to teach you how to use the camera. Happy Birthday sweetheart."

I went back into the other room. "Okay let's eat.

Everybody to the table." I proceeded to bring the food out of the kitchen. When we were done eating, Ben and Bridgette did the dishes. I turned to Tom. "How about a walk along the beach?" I could see that he was upset with the fact that I was going back to Ontario.

"Sure. It's a nice out there tonight," he replied as he grabbed my hand and started toward the doorway.

The waves were lapping up against the shoreline as the sun was starting to set. I put my hand up and followed the cheekbone of his face. "You know that I wanted to go back, but you also know that I will be coming back in a week. Don't you trust me when I am out of your sight?" I asked him as I drew closer to him and slowly gave him a kiss. When we broke from the kiss I asked, "Well?"

"You know that I trust you no matter where you are. I'm just not sure of this guy Dave."

I pulled him closer to me and just before I kissed him again I said, "Tom all you have to do is trust me and leave Dave up to me. Just remember, I'm coming back to you." Then I slowly embraced him.

"Okay then, but I will drive you to the airport. I don't want to have you leave me any faster than necessary," he said as if he were still in control of the situation. As we walked along the beach, the sun slowly sank out of sight. When it finally was out of sight we walked back to the house.

The next day Sandy came over to find out what I got for my birthday. What she really wanted to know was what Tom had given me, and then when she found out that I was leaving the next day for Ontario.

"Stephanie, are you sure that you want to go and leave Tom?"

"Hey Sandy, I have been waiting to go back for quite sometime. Besides, Tom knows that I'm coming back in a week's time. He's been quite good about it. In fact he is taking me to the airport."

"All the same, the two of you just started seeing each other. I don't know if I would leave him by himself since he is a good looking guy." She said this as if I was the jealous type and I would be worried at leaving him with her.

I continued packing as we were talking. "Look Sandy, I trust him and he trusts me, so there is nothing to worry about, and after this year I think that I deserve a break."

Chapter Fourteen

Tom picked me up and drove me to the airport; we got there with enough time to spend some time alone before I had to board the plane. We were sitting talking when we heard, "Now boarding for Toronto at gate ten."

"Well, I guess that is my call to say good-bye," I said as I was rising from my chair. Tom stood at the same time and pulled me close to him, and he started to give me a long kiss.

"Tom if we keep this up, I am going to miss my flight."

"That is the whole idea," he said as he gave me another kiss.

"I thought that we had settled this. I'm going for the week and than I'll be back. Now I must go." They were making the final boarding call so I turned and ran for the gate.

I had booked a window seat so that I could watch and see Tom as I flew off and see Stuart as I was landing. I no sooner got in my seat than they announced that we should do up our seat belts. The flight attendant started going through the emergency procedures. I was watching out the window all of the time. Tom had said that he was going to the observation deck to see the plane take off. I looked and sure enough there he was. The plane's engines revving up stirred something in me, and then all of a sudden I could feel the plane taking off into the sky. It wouldn't be long before we would be in the clouds. Up there all your worries seemed to vanish and you could go off into a dream world. This dream world would last until they announced that we were approaching Toronto and asked us to put our seat belts on and return our chairs to an upright position.

I looked down to see the skyline of Toronto, and soon there was the racetrack that meant that touchdown would be soon. I hurried through customs after locating my suitcase. When I got to the other side of the customs gate, I stopped. Where was Stuart? He was late. I looked in every direction but he was nowhere in sight. I decided to have him paged, so I headed toward the information desk.

"Hey gorgeous. Can I give you a ride somewhere, like maybe my place?" this guy was saying as he was grabbing my suitcase, and at the same time putting his arm around me. I didn't stop to see who the guy was. I just brought my elbow back and hit the guy. After I did that, I turned around to see who my victim was. There was Stuart bent over in pain.

"Stuart, what was with the phony voice? Don't you know that I could have hurt you?"

"Hey, I'll remember that the next time that I decide to surprise my cousin. I didn't think that you were that strong. Do you do that to all your boyfriends?"

"No, just the ones who get out of hand. Now did I hurt you?"

"No, just let's get you home before you do anymore damage to me," he laughed.

We got to the car and there was Charles. "Did you have a nice flight, Lady Stephanie?"

"Very nice, thank you Charles. It is very nice to see you again," I replied as I got into the car.

In the car Stuart and I caught up on what had gone on since the last time we had seen each other. I told him all about the twins being almost fully recovered and about Mother's relapse, how things were going back there, and how I was doing in school. He told me about how things were going at his school, and that he would soon be going to college if his marks were good enough. Deborah-Anne wouldn't be around during my visit and that brought a smile to my face.

"I thought that would make you happy. You haven't changed a bit," he laughed.

"I might have grown up a bit since you last saw me, but I'm still the same person."

"Have you done any riding since you left?"

"No. In fact we were just arranging a riding trip just before I came out here."

"Well, I know someone that will be glad that you are back," he said with a smirk on his face.

I didn't know whether he was referring to Stephanie's Fury or if he meant Dave. I was surprised that Dave wasn't there to greet me at the airport. I thought that I would just leave that last comment without a reply since we were now turning into the driveway. As we approached the house I felt as though I was coming home again.

"Come on Stephanie, we should let them know that you're home first," he said as though he was reading my mind. I didn't really want to go into the house first. We went into the family room and there was Uncle Pat sitting reading his newspaper.

"Hi Uncle Pat. How are our stocks doing anyway?" I called out to him.

"Stephanie, it's good to see you again. The stocks are doing fine. Did you have a good flight?" he asked with a smile.

"Look Uncle Pat, I would love to talk to you, but there is somewhere that I have to go to now."

"Go ahead Stephanie. I know that she is waiting to see you too," he said as he started to laugh. "Well get going, she is waiting for you."

"Stuart, are you coming?" I called back to him as I started in the direction of the stables.

"No, I think I will pass. I'll see you afterwards."

I got to the corner of the stables and I heard a familiar neigh. A smile came across my face. Stephanie's Fury could sense that I was there. I went into the stables and up to her stall. She started to nudge my hand as I patted her. "Do you think that I would forget my girl?" I said as I reached into my pocket and brought out a carrot. "There you go girl." I gave her a hug. "Have they ridden you yet today girl?"

"No, I thought that you might like to ride her when you arrived."

I was startled I didn't expect an answer. As the voice answered a rose was placed along the side of my face. I turned around and there was Dave.

"Stuart told me that you were coming home and that you be arriving in time to get a ride in. Would you like me to saddle her for you?"

"No, I can do that for myself. I wondered where you were at the airport. I thought that maybe Stuart had found you a girl who was keeping you busy."

"He has tried but it hasn't worked yet. Would you like company on your ride?"

"Yes, I would like that." All that time our eyes never left each other.

"I thought that you might say yes, so I asked Stuart if I could ride his horse."

We saddled the horses and headed out of the stable doors.

"Do you want to go on the circuit, Cat?" Dave looked across at me.

"You know me pretty well, don't you. You know darn well that I have missed the circuit more than anything. Shall we race against each other then, and may the best team win." I smiled back at him as I started to gallop my horse.

He knew that I might be rusty but he also knew

that once I got back in the saddle I was a threat to anyone. We raced up to the circuit area and then let our horses catch their breath. I asked him to go first so that I could recall the routine.

He agreed saying, "I'm only letting you get away with that one, but I know that you'll never forget the routine. If you think that you got me with that one, then you are wrong. Your smile gave you away." He lined his horse up at the starting line and I gave him the signal to start. He did pretty well. "Gee, I don't know, that is going to be pretty hard to beat."

"Yeah that's what you say. You could more than likely beat that time with your eyes closed. Now on your mark go."

He sat back with a smile on his face. His Cat was back, jumping over the jumps close to her horse and sitting pretty when she wasn't jumping. What a shame that she couldn't continue competing. Not one fault and her time was under his. I finished the run and proceeded over to him. "Well how did I do?"

"Do you really have to ask?" he laughed.

We raced the horses back to the stables and gave them a rub down. As we put the tackle back, I turned to Dave. "You know Dave, it's as though I never left here."

"Maybe to you it seems like you never left, but there are two here who know that you left. We are however glad that you are back. I'll tell you something else you may have left as an attractive girl, but you have come back as a beautiful young lady. By the way, I took the liberty of arranging dinner for tonight. I have already cleared it with your Uncle Pat. I am taking you out for your birthday and I am not taking no for an answer." He looked at me with a look of authority and as though he was in charge.

"I wasn't going to say no. After all, how could I say no to someone who greets me with a rose, which I never said thank you for." I stepped closer to him and gave him a kiss.

"Cat I will pick you up at six, okay?" He looked at me waiting for an answer.

We started to walk back to the house together. "Six it will be. Any particular dress that I should be wearing?"

"No, just look great like you always do," he laughed.

He left me at the house and I went up to get washed because no matter where we were going, they definitely wouldn't appreciate us smelling like horses.

"So did you ride Stephanie's Fury?" asked Stuart.

"Yes, it was such a great feeling to be back on her," I exclaimed.

"Is that all that you did down there? Wasn't there anything else?"

"If you mean was Dave there. Yes he was, but I figured you knew that already. I supposed you also knew that he was going to take me out for my birthday too, didn't you?"

"Yes, I knew all that but he made me promise not to say a word to you. You know that guy is really taken by you. I have tried everything to match him up with some girls, but he just keeps comparing them to you. Oh, he goes to dances with us and he enjoys himself, but that is as far as it goes."

"I guess then that you know where he is taking me to tonight, don't you?"

"Yes I know, but once again lady I am sworn to secrecy. You will just have to wait and find out for yourself. Don't you know that curiosity killed the cat?" He laughed.

"Yeah Stuart, but don't you know that this cat has nine lives."

"I'll tell you this much Stephanie, put on your

nicest dress, and prepare to dance the night away."

"Thanks a lot Stuart."

He left, and I started to look for a dress that would be appropriate for the evening. I finally found one, a pretty pink one that was slightly low cut but not too low, just enough to accentuate my figure. I went downstairs to wait. The family had finished their dinner and was sitting in the family room. When I walked in Uncle Pat looked up from his paper and said, "Look what we have here."

"Stephanie, you have matured since you left here," exclaimed Aunt Elizabeth.

"It is nice to see you again Aunt Elizabeth, and I must thank you for teaching me all the things that you did when I was here. They really came in handy when I went back home." I didn't know if she would be pleased with that or if it would make her mad. To think that she actually helped me in the process of punishing me. She had taught me to do chores and accept responsibilities.

"You know that I don't know if I should let Dave take you out or punch him in the nose and take you out myself. You look like the most attractive lady that I have seen in these parts," Stuart exclaimed.

"Now that's enough. I'm still the same girl that I was when I left here. I don't look any better than I did then," I replied , blushing as I was saying it.

All of a sudden, there was a knock on the door. I turned to see Stuart looking at me. "Well Lady Stephanie, this is the moment you have been waiting for." He got up to answer the door, and for the first time Aunt Elizabeth didn't tell Stuart off for calling me Lady Stephanie.

"You know for once Stephanie I must agree with Stuart. You do look like a lady," Aunt Elizabeth commented.

I could hear Stuart joking with Dave in the other room. Their voices were getting louder as the closer they got. When they came through the doorway, Stuart was chuckling. "I have already told Dave to have you home before eleven and to keep an eye on you, so that some other good looking fella doesn't snatch you from him."

"Stuart said that you looked great, but he didn't say that you looked that great," Dave said, as he looked me over with stunned look on his face.

"Now Dave you can forget what Stuart said. Just take Stephanie out and have a good time," Uncle Pat said to Dave from behind the newspaper.

"Okay we will and thanks," Dave said as he took me by the hand and escorted me outside to where his sports car was waiting.

"Are you now going to tell me where we are going, Dave?"

"No, not until we are there and maybe not even then. Stuart told me that you were trying to get it out of him," he said laughingly. "You really haven't changed a bit. You always needed to know everything that was going on, otherwise you didn't have the upper edge in a situation. Well, lady this is one time you aren't having the upper edge."

"You are definitely not going to tell me anything, even if I resort to crying?"

"I know you better than that. You wouldn't resort to tears because your face would be all red when you got to the place, and you wouldn't like that because everyone would know that you were crying."

"I have to admit you sure did your homework on this one, didn't you."

"The main point of this evening is to make sure that you have a great time, one that you will never forget, and one that will make you never forget me."

"Boy, you sure have your work cut out for you tonight, don't you?"

"Yes, but I know that I can accomplish everything that I set out to do, so just sit back and enjoy the ride."

I've got to admit I was having the time of my life, and I already knew that I wouldn't be able to forget tonight no matter what. I thought of Tom for a split second and thought what he would say if he knew that this was happening. I knew too that I could never tell Tom about this evening, well at least not the whole story. I would tell him that we went out to dinner to celebrate my birthday and that would be all. We kept driving until Dave put on the signal to turn into a driveway.

"This is the place, isn't it?" I asked like a little school girl.

"I told you that I wasn't telling you anything, so you might as well forget about asking," he said sternly. Yet, he still had a smile on his face.

We drove up the driveway to a quaint cottage like setting. As we got out of the car, somebody came, collected the keys, and drove it away. We went inside and the gentleman inside said to Dave, "Your table is ready for you Mr. Thompson."

"Everything the way I requested?"

"I'm sure you will find everything to be satisfactory," the man replied, as he led us to a table in front of a fireplace. There on the table was a candle and on my plate there was a single rose. The gentleman sat me down at the table after pulling my chair out. Shortly after we had been sitting at the table, a waiter brought us each a drink in a fancy glass.

"Dave, is there anything that you have forgotten. I mean the fireplace, the candle, the rose, you even had the drinks ready. What else could there be?"

"Just sit back and enjoy this evening. It is just beginning," he said to me as he gazed at me with a smile on his face.

We were served dinner. As we were eating, music could be heard playing in the background. They started to play a certain tune that I didn't know, but it sounded so romantic.

"May I have this dance? I think that they are playing our tune," Dave said as he stretched out his hand toward me.

We danced around the room cheek to cheek. As he held me close to his body and we moved around the room, there seemed to be an electric current flowing from him to me. The atmosphere was perfect for him to capture my heart. I don't know how to express it, but what I felt was totally different from what I felt when I danced with Tom. With Tom, I felt that we danced as one and were the only ones in the room. This was different. It was as though Dave had taken full control over me. His eyes were looking right into my soul and he knew what was needed to control this cat. I knew that he was the one that had the power to control this cat, and that I had to keep my guard up or lose to the master. He also knew that I loved every minute of the night so far, and that he intrigued me.

During the rest of the meal we danced several times, but none were as special as the first dance. We were sitting having our tea when the waiter brought over a very small cake with a sparkler on it. My face went red with embarrassment. I mean everybody was watching the waiter to see where he was going with this cake. After we finished our meal, we left the restaurant in his car.

"Dave I have to admit there is no way that I will ever forget tonight or the person that made it possible."

"Don't thank me yet. The night isn't over yet."

"What else could you have planned that could possibly top this evening?"

"Just sit back and watch," he said as he glanced at me. We drove for a while, and then he turned into the parking lot. We got out of the car and walked for a while. Here we were at the beach with the water lapping against the shoreline. He really had thought of everything to make the evening perfect. As we walked along the beach he stopped all of a sudden. Turning to me, he reached into his pocket.

"Now for your birthday gift," he said as he handed me a small package.

"Dave, you didn't have to get me a gift. This evening was more than enough for a gift."

"No, it wasn't not for your sixteenth. I told you that I was going to make this an evening that you wouldn't forget it or me, and I meant every word of it. So here is your birthday gift," he said as he handed me the tiny wrapped gift that he had pulled from his pocket.

As I opened the small box, inside was a small ring. My look must have been one of total astonishment. Dave took the ring out of the box. "Here read the inside before you say anything." He lit a match so that I would have some light. Inside the ring I read the following engraving, "H/B 16th Cat, Dave."

"Cat, whenever you are in trouble, or just need a friend, just look at that ring and call me. I know right now that all we can be is friends, but maybe someday we could be more. Right now, you have things to learn and to experience, as do I. Please accept the ring; the stone is your birthstone, so that is all anybody needs to know." He took my right hand in his and then placed the ring on my fourth finger. He came closer and gave me a gentle kiss on the lips that seemed to linger forever. When he stopped he said, "Happy Birthday Cat." He no sooner got the words out than I brought him back close to me. "I haven't thanked you yet for making this an evening that I will never forget." I returned his kiss. I no longer felt like a little girl. I felt that I was starting to venture into the world of being a woman.

"Now, I'm sorry to say, but it's time to take you home before I forget myself and do something that would ruin this evening."

We got back into the car and headed for home. When we got home, he opened the car door and helped me out of the car. He put his arms around me and gave me one last kiss. "Now you can dream about tonight and I will see you tomorrow."

I went into the house and up to my bedroom. As I opened the door to my bedroom there was Stuart sitting on my bed.

"Gee, I thought that you were never coming home. How did the night go anyway, Lady?"

"I thought that everyone in the house was in bed and besides, I thought that you knew what Dave had planned for this evening."

"Well, I knew most of the evening, but I knew that Dave wouldn't tell me everything just in case you managed to get it out of me. So did you enjoy yourself? I know that is a crazy question. Just by looking at you I can see that it will take all week to bring you down from the cloud that you are on."

"Stuart I never knew that life could be so good. We had a perfect evening. He thought of everything."

"Well cousin, you better get some sleep because we have a busy day tomorrow. Maybe I should tell Dave to keep away for the rest of the week, so that I can have some time with you."

"Good-night Stuart," I said as sternly as I could.

He was right. I was on cloud nine and sleep seemed to be the furthest thing from my mind, but soon I drifted off to sleep. Morning seemed to come quicker than usual.

"Come on sleepy head, rise and shine." Stuart opened my bedroom door and yelled.

He went downstairs and was having breakfast when I got down the stairs. "Hurry up and eat, we have a lot to do." I ate my breakfast and then we went outside and down to the horses. First, we groomed them, and then we raced each other. We took the horses slowly over to the pond that still had ice on it, even though this year the weather was considerably milder for this time of the year. When we got the horses back to the stables, we gave them a rub down and put them back in their stalls.

"Now go in and get cleaned up. We are going to meet Father at work for lunch, so don't be too long," he said as we walked back to the house.

Charles drove us into Toronto, where Uncle Pat worked was a Senior Partner at the investment firm of McConnell and McBean. He was standing outside the building waiting for us. He got into the car and directed Charles to go to the Stock Exchange building on Bay Street.

"I thought that while you were up here visiting, that you might like to see the stock exchange and see where your stocks are being traded," said Uncle Pat.

"I've arranged a tour for us, and then we will go for lunch."

We went into the Stock Exchange and were greeted by a man who was waiting there for us. He greeted Uncle Pat and then came over to Stuart and myself.

"Pat has told me about his young niece and her interest in the stock market. He has also told me how well your stocks are doing. So Stephanie, how about if we show you where it all happens?"

We went into a room that overlooked what they called the floor. There was paper all over the place and people running about with the papers in their hands. Above them was a board with numbers going across it showing which stocks were trading at present, and what price there were trading for. Then there was another area in which the stock brokers were sitting talking to their customers on the phones. The whole atmosphere absolutely fascinated me. After the tour, the man turned to me and asked, "Well what do you think? Would you like to work here someday, Stephanie?"

"No, I think I'll stay on the investor side of the business," I replied. We then proceeded to have lunch and then dropped Uncle Pat off back at his office and Charles took us home.

As we were driving home Stuart said, "You had better get a good night's sleep tonight, because tomorrow we are going into Toronto for the day. We will ride the horses when we get back."

"Are there any other plans that you haven't told me about?" I asked with a laughingly. "You know if I had known that you had all this planned, I would have brought my roller skates with me."

"Well I thought that we would go to the museum tomorrow, and the day after that I thought maybe we could go ice skating. After all, you are supposed to be on vacation. That will bring us up to the weekend. I thought that you could rest on the weekend before we take you to the airport on Sunday. Why is that too much for you?"

"No, but for a minute there I thought that you were trying to keep me away from Dave." I looked at him with a gleam in my eye.

"I have to admit that I like being seen with such an attractive girl, and if Dave were there, he would be around you more than me. Anyway, knowing Dave he will be around sometime or the other. If he happens to be here when we are going, then he can come along too."

That was how the week went, Dave came along with us on some of the outings and on the days that he didn't, we usually saw him at night. During the whole week it seemed like there was competition between the two of them as to who was going to be with me. This trip was nothing like the time I spent here before. This was the most beautiful time in my life.

The time went by too quickly, and soon it was

Sunday and time to leave. Dave came over to take me to go the airport. He and Stuart had both wanted to take me to the airport but Dave got to take me. His theory was that Stuart had picked me up at the airport, and therefore it was only fair that he got to take me to the airport. So after good-byes were said, Dave and I set off to the airport.

We got there in plenty of time and I put my suitcases through customs and then we went to the coffee shop, to kill some time.

"Cat, promise me that if ever you need my help, or you just need to talk to someone, you will call me," Dave said as he clutched my hand.

"I promise that when things get tough, I'll look down at my ring. I'll remember the guy that gave it to me, the night that he gave it to me, and that he is only a phone call away. If things get too bad, I promise that I'll call you."

We started to walk to the gate. "I won't say goodbye, because I know that we will see each other again," Dave said as I was about to go through the gate.

I reached out and pulled him close, and gave him a big kiss. I said to him, "This is to last you until the next time we meet."

Chapter Fifteen

The plane landed as scheduled and Tom was there to greet me. All of a sudden, I had to put Dave out of my mind or at least at the back of it. The first time that I noticed him was when I went to pick up my luggage. There was this man running toward me, at first I didn't recognize him, until he grabbed me, pulled me into his arms and started to kiss me. At first I thought, who is this stranger, and what does he think that he's doing kissing me. I recognized the kiss, and oh what a kiss. As we came out of the embrace I looked at the smile on his face. "I don't need to ask if you missed me. That kiss told me everything."

"I just hope that you missed me as much as I missed you."

"I can't tell you how much I missed you," I replied looking at him with eyes that seemed to say, "You're the only one for me. Why do you have to ask?"

"I told you that you had nothing to worry about, that you are the only one in my life. You must realize that I grew up there and that it will always be part of my heart. I grew up more there then I did here. The luxury that they live in, the horse back riding, and the people I met will always be special to me."

"I do realize that, but I am so glad that you are back here in my arms. Now I suppose that we need to take this stuff back home, heh?"

I decided then that I must learn how to keep my feelings for Dave and everyone in my other lifestyle to myself. After all, this is where I had to live and not in the mansion. We drove back to the house and I took my luggage into the house. Things hadn't changed much since I was away. Ben and Bridgette were the same and Mother's health hadn't improved. When we arrived at the house the doctor was there checking on Mother.

Tom stayed for a while, but decided to leave before the doctor came out of Mother's room. I was glad that he had since I had to unpack and get a bit of a rest. "Look, if you feel like it, give me a call later. If you don't, then I will see you tomorrow at school." He bent over and gave me a good-night kiss at the doorway. I watched as he went down the driveway and out of sight.

I started to put my clothes away and was just about to put the suitcase away at the top of my closet when there was a knock at the bedroom door. I turned around, to see Ben poking his head around the corner. "I thought you would like to know that the doctor just came out of Mother's room."

"Thanks Ben, I do want to know what he has to say." We went into the living room where the doctor was talking to Father.

"All that you can do now is keep giving her the medication and pray that it starts to work soon. The fact that she relapsed without building up her strength doesn't help matters. I would also advise that somebody be in the house with her at all hours of the day. I am sorry that I can't say anything that is more optimistic." The doctor shook Father's hand as he was going out the door. He said, "Take care and I pray that the medication starts to work."

"Thanks doctor for what you have done. I guess that it is now up to the Lord." Father turned away and headed for a chair in the living room. He looked as if he had been through a war or something. He was distraught, tired and finally let his emotions take control. He began to cry.

I knew from what the doctor had said that things got worse since they decided to let me go on my vacation. I also knew that I had to comfort the rest of the family since I grew up away from everything that had happened to this family. I didn't seem to be going through the same pain. I walked over to Father, put my arms around him, and I gave him a little hug. I gently massaged his shoulders. "Don't worry. I will stay home with Mother, while you go to work. I will get Tom to bring my schoolwork home for me and he can take the assignments back to school for me. You have to go to work in order to take care of the family, and the twins must go to their school. It is only logical that I take on the responsibility of caring for Mother. Besides, I just came back from my vacation so I am well rested."

"I know that what you are saying is right, but I just don't like taking you out of school. What happens if you have an assignment that you don't understand?"

"I leave it until you get home. After all, that is the joy of having a father who is a teacher."

So it was settled, I went back to my old routine again with the exception that I didn't go to school. Every day, I did the same stuff over and over again, but now I no longer had time for Tom. I ended up telling him to send my work home with Sandy. She had to pass by my house on the way home anyway. The only time that I wasn't working now seemed to be when I was sleeping and then my father was with Mother. Due to the fact that the pneumonia had settled in her chest, Mother now wheezed when she breathed. As long as you heard that noise coming from her room, you knew that she was resting.

By the beginning of the second week I was starting to get the feeling that I was nothing more than a built in maid service. However, a maid had it better than I did. Her shifts would come to an end, and she was allowed to go home or go to the sanctuary of her private room. My shifts however, never seemed to end.

One of those days when I had just finished doing the dishes in the morning, and was just about to start my homework, I suddenly had a strange feeling. I didn't know what it was, but I knew I better go in and check on Mother. I went into her room and there she was awake. I couldn't believe my eyes so I rushed over to her.

"Mother, you are awake. How are you feeling?"

"Come here Stephanie. Your Grandfather McConnell asked me to tell you to trace your family history back to him, to find your destiny. Now I must go to join him." She slowly dropped my hand and closed her eyes..

"Mother wake up, don't leave me, wake up, wake up," I cried. I knew what was happening and I couldn't stop it. "Mother, don't do this to me, I just got you back. We have so much to do, there are so many things that you have to show me. If you die who will show me how to work your camera. Mother, come back to me." I lay my head on her chest to see if I could hear her heart, but here was nothing there. The tears started to flow. I couldn't stop them. I phoned the doctor who said that he would rush right over, and then called my father to tell him to come home.

The doctor was there before I knew it; he met me in my Mother's room where I was still trying to bring her back even though I knew that it was useless. "Why don't you go and make yourself a cup of tea and try to relax Stephanie." So I left him to check on Mother while I made a pot of tea knowing that Father would be there soon. The doctor came back into the room before the tea was even made. "I'm sorry Stephanie, but she is in his hands now. Take one of these with your tea, it'll help you calm down." With that he took some pills out of his bag and offered them to me.

"I don't want a pill to calm me down. I just want my mother back," I yelled at him. Just as I was doing that my father walked through the doorway.

He started to cry when he heard me and ran into her room.

"No, they didn't have to take you away from me. What did we do so wrong that he's punishing us like this? First the twins and now they have taken you away. Why?" We could hear him screaming. When he finally did come out of the room, the doctor embraced him the same way that he had done with me.

"I know doctor that you did everything that you could for her, but why did she have to die?"

The doctor left us and I went to make the phone calls to the family. As I went to get the numbers Father poured himself a drink of scotch. When the twins came home the crying started over again. I finally managed to get the call through to Uncle Pat.

"Uncle Pat this is Stephanie, I have some bad news for you. Mother... (I started to cry again, then I caught a hold on myself), Uncle Pat, Mother just passed away."

"Stephanie, are you and the family okay?" Uncle Pat asked.

"We will be okay. It's just the shock of it right now," I sobbed. "We still have to make the funeral arrangements."

"Stephanie, tell your father that we are sorry to hear about your mother, and that I'll be on the next flight to be with the rest of you."

After hanging up the phone, I relayed Uncle Pat's message to Father. There wasn't any other family to notify since there was none of Mother's family left and Uncle Pat was Father's only family. It would now just be a matter of notifying friends of the arrangements.

They came and took Mother's body away from the

house and it was Father's job to make the funeral arrangements at the funeral home. This wasn't the kind of place that I would have liked to go to, but I went merely to support Father. He had decided the funeral would only be two days and that should be enough time for everybody to say their good-byes to Mother.

On the casket there were two large bouquets placed. One was a bouquet of roses with a ribbon on them that read, "To a loving Mother." The other one, made of red and white carnations had a ribbon that said, "To a loving Wife." Just over from there we placed three pictures, two of them were of the family at Christmas and the other one was one that was taken of Mother over in Africa. She had a pretty white cotton dress on that she used to wear on Sundays when we were there.

Uncle Pat, Aunt Elizabeth and Stuart had arrived for the funeral. They had booked into a hotel since they already knew that we didn't have enough room to put them up. Uncle Pat greeted each one of us with a hug and a kiss, then he went to see Mother. He thought that no-one was close enough to hear, but I was. "Valerie, why did it have to be you. Why couldn't you have married me instead? Then none of this would have happened to you. I loved you so much." After he finished saying his good-byes he secretly wiped the tears from his eyes.

Aunt Elizabeth in the meantime, was comforting Father. "Are you okay, James? Is there anything that I can do for you?"

"Elizabeth, I keep wondering if this isn't the way the Lord is getting back at me for that last time that we were together. I know that you are trying to comfort me, but I can't help wondering if I'm being punished."

"James that was a long time ago, both of us have been happily married until this happened. Valerie just had to much handed to her on her plate, I mean all that happened to the twins and then the pneumonia. Either one of those things take their toll on the human body, but to have both things happen at the same time is just too much. James, just look at it this way. She is at rest now and you must go on for the sake of your family." Aunt Elizabeth comforted Father which she seemed to have done before in the past.

Stuart had now caught up with me. He gently embraced me and asked, "How are you holding up Stephanie?"

"You know me Stuart, after the shock wears off I'll be okay. It's the twins and Father that I worry about. They have been here all along, I just came back to this family. By the way, have you met the twins yet?"

"No, I thought that I would come and see how you were doing first. Dave sent this for you." He handed me an envelope from his pocket.

"I will open it later. Now I'll take you over to the twins." We walked across the room where the twins were comforting each other. I put my arms around them. "Come on now we've got to be strong. Isn't that what Mother would have wanted? She would have said that we didn't come this far to fall on our faces. Now chins up, we still have a long way to go. There now do you feel better?" They were both drying their tears.

"Okay. Now I would like you to meet your cousin Stuart. I would have liked this meeting to have been under different circumstances. However, Stuart this is Ben. Make sure that when you talk to him, you are facing him," I said as I pointed toward Ben. "Stuart this is Bridgette and since you do not use sign language I would advise that when you talk to her that you have Ben or myself around or a piece of paper."

By now my friends had arrived, some with their parents, others just by themselves to pay their respects. When Tom arrived with his Grandmother, I took them over and introduced them to Stuart. Then Sandy and her parents came along with Jenny. When I came back from talking to some of the other people that were there, I found Stuart talking to Tom, Sandy and Jenny. "Stuart you don't know how glad I am that you are Stephanie's cousin. With your looks then I definitely would have worried about her going to Canada to visit a couple of weeks ago."

Stuart's dark hair, his dimpled chin and his sexy looking eyes had not only caught Tom's eyes but also those of Sandy. "I'm glad too that you are her cousin, because that means that I can try and convince you to come and visit more often. By the way, when will you be going back?" Sandy was saying to Stuart, not wasting any time in trying to get to know my cousin.

"Stuart, shall I save you from all these questions my friends seem to have found for you?" I waltzed over and took him by the arm. "We will be leaving soon for the evening. I was going to see whether or not your parents would like to come over to the house for a while. Would you mind coming with me while I ask them?"

"I don't know about them, but I would like to come back with you, so let's go ask them."

We went over to Uncle Pat and Aunt Elizabeth and they agreed to come back to the house. When we arrived there, I made a pot of tea and a platter of sandwiches, since it was a long time since anyone had eaten anything. I put out our best cups and saucers, trying to make everything look right and then served the tea. Stuart and I left the rest of them having their tea while we walked down to the beach.

I had already taken time to read Dave's note, which simply said, "Sorry to hear about your mother, Cat. Remember the ring if things get too tough. Love Dave."

"Stuart would you do me a favour?"

"Sure Stephanie, what is it?"

"Could you tell Dave that I will remember. He will

know what I mean."

"Yes I will do that, but he also told me to do something for him."

"What was that?"

We had been walking along the beach while we were talking, but when I asked him what Dave had asked him to do, I noticed that he no longer was beside me. I turned around and looked at him. "What is it Stuart?" He held his hand out to me, I reached out and took it. As he pulled me close to him, he quietly said, "He told me to hold you close so that you could let everything that is pent up in you out, and then to make sure that the hurt goes away. So Stephanie let all that hurt inside of you out and just let those tears flow."

I started to cry, the more that I cried the closer that Stuart held me. Then all of a sudden Stuart said, "Okay Stephanie I think that all of the hurt should be out of you, now it is time to make you feel better." Still holding me close, he kissed me on the forehead, then the cheek, and next on the lips. When he got to the lips, he gave a short quick kiss and then a slow lingering kiss. "I guess that I am not as good a Dave is, but has the hurt started to go away?"

"That helped a little, but I think that I could use a little more first aid." I looked back at him with my head slightly tilted, my eyes shining up at him in the moonlight. With that he took me in his arms again and slowly started to kiss me again. I needed to feel loved that night and Stuart sure was doing a good job of making me feel that way. Slowly, he worked his way down from my lips to my neck and then slowly to my breast. They started to tingle; they never felt that way before, and that triggered off my cat instinct. "Stuart, I think we ought to stop this."

"Stephanie doesn't it feel right, don't you feel good?" he replied, looking at me with those sexy eyes of his.

"That's the problem Stuart. It feels too good, too right, but you are my cousin."

"Don't worry Stephanie I would never do anything to hurt you. I love you too much to ever do that. Since I saw you in that pink dress the night that Dave took you out, I have wished that you weren't my cousin. You need to feel loved tonight and I am here. I promise you that I won't do anything that would hurt you, besides we could be like kissing cousins, couldn't we?"

"Kissing cousins, I like that but Tom won't." He pulled me back to his side and continued to kiss me from the mouth down to my breasts and back again. Then he said we should be going back to the house. All I wanted was more of his petting and kisses. He had started a fire in my body, one that would never go out.

The next day was the funeral and we laid my mother to rest. After the funeral, we had a tea back at our house. When everybody had left, we now had time to say our good-byes to Uncle Pat, Aunt Elizabeth and Stuart as they left to catch their flight home. Now with everyone gone it was time to get on with our lives.

Chapter Sixteen

Back to reality and getting on with our lives. The twins were back to their special school, Father was back at work and I went back to school. I had my routine down pat. I organized everybody's schedule along with their meals. The twins had now started to assist with things around the house, and things seemed to be running a little smoother.

I signed up for the photography course at school. With Mother gone, I had lost the best teacher in that subject area that I could have asked for. The fascination of looking through the lens of the camera was unbelievable. It was almost as though my mother was with me, helping me every step of the way. The information that my teacher gave to me came almost as if it were second nature. My assignments were a breeze because they provided me with such pleasure and relaxation.

Mrs. Black, my photography teacher came up to me one day in the hall. "Stephanie there is a contest coming up in two months. I think that your work is worth being entered. I was considering Tom's and Deborah's work along with your own. I think that all three of you have potential. Could you give it some thought and let me know if you want to enter?"

"Do you really think I have a chance, Mrs. Black?"

"Your work has the quality that makes the pictures seem to be jumping out at the person looking at them. As if the subject isn't a picture but the real thing. By the way, to help make up your mind there is prize money involved. It isn't much, one hundred dollars for first place, fifty dollars for second and twenty-five dollars for third. The pictures will be up against other High schools in the area."

I left Mrs. Black saying that I would think about it. When I got home I made the supper and then sat down to look at some of the pictures that I had photographed. I left them sprawled over the bed when I heard the rest of the family come home. It was now a family ritual after supper that we all sat down and did our homework, every one of us including Father. After Father had finished his homework, he started to do the bills and when I looked at him he had a very sad look on his face. He got up and poured himself a drink of scotch and then returned to the table to continue going over the figures.

Going over to him and placing my hand on his shoulder, I said to him, "Is it all bad news Father?"

"It sure doesn't look good. The bills seem to be more than I bring in. The insurance covered your mother's funeral expenses, but the medical bills mounted up in the meantime. We were just making it before your mother got sick."

"Then why did you send me back to Uncle Pat's place in March, if we didn't have the money?"

"That was at your mother's request. She said that we could manage without you and that you had been working too hard."

"Well, then how about if I get another job. I am sixteen now so I can get a job in the store. I can handle my school work at the same time. The twins can help around the house, but they must continue to go to their special school. It is helping them so much."

"Your mother wouldn't like to think that you had to work hard again to make ends meet, but if we don't get extra money then the twins will have to forfeit their school."

During this little talk with Father, I made up my mind about entering the photography contest. I would enter my best picture, but which one would that be? The next day after school I would go out and apply at the stores for work after school.

I went into store after store and soon I thought that I wasn't going to be so lucky. Finally, I got a job at the last store that I applied at. It was a fish and chip store where I would have to wait on customers and operate the cash register. The pay was nice too; I would be paid four dollars and fifty cents an hour. I would be working from four o'clock to six o'clock on Mondays through Wednesdays; from four o'clock to nine o'clock on Thursdays and Fridays and on Saturdays it was from twelve o'clock to six o'clock. This schedule would leave me Sundays to do my homework and maybe an hour or two for myself.

With all these things that were going on, I had to make sure that my marks didn't suffer in the process. I had to be sure that I was one step in front of everybody. I knew that if I was careful when I did it, I could find out what tests were scheduled and when. Simply by coming up quietly behind the teachers when they were talking, checking out their calendars on their desks, or just by plain eavesdropping outside the teachers lounge. Just by doing these few simple tricks I could find out lots of facts, and with this information I could plan so that I could study extra for a test in advance.

This was great until one day when Tom asked me to go out with him. "Come on Stephanie, you have been working, and doing homework. You need a break. We will just go for a walk along the beach, what do you say?"

"I can't Tom I have to study for the test." All of a sudden I realized that I had made a slip, the test had not been announced yet. I had tipped Tom off; now I will have to do some pretty fancy footwork to get out of this.

"Stephanie, I know that there are no tests scheduled. Does this mean that you don't want to see me, or is there something that you're not telling me?"

"Tom I have changed my mind, I think that a walk on the beach might be just what I need. I seem to have tests on my brain." I said hoping that this would put him off track. I grabbed him by the arm and led him toward the door. "See, you're right. I have been working too hard, I can't seem to think straight any more."

As we walked along the beach, we stopped here and there to give each other a kiss. The wind was blowing gently on our faces, blowing my long black hair around in a whirlwind. "Now, don't you feel better for a little R& R. What test were you going to study for, anyway?"

"There was no test. Let's get back to that R & R you were talking about." I bowed my head and looked up at him with eyes sparkling in the moonlight. Eyes that seemed to say, "That's enough talk for now." I moved toward him and gave him a slow seductive kiss that seemed to say everything that needed to be said.

He responded by slowly kissing me back on the lips, then down the neck. His hands seemed to follow his kisses down my body. We slowly slid down into the sand below us. The wind slowly caressed the open skin that Tom had uncovered while placing his sweet kisses over my body. "Steph, do you know how long I've wanted to do this with you. I love you so much, he said to me as he slowly went back to gently caressing my body with gentle touching and kisses. As he kissed around my breast, I felt my body arch to his gentle touch. I pulled him back up to my face area and passionately kissed him. "Do you want me to stop?" he gently asked.

"I don't know. It feels so right and yet it feels so wrong. Why do I feel this way? I know that I love you and that should make it right, but yet I have these reservations."

"I can't make you do anything that you don't want to do. All I can say is that once we do it, you will know that it was right, and you will enjoy it as much as I will. What is it going to be Steph?" He pulled me close to him and with his next kiss we were lying back in the sand, his hands exploring every part of my body. He slowing undid the buttons of my top and the front of my slacks. His body was next to mine, his seductive kisses captivating me all the time. My body arched as he passionately touched me from my breasts to my crotch, then he finished with his body joining mine. We separated and we lay there, our bodies slowly relaxing.

I turned to him and he turned to me we both had smiles on our faces. I knew that I felt totally relaxed, and I knew that I felt that it was right because we both loved each other and that we were making it right. As he slowly took his hand and brushed my hair out of my eyes, he spoke very gently. "Well, was it right? Did you enjoy it, did it feel right? You aren't sorry that you did it, are you?"

"I enjoyed it and I am not sorry that we did it, because making love with the one you love and the one who loves you makes it right." As I looked down at the exposed skin I started to blush as I slowly did my clothes back up. We brushed the sand off of us and slowly headed back to the house, hand in hand, exchanging kisses as we went.

As we walked back to the house Tom stopped. "You know that when we make love again, if ever, and you don't want to then say so and I'll respect your wishes. The only thing that matters to me is your happiness." We got up to the house and after he kissed me good-night he turned and said to me, "Now no more of this work, work until you get confused."

I went into the house satisfied that I had put Tom off the track concerning how I was able to know about tests. After all, if this got around school then I would have every student down on me to give them information and not just test dates. There was also the chance that the teachers would find out and then I would be suspended. I couldn't let that happen. Tom had also satisfied me in ways that he would never know and in doing so made me feel even more like a woman. The fire that Stuart had started Tom managed to satisfy for the moment. The fact that I did love Tom made it even better. I went off to a peaceful sleep with dreams that Tom and I would someday live happily ever after.

The next few days at school I was so happy that Tom and I had sealed the extent of our love by making love that I let my guard down. There I was checking out when the next three tests would be, forgetting the most important rule, and that was to make sure that no-one was around. I was checking the calendar on the history teacher's desk and for once my cat senses were clouded with feeling so good that I didn't notice that Bill was standing there watching me. Then when I went to see what I could get from outside the teacher's lounge, I didn't notice him there either. I rose up from my position of pretending to tie my shoelaces and started to walk along the hall, when Bill popped up in front of me. "Would you like to take a walk with me Stephanie?"

"Sure Bill, what's up?" I replied still not knowing that he had been watching me.

"Would you mind telling me what you were doing outside the teacher's lounge? You weren't eavesdropping now, were you?"

"No, I was just tying up my shoelaces," I replied looking at him with questioning eyes, trying to find out just what he was getting at.

"Then what is your excuse for what you did in the history room?"

"What? Is this a follow Stephanie around day?

What I was doing is none of your business or anybody else's." I was starting to get mad. I didn't like being followed, much less being accused of things even if the things I was being accused of were true.

"I know of several people that would be quite interested, namely the teachers or how about Tom. Yeah, what about Tom? Does he know that you are going around snooping? What would he think of his sweet Stephanie, then?"

"Bill, I didn't know that you were the kind of guy that cares what everybody else is doing. I thought that you were a nice guy. Look if you want to know the truth, I need an edge on everybody else because I have to work to make ends meet. I can't afford to let my grades drop. Besides it's not like I am stealing the test papers, I'm just finding out when they are so that I can fit in extra time for studying. Now you aren't going to tell anybody, are you?" With my last words I looked at him with the saddest eyes I could muster, trying to work on his compassion.

"Well, give me one good reason why I shouldn't, Stephanie? After all, I don't see what keeping quiet will do for me."

"One is that you are a nice guy, and another is that you are my friend, or at least I thought that you were."

"Tell you what Stephanie. You share your information with me and I won't tell anybody about your spying tactics. How about that?"

"It looks like I have no choice in the matter, doesn't it? I guess I will have to go along with you on this. Just remember that no-one is to know, absolutely no-one."

Bill had me and I knew that at this moment there was nothing that I could do, but I also wasn't going to let him get away with it either. As the two of us were ending our discussion, Tom came up behind me and put his arm around my waist. "Now should I be jealous, finding my best friend with my girlfriend?"

"Now you should know better than that Tom. Bill and I just had some things to talk about. I was just getting ready to leave for work," I said flashing my cross eyes back at Bill. If looks could kill, there would have been one corpse lying at Tom's feet.

"Wait a minute and I will walk with you. I just want to talk to Bill for a second."

"Okay, I have to get some things from my locker, so I will meet you there." I turned and walked away from the two of them leaving them talking to one another. I never thought that Bill would turn out to be an enemy of mine. He always seemed so understanding.

I was just putting my lock back on my locker when Tom reappeared. "Come on, I'll carry your books to the store for you," he said as he put his arm around me and we walked out of the school. "Are you going to tell me what that was all about back there or not?"

"There was nothing going on. We were just talking about school work, that's all."

"Stephanie I know you better than anybody. Remember this is me that you are talking to now. I know that what was going on back there wasn't just about school work."

"Look it's nothing, just something that Bill and I just have to settle. Now don't worry anymore about it." I smiled back at him to reassure him that everything would be okay.

"I hope that it's nothing. I can't stand to see you mad and hurting, especially if it's my best friend that is the cause of it."

He dropped it for the time being and we continued on to work. There he handed me back my books and gave me a kiss good-bye. "Now don't you work too hard, you hear."

"No way! Not this kid. Not unless I want some R & R with a certain cute looking guy that has my heart in his hands."

"Well if you put it that way, you can work till you are just about ready to drop," he laughed as he turned and waved good-bye.

There was nothing that I could do about Bill right now, but sit and wait for him to make the wrong move. I began to keep my eye on him, watching every move that he made. I would only have to put up with this blackmail for a couple more weeks since summer was approaching quickly. When summer came I would be working more hours, which would please me but not Tom. Since it would be like we were still in school with the amount of time that we would be able to spend with each other.

The results of the photo contest would be announced in the last week of school. I could hardly wait for the day to arrive. No one would know who had won until the pictures went on display in the mall on the Saturday before school was out for the summer. At that time, they would announce the winners and present them with their prizes.

I had to work that day, but luckily the store was in the same mall, so I figured that I could look at the pictures on display on my break. I was busy taking some orders when Tom came into the store. Patiently he waited for me to get free. "How did you do in the photo contest, Tom?"

"Second place. It wasn't bad considering the competition was so tough. You should see the pictures that we were up against. Some of them are just beautiful. By the way, how about dinner after work to celebrate my winning second place?"

"Sure. I'll phone home and tell them that I'll be late coming home and not to keep dinner for me. Were the pictures that good?"

"When are you going down to look at them?"

"I thought that I would go on my break. It will be in another fifteen minutes. Will you be around then?"

"I suppose that I could walk around the shops and come back and meet you then."

He left and I went back to serving my customers. It seemed like he had just left when Tom returned with a pop and some potato chips for me to eat while we looked at the display. He was right when he said that the pictures were good. In fact, I wondered how we even had a chance. I kept looking for mine since Tom never mentioned seeing it and I was sure that if it had won anything that he would have said something.

We were just about finished looking at the pictures and still I hadn't come across mine. I was starting to get depressed "What's the matter? I thought that you were happy about me winning. What's with the face?"

"I was just hoping that mine might have won something, even an honorable mention."

"Well, we haven't finished going through the honorable mention winners yet. Maybe yours is in there." We kept on walking. Still my picture was nowhere to be seen. We turned the corner of the pictures that had won honorable mentions. The next one had a third prize ribbon on it, but it wasn't mine. Then the next picture was Tom's with a second prize ribbon on it. "Looks pretty good with the second prize ribbon on it, heh?" he said as he stood beside his picture.

"Yeah, it looks pretty good. Now where is the one that beat you out of first prize?"

"It's over here. The photographer that shot this picture is out of my league. In fact, I can't believe that he is in High school." He took me by the arm as we went over to the picture with the first prize ribbon on it. As soon as I caught a glimpse of the picture I realized that I had won first prize. The eyes of the Black Jaguar in the picture that I had shot seemed to be following me. The picture was of a mother jaguar carrying a baby jaguar over to where the father jaguar was lying looking at me. The way that I had captured the shot, the picture seemed to come alive. The male jaguar's tongue was out of its mouth just a bit and the facial expression on the cub was perfect.

"I told you that the photographer was great. I even heard that she might be up for a scholarship in photography if she is still into it next year. Come with me now and we will collect your prize money."

"Tom, I don't believe it. You are joking about the scholarship, though, aren't you?"

"Yeah, but anything is possible," he said as he took me over to where they were handing out the prize money.

"You have a great talent with the camera. Are you intending to take up photography as a career, Stephanie?" asked the person handing me the money.

"I enjoy it, but I had intended on studying law and becoming a lawyer," I replied.

"Well, keep in mind that you could try selling your photographic work to pay for your schooling. We have had offers for the first, second and third prize winning pictures already. If you want to sell your picture, let us know." They handed both of us a card with their names on it along with their phone number.

"Tom, can you believe this? We both won." I was on cloud nine.

"Stephanie I hate to be the bearer of bad news, but you do have to go back to work, remember."

He was right, of course, but how was I supposed to work when I had just won first prize? I went back to work and told everybody my good news. I had won first prize in the photo contest. It seemed it was impossible to work even though I knew that I had to, but the Lord seemed to take care of that. When I came back from my break business was slow. After about an hour had gone by we had a line up almost out the door, so my high feeling soon disappeared as I went back to serving the customers. When six o'clock came I was totally worn out. All I wanted to do was put my feet up and rest. Then I saw Tom at the window of the store and I remembered that it wouldn't be so.

"Are you ready to celebrate?" Tom asked as I opened the door.

"I guess I am as ready as I ever will be. Please just tell me I don't have to walk too far," I pleaded with him.

We just walked down the mall to a little pizzeria. This is where most kids liked to go. Inside you had the choice of whether you sat in a booth or a little wooden table with fresh cut flowers on them. We normally took the booth so that we had more privacy. They always had nice soft music playing (not out of date music like what Mother and Father listened to) but modern soft music. The kind that allowed you to hear what the other person was saying to you, without telling everyone in the place what you only wanted the person you were with to hear.

We ordered our usual, a pizza with green peppers, pepperoni, onions, double cheese and a pitcher of coke to celebrate with. Tom was looking over at me. His eyes were hypnotizing as he reached over and took my hand in his.

"Well, how does it feel to be a winner? Does it feel the same as when you won riding or are you getting immune to the feeling?" He was joking I knew, but there was truth in what he was saying.

"It feels great. I don't think that you ever get used to winning. Every time feels like the first time when you take first prize. How do you feel about taking second prize? After all, you are a winner too; you must feel like you're on cloud nine too."

There was another good thing that the teenagers liked about sitting in these booths. You could sit close to your boyfriend. As I asked him how he felt about being second, I put my hand gently along the side of his face and looked intently into his eyes.

"I have to admit, Stephanie, that when I saw that I was only second I felt pretty damn low. I thought, I guess I better work on my camera work a little bit more if I ever thought that I could take first prize. Then, when I walked along and saw the picture that you had entered and there was a first prize ribbon on it, well, then, I didn't feel so bad. I mean, that if I was going to lose out to somebody then I was glad it was you. I don't know how you did it or where you got that shot. All I know is that the way the cat's eyes follow you wherever you go, they must have hypnotized the judges. Anyway, when you looked at that picture it had winner written all over it. No wonder you wouldn't let anybody see it before you entered it."

"The eyes in that cat are mysterious, aren't they? That's what attracted me to the cats when we were in Africa. Over there the little cubs had such sensitive, warm caring eyes that seemed to say that they wouldn't hurt anybody. The parent cat's eyes were mysterious, deep and dangerous, almost hypnotic at times. I shot that picture at the zoo, the last time that we went there, don't you remember? By the way, when did you shoot that picture of me that won you second prize?"

"Strangely enough, at the zoo that very same day you shot your picture. It must have been a lucky day for us," he said, laughing.

"Just goes to show that you can't see everything when you are looking through the lens of a camera. When you're shooting the picture of something, then somebody else may be taking a picture of you, heh?"

"I guess I am going to have to be on guard for any extra eyes that might be watching me. Catching me doing things that I don't want anybody to know about," I replied, as I looked at him with my head slightly bent watching him with the top of my eyes and a slight smile. Now our pizza had come and Tom poured us another drink of pop.

As he cut a piece of pizza and placed it on my plate he commented. "You know, when you look like that, you have the same cat eyes that the cat in your picture had. Maybe I should be careful of you."

"Why would you have to be careful around me? What could possibly happen to you?" I hadn't changed my expression as I spoke.

"I don't know but if you end up having the same personality as that cat, then I could be in danger if ever I crossed you." Shaking his head he started to laugh as he placed a piece of pizza on his plate.

I took his hand in mine, "Luv, there's one thing that you must remember about cats. That is they take care of their own, so as long as we love each other then we are each other's."

We left the pizza place for the show. There was a comedy playing. It was called "The Day of Monkeyshines," all about these crazy and hilarious situations that a bunch of kids get into. We sat and laughed so much that our sides were hurting by the time we came out of the show. Tom had the car, so we didn't have to walk home. We took the scenic route home along the coast so that we could gaze at the stars. The stars were so bright that they looked like they were close enough to be picked out of the sky and put in your pocket. A gentle breeze that was blowing in from the ocean felt fresh on our faces as it blew in through the car windows. We pulled off the road into what they called a scenic outlook point that was found all along the coast.

We left the car and walked along the beach slowly embracing each other as we walked, stopping only to exchange kisses with one another. As we stopped and exchanged a loving embrace, I could feel the passion from Tom's hand as they gently felt their way over my body like a blind man reading Braille. He looked up into my eyes to see whether or not he had read me right or not.

I looked back at him, "Not here. It's too public and besides, I must get back home."

"Like always I guess that you are right, but we will be together again soon, won't we?"

"When the time is right, we will both know it but tonight is not it. You know how I feel when I'm with you. There is no other feeling like it."

We drove the rest of the way home in silence. I knew that I had disappointed him by saying "no" tonight. He had wanted to celebrate tonight in every sense of the word and sharing our love was to him the ultimate way of celebrating. We pulled into the driveway, and bending over toward him I gave him a long sensual kiss. As I kissed him we could feel the icy wall that had been forming between us on the ride home, slowly start to melt away.

"You said you would understand whenever I said "no" to making love. Now show me that you do understand why I said "no" tonight." He pulled me back closer and returned the kiss that I had given him. The temperature between the two of us was rising to boiling point and I knew that it was now time for me to leave.

With just enough smile, he said, "I do understand. I don't like it but I do understand."

"It's time for me to go in now," I said as I bent over and gave him a good-night kiss. He pulled me back and gave me one last kiss.

"Good-night Steph, I'll catch you tomorrow."

"Yes, until tomorrow, then." I stepped out of the car and went into the house.

Chapter Seventeen

Time was going by; Tom and Bill were in their last year of High school. Ben and Bridgette were in the equivalent of the fourth year of High school as were Sandy, Jenny and myself (the twins had lost time at school when they first fell sick). We had all reached the stage in our lives where we had to decide whether or not to pursue a college or university or to go out into the working world.

Tom had decided to take up the study of oceanography and major in photography at the University. Bill, on the other hand, decided to pursue general business in the hopes that someday he would be running his own business. Sandy, who was like an accounting machine, chose to continue in that field and pursue a chartered accounting degree. Jenny being sick and tired of school was just glad to get out of school and into the working world and couldn't wait until she received her first pay cheque. Bridgette, although she still could not talk, had been studying dramatics at the school that she had been attending and wanted to continue. Although she was quite good in dramatics she also knew that jobs for actresses that couldn't talk were quite scarce. Ben, who was majoring in mathematics and a new thing known as data processing, would take further classes in College and then University. I still wanted to be a lawyer. Even though there weren't many woman lawyers, it was still a dream of mine and right now the cost and time to do this was just against me.

Still keeping in touch with Stuart and Dave, I

found out that they had both started college this year. Stuart had started the process of becoming a lawyer someday. I thought that this would be just great if someday we both went into a courtroom, but were on opposite sides of the law. They would introduce us as McConnell for the defense and McConnell for the state. Wouldn't that be confusing? Dave had started his education to become a doctor. My God! What a doctor he would make and what a bedside manner he would have! Since they were both in college, it meant that Dave couldn't ride Stephanie's Fury all the time. Stuart had finally won out and had Dave dating other girls, which was great for him since he knew that I was going steady now with Tom.

Father was still working hard at the University, but had now started to drink a little more than I liked. Ben told me that I was being harsh on him and that it wasn't harming anybody. I understood it when it was shortly after Mother's death. I figured then that it helped him to cope with things and his loss.

This year was harder for all of us at school because we were all trying to have high enough marks to receive scholarships. I had forgotten about Bill and how he had caught me snooping last year or at least I thought that he had forgotten. I went about my business checking out the schedules, finding out people that were tops in the subjects, getting information wherever I could find it. The edge was what I needed and the edge was what I was going to have. My photography was coming along just fine and with the use of a telephoto lens I could take sneak shots of people without them seeing me. This came in particularly useful when I joined the school's newspaper.

Shortly into the new school year, Bill came up to me, making sure that Tom was nowhere in sight, and cornered me so that I couldn't avoid him. "Well

Stephanie, are you snooping again this year? You did so well last year that I thought that we could be partners in it again. You doing the snooping and I would keep quiet at how you did it." He was looking at me with an untrusting smile. How could I have been so wrong about this guy? When I first met him I wished that he would ask me out on a date, but now I just wish I could get rid of him.

"Bill, I thought that I would leave snooping out of it this year."

"Stephanie, I don't think that would be such a good idea. Tom just might find out how sneaky you can be when you want something, and I don't think that he would understand, do you?" I knew he was right. Tom wouldn't understand. Bill had me and he knew it.

I had to find out something that I could use against Bill. However, until I had the goods on him, I would just have to play his little game. I had started to carry a camera around with me at school due to joining the school's newspaper as one of the photographers, having carte blanche to what shots I could shoot in the school. If I wanted to take a picture of anyone, all I would have to do was to say that we were doing an article for the paper and their picture just suited the story. With the telephoto lenses I could capture different activities that were going on without anybody noticing me. The fact that I carried a camera around with me at all times made Bill a little uneasy. After all, he had to be twice as careful now if he wanted to be on top of the situation with me.

By this time, I was known for being the sneakiest newspaper person in the school. People in the school never knew if they were having their picture taken or not, or if what they were saying would show up in print that week. One moment I wouldn't be standing with one group of people, and the next moment I would be adding my two cents worth to the conversation. The fact that I was liked since I started this school helped immensely in this area. However, one of my newspaper colleagues thought that a story about me would make a great article and ran the following headline, 'The fastest rising newspaper person, The Cat.' Underneath the headlines was a picture that Tom had shot of me lowering my camera. Come to think of it, he was shooting good pictures if not better than my own. The article below the picture started, "Stephanie McConnell is getting to be known as 'The Cat' around the school because of her ability to take pictures of things going on around the school that no-one knows are being photographed. Also, she has an ability to appear and disappear without anyone knowing of her presence or her disappearance. She has the ability of a cat to take people by surprise and to captivate her audience with her work and personality." The article continued on and ran for about half of the page. When I received my copy I made several photocopies of it and sent one copy to Dave. All around the school, I was now known as 'The Cat,' a nickname that I thought would only be used by Dave was now becoming a public nickname.

I was still holding down my job at the fish and chip store at Christmas time, but I wasn't doing as many hours as I was when I first started. I needed time for all the extra curricular activities that I had started; the newspaper, the photo club and of course Tom who was still the most important person on my mind. With all these things going on I wanted extra money for Christmas, but I didn't want to give up anything either. Tom suggested that I see the people that were interested in my pictures during last year's photo contest and maybe they would still want to buy them. He said that we could check out both possibilities since they had been interested in both our photographic skills and his model, who just happened to be me.

After phoning them and making an appointment to meet with them, we put together some of our best pictures or at least we thought that they were our best. When we arrived at the office we could tell by just looking at each other that we were nervous, but neither one of us wanted to admit it. When the secretary took us into the office, there was a gentleman sitting at a desk who rose up from the chair when we walked in. "Stephanie McConnell and Tom Brennan, nice to see you again," he said as he shook our hands and offered us a seat. "I see that you have brought some of your work with you. That's excellent. Now, won't you have a seat?"

"Mrs. O'Donnell will be joining us shortly. She is the art director for our firm. Now, before she comes in I will give you a bit of insight as to how we work things here. If we buy one of your shots for a magazine front page, then we will pay you five hundred dollars. If we use it for a center story then we will pay you three hundred and fifty dollars. At all times, you have the rights to your photo, so that you can re-sell the shot again. We will have you sign a contract saying that we have first choice of your shots, however. Do you have any questions about this?"

"I have one. I am on the school newspaper and we are both still in competitions. How will this be affected?" I questioned.

"Yes, how would that affect our work as far as competitions or, for the fact that I am planning to major in photography next year in college?" Tom remarked.

"You are still free to enter all the competitions that you want. In fact, the more competitions you enter the more drive you will have to improve on your work, and to strive to be number one in the field. After all, Tom, how did it feel to find out that you were in only second place? Didn't it make you want to do better so that next year you could be number one? Stephanie, didn't you want to strive to hold on to the number one position?" We both had to agree with him. "The only thing that we require is that after any competition that you enter, we get the first chance at the picture. Now, if you are ready we will have Mrs. O'Donnell come in and view your work." He picked up the phone and soon the door opened. A woman came in wearing a beige skirt suit. Her hair was down to her shoulder with bangs that were off to the side of her face. She carried a note pad in her hand as she walked over to us and greeted us with a pleasant smile on her face.

"Mrs. O'Donnell, this is Stephanie McConnell and Tom Brennan. They were the first and second prize winners at this year's photo contest for High schools. I think that you will find their work very interesting."

She proceeded to sit in a chair at the desk after shaking both of our hands. "Shall we start to look at Stephanie's work first?" I handed her my portfolio. Inside there were several other shots that I had done along with the picture that had won me first place. The butterflies in my stomach started to flutter again as I sat back and waited for their opinion. I knew that everyone thought that my work was good, but they were mainly my friends. Now we were seeing what the professionals thought. Sure, these pictures made it through the competition and won money, but this was different now. Mrs. O'Donnell looked them over with a critical eye, picking up shot after shot, then she would look down at a note pad that she had brought with her. She looked up from the note pad and said, "Okay, now let's take a look at Tom's."

After Tom handed over his portfolio he sat down rubbing his hands. I knew what he was going through since I was going through the same thing. Mrs. O'Donnell went through his work with the same scrutiny that she had with mine. Then she said to the gentleman that had greeted us at the door, "Mr. Conrad, can I review these with you for a second?" He went over and studied several of the pictures with her. They were whispering.

Then, they finally looked up from the pictures and we heard them say to each other. "Yes I tend to agree with you, we can't use the standard agreement here. I'm sure that we can work something out though." They turned to us and Mr. Conrad started to speak. "We have a slight problem, but it isn't anything to worry about. The problem is that we want Stephanie's work for the magazine, but we also want to sign Tom to be a photographer for shooting models for our fashion magazine. Now you may be wondering what the problem is. Well, the shots that Tom has presented are all of Stephanie who is portraying the perfect model image. Therefore, we also want to sign Stephanie on as the model that Tom would be shooting. Now due to the fact that the two of you are still in High school, that means that most of the work would be done on the weekends. The next question is would Stephanie be willing to be in front of the camera as well as behind the camera?"

"What does it mean in dollars and cents?" I asked. After all, that is what I was there for.

"For the pictures that we buy for the magazine, you will get paid as we discussed before. For being a model, you would receive a flat fee of six thousand dollars a year paid to you monthly. Tom, on the other hand, because you would be a junior photographer we would be paying you a yearly salary of seven thousand a year, also paid to you monthly. Now Stephanie, because you are still under eighteen, we would have to have your parent's or guardian's consent before we could finalize the deal. Do you think there would be a problem with that?"

This would be paying more than my job at the fish and chip store. Even if there was a problem I would find a way to overcome it. "No, I don't see that there would be any problem with it. If you give me the papers that I need signed, I'm sure that I could have them back tomorrow, that is if Tom is in agreement." I knew darn well that he would be since it was a perfect arrangement for him and me to be working together and spending all the time in the world together. We all turned and looked at Tom for his answer.

"Well, as far as I'm concerned, we have a deal," he finally answered.

"I'm so glad to hear that. You are both promising artists in the field of photography. Stephanie, you lucked out twice by having the looks and being a great photographer. I'm glad to have you aboard. While you are here, if you have any questions about anything please feel free to ask," Mrs. O'Donnell told both of us as she shook our hands.

"Well then Tom, do you want to sign now or do you want to sign when Stephanie does?" Mr. Conrad asked Tom.

"I will sign now. I know that if Stephanie says that there is no problem then there won't be one." He looked back at me and smiled as he took the pen and signed the contract that Mr. Conrad had placed before him. Mr. Conrad then took out two more contracts and a permission form for my father to sign. As he gave them to me he pointed out where my father had to sign.

"Well, I guess that's just about it. We will start the model shots this Saturday after Stephanie brings back the contracts. At that time, we will have a cheque ready for the pictures that we are buying. As Mrs. O'Donnell said it's nice to have you aboard. I guess we will see you when you bring the paperwork back," he said as he shook our hands at the doorway.

As we got outside the office Tom picked me up and swung me around in the air. The smile on his face was enough to tell me how happy he was, "Do you know what this means Stephanie? We get to work with each other, never again do we have to work out ways to be with each other and better yet we are going to get paid for it. God I couldn't be happier than I am right now. It's like all my dreams have come true." He picked me up again, swinging me around slowly and bringing me back down to meet his lips in a slow lingering kiss. "Stephanie, tell me I'm not dreaming, that there is a God and he has granted me my every dream."

"Tom, do I look like a dream, or better yet does this feel like a dream?" I pulled him close to me and placing my lips against his as I gave him a overpowering kiss. "Well?"

"No, but if it was I hope that nobody ever wakes me up," he replied with a smile on his face. "Now let's go and tell everybody."

"Tom, can we hold off on that until I get my father's signature on these forms?"

"Hey Steph. You don't think that you will have a problem now do you?" A worried look came over his face.

"Don't be silly, I just want to handle it myself, okay? So don't worry. After all, who is your girlfriend anyway?" I looked at him with the look I get on my face when I know that everything is under control and that I am going to get what I want.

"I know that you're starting to get known as 'The Cat' but even cats get hurt; they don't always know what is going to happen."

"But they always land on their feet and that is what I intend to do," I replied. I gave him a little peck on his cheek.

"Now let's go home so that I can get these papers signed," I said as I grabbed him by the hand and started to run with him to his car.

I knew I might have a problem with Father since he didn't like me working anyway, but I knew that I could get around it. When I got home, I waited until after we ate supper and then decided to try out the water. "Father, Tom and I went to see Mr. Conrad from the photo contest today and he offered Tom and me positions there. They offered me two positions, one of them is that they are willing to buy my pictures outright and the other is to model. The pay is great and I will be getting paid more than I make at the fish and chip store. I brought the papers home with me for you to sign. They need your permission since I am just under eighteen. Will you please sign them for me?"

"I don't think so, Stephanie. After all, you don't need to work that much. The fact that you work at the fish and chip store should be enough for you," he replied with a tone in his voice that usually meant that the subject was closed. I had news for him; the subject was far from closed. It was just put on temporary hold.

I did my work around the house as he sat down with his drink of scotch after supper. I would just wait till the moment was right, until then I would do my homework. I went into the living room where my father was sitting with another glass of scotch in his hand (this was about his fourth by now). "Father won't you reconsider signing the permission slip for my photos? After all, this is something that I want to do. Look it's something that comes naturally to me and I am good at it too. You might even say that Mother knew that I would be good at it when she gave me her camera equipment. Now is my chance to prove that she was right, I need your signature on the permission form. Please, Father, won't you do it, if not for me then for Mother?" I didn't like using Mother's memory to get what I wanted, but I knew that when Father had a couple of drinks, the mention of Mother was the best way to get what you wanted.

"You really think that your mother would have

signed this permission form, do you?"

"I know that she would have. She believed that I was the one gifted in that field. Please Father, sign the form and let me prove her right," I said in almost a pleading fashion.

"Well, okay. She did give you the camera equipment. Maybe that was her sign to let you go ahead with this then," he said as he picked up the pen and signed the form.

I wouldn't need my job at the fish and chip store any longer, so I quit my job there.

I started my new adventure into the world of photography and modeling. The photography part was great since this was something that I enjoyed doing. However, the modeling part I had to get used to, but with Tom behind the camera it made it a lot easier. We went back with my papers signed and Mr. Conrad presented me with a cheque for my pictures that came to a sum of twenty-two hundred dollars. They also had a cheque ready for Tom that he wasn't expecting for the amount of five hundred dollars.

"When we were going through your portfolio Stephanie, we came across the school newspaper clipping about their budding new photographer who they had nicknamed 'The Cat.' Well, if you don't mind, we want to run with that in the first issue that you are shown in. From now on your work will be known as the work of 'The Cat.' Will you go along with this, Stephanie?" Mr. Conrad asked with a inquisitive look on his face.

"What can I say?" I replied.

"You see, your pictures will be in our animal magazine, headed up with, 'The work of The Cat, the works of a future star in the world of photography.' Meanwhile, in the fashion magazine we will head it up with' The Cat strikes the fashion world from Oceanville High school.' We will run the picture that Tom won second prize with on the front cover and the follow up shots. He can shoot while you are at school. We of course, will supply you with a wardrobe to wear. How does it sound to the two of you?"

"It sounds great to me. What about you Cat?" Tom had turned to me laughing when he called me Cat.

"What can I say? I get a new wardrobe out of the shoot or at least when the shoot is on. I just can't get over this nickname going as far as it has," I replied.

We left as happy as we were the first day that we came out of the office. All of a sudden things were getting to look like someday I would have the mansion on the hill. This Christmas I could once again provide a Christmas that I liked to provide. It would be a Christmas with gifts, turkey and a Christmas tree and a future of happiness. Although we had our sad moments due to the fact that Mother wasn't there to share in our happiness, we managed to think that she was there enjoying the pleasures that my new job had provided.

I had taped the Christmas cards up on the wall to decorate the house a bit. In Dave's card to me, he had sent a little note saying, "Merry Christmas, Cat. Now I can call you that in public, Love always Dave." He had received the copy of the school's paper article. Wait until he sees the magazines that were hitting the newsstands next month. Won't he be surprised then?

Chapter Eighteen

"Stuart? This is Dave. Have you got time to meet me for a coffee? I have something to show you." Dave was on the phone with Stuart; his voice was full of mystery. He had just been in the store when the girl in front of him was paying for a magazine. He looked down at the magazine and he couldn't believe his eyes. There she was looking back at him, his Cat. He went back to the magazine section to see if he could find the magazine. When he did, not only did that magazine catch his eye, but so did another one. He reached for the second magazine that had caught his eyes. There was a beautiful black jaguar family on the front cover. The larger of the cats caught his eyes, 'The Work of The Cat.' He picked up both magazines, took them to the counter and paid for them.

Leaving the store he went to the nearest restaurant, ordered a coffee and began to look at the magazines. First he took the animal one. There was a layout of the photographer's work and a picture of Cat. It was her work. Sitting in a daze almost as if he had seen a ghost, he started to go through the fashion magazine. The shots of her showed that she not only surpassed Deborah-Anne in beauty, but now Deborah-Anne would have to take a step back and take notice. Dave went over to the phone booth to call Stuart and now it seemed like forever for Stuart's answer.

"Well, I don't know, Dave. I am pretty busy right now. Couldn't it wait?" Stuart finally replied.

"No, Stu. I think what I have to show you, you won't want to wait to see. In fact, I think that you will be quite proud of Stephanie when you see it." Dave knew that once he mentioned my name then he would get Stuart's attention.

"Okay, but where are we going to meet?" he asked.

Dave gave him the location and sat back with another coffee to wait for Stuart to arrive. As he waited for his friend, he went back through the magazines again studying the pictures of my work and me. Finally, Stuart arrived at the restaurant and came over to the booth.

"Okay. Now what's this all about? Did Stephanie send you another letter or something? What am I going to be proud of her for? I'm always proud of my cousin." Dave didn't say a thing. He just put the magazines in front of Stuart. "Now I know that you have flipped when you start to read fashion magazines."

"Stuart, have you gone blind? Look at the front cover," Dave said to Stuart almost yelling at him.

"Oh my gosh! It's Stephanie. What, she's become a model now? I don't believe this. The last thing that I heard was the she was working for a fish and chip store. God, she is beautiful though! She always had a special look about her. What's this one about?" Stuart was now fascinated.

"Your cousin is not only a beautiful woman, but she also has talent. The second magazine is showing her work as a photographer," Dave explained. "By the way, do you want coffee while you are looking at that one? I am getting another one."

"Yes, get me one too," Stuart said as he started to look at the pictures in the nature magazine. His look on his face showed his total amazement with the pictures that he was viewing. They were just amazing.

Dave came back to the table with the coffees, placing them down on the table, "Well, now what do you think of your little cousin?"

"Well, for one thing, my little cousin isn't little any more, and as far as her work goes she is a fantastic photographer. I never knew that she was into this kind of stuff. What I would like to know though is where did she pick up the nickname 'The Cat' from?" Stuart replied while taking a drink of coffee.

"Then I take it that she didn't send you a copy of this?" Dave pulled his wallet from his pocket and took out the copy of the school newspaper clipping, and slowly passed it to Stuart.

Stuart sat there reading the article, and then slowly started to laugh. "I don't believe this is my little cousin." He started to read the magazine for the fashion shots. A name suddenly caught his eyes, photographs by Tom Brennan. A look came over his face and then he kind of nodded his head. Without thinking he quietly said, "Yes, that is just like my cousin. If you are going to do something then you might as well call the shots."

"What was that Stuart?" Dave hadn't quite heard what Stuart had said.

"Oh nothing, nothing at all," Stuart replied with a quirk of a smile on his face.

"Look, Stuart, I thought that during March break that I would go down and surprise Stephanie to congratulate her on her success. What do you think, do you want to come along?" Dave was concerned with the fact that Stephanie's face was on the cover of the magazine. He didn't know if he liked it or not. However, there was another reason that he wanted to see me. Looking at these magazines he got the strange feeling that I wasn't safe.

"Dave, I don't think that would be such a wise move. Besides, do you think that Susie would understand?" Susie was the girl that Dave had been seeing and they were getting pretty serious, this much he had said in his letters.

"No, but that is why I would have you go along, to cover up the real reason why I was going." You had to give Dave credit. He was sure thinking in advance.

"Dave, before you think anymore about it, I think you ought to know that the guy that took these pictures of Stephanie is no other than Tom Brennan, Stephanie's steady boyfriend."

"That is the guy that is going with Stephanie. I don't think much of his style then, there is no way that I would want my girlfriend modeling for a fashion magazine. Doing that puts her in all kinds of danger with the nuts that are running around out there."

"I am sure that Stephanie had something to do with this. After all, she is a photographer and they don't usually get in front of cameras. Not only that, just think how Tom must feel knowing that all the guys that see her pictures in the magazines want 'The Cat', and he knows that he is the lucky guy that won her heart."

This of course, was not what Dave wanted to hear. 'The Cat' had won his heart first and he didn't want all the other guys in the world wanting her. "What do you know about this guy Tom anyway?" Dave asked with curiosity in his voice.

"I know that Stephanie has been going out with him almost from the time she went back home. I met him at her mother's funeral. He seemed like quite a nice guy at the time, totally faithful to her and very jealous of anybody that came near her. You don't have to worry about her safety with him around. If Stephanie ever feels that he is putting a wall around her to protect her, then somebody should worry about his safety. He just might see the wildcat in her come out if that happens."

"Stuart, I know that you think that I am crazy, and that I haven't let my love for her rest, but I have this feeling about this modeling career. I feel that she is in danger," Dave said with worry in his voice and on his face.

"Look, Dave, if you would like it I can give her a call. I will see what the story is. I now understand how she is able to send money up to Father so that he can invest it for her. I was wondering where she was coming up with it," Stuart said laughing at the same time. "Just leave it up to my cousin to come up with something like this. By the way where did you get these magazines anyway?"

"The smoke shop in the mall," Dave replied still in a daze as he stared at the fashion magazine.

"Good. I will stop off there and get a copy of each for my parents and myself. My parents will be shocked just like you were. Hey, Dave, don't worry. I will call her tonight and I will call you tomorrow."

Stuart left Dave staring at the magazines, and stopped to pick up copies of the magazines on the way home. He phoned just as he had told Dave that he would.

When the phone rang I was out in the kitchen, and yelled to them that I would get it. I ran to the phone, picked up the receiver and said, "Hello." A voice responded, "Hello, cousin. Didn't you think that I at least deserved an autographed copy of the magazines when they were published?"

"Stuart, you have already seen the copy of the magazines?"

"Well Stephanie, or should I call you The Cat now? I didn't have any choice in the matter. Dave called me from the store as soon as he saw them."

"He saw them too, did he? What did he think?"

"He thought that they were great. In fact, we all thought they were great, but Dave for some reason got the feeling that you are in danger when he saw you in the magazines. I told him that I would check the story with you. I told him that Tom wouldn't let anyone harm you. He is afraid that some nut bar out there is going to want you just because you are on the cover of a magazine. I told him he was nuts."

"Stuart, you can put his mind at ease. Tell him I am doing something that I am good at and that I like. Besides, I don't really have to work either. Tell him that Tom keeps a very watchful eye on me and that I am perfectly safe."

"Okay, I will tell him that, and by the way, your photographic work is superb. You will make your mark in society in no time at all."

"How is school going now, Stuart? Is it really hard?"

"It is hard, but anything that you want, you know that you have to work for. I guess this is what you are going to be when you leave school, heh? I guess that you won't venture into the university area, will you?"

"Sorry to ruin those thoughts Stuart, but this is my way of paying my way through school to become a lawyer. So if you thought that you were the only McConnell that will be in the courts, well I am just going to prove you wrong."

"Well, now I know that everything is okay, and I know what to tell Dave. "The Cat is just waiting to attack the world of the courts." Stuart was killing himself laughing now at the thought that we might see each other in court. "Well take care Stephanie."

"Yes, you too Stuart, and give my love to everybody up there especially Dave. Try to get him to stop worrying. Okay? Bye now, Stuart."

Stuart called Dave the next day as he said he would. "Hey Dave you don't have to worry about Stephanie. She has all four on the floor. She is using the money from the magazines to put herself though law school so that she can beat me in the courts. He started laughing again. She also said to tell you that Tom keeps a very protective watch over her so that nothing will happen to her. She also sent her love and said not to worry about her. So are you happy now?"

"Yes, I guess that makes me feel a little bit better, but I still have this feeling. I will try and put it to rest. Talk to you later Stuart," Dave said as he hung up the phone but the feeling that The Cat was in danger still persisted.

Chapter Nineteen

Time went by and I was putting more money away for my schooling and the twins' schooling. For even if we all lucked out and received scholarships, it would still cost a lot of money. With summer coming up, Tom and I just finished doing the spring line up. We got into a routine of doing the fashion shoots with no problems. I just had to act normal and Tom just took the pictures of me. I would fit the photographs that I needed to shoot into a day that we didn't have anything planned. I would just take me camera out with me and let my moods take me away. The warmer weather was coming and we were able to do the swimwear shots down on the beach. This allowed the twins to come down and watch. They thought that I was so lucky that I had everything going my way. I had the publicity that my sister wanted, and I had the money to spend too. The only thing that they didn't realize was that I did everything so that we could all get ahead.

One night, I had finished doing my work around the house and for a change I had no homework. I thought that I would take advantage of the blue sky and the warm air. I grabbed my camera and headed down toward the beach. The shots that you can get as the sun is setting change every time you click the shutter on the camera. With the warm air blowing over me I got in the mood for just letting my creative mind go to work. I started to shoot pictures of the crabs going along the sand on the beach, then the gulls on the rocks with the water slowly receding. The sun was giving a multitude of colours, variations of oranges and mauves that gave the objects different characteristics. With one whole roll of film gone, I sat back to enjoy the evening, something that I hadn't done in quite sometime.

With the warm breezes caressing my face, I walked over to the rocks to sit on them for a while. I took in all the beauty that was being created before my very eyes. This time in the evening, with the warm breezes coming in from the ocean, had always made me feel so peaceful. It was as if this was my own little world. This was a place that was always beautiful even if I had a rough day. I could always come here and soon I would feel better. It just always had that effect on me.

It was getting dark out and the stars were slowly coming out. Gazing up into the sky at the stars always fascinated me, as though I was looking up at all the pictures that the constellations drew in the sky. If you looked up at them long enough you could see the earth moving under them in an almost hypnotic fashion. That is just how I was starting to feel, so relaxed, when all of a sudden someone grabbed me from behind. Whoever it was pulled me off the rock that I had been sitting on, which knocked the air from my body. Stunned by the shock to my body, my assailant dragged me partially to the caves. By the time we had reached the opening of the caves, I managed to get my breath back. I started to fight. Nobody got away with doing anything to me that I didn't want to happen, and I knew that what was happening I didn't want. My assailant had placed his hand over my mouth so that I couldn't scream and with his other hand had started to undo my dome fastened top. I started to struggle, but as I struggled I could feel his hand feeling my breasts as his breathing started to get heavier. I struggled even more to break his grip, but he only tightened his hold in order to keep the upper hand in our confrontation. While we struggled his hand moved slowly from my breasts to the bottom of my skirt and groping at my bottom. All the time I struggled I could smell this disgusting smell of liquor so strong that it was almost turning my stomach. He finally spoke as we struggled in the most incoherent voice. "Don't go struggling so much. Isn't this why you put your picture in all those magazines?" That voice made me struggle even more; the fury and the fear seemed to come together. I received a burst of strength from inside, and pushing back on him I managed to knock him off his footing in the sand. As he fell backwards his head hit the ground. As I ran from his grip I turned to look back to confirm what my head and heart didn't want to believe, but what they heard as my assailant spoke. I looked back to see my assailant and there lay my father on the ground. Why had he attacked me?

I backed up, picking up my camera as I went. Doing up the domes on my top, I proceeded back to the house. Maybe I was in a state of shock. I don't know, but I thought that I would confront him with what happened in the morning. When I got to the house I went in and drew myself a nice hot bath. The twins had only heard me come in and had not seen the tears on my face. As I came out of the bath I asked where Father was, they didn't know only that he had gone for a walk. I went to bed after saying good night to them.

The next morning when Ben came out for breakfast, I asked him to go and get Father from the bedroom for breakfast as it was getting cold.

"Father is not in his bedroom. In fact, it looks like he never even slept in it."

"Well, you two go out and look around the house for him maybe he is just outside somewhere." It was as though I had blocked that part of the night out of my mind. So they left to see if they could find Father but it wasn't to long before we were startled by a girl's scream.

"Come quickly, I found Father." Bridgette was screaming at the top of her lungs.

We all ran to where she was and there before her was Father exactly where I had left him last night. I went into a daze that everybody put down to shock due to the fact that I had just been reunited with my family and now I had lost both parents. I just stared at him, I couldn't move. Ben went over to him and as he returned to us said that we had better call the police that he thought Father was dead. Bridgette was crying all over the place but nobody noticed that she was talking. Ben went and called the police, when they came they ruled it accidental. That he got drunk, lost his footing, fell and hit his head on the rocks. When the tide came in, well, if he wasn't already dead then the tide finished him off. Once again we phoned Uncle Pat to come to another family funeral, and once again they passed on their condolences.

"What are you going to do now?" Uncle Pat asked when he arrived. Is there anything that we can do to help you?"

"Thanks Uncle Pat, but I have been like the head of this family ever since I came back, even though I am the youngest. I will continue in that role now. I will take on a permanent job and keep up with the modeling and photography on the side. That way we can manage the bills and the twins can continue their education."

"What about your schooling and your dreams?" Stuart asked.

"They will go on hold for the time being, and when I have enough saved up, then I will go to night school. Right now the fact that Bridgette got her voice back means that she will need further training in how to use her voice. Don't worry I will be in court against you as a lawyer someday. It just won't be as soon as I would like it to be, that's all." My mind blockage didn't affect the way that I saw things; just how I viewed sex.

Therefore no one really noticed a difference in me. When we found Father's body I was in shock and the doctor gave me something to calm me down. After that I went back to being my normal self.

"Look if there is anything that we can help you with, you just call now, you do understand don't you?" Uncle Pat was very demanding at this point. I noticed that he wasn't as grief stricken at this funeral as he was at Mother's, yet instead Aunt Elizabeth was. She was over at the casket and her eyes never seemed dry.

"Tom, tell me truthfully. How is Stephanie?" Stuart asked Tom.

"To tell you the truth Stuart, I am worried about her. Ever since this happened, she has this look in her eyes. I just can't put my finger on it," Tom replied with concern in his voice and on his face.

"That look is what I picked up on too. I wish I could take her back home with us and away from this, but I know that she won't go, not now anyway." Stuart said as he looked over in my direction.

I caught them looking at me, as I headed in their direction. I graciously accepted people's condolences. The look on their faces told the whole story about what they were talking about, and the subject just happened to be me. I went up to the two of them, put my arms around both of them.

"By the look on your faces there seems to have been a heavy discussion going on here before I arrived. I just hope that I wasn't at the center of it?" I looked from one to the other with a look of displeasure, if that was the case.

"Stephanie, can we help it if the men in you life care about you enough to worry whether or not you are okay?" Stuart started to explain. He looked at me with eyes that showed not only the love that he felt for me, but also the concern he was feeling.

"I keep telling everyone that I am okay. I will survive or rather we will survive. The twins and I, that is. I have a full time job to start with, and with my photography and the extra money from the modeling shoots, we will do just fine. I just wish that someone had just listened to me with regards to Father's drinking. Then maybe he would be here and we wouldn't be at this place." That was just how I was looking at his death, as if I hadn't even seen him that night. I had blanked everything out of my mind about that night. All I could remember was that I took some lovely shots. They were of the sunset and they sold when I took them in to work. Also, I took a nice relaxing bath when I returned to the house.

We buried him next to Mother. Now, it would just be the three of us, Bridgette, Ben and I; no one else seemed to matter. I invited the family back to the house for tea along with some of my friends. I served it as a perfect hostess would. This struck everyone in the house as being rather strange. I had just been reunited with my family only to lose both Mother and Father, yet I was unable to express the loss.

"Stuart, would you try to get her to open up before you leave?" Tom asked Stuart with almost a plea. "You know that I can't stand to see her this way. I know that she is hurting, but there doesn't seem to be anything that I can do to help her."

"I will try because to tell you the truth, I don't want to leave seeing her this way. I will see if she will go for a walk with me.," Stuart replied.

"Stephanie, come with me for a walk. We won't be able to do this for a long time now." Stuart placed my hand in his and started to lead me from the room full of people without waiting for my reply. He gave his father a wink and he nodded back in agreement.

"Stuart I know what you are trying to do," I

replied to him as we walked along.

"What is that, Stephanie? All that I see is that I am walking with my kissing cousin whom I love very much, and who I am not going to see for a while. Don't you think that I miss having you around to talk to, to share my feelings with, to tease you (he laughed a bit) and to make your pains go away. Won't you share some of those feelings now with me, Stephanie? It isn't good to keep them pent up inside you." He was looking at me with St. Bernard eyes that were so sad.

"Stuart, I have to be the strong one now. I can't let my feelings show. What good would I be if I go to mush? I won't be useful to anybody." I was almost yelling at him but I couldn't help it.

"Stephanie, if you don't let go with me, then you won't be able to hold on and be that strong person that you talk about. Instead you will just break into pieces. Please talk to me." Now he was yelling at me. It was the first time that this ever happened. We had never yelled at each other before, we were always on the same side. He grabbed hold of me and began to shake me.

"I can't talk to you. I can't tell you my feelings if I don't feel anything. I know that I should be crying, but I can't and I don't understand why. You have to trust me on this one. I will mourn when my system is ready, but right now the will to be strong is ruling my body. You know that if I needed help you are the first one that I would come running to. You are more of a family to me than what I knew here. I don't want you to leave with us yelling at each other. Please say that you understand?" I held out my hand for him to take it.

"Stephanie, maybe I should stay down here for a while, just until you get through that part at least?" He had now taken my hand in his and was looking directly into my eyes.

"No Stuart, this is something that I will have to do

on my own. If I need you, I know that you are only a telephone call away." I had calmed back down and spoke with a calm voice now.

"Providing that you remember that I am only a phone call away, then I will go back with my parents." We walked back to the house where Tom was waiting to see whether or not Stuart had any luck with me.

"I am going back home with my parents. Stephanie has given me her word that if she needs us for anything that she will call us," Stuart told Tom. "If you think that she is getting worse or that she is getting depressed then you call me, Tom. Right now I think that she seems okay. She says that she can't mourn right now, but when she starts then she will need all of us around. Until then, as she has to do what she thinks is right, you can't try to push her."

"Okay, then if I think that she is getting depressed, I will give you a call," Tom replied, never really taking his eyes off me.

"Now that she has been nicknamed 'The Cat' let's hope that she behaves just like a cat and lands on her feet. Up till now she has been pretty good at doing that." Stuart looked over at me, while he was saying that last line to Tom.

After talking with Tom he came over to say his last good-byes to everyone. His parents were just ahead of him. As he bent toward me to kiss me good-bye, he turned and looked at Tom, "Now you take good care of this one."

We waved good-bye to them as they drove off and out of the driveway. I went back into the house to start to tidy up and to plan our next move. Tom was the only one left. Sandy, Bill and Jenny had left about the same time that Uncle Pat and his family had. Tom came over and put his arm gently around me. I knew that he was trying to console me, but all the same I pushed him away. This was the first time that I had ever rejected a hug from him.

"Tom not now I have work to do," I said as an excuse.

"Stephanie all I was trying to do was give you a little bit of comfort. Won't you even let me do that for you?" Tom was trying to explain his actions, something that he really didn't have to do.

"Tom I don't want to be comforted," I yelled back at him, raising my fists at the same time ready to hit him. He blocked my fists, and grabbed hold of my wrists. Feeling the strength in his arms, I could feel my strength weakening. As the strength ran from my body, I could feel the pressure releasing in my head and the tears started to flow from my eyes. Not only was I fighting with Tom, but I was fighting with my body to keep it under control. I seemed to be losing. Tom knew this and gently let my body collapse in his arms, as the tears started to flow more freely.

"Let it go Stephanie. It's not wrong to cry or to show your feelings. When it's over you'll feel better, believe me." Tom was gently stroking my hair as he comforted me. Holding me in his arms I sobbed on and off for more than an hour till I slowly drifted off to sleep. He carried me into my bedroom. Coming back out of the room he turned to Ben and said, "Are you guys going to be okay or do you want me to stay the night? She should sleep straight through."

"No Tom, you have been just great, but I think that we have to get used to the fact that we are now on our own. If we need you, we know where to call." Ben looked over at Bridgette while he was answering making sure that she agreed. Tom comforting me was the last thing that I remembered that night, the next thing that I remembered was waking up the next morning in my bed.

Chapter Twenty

I managed to take my final exams ahead of everybody else, so that I could take on a full time job that I had lined up. Completing the fourth year of High school, I at least had my High school diploma. The full time job that I had was at the factory in town. After work there, I would go home grab a bit of supper that Bridgette made. I would either go for a modeling shoot, or if there wasn't one available, I would take the camera and shoot some pictures to sell.

Ben was now walking with a cane, so that you might say that he was almost healed. The doctors said though that his hearing could be fixed with an operation. In the meantime though, he could be fitted with a hearing aid to assist him in hearing. The operation would be expensive and we just couldn't afford it right now. The hearing aid was more in our price range and we made arrangements for him to be fitted with one. He was now able to get on with his life and go to a normal College or University with the use of the hearing aid.

Bridgette they said should be able to enter the dramatic art college in the fall, providing that she continued her special speech therapy classes during the summer. Her voice was coming along and soon there would be no trace that she hadn't spoken in years. She had now started to do the housework, so that all I had to do was be the bread winner. The two of them constantly asked if I didn't want them to quit school, and help supply the money that was required to make ends meet in running the house. I repeatedly refused their offer knowing that if they were to make anything of themselves that they needed further education. I could pick up my education later on at night school or through correspondence courses.

Tom would pick me up for the modeling shots but things were just not the same with us. He still had the power to get the shots out of me that the other photographers couldn't. We had become the number one model and photographer team, any shot that the magazine wanted, between the two of us we could come up with the effect that they wanted. I was pouring more of myself into my work. We would work longer hours, so that by the time that we were ready to go home I was exhausted and would almost fall asleep in the car. Then when we got home Tom would have to carry me into the house. I would be back up at six in the morning leaving the house for my job at the factory.

Tonight when Tom brought me home, after he had put me in the bed, he went out to the living room to talk to Ben and Bridgette. Shaking his head as he came out of my room, he started to talk to them. "Is there any time that she isn't on the go now? Does she ever just sit down and spend time with the two of you or for that matter does she ever just rest?"

"We have tried to get her to slow down, but she just won't listen. Have you tried to get her to take some time off?" Ben asked. "Maybe if you suggest going scuba diving or horseback riding, then maybe she would consider it."

"You know you might have a point there. I know that she has a new waterproof case for the camera that she hasn't tried out yet. It is worth a try, anyway or if I could get her to go shoot pictures of the horses she would still be resting a bit." Tom thought that he had finally figured out a way to get me to rest, now came the hard part to get me to agree.

By the time he figured out how to get me to take

time off for some R & R, I had already figured it out. If I didn't take some time off, something was about to snap. I could feel the little spring inside of me starting to tighten, and I knew that if I didn't do something soon that I would be in trouble. Today, when he finally got around to asking me to go scuba diving on Sunday, which was the only day that I had free, I surprised him and agreed to go. He was sitting on a stool at the time that he asked, as he was fooling around with the camera.

"Stephanie how about on Sunday we get a couple of tanks of air, take that new camera stuff that you got for underwater and try them out?"

I had just finished striking the pose for the next shot and answered him back quickly. "Sure that sounds great." I guess he was all prepared for me to turn him down because the poor guy just about fell off the stool he was sitting on.

"Did I hear you right? Did you say that we could go scuba-diving?"

"That is right. I figured that it is time that I got a little R & R time in."

"Well that's more like my girl. I think that 'The Cat' has just sprung back. It sure is good to have you back, girl." Tom had a smile on his face, not just a smile but a joyous smile.

"I told you guys to let me handle things. I know what this body can take and what it can't. I just wish you guys could understand that. Now you can write Stuart and tell him that 'The Cat' is back. She has landed on all fours again," I said to him in a sexy but almost cat like tone, almost as if I had found out something that I wasn't supposed to know.

"You knew that I was keeping in touch with Stuart?" Tom answered with a shocked tone of voice.

"If you think that you could do something like that without me knowing about it, then you don't know me as well as you thought you did. I know Stuart and because he loves and cares for me so much, he would never have left, trusting me to keep in touch. Especially in the state of mind that he thought I was in when he last talked to me. I knew that he had to have somebody reporting that information to him, somebody that was close enough to me so that I wouldn't catch on, and that somebody could only be you." I said to him as I came out of the change room. I had just put on a black skirt with a slit up the side, a black silk top with a low cut style, and a belt that emphasized my waist. I had on high heels and was slinging a black leather jacket over my shoulder.

Tom was bent over changing the lens on his camera as I came out of the room. His eyes met the bottom of my leg and seemed to follow the leg to the slit of the skirt, then to the V neck of my top that showed just enough cleavage to entice. "Are you sure that you want to continue to shoot? It seems to be becoming awful warm in here."

"I didn't notice that it was warm in here," I replied looking at him from the top of my eyes.

"Yeah, I think that we can call it a night. Maybe we could stop for something to drink on the way home." He picked up his camera and started shooting. Every time that the camera clicked I struck a different pose till he came up for a close up. "Perfect, now let's call it a night," he said as he put his arms around me and gave me a gentle kiss on the cheek. "What do you say to an early night?"

"Sounds good to me, now just let me change," I said as I kissed him gently back. The outfit had put me in an exceptionally sexy mood and Tom was picking up on that mood.

"While you are doing that I will just put the camera and stuff away." He started to clear away our stuff as I went to get changed. He thought that he had died and gone to heaven. Everything seemed to be going his way or our way whichever way you looked at it.

I came out of the changing room with my V neck angora sweater on that seemed to mold every curve of my body along with a tight pair of blue jeans. I could see from Tom's eyes that he was enjoying everything that he saw. He came over and took me into his arms. "You look so gorgeous that I can't take my hands off of you."

"Well, if you don't take your hands off me then we aren't going anywhere. If that be the case then we might as well do some more work then." I laughed as I was saying it to him because I don't think that I ever saw Tom move so quickly in my life. One moment his hands were around my waist, and then the next second they moved from there to grabbing my hand and pulling me toward the door. He wasn't taking any chances at ruining this moment, a chance of getting me out of this place without me falling to sleep. We got to the car, and stopped only to pick up a few drinks for later. We arrived back at my place for a moonlit walk along the beach. We placed the blanket down on the sand to sit on and the drinks in the sand so that the water could wash up on them to keep them cool.

We walked along the beach hand in hand, something that we hadn't done in months; there never seemed to be enough time. As we got back to the blanket he traced my moonlit face with his hand ever so gently stopping at my chin. He looked at my eyes that seemed to sparkle in the moon light. With my chin still on his finger tips he bent closer to me stopping just above my lips, our eyes meeting one another. His seemed to be saying, "I have missed you so much. What are we waiting for?" He continued to move in closer till our lips met and he gave me a slow lingering kiss. Slowly I moved my hands so that they were following the curves of his back. He gently braced my back as we slowly and gently sank onto the blanket. He gently showered my body with loving kisses that seemed to massage my overworked body. Like two blind people fondling works of Braille, our hands gently and carefully undid garments that covered the works that we were trying to read. Then like the waves against the shore we joined as one, only to part as the air exhaled from our exhausted bodies. As we lay there resting, Tom was following the curves of my body under the moonlight with his fingertips. His eyes watching every move wondering what I was going to do next. I felt so restful and relaxed just like the first time. I lay there next to him looking at his muscular physique, knowing that I did love this guy. I loved making love to him, but as he touched me more and more I started to feel dirty. I knew that what I was doing with him wasn't wrong as long as I did it with him, but now this dirty feeling was coming over me. I slowly pushed his hand away and started to rise from the blanket.

"What's wrong Stephanie?"

"Nothing's wrong. I am just going for a moonlit swim, do you care to join me?" I glanced back at him, I couldn't tell him what was wrong. I couldn't understand it so how could he. I proceeded down to the water and he followed after me. All I wanted to do was have the water pour over me. I wanted it to clean me and get rid of this feeling of being dirty. The water felt so good over my body, so very refreshing. This was one of the joys of having your own private beach that was sheltered from everyone else's eyes. You could go swimming in the nude and nobody would be any the wiser. Using the blanket as a towel we dried off and got dressed, grabbing our drinks to have as we walked back to the house.

"Are we still going scuba diving then on Sunday?" Tom asked, thinking that if I had broken down and relaxed tonight, then maybe I had changed my mind about Sunday.

"Yes, in fact I thought that we would make a picnic out of it and the twins could come along too. I will make a picnic lunch and you just bring the tanks. How does that sound?" I was looking down at the ground as we walked.

"That sounds great and it sounds like my old Stephanie too. Welcome back." He turned to me and gave me a kiss on the cheek.

"Did I seem far away all this time?" I questioned him.

"You will never know how far away you seemed to be." The smile was back on his face, something I couldn't recall seeing in the past few weeks.

"I will see you tomorrow then. I have to get some more sleep before the camera starts to pick up those dark circles under my eyes that you get when you don't get enough sleep." I chuckled and gave him a kiss on his cheek.

Chapter Twenty-One

Time went by and although we had now worked things out so that I could have the odd night off and relax, things were still not quite right. The twins tried to arrange things so that I didn't have to worry too much about things around the house. Bridgette was progressing with her talking so well that you would never believe that she hadn't been talking. Tom and I would work on the shots discussing which way we thought things should be done. I had my choice of wardrobe providing that it met with the theme that we had to promote. I would plan ahead on nights that I wanted to call it quits early to have a relaxing evening with Tom. I would decide early what order the clothes would be for that evening shoot, making sure that the sexiest outfit was put on at just the right time. Now that the twins were able to get out and live pretty normal lives, the house would be empty some nights and it would be on those nights that I would plan to leave early.

I loved making love to Tom, but I hated the feeling that I got afterwards, the feeling that I was dirty. I never had this feeling until that evening with Father that I was still blocking out of my mind, so I couldn't understand the feeling. Every time that we would make love, after Tom would leave I couldn't wait until I got into the shower to wash my body in order to make myself feel clean again. The feeling was starting to pull my mind apart. One side of me said that there was nothing wrong with what I was doing, that here was a man that loved me, who showed me that he loved me by making love to me and made me feel loved. Then, the other side would say that what I was doing was wrong; using my picture in the magazine to attract men to make love to, and that I was no better than a tramp. Now I know that Tom was the only man that I made love to and that it shouldn't be wrong, but here was my body being torn apart. I didn't know how much more I could take. I didn't want to confront what happened that night, nor did I want anybody else to know about it, but what was I going to do.

The war within my body kept on going every single day, even when we didn't make love. I started to feel as though everybody knew what had happened and that they thought that I was a tramp. I managed to hide my feelings in front of the camera, but Tom was starting to think that something was wrong. He would come out with sayings like, "If you don't want to make love, then we don't have to. The decision is yours." I guess I was giving out the feeling that I no longer felt the pleasure that I once had felt when we first made love. It seems like in bed, I just couldn't hide my feelings.

I decided that I didn't like this feeling anymore, so I took a day off from work and decided to go swimming and just relax. I grabbed my towels, a small picnic lunch and headed toward the beach. I put my food down on the blanket and headed for a walk along the beach toward the caves. I hadn't been over to the caves since the day that Bridgette found Father. As I got near the caves, I decided to sit on the rocks. Suddenly the nightmare went racing through my mind. I jumped up and ran to the ocean, trying to get rid of that feeling that his hands were all over my body. In and out of the waves I went, diving into the surf catching breaths as I broke the surface. I was getting tired, but I had to get rid of this feeling. I couldn't stop until it was gone. Slowly, weakened, the surf pushed me onto the shore. As I lay there totally exhausted, my one hand reached over to the other hand with Dave's ring on it. As I touched it, I heard myself whisper, "Dave help sorry." After that I heard nothing more.

There was somebody's mouth on mine. They were trying to give me mouth to mouth resuscitation, but who was it. I couldn't make them out only that it had to be a male because he had rough skin. He blew another breath into my system and I started to gag. He rolled me over on my side as I started to bring up sea water that I taken in. I started to cough and gasp for air. The person put their arm around me and then covered me with a towel.

Still groggy, I heard the person speak. "Don't you know that Cats aren't supposed to try to swim, well at least not alone in case they get into trouble." That voice was Bill's, but what was he doing here? "What are you trying to prove anyway, that cats have nine lives, by trying to kill yourself?" Was I really trying to kill myself? I didn't think that I was.

"Thanks Bill for coming to my rescue, but what were you doing here anyway?" I asked him through my coughing fits.

"I was supposed to meet Tom here. It's a good thing that I found you and not him. He would never let you anywhere near the water after this. What the hell happened anyway? I know how good a swimmer you are." Bill was now sitting on the sand beside me.

"I went out for a swim. I must have been more tired than I thought I was. Anyway the tide tired me out quickly and the next thing I knew I was washed up on the shore without the strength to move."

"Are you sure that is what happened Cat? Are you sure that you weren't trying to kill yourself for what your father tried to do to you."

"What are you talking about?" Suddenly I became defensive.

"Cat I know that your father was drunk that night and he tried to rape you, but you managed to break loose from him and he hit his head on the a rock." Bill was looking at the sand as he was telling me this.

"How can you sit there and talk such nonsense?" I looked at him crossly, how could he possibly know what happened that night.

"Cat I was there that night. I was over there in the bushes watching you. I never thought that your father would hurt you, so I sat there watching. I saw him getting ready to molest you and I was getting ready to come out of my hiding spot to save you whichever way I had to. Then all of a sudden you seemed to get this hidden strength and I knew that you were okay." Bill was looking at me with saddened eyes.

"Why didn't you say anything?"

"I thought that maybe it was best to leave it alone, and let you forget it, maybe I was wrong. If you knew that I knew then maybe you could have talked to me and you wouldn't have tried to kill yourself." Bill got up and walked to the shoreline and started to throw stones into the surf.

"I didn't try to kill myself, but you still haven't said why you were there that night."

"I have always liked you. The fact that you date my best friend didn't help. When we were at school and I caught you snooping, I thought great I had finally found a way to be with you, so I used it in that way. When you left school I had to find a different way of watching you or being near you. I would come around here hoping that I would see you and maybe even talk to you."

"Why couldn't you have just come out and told me, asked me out or something like that? Now you will have to promise me that you won't tell Tom about this afternoon." I pleaded with Bill.

"How could I tell you how I felt. You were going

out with my best friend. If I told you, that friendship would have been damaged. Since Tom is my best friend you have my word that I won't mention this afternoon to him." He kicked the sand with his foot.

"Bill it looks like we always seem to have secrets between us, doesn't it?"

"We may have secrets, but now you have somebody to talk to about anything because I always seem to know your secrets. Besides, what happened to you doesn't bother me because I was there and I know what happened. The truth is you did nothing wrong so stop blaming yourself."

"I know that I have done nothing wrong, but I still can't get rid of this feeling of being dirty and being a tramp ever since that night. I want to be close to Tom like it was before that night, but I can't as long as I feel the way that I do." I looked out at the water and then back at Bill.

"Did you ever think of telling Tom. If he loves you the way he claims to, then he should understand." He had walked over toward me putting his arm around me in a comforting fashion.

"How could he possibly understand when I can't understand it?"

"Look if you don't, then it is going to drive the two of you apart." He looked at me with concern in his eyes as he spoke. "Do you want to loose him? I don't think that you do. I have watched the two of you since you met. I could tell back then that the two of you belong together, that you cared for each other. That's why I had to take the back seat with you. Now, as a friend to both of you I don't want to see you make a mistake that you will regret later on in life."

"Bill, I don't want to loose Tom, he was the best thing that came into my life when I came back here. He was what I needed then, caring and loving, someone to make me feel important and loved, but now I feel us drifting apart. It would be easy if I could tell him, but I really don't think that he would understand. I'll tell you one thing though I feel better for finally being able to talk to someone about it. Maybe I pegged you wrong from the start. When I first met you I actually wanted you to ask me out, but I guess that we were just meant to be friends and we just never knew it." I looked at him with grateful eyes and took him by the hand to show him that I was willing to accept his friendship, and that I was glad to have him to talk to.

"Stephanie, now that you know that I am on your side, I want you to call me whenever you want to talk about anything that is bugging you. I don't care what it is, if you can't talk to anybody else about it, call me. There isn't anything that you could say to me that would upset me. Look if you want moral support, if you decide to tell Tom, then just say the word. I will be there, but if you decide to go on keeping it a secret, then I will honour your wishes too." He was looking down at me with eyes that had reassurance coming from them.

"Thanks Bill. You don't know how that makes me feel." Gradually a smile was coming across my face as we held hands.

"Well, what is this. I thought that you were at work, how come you're not there, you don't look sick." Tom was questioning as he stormed through the brush that was just before the sand of the beach. "In fact this looks kind of cozy."

"Hey Tom, I think that you're way off base. You knew that I was meeting you here. Stephanie just happened to be here when I got here so we were just talking." Bill explained the situation to Tom, trying to calm down his jealous friend. I realized then that Bill was right when it came to seeing me. His friendship with Tom would be in jeopardy. When Tom had came onto the beach we dropped each other's hand after being startled by his outburst.

"I know I was meeting you here Bill, but when did Stephanie decide to join you?" Tom was furious and frankly I couldn't understand why.

"I didn't know that you and Bill had decided to meet on my beach when I decided to take the day off to be by myself. Bill came and said that he was meeting you here, so we sat and talked." I was massaging my neck as I walked. His outburst, that something was going on between Bill and I made me tense. "What seems to be your problem? Don't you like the fact that your best friend and your girlfriend are able to carry on a conversation together while they wait for you?" I was yelling now, nobody was my keeper and nobody could put me in a glass cage, to be looked at only when they say that it is permissible. If Tom thought that he could do that then he was in for a big shock. Bill was now sitting back on the sand watching me very carefully. I had turned on Tom like a wildcat.

"Well, how do you think that it looked to me when I came to the crest and saw the two of you holding hands. What am I supposed to think?" Tom was pleading his case but was doing a poor job of it.

"You're supposed to think that gee that's strange I didn't know that Stephanie was off today. Isn't that nice that she is able to join us and that it was good that she was there to meet Bill, and keep him company since apparently I was late. That was what you were supposed to think and not jump off on some jealous notion that your best friend and your girlfriend were up to something behind your back. I thought that love was based on trust, but apparently you don't trust either one of us." I started to walk away from him and then I made a quick about face. "I thought that you knew that you are the only one that I ever wanted. That nobody could ever make my eyes stray from you. The only one that ever could do that is you. If you let your jealous fits continue, then maybe you don't believe that I love only you. Maybe you don't really love me, if you can't trust me." That last line really struck home. He ran over and grabbed me by the arm, and turned me around so that I was facing him.

"Stephanie I'm sorry, you know that I love you and I do trust you," he said as he pulled me close to him and slowly gave me a seductive kiss.

"I'm not the only one that you owe an apology to. You also insulted our friend Bill by accusing him of things that you knew that he would never do to you." I looked at him with stern eyes that felt that they would burn a hole through him if he didn't do as I asked. I still hadn't accepted his apology yet.

Bill was sitting back in the sand taking this all in. He winked at me behind Tom's back. Tom looked over his shoulder to Bill and called back to him. "Sorry Bill I should have known better." He turned back to me, "Does this make you happy?" He turned to Bill once again, "No hard feelings?"

"No, I guess that if I had a girlfriend that was as attractive as 'The Cat', and I saw her with my good looking friend, I guess I might be a bit upset too. I just hope that if you happen to see us talking again, that you won't blow up like you did this time. I thought for a moment that I might have to deck you," Bill said as he slapped Tom on the back. "Now shall we enjoy this wonderful weather?"

"Yeah, let's do that," Tom said as he took off his top and put his arm around my waist as we walked over to the blanket on the beach. They went swimming as I rested on the blanket. The sun's rays felt great on my body as I lay there resting. By the time that evening rolled around, and it was time to go to the studio to do our modeling shoot I was well rested. What Bill and I had talked about was still on my mind during the evening. He was right. It was my decision whether or not to tell Tom. After the way he reacted this afternoon, I didn't think that he would be so understanding if he knew that Bill was also there that night.

Chapter Twenty-Two

Tom and I seemed to drift apart even more after that day on the beach, and today I decided that this wasn't going to work. I met with him to go to the studio and after the shoot I turned to him. "Tom how about if we call it an early night, I really would like to talk to you."

"Sure anything you say Stephanie," he replied.

As he packed up things, I got changed and we headed out along the road to outlook point. When he parked the car, I got out and started walking without even waiting for him to get out of the car. I looked out toward the water hoping that the sound of the waves could put me at ease so that what I planned would be easier. He came up behind me and put his arm around me.

"What's bugging you Stephanie? You seem to be a million miles away," he said quietly in my ear.

"If I were a million miles away then this would be easy, but because I am here it is the most difficult thing that I have ever had to do." I turned around so that I could look him in the eyes. His eyes had become sad at the thought of what it might be that I had to do. "Look, there is no easy way of doing this so I might as well just say it." He was getting defensive as I was saying this. "You know as well as I do that our relationship hasn't been going well for some time now. I think that it has come to the time for us to go our separate ways and for you to meet someone new."

"Do I have a say in this or have you thought it out for the two of us? You say that I can go and find somebody else, what about you or have you already found somebody new?" He pulled me close to him, hurting me with the force that he grabbed me with.

"There is nobody else in my life and there isn't going to be. I'm not doing this because I want somebody else. I'm doing it so that you can find somebody that could make you happy. I can't and I know it. When we make love, I don't enjoy it anymore and you know it. Don't you think that I would like things to be different? I always thought that you would be the one I would marry, but now I am facing facts and they add up to letting you go. Don't you understand that I am doing this because I do love you and not because I hate you? Maybe I am wrong, I'm not saying that I am right, but I am willing to give you a chance to find out if somebody else could make you happy."

"Maybe I don't want anybody else. Can't we work this out?" He was angry and I couldn't blame him. Our quiet discussion was becoming a cross between raised voices and a yelling match.

"All week I have been running that through my mind. The only answer that came back was that if we were meant to be together then we would be together. That we would make it through the separation, but in order to find this out, we must try to find out whether or not we are truly for one another. The only way to do that is to set you free."

"Do you think that you could stand to see me with other girls? How about at the studio? We still work together." When he questioned me he had fury in his voice.

"I can handle you dating other girls. After all, I am the one that is ending our relationship. As far as work goes if you can't handle working with me, I can always request a new photographer and you could have another model. I would hope that it wouldn't come to that though. I don't want our friendship to end, just our relationship."

"Christ you've figured out every last detail, haven't you? Well, there's one thing that you didn't figure out, did you?" He yelled at me as he turned and rushed toward his car, slamming the door behind him. With the sound of the tires spinning in the dirt, he raced out of the parking space and down the roadway. I stood there looking out at the water, crying my heart out. I knew that what I was doing was the right thing, but why did it have to hurt so badly. He could never know how bad it hurt me to do this to him. I looked into the stars and prayed that the Gods would keep him safe while he was driving home that night. I knew that I had hurt him, but it couldn't be helped. I walked around until I regained my composure. I knew that I had a long walk home but that didn't bother me. I had done it many times before when I was growing up, but there had always been somebody with me. Now, it was time for me to make the journey by myself. I started out of the parking lot and down the long road that would lead me home.

In order to keep out of the paths of the cars I walked on the shoulder of the road. I started to think that this was a jungle and I was a jaguar blending into the night. My mind was wondering, helping to perk up my mood. I watched everything that moved, and listened to every sound. I knew that it would be a long time before I got home tonight. I got used to the cars passing by and was no longer paying attention to them. So I didn't notice the one that passed me by on the other side of the road, or the fact that it had suddenly turned around down the road.

I just kept on walking, my mind wondering from time to time. It's kind of an occupational habit with anybody in the creative field that you seem to let your mind explore the unknown worlds. My mood had lightened enough by now that I wasn't totally saddened by the happenings of the night. The night air had cleared my mind and I was able to accept what seemed to be unfair punishment from Tom, for making me walk home by myself. I started to sing little songs to myself. I moved over a little bit more from the pavement as I heard another car approaching from behind me. Just as I did, I felt such pain, as if my body was being torn apart and then nothing, just the feeling that I was unable to move. My head hit the ground so that one eye watched the tail lights of a swerving car leave the dirt.

Chapter Twenty-Three

Where was she, Tom had said that he had left her at lookout point. I should have come across her by now. Let's hope that one of us soon finds her. I told the twins that I would call once I got to lookout point, and Tom was to check back in when he had checked around the town area. I hope that I find her first so that I can calm her down. Maybe I can get them to talk when we get back. Oh my gosh! What are those flashing lights ahead? I don't like this feeling I'm getting. Bill sped up the car in order to get to the lights. He pulled off to the side of the road and went to investigate.

"You can't go over there," a cop who was directing traffic around the area yelled.

Bill didn't listen he just pushed his way past the cop, rushing to the area where the ambulance was. Just as he got close to the accident scene, he saw the battered body of a girl. He recognized it right off the bat. It was Stephanie. "Stephanieeee," he yelled at the top his lungs, as he ran closer. The cops tried to hold him back. "I've got to see her. Is she going to be okay?"

"You know that girl? The cop asked as he was holding him by the shirt.

"Yeah, she's Stephanie McConnell. She is a friend of mine. She's going to be okay isn't she?" Bill yelled at the cop, crying at the same time.

"We don't know that until we get her to the hospital. Is there any next of kin that we can notify?" The cop replied. They were loading Stephanie into the ambulance.

"Yeah, there's her brother and sister. They are at

four, four, four sixty one hundred. Look I'm going to follow them to the hospital." Running to his car he followed after the ambulance to the hospital.

If anything happens to her, I'll kill that son-of-a-bitch Tom. How could he be so thoughtless as to leave her out here. They reached the hospital and rushed Stephanie through the emergency doors, leaving Bill outside in the corridor. Bill went into the waiting room, pounding his fists into the wall, waiting for some kind of word from the doctors. He was sitting with his head resting in his hands when Bridgette and Ben walked through the door.

"Bill how is she?" Bridgette asked. There was panic in her voice.

"I don't know yet. They took her into the emergency room, it seems like hours ago." Bill started to cry again.

"What happened anyway, Bill?" Ben was doing the asking now.

"They say they figure it was a drunk driver, by the marks on the road." As Bill finished saying that, he looked up and saw Tom come into the room. Running across the room he punched him in the face. Ben jumping up and came between the two of them.

"You son-of-of-a-bitch. Why the hell couldn't you at least see that she got home? You didn't have to talk to her, but you could have at least seen that she got home." Bridgette put her arms around Bill and led him to the chair. He was sobbing and shaking his head. "Why did this have to happen to her?" he cried out loud.

"I was mad. I wasn't thinking straight. If I was, do you think I would have let her go home by herself? I couldn't believe that she wasn't home when Bridgette called looking for her. I was still mad at her when we went out to look for her, that is why I let you take the route that I was sure that she would take. I knew that if I found her, that we would just have another fight. If you found her, then you would try and straighten things out."

"All I know is that because of you she's in that emergency room," Bill cried out as he flung his fist at him again.

"All this fighting between us isn't going to help Stephanie. We have to pull together." Bridgette was saying as she tried to calm everyone down.

"McConnell Family," the doctor said as he came through the doorway.

"Yes doctor," Bridgette said as she jumped from her seat and went toward the doctor. "Is she going to be okay?"

"Amazingly enough yes. She has several broken bones and a slight concussion, but other than that she will be okay. I couldn't believe that is all she came out with considering the impact," the doctor said as he rubbed his forehead.

"Can we see her now?" Bridgette asked in an anxious voice.

"Yes in a moment. They are just taking her to her room now. I would advise that you go in one at a time though. She is quite weak right now, though she should be able to go home in a few days," said the doctor as he was getting ready to leave the room.

We waited patiently in the waiting room until a nurse came and told us that we could now see Stephanie. Bridgette was the first to go in. "Hey I guess you do have the lives of a cat Stephanie, but I sure wouldn't do a photo shoot right now."

"That bad, heh?" I managed to say.

Then Ben went into the room. "Hey Sis, are you trying out for the Mummy's next movie or something. All joking aside, how are you? I wish you would quit giving us such scares."

"Ben, you have to look after the money for a while

now. The bank book is in my bedroom," I whispered to him.

"Look Stephanie, you will be out of here in no time, so don't worry about things, at least not yet," Ben said with a smile on his face.

That left Tom and Bill out in the waiting room. "Are you going into see her?" Bill posed the question to Tom in a not too pleasant tone as he watched for his reaction.

"Christ yes, I'm going in. Do you have a problem with that?" Tom snapped back.

"Do you think that she really wants to see you?" Bill snapped back.

"I'll let her decide that," Tom replied as he pushed by Bill. He opened the door and as he did he took one step back. There ahead of him in the hospital bed lay Stephanie. Her head bandaged, eyes blackened and arms and one leg in a cast. "My God Stephanie, couldn't you have picked a better spot to break up so that this couldn't have happened."

"It wasn't my idea that I was going to be walking home or that I was going to be hit." Tom was bowing his head down. "Look I don't blame you. Can you do me a favour though? Could you tell them at the studio that I won't be working for sometime now? See the Lord thought it would be good to separate us for a while. By the way, what happened to your face?" I was tired but I knew that I had to get these things out.

"Bill decked me once I got here for leaving you out there. I guess I deserved it. Do you mind if I stop in and see how you are doing?" Tom said as though he wanted to know whether or not it would be safe for him.

"Yes, you can come by whenever you want. I told you that I didn't want our friendship to suffer because of this."

Tom left and Bill showed his face around the

corner of the door.

"I hear that you decked Tom, you really shouldn't have." I was starting to whisper now.

"He had it coming and I just couldn't resist any longer." Bill laughed as he looked toward the floor. "But how are you? I thought for sure we had lost you when I saw you at the accident scene."

"I'll be okay, in case you haven't noticed. I intend to be around for a long time yet. Besides that, I've only used up three of my cat's lives so far."

"Yeah, but if you keep this up you won't live to see forty." Now he was joking with me. "By the way, do you remember anything about who hit you? I know that the cops say it was a drunk driver but do you know anything?" He had become serious now.

"I can't remember anything only that I was walking along, then the next thing I was on the ground watching the tail lights leaving the scene."

"Well don't worry about it now, just rest." Bill bent over and gave me a kiss on the cheek.

Bill drove Bridgette and Ben home that night. "Bill, do you know what happened tonight?" Bridgette finally asked.

"Tom and Stephanie left the studio early to talk. They stopped at lookout point. Stephanie told Tom that she didn't want to go out with him any more, that she wanted him to date other girls. He got upset and drove off in a huff, leaving her to get home on her own."

"So that's why you hit him in the hospital. You blame him don't you?" Bridgette hit the nail on the head, Bill did blame Tom.

Everyday Bill would bring me flowers at the hospital. Tom only came by once making sure to avoid Bill when he came. The day came that I would be released from the hospital and it was Bill that came with Bridgette to take me home.

They got me home and set me up on the chesterfield in the front room, giving me instructions to call them whenever I needed anything. As I sat down, I noticed that there was a lovely bouquet of flowers with a card attached on the table.

"Bridgette, who brought the flowers?" I yelled to her as she was making some tea in the kitchen.

"I don't know who they are from. They were delivered this morning just before we left for the hospital. It came with a card. Maybe Bill could give it to you to read."

Bill handed me the card, I now had one arm that was out of cast since it wasn't actually broken so at least now I could hold the card myself. The card read, "Cat I do wish that you would quit these close calls with death. My heart can't take much more. If you aren't more careful, then I will have to come down there and take care of you myself. Hope you feel better. Love Dave."

"Were you in touch with Stuart or Uncle Pat, Bridgette?" I called to her as I played around with my ring.

"Yes, but you also made the newspapers. We kept them under the table."

Bill handed me a few papers. I read the headlines, "Model 'The Cat' Hit by drunken driver". I never thought that I would make the newspapers for the accident. Even though I was a model, I wasn't making as many waves in that field as I had when I first started. Sure I was one of the lead ones for the younger generation styles, but as far as I was concerned I was a small fish in the ocean of models.

"I take it that the flowers were from somebody in Ontario, heh?" Bill said with curiosity.

"Yes, it seems they keep a very watchful eye on me all the way up there." The phone rang as I finished saying this to him.

"Bill, could you help me get that invalid to the phone? it's Ontario calling," Bridgette called from the other room with a laugh in her voice.

"Yeah sure. See we speak of them and they hear us talking. Pretty amazing. Too bad that they can't warn us when something bad is about to happen to you. Then maybe, we could protect you." He laughed as he helped me up and to a chair in the kitchen where the phone was.

"Hello."

"Stephanie, how are you feeling?" Stuart asked.

"I'm okay now, just a few broken bones to heal, then I'll be as good as new," I laughed.

"Hold on for a minute then," Stuart said and then there was a sound as if the phone was being passed around.

"Cat, could you do me a favour and not make so many headlines like these last ones." Dave had taken the phone from Stuart.

"I got the flowers, they are just beautiful. I was so surprised to see them." I could feel the redness in my face as I talked to him.

"Cat, how did this happen? I thought that they were watching you down there."

"I guess you could say that it was partly my fault. I chose to break things off with Tom out at look-out point not expecting him to leave me out there to make it home by myself. Then when I was walking home a drunk driver hit me. But I'm okay now. I just won't be able to work for a while."

"If you say the word I'll catch the next plane down and look after you while you recuperate." I could almost see his face through the phone as he made his offer.

"Thanks, but no thanks. I will do just fine. You know I always do. Remember, I am 'The Cat'. I always land on all fours. I may have the tar kicked out of me, but I'll come back stronger than before, just you watch."

"I guess that I better put Stuart back on, just remember I love you Cat."

"I love you too," I said to him just before he passed the phone back to Stuart.

"Well Stephanie, do I have to accompany Dave down there or are you going to be okay." Stuart said with his usual chuckle.

"No, you don't I think he is satisfied. Keep in touch okay, I love you Stuart."

"I love you too, Stephanie."

I hung up the phone and Bill helped me back to the chesterfield where Bridgette had poured me a cup of tea.

"Well, are they satisfied that you are okay?" Bill asked.

"Yes, hearing my voice put their minds at ease," I replied with a smile.

"Well, they seem to have given you an extra lift. You look like you got a shot of sunshine over the phone. Now it's our turn to take care of you like you did for us while we weren't well," Bridgette said. "Anything that you want, you call one of us."

They were just great while I was recuperating. Bill would check in on me periodically, and if he didn't then his sister Sandy would. Tom was still keeping his distance and would only stop by with news from the studio. The friendship that Bill had valued so much had quickly come to an end. Tom and he would talk politely to each other when they met, but they would never go out of their way for each other as they had in the past.

My brother and sister never could understand why I would ever want to break things off with Tom in the first place. We always seemed to make such a nice couple and we had gone through so much together. The only one that did understand was Bill, but he just couldn't understand Tom leaving me out there. Sandy couldn't understand it either, but didn't hesitate to ask whether or not it would bother me if either she or Jenny dated Tom, or if they even modeled for him. I told her that it was between him and them, and that it didn't bother me. Bill couldn't believe his sister when she came out and asked it. I could, after all, Tom was an attractive man and was a fine catch for any girl; he just wasn't the right catch for me.

      I got Bill to pick me up some law books from the library, I mean there is no sense in being bored doing nothing and wasting time when I couldn't do anything else. I had already started taking correspondence courses that would lead me to my law classes before the accident, so I might as well get as much reading in as possible. They brought out Ben's old wheelchair so that I could get around a little bit better on my own, and I was counting the days until could get these casts off.

Chapter Twenty-Four

The day finally came when I could get those darn casts off. It was a day that I thought would never come but at last it was here. Bill took me to the hospital to have those dreaded things removed. I would finally get back to normal I thought, and then the doctor nicely reminded me that now the therapy would begin. The good news was that I could go back to doing a bit of modeling as long as I felt up to it and I didn't overdue it. The factory work was still out of the question. I was glad to hear that I could go back to modeling as our funds were starting to get a little low. Oh, we would still be able to get by for a little bit longer without real panic, and I still had my stocks if things got worse.

I turned up at the studio the following week feeling stronger. I walked into the room where Tom was doing a shoot with a new model. As I walked in he looked up from his camera.

"Good to see you, Stephanie. Do you feel up to working? They said that you would be coming in today." Tom was smiling as he was talking to me, but he seemed distant as if he wasn't even in the room with me.

"Yes, I am ready. Who is the new one, she seems pretty good," I replied as I nodded my head toward the new model.

"Stephanie this is Melanie." He motioned to Melanie to come over to meet me.

"Hi, I'm sorry to hear about your accident," Melanie said as she extended her hand to shake mine.

"You look good up there," I told her.

"Melanie you can get changed now, while I do

Stephanie's shots," Tom commanded to her.

"How are things going Tom?" I asked Tom as I was changing.

"Things are going great. I have been offered a permanent photographic job with another fashion magazine upon completion of my year at school," he replied.

"Are you going to take it?"

"I think that under the circumstances that it might be the best thing that I could do. It would mean going to Montreal, Quebec."

I came out of the dressing room in a three piece pant suit. Mr. Conrad thought that I should wear clothes that would cover up my injured spots until I was completely healed. "So in other words, your mind is already made up?"

"There's something else too, Stephanie. I told Mr. Conrad that I would try to be your photographer. However, if I found out that it wasn't working he would ask Richard to take over. So we will try it for one week and see how it goes."

"I never thought that it would come to this Tom. I hope that you believe me."

"I do believe you, I just can't accept it. Now shall we get on with the shoot?" He motioned with his arm, pointing to the spot where I was to stand.

We lasted about one week, and then Richard took over from Tom. Modeling which started out as something that both Tom and I enjoyed because we were doing it together, was now turning into something that I had to do because it was my job.

Tom took off to Montreal as he said he would. Ben finished his schooling and got a job with an architectural firm as an apprentice. Bridgette managed to get work with a small drama club. We had just received word that our dear sweet cousin Deborah-Anne was getting married. Stuart wrote in his letter, "Of course, I know that you are not hurt for being left off the guest list." Boy he couldn't have been more right, that was one wedding that I was glad that I wasn't going to, even though it would be the fashion thing of the time. We had weddings here of our own. Sandy was marrying John Borringsworth. She had known him all her life, but they hadn't started to date until the last year or so, then things just seem to take off.

I was her maid of honour and Jenny was the bridesmaid. John was having his brother Derek as his best man and Bill was an usher. They had Tom come in from Montreal to do the photography.

The church was all decorated with white ribbons on the pews and white flowers on stands. When we arrived at the church they started to play the wedding march. Standing at the front of the church were the minister, John, Derek, and Bill. They were all looking toward the back of the church where we were standing. First Jenny started down the aisle, and then I started down followed by Sandy in an antique wedding dress that had been passed down from her Grandmother to her mother, and now to her. Jenny and I had matching gowns that were designs from the Victorian time period, but in different colours. After the ceremony we went back to the reception hall. There Tom was joined by a very attractive woman, who caught everybody's eyes as she came into the room.

When the dancing started up, we never seemed to be off the dance floor. Finally Tom came over and asked me to dance.

"Stephanie, can I have this dance?"

"Sure Tom, I would love to." I got up on the dance floor with him and we floated around the dance floor as we used to do.

"When we are on the dance floor it seems as

though nothing has changed. We still seem to dance as one. How are things going anyway?" he whispered to me.

"Everything is going just fine. I will be entering night school to study Law. It looks like things are going okay for you," I said, motioning in the direction of his date.

"I thought that you said that my going out with other girls wouldn't bother you?" He looked down at me with eyes that almost said, I told you so but with also the question you mean you still care.

"It doesn't bother me. I just couldn't help but notice her. If I didn't know better I would swear that you did it purposely to see if you could strike a nerve with me."

I looked him right back in the eye. "Are you two happy together or am I jumping the gun in thinking that there is more than a friendship there?"

"I met Monique shortly after going to Montreal, and yes, we are happy. The two of us get along well together. What about you, have you found someone else?"

"No, I told you that wasn't the reason for breaking it off with you. When I go out we go out in a group so I don't need anyone who is mine alone."

"Would you like to meet Monique?"

"Yes, that would be nice." He took me by the hand and we headed over to where Monique was standing talking to some people.

"Monique, I would like you to meet Stephanie McConnell," he said to her.

"So you are 'The Cat'. It is a pleasure to meet you Stephanie. Tom has told me so much about you," she said with a slight French accent. She seemed very nice.

"He has, has he? I am so glad to see that he has met someone as nice as you. You seem quite charming."

"Would the single girls come up to the front of the

room for the throwing of the bouquet," the Master of ceremony announced.

"Well girls, they seem to be calling you," Tom said to the two of us.

"Come on Monique. Let's go and see who catches the bouquet." I said to her. We walked up to the front of the hall where all the other girls were standing. Sandy turned around and threw the bouquet. I knew that she was trying for me and she managed a perfect throw right into my hands.

Then came the turn for the bachelors, Tom went up and alongside him were Ben and Bill. John slipped the garter slowly off Sandy's leg, and turning around threw it right into Tom's hand. The announcer then asked the gentleman that had caught the garter to place it on the leg of the girl who had just caught the bouquet. I sat down on the chair and slowly lifting my dress to show the shapely leg that was hiding under the dress. As I was doing this, I was looking down at Tom with the sexiest cat eyes that I could possibly show, enticing him all the way. He slowly put the garter on my leg gradually coming closer as he got to the thigh of my leg. They started to play music for us to dance to. He gracefully took me in his arms and we danced around the room in complete unison as our bodies became one for one more time. We had everybody in the room wondering whether or not there might be a reconciliation in the air.

Chapter Twenty-Five

The day came for Deborah-Anne's wedding and in the social section of the newspapers were pictures of the festive event. There were pictures of the bride and groom, her family and his. She was marrying Doctor Michael Burnaby, quite an attractive guy too if I must say so. It was such a shame that he had to end up with her.

Deborah-Anne's wedding had caught my eye, but something else caught my eye on the page. There was another announcement on that page, "Mr. and Mrs. V Hancock are proud to announce the forthcoming marriage of their daughter Susan to Mr. David Thompson on September Twentieth at four o'clock."

How could this be that Stuart, or better yet that Dave himself hadn't written and told me about this? I picked up the phone and called Stuart.

"Stuart I just saw the pictures in the paper of Deborah-Anne's wedding. I see that everything went well, but something else caught my eye in the newspaper. I see that Dave is getting married. Why didn't you tell me that in your letter?"

"Stephanie, I was supposed to call you and tell you. Dave asked me to do that for him."

"Just tell me something. Is she a nice girl? Can she make him happy?"

"She is very nice and she can make him happy, but she will never take your place in his heart. He said to tell you that if you are ever in trouble that you are still number one in his books. He will come running to get you out of trouble. All you have to do is to call."

"That's all I needed to know, thanks cousin," I

said as I hung up the receiver.

I would send him a wedding card to congratulate him. It seems like everybody was finding the right person to settle down with except for me. Ben was seeing a very nice girl from the office and Bridgette had found somebody nice too. I went back to my law books as they seemed to be my partner right now.

The day of Dave's wedding came and the pictures of his wedding were also in the social section of the newspaper. It almost tore my heart out as I looked at them. I knew that I had no hold on him, but there had always been a special bond between us, something that seemed to draw me to him and him to me. I got through my first set of exams, pulling through at the top of my class. If the next couple of years would be that good to me, then I would have nothing to worry about in becoming a lawyer.

We were able to set aside a little bit of money for a rainy day. That meant for me the last year of schooling could be done alone without working at the same time. Uncle Pat was still keeping me posted on my stocks. Money that if I wanted to, I could use to get through Law school, but I chose not to go that route.

Ben was getting into the architectural business along with this new computer technology that they were bringing out. He was learning to design buildings with the use of these machines. Bridgette was starring in dramas that were put on in the theatre in our town. She was getting excited since there was going to be a producer from Los Angeles at one of the showings.

Ben came home tonight and approached me rather seriously. "Stephanie how about if you stop working this year so that you could try for your bars at the end of the year?"

"What brought this on Ben?" I questioned.

"The truth of the matter is that I am thinking of

getting married next year, which would leave you without my pay cheque coming in. That would mean it would take longer for you to get your degree."

"Have you discussed this with Bridgette yet?"

"No, not yet, but I am sure that she would agree that you should go for it. If you want, I can call her in and we can ask her." He was determined to get his way.

"Yes, call her in because this involves her too."

He went and got Bridgette from the other room where she was drying dishes.

"Bridgette, I have just suggested to Stephanie that she takes time off from working this year and go back to school full time so that she can try her bar exams next year. What do you think?

"I think that is a great idea. We can manage to carry the family on our salaries," she replied with a smile on her face.

"Bridgette, there's something that Ben didn't tell you."

"What's that?" she asked.

"At the end of next year, he is planning on getting married," I said with a smile on my face.

"Why that's great. We can plan for you passing the bar and his marriage together." She ran over and gave her brother a big hug and a kiss.

So it was back to school full time. I hit the books twice as hard now, since I had more subjects to cover if I was to try the bars at the end of the year. I took in all the information that I could. I visited the courts taking in court room procedures. Time seemed to fly. I couldn't believe that a year could pass by so quickly. Before I realised it, it was a week before the bar exams and I was wishing that I had another year. Ben and Bridgette made sure that they were out of the house every night that week so that no-one bothered me while I was studying. Now today I had such a bad case of butterflies that I didn't know whether or not I would be able to write them, but I did. I thought that writing this exam had to be the worst thing that had ever happened to me, but somehow I managed to pass it.

Now after getting this far, the next step was to land a job. I sent my resume to law offices far and near. As I waited for the replies to come back, I continued with my modeling and shooting pictures so that we would have extra money for Ben's wedding. Then it happened; I came home from work and there in the mail box was a letter from the firm of Beachly & Beachly in Toronto. I opened it with trembling fingers. Ben and Bridgette watched patiently. I finally got it opened.

"Dear Miss Stephanie McConnell:

After reviewing your marks and your resume, we request that you be in our office on November 10 at ten o'clock for an interview. At which time we will inform you whether or not you will be asked to join our law firm.

If you are unable to keep that appointment, please contact the undersigned immediately, otherwise we remain.

Yours truly;
S.Beachly

Q.C."

"Well I guess this is it, then Stephanie. It looks like you will be moving to Ontario," Ben was saying to me.

"Hey nothing is for certain yet. I haven't got the job yet."

"Maybe not, but we know that you will, don't we Ben?" Bridgette put her two cents worth in.

"Are you going to call Uncle Pat and stay with them?" Ben asked.

"No, I thought that I would look for a hotel in the city, and maybe call them after the interview."

The hard part now came with actually landing this job. Could I actually pull off the interview? Was I really good enough to be a lawyer? Would Stuart and I actually meet in court someday? He had been a lawyer for a year now. The time for the interview was drawing closer and these questions would soon get answered.

Chapter Twenty-Six

I look on that day when Ben suggested that I take a year off and try my bar exams, and think that I could never repay them for that. I had started at the bottom in the law firm after that interview, but worked hard and proved that they hadn't made a mistake hiring me. The more cases that they gave me, added fuel to the reputation that was starting to follow me in the law field and my nickname followed along with it. I was a prosecuting lawyer and I specialized in certain cases. I got the cases if they were about child abuse, molesting of any type or drunk driving. I would do my homework left, right and center to make sure that I got a conviction if the person charged was guilty. For these cases, I threw my whole body and soul into it, using every trick in the book, because of this I soon became disliked by many people.

The legend of 'The Cat' soon echoed through the halls of the courts. Stuart and I had never had the opportunity to go against each other on a case, and I guess that we were grateful for that. We would joke about it on weekends when we would got together with the families at the mansion. Stuart now married and had a beautiful daughter named Erin. At these family get-togethers the question about when was I going to settle down always seemed to come up. Ben was now married and so was Bridgette, so everyone wondered when I was going tie the knot.

I couldn't see that ever happening because of my past, but I couldn't tell them that. I would have loved to have been married and have children that I could pass things down to, but that sure didn't seem like it would ever happen. I had started to do research into the family name, trying to find out what mother meant, when she said that I was to trace Grandfather McConnell and that he was looking for me. Now, that I was a lawyer and doing rather well at it. I now had the funds and the ability to have this done. So at one of these family get-togethers I informed the rest of the family of what I was doing, and the response that I received was very strange.

"I've hired a investigator to trace our family history," I said casually.

"Why on earth would you want to do that?" Stuart came out with.

"I have this feeling that I need to know the history of my family," I explained.

"I think you should leave well enough alone," exclaimed Aunt Elizabeth.

"You know the old saying that curiosity killed the cat, please leave things alone Stephanie," Added Uncle Pat. This was strange coming from him. They now had aroused my curiosity to continue even more than before.

I went back to the investigator, and asked if he could possibly get a copy of my Grandfather's will. Also, if he could find out anything about my parents, Uncle Pat, and Aunt Elizabeth from people that knew them, when they were just going out with each other. I knew that the answers to these questions were the answers that I needed to answer this puzzle about my family.

The following week I started on a new case concerning child abuse. Stuart had also been assigned a new case.

"Who's the prosecutor on this case?" Stuart asked his colleague.

"Well Stuart my boy I don't envy you this case. They say you will be up against 'The Cat' and you know what her record is. God she'll tear you apart in the courtroom."

"I can't take this case; The Cat is my cousin!" exclaimed Stuart. "You have to take this one."

"Cousin or no cousin, there is no way that I am going up against her," his colleague exclaimed. "She has this way of getting the accused to sometimes confess to the crime right there on the stand. Sorry buddy, but this one is all yours."

In the court room, we stood before the judge before picking the jury. The judge looked at the two of us.

"Isn't this a little irregular, the defense and the prosecution being of the same family?" The judge questioned us.

"Your honor the fact that my cousin is defending the accused has no bearing on how I will proceed in this case. If the accused is guilty as I believe he is, then I will prove it beyond a reasonable doubt. I am sure that my cousin will not let the fact that we are in the same family cloud his judgment in presenting a fair case. So if your honor accepts this situation as such I move that we continue to pick the jury for this case." I presented to the judge in charge of the case.

"Mr. McConnell, do you agree with how Miss McConnell has presented the situation?"

"I agree with Miss McConnell, that the fact that she is my cousin will have no bearing on this case whatsoever," Stuart replied.

We proceeded to choose the jury, after which I told Stuart that I would not be at the family gatherings until after the case was over, in fairness to the case.

The case started with very feisty opening statements from both sides. The press however was having a field day by releasing such headlines as, "The Cat eats cousin in the Courtroom," when it seemed like I was winning in court that day. Then when Stuart seemed to be winning, the headlines would read, "McConnell stomps on The Cat."

It came down to the last day of the trial, which we both were glad of. Although, neither one of us would admit it, we hated having to battle against each other. I had one last trick that I was going to use in order to get a conviction.

I had the accused on the stand, as I walked back and forth from the desk to the witness stand.

"You have two children of your own, do you not?" I asked.

"Yes, I have two little girls," the accused replied.

"How would you feel if somebody sexually abused them?" I looked him in the eye.

"I would kill whoever did it," he replied.

"Yet, you did it to this little girl?"

"I object your honor. That is purely conjecture." Stuart stood up and exclaimed.

"Counselor, please stick with the facts. Jurors please dismiss that last statement." The judge cautioned me.

"Do you know the child that was abused in this case?"

"No, I do not know her."

"I would like to remind you that you are under oath. If it pleases your honor I would like to present a video of the child involved in this case. The video was taken when the doctors were examining her." I approached the bench.

"If there is no objection from the defense, I will allow it." The judge motioned to Stuart to approach the bench.

"I have no objection at this time. However, I am curious as to where the prosecution is going with this?" Stuart replied.

"As you watch this I want you to think of your

daughters. I want you to tell me that you have never seen this little girl before. I want you to watch how this little girl won't let a man near her, not even her father. I want you to think of the pain that this father felt knowing that he has done nothing to cause his daughter to hate him, so much so that she won't even let him near her. How do you feel? Do you still say that you have never seen this little girl before? Are you still going to sit there and tell the court that you didn't sexually assault that little girl,?" By now Stuart was on his feet.

"I object! The prosecution is badgering the witness," Stuart yelled at the judge.

"Miss McConnell would please refrain from your line of questioning." The judge was saying to me, but I just kept on going.

"Well are you still saying that you didn't touch that little girl. Please take a close look at that screen, and listen to her screaming. Think of your daughters. Are they still safe with you in the house?"

"Your honor please," Stuart was standing again.

"Well?" I asked the accused. "Are your daughters safe in the house with you?"

"Answer the question please," the judge requested.

"They are safe in my house. I would never do to them what I did to her," the accused replied. There was a wave of muttering going through the courtroom.

"Then you did sexually abuse this little girl that night?" I posed the question to him.

"Yes, I didn't mean to. I had too much to drink." He started to cry. "When I sobered up and realized what I had done, I just wanted to forget about it."

"Did you think that little girl would forget it?"

"No, I'm sorry. I'm so very sorry."

"Your honor I have no further questions," I said to the judge and proceeded back to my seat.

"Mr. McConnell," the judge said to Stuart.

"No further questions. The defense rests under the circumstances."

I had done it again and the newspapers read, "The Cat turns into a wildcat and scares the truth out of the accused." I was glad that it was over. Now Stuart and I could enjoy some time together. That weekend I had Ben and Bridgette and their families up to the cottage that I had on one of the islands in the Georgian Bay area. Only the people that I wanted to know about this place knew where to find it. I told Bill to come up too, then we would be coupled off although I hadn't seen him in years.

I had business that I wanted to discuss with Ben about starting up our own architectural and construction company. I now had the funds, but I couldn't be seen as the head of it at least not in the open. I wanted it to be set up through a holding company, so I also had Uncle Pat join us in order to advise us on how to go about the whole thing.

I had done my homework as usual and there was another reason for me asking Bill up. I had him checked out and found that he was one of the people at the top in the construction field. I wanted him to run the construction part of the business, and Ben would run the architectural side. When I ran it past both of them, they thought that it was a great idea, but that meant that they would all have to move up to Ontario. That is why I had them bring their families. Bill hadn't married, so I could see no problem there. Ben I knew could twist his wife around his little finger, if he wanted something badly enough. It would take just a bit of explaining but he would get his way. I told everyone to enjoy themselves, after we had talked about the business and had covered all aspects of it. I asked them to think about my proposal.

"Bill, do you feel like some scuba-diving? I have a couple of tanks just waiting to be strapped on," I said to him as we walked out of the main cabin.

"You seem to have thought of everything, haven't you?" he said as he picked up one of the tanks.

Where the island was located, the water was so blue and clear; it was like diving down south. We went down in complete solitude except for the air bubbles being released. The fish seemed to have accepted us as one of their own. Looking up to the surface, the sun rays were filtering down like stardust. We came to the surface and slowly swam to the shore. On the shore we lay back and rested.

"That felt great, just like old times, heh?" Bill said as he turned and looked at me.

"Yes, just like old times. Bill, why didn't you ever marry?" I thought that I knew the answer, but when he first mentioned it, it was so long ago. I had been away from him for about ten years now.

"I think that you know the answer to that Stephanie," he replied looking me in the eyes.

"I think that I do, but I have to know for sure."

"The reason that I never married was because I never stopped loving you. I couldn't find someone that I loved more than I loved you. I still love you." He moved a little closer. "The same question goes to you. Why didn't you ever marry?"

I stood up and started to move away from him. "I think that you know the answer there. I've never found a person that I thought I could trust to know the truth about that night. Without them knowing about it, I didn't know whether or not I could make love to them without feeling dirty and like a tramp. I couldn't stand that feeling so I just avoided the situation." I left him sitting there by himself as I walked up to the main cabin with my tank in my hand.

The way that the island was arranged was there were two guest cottages; both were fully equipped with everything the family using it would need. That way they wouldn't have to bother me and I didn't have to bother them. We all had our privacy if we wanted it. The standing rule was not to bother Aunt Stephanie unless it was necessary or unless she invited you.

Since Uncle Pat and Bill were on their own there, they had the use of the master cabin along with me. I always served dinner at six o'clock and no matter where you were, you made sure that you were back in time for it. At the cottage, I made the meals and did the cleaning. Back in the city I didn't have to; as my income from being a lawyer and a photographer was sufficient, so that I could afford a housekeeper. I had reached a time in my life that I didn't worry what the next day was going to bring. I still played the stock market, and now knew that it was time to start to expand my finances into something that would become my dynasty, to be passed on in the family. That was the main reason for calling everybody together this weekend.

After I finished the dishes, I grabbed my camera case and with my tripod over my shoulder, headed to the other side of the island where I could get the sunsets. When I reached the spot, I set up the tripod so that I could sit on the rocks instead of standing all of the time. I looked around listening to the quietness of the area, watching the water slowly become a mirror before my very eyes. This is why I bought this place, the peacefulness that it provided after a hard case was the best medicine that anybody could have. I sat there watching and listening until I heard the rustle of leaves. I turned the camera in the direction of the noise. There I saw a small chipmunk with an acorn in his mouth, his tiny hands shoving it further into the pouch in his mouth making him look as though he had the mumps. I kept shooting the camera getting every move that he made on film, until finally he left.

The area was a photographer's delight. Everyplace that you turned there was something different to shoot. I specialized in nature shots now and it didn't matter how many times I shot an animal, bird or sunset; I still got the same feeling of seeing something special for the first time. I sat there now taking in the sun as it slowly started to sink from the sky, taking a shot every now and then.

"The sunset is beautiful, isn't it?" A voice suddenly broke through the silence. I turned from my camera and saw Bill standing above me.

"It sure is. It's one of God's greatest gifts and you know that no two sunsets are the same. There's something different about each one, that's what makes them special," I replied as I leaned back on my arms.

"Do you come out here much?" he asked as he sat down on the rocks beside me.

"Every time that I am up here, I come out here with my camera and every time, I see something different." I no sooner spoke than a mother duck and her ducklings started to pass by us. I reached for the camera, focusing the camera I motioned to Bill to come closer. "Here take a look at what I mean." He looked through the eyepiece of the camera, to see an adorable little duckling struggling to keep up with the Mother duck.

"Cute little fellow, isn't he," he remarked.

I reached for the camera to get the shot of this irresistible fellow. Bill watched every move that I made. "You love it up here, don't you?" he asked.

"I love the beauty that I find up here along with the peacefulness I could never find anywhere else." I glanced over my shoulder at him.

"There is a certain beauty up here, but wherever you go, so goes beauty." I felt my face go red on hearing his comment.

"Bill you must be getting blinded by the light. I'm

not that beautiful girl who used to be on the cover of the magazines."

Bill thought who was she trying to kid. Her body was still firm and fit and there wasn't a crease on her face. The gray hair that was slowly starting to grow in was kept in check with trips to the hairdresser, but she was still very attractive.

"You could still put the others to shame, if you were to go back to modeling," he said just as we heard a loon calling out.

"See that, the loon is trying to tell you that you're loony to think that way," I chuckled.

"The only thing that I might be loony for is never showing you how I felt about you." He started to move closer to me.

"You told me or don't you remember?" I replied as I looked straight into his eyes. His eyes were changing. They were becoming commanding.

"I may have told you but I never showed you." With that he came closer and put his arm around me. He slowly kissed my lips. I didn't resist his kisses and then slowly he picked me up in his arms all in a matter of seconds, moving me over to where the moss was at the beginning of the rocks. Never letting his lips leave mine, he slowly continued to kiss me and then as the sun finally melted into the water, he started to caress my body. I started to pull away, but he gently brought me back nearer to him. "Don't worry Stephanie. There isn't anything wrong with this. I love you and there is nothing that I would do to hurt you. What we are doing is not dirty and you're not a tramp. You are a lady. What more, you are my queen." He started with a lingering kiss from my lips, to my neck, then my breasts. I started to squirm at the feelings that were rushing through my body, as his lips were caressing everywhere that his hands were not. I felt his body against mine. Part of me wanted him off, the other did not. His lips once again were against mine while the final part of the puzzle slid gently into place. The feeling felt nothing like when Tom and I had made love, but instead the feeling of dirtiness seemed to have lifted, as though I finally found the one that I should be with. As he slowly started to move away from me, kissing me every second that he was doing it, he whispered. "Well how do you feel? Do you feel that this was wrong?"

"No, I feel like a big burden has been lifted off me." I smiled back up at him.

"You don't feel dirty or like a tramp?" He looked down at me with a questioning look.

"Completely the opposite! I feel like a queen with her king." I reached up, putting my arms around his neck I pulled him back down to my level. I started to kiss him passionately from his lips to his chest. He responded with kisses to my body.

"Cat, I was such a fool to have waited so long for you," he whispered in my ear.

"Well, we are together now and that's all that matters," I whispered back.

"Cat, now that I have found you I don't ever want to let you out of my sight again."

Passionately we made love again and at the end he helped me off the bed of moss, our naked bodies glowing in the moonlight, kissing me gently on the lips.

"I know that we have just met again, but I have known from the very first time that I saw you that I wanted you as my wife. Stephanie, please say that you'll marry me." Bill was looking straight in the eyes with these commanding and yet passionate eyes of his.

"I can't say yes just because of what we both just experienced. I want some time to get to know you again, stay here in Toronto with me for a while," I said quietly back to him, kissing him on the lips.

The next morning I called everyone to the main

cabin to find out the decisions that everyone had made. The vote was unanimous, they were all in favour of the business. First on the agenda was to arrange for work permit for everyone.

Chapter Twenty-Seven

The Company had been set up for sometime now, giving Bill and I time to get to know each other again. We decided to set a wedding date, since we both agreed that this was what we wanted. We wouldn't have anything too extravagant like Deborah-Anne's, just family and some friends. We decided to make the announcement at one of the family weekends. The same weekend I told Aunt Elizabeth that I had heard back from the investigator. The one that I hired to trace the family history, and that he had informed me that she and my father knew each other before she married Uncle Pat.

"Yes, I knew your father back then, but I also knew your mother too. We used to go out to places together," Aunt Elizabeth commented.

I knew that there was more to this than what she was letting on, but I couldn't very well treat her as I treated witnesses on the stand. I wanted the truth and I was bound to find it.

"You know Stephanie, I do wish that you would leave the past in the past," she continued. Why did they want me to leave things in the past? I needed to know the answer to this. Bill and I got into my car, (a green jaguar with a license plate that read THE CAT, the plates were a gift from Stuart) and headed home.

"You know Bill there's something buried in the past of this family that nobody wants me to know, but I have got news for them. I am going to find out what it is."

"Maybe you should leave things alone Stephanie," he said showing concern. "Maybe what you are going to find out will be something that would hurt you."

"That doesn't bother me as much as not knowing what it is."

That night when we got home I received a strange call.

"Cat is that you?" It was Dave on the other end of the phone.

"Yes Dave, what is it?" I replied sensing that something was wrong.

"Are you okay?"

"Yes, I'm just fine. What is this all about?" He had my curiosity aroused.

"Thank God for that. I just got this weird feeling that something happened to you."

"Well I am just fine. In fact, I couldn't be better. Bill and I just announced our wedding date to the family."

"Well that's great news. I'm glad to know that the feeling was not supposed to be a negative one. That it was good news about you instead of bad."

"Thanks for your concern though Dave. Glad to hear that you still worry about me."

"Well, I'll let you go now. Pass on my congratulations to Bill. He's one lucky guy."

"Bye Dave," I said as I hung up the phone and headed over to sit with Bill.

"What was that all about, Stephanie?" Bill asked as I still had a puzzled look on my face.

"That was Dave, he says congratulations to you and that you got a great girl." I was still looking distant. I could not shake what Dave had said.

"But why did he call?" He was persistent now.

"He wanted to make sure that I was okay. He had this feeling that I was hurt or in trouble," I said still with a confused look on my face.

"Is there any reason that we should be alarmed by

this feeling of his?" Bill questioned.

"He had one of those feelings shortly before my father attacked me and when you found me on the beach. You see, there is something about Dave and I. We can sense when the other one is in trouble, but I never seem to listen."

"Maybe then we should take no chances this time. I don't want anything happening to you before the wedding or after the wedding. It has taken us too long to get together to have anything wreck it."

"After I told him that we were getting married he felt that it was good news that he was supposed to hear about me and not bad news." I still had a distant look on my face. I couldn't shake this feeling that Dave felt that there was trouble ahead and that I should be careful.

"No matter, we are not taking any chances. I am escorting you wherever you go, is that understood?" He looked at me as though he was a figure of authority.

"Yes okay, if that will make you happy," I joked with him. He thought that he could protect me which was kind of silly since I was in the media most of the time with my court cases. I had always taken precautions in not letting it be known where I lived. They had increased the security around the court house, so I really didn't know where I could be in danger. Just the same I took the added precautions to make him happy. The case that I was working on had gained me a few new enemies, but no more than usual. This was normal and went with the trials, especially if the case didn't go the way the people involved wanted it to go.

Bill dropped me off at the courthouse as usual. I went inside and there was a message to meet my investigator friend. I called Bill up and told him to pick me up at the investigator's office instead of the courthouse. He was not amused with the idea. However, after fighting with me on the phone for ten minutes, he finally agreed to do it my way.

The investigator had a copy of my Grandfather's will which he handed to me. I started to read it, and half way down the page a clause jumped out at me. "In the event of my death, the entire estate shall be given to my eldest son Patrick with a modest sum of ten thousand dollars going to my other son James. In the event however, that there is an offspring from either son and that the offspring is born on the full moon, then as my father before left the estate to me, I shall leave my estate to that child." I was that child, I was not only born on the full moon, but I was born just before my Grandfather died. The estate was rightfully mine, so that is why nobody wanted me digging around. I thanked him and told him to keep up the good work. I let my guard down as I left the office, looking all over the street for Bill. I saw the jaguar pulling up, so I ran over to it. As I opened the car door to sit in the car, keeping my eyes on Bill at all times with a glowing smile on my face I said as I started to get into the car. "Wait until you hear this I have found out why they didn't want me digging around in the past." I slowly slid into the car. Bill reached over to give me a kiss as I entered the car, and as he put his arm around me he felt something wet. Pulling his arm back he screamed as he saw it was covered in blood.

He yanked the door shut and with the tires squealing on the pavement he rushed me to Southern Metropolitan Hospital. There they rushed me into the emergency room. I was still grasping onto my Grandfather's will. Dave came into the emergency room. "What do we have here?" He questioned the nurse tending to me not knowing that it was me on the table.

"It's an apparent shooting. The patient is female, maybe about forty. Apparently she was getting into her car and slumped. The boyfriend felt her back only to get a handful of blood." He still hadn't looked directly at the body that was before him. He walked over still putting his surgical gloves on and then he stopped dead as he looked at the body before him.

"Oh my God it's 'the Cat'!" he exclaimed.

"You know the patient, Doctor?" the nurse asked.

"She is a good friend of mine. Let's get to work, we have to save this one for sure."

The nurse took the paper out of my hand and put it over to the side. They got me ready to go to surgery and as we passed Bill in the hallway Dave called out to him, "Don't worry Bill, she is in good hands. I would never let anything happen to her." Then he continued rushing down the hall.

Bill spent another agonizing time in the emergency room waiting room for me. The time seemed to stand still while he was waiting for some word on his precious Cat. All the time he was wondering why this had to happen to her. Who would want her dead so badly? The questions seemed to be swirling around in his head. Would they ever see their wedding day? The hours passed by then the police arrived and started to ask him the same questions that he had been asking himself. The questions that no-one had the answers to.

"Does she have any known enemies?" the police asked.

"None that are known. She often makes them on cases that she is working on, but there's never been an attempt on her life before. God what's keeping them so long?" Bill was pacing back and forth as the police tried to comfort him.

"Have you notified her next of kin?" One of the officers asked.

"No, I've just been running through my brain who would want to do this to her."

"Give us the numbers and we'll have somebody make the calls." The officer said to Bill. "Now don't worry she is going to make it. She is a pretty gutsy lady. I have seen her work in the courts," the officer said as he patted Bill on the back and took down the numbers.

Finally, Dave came through the doors, wiping the sweat off his brow. "Bill we got the bullet out. I thought that we were going to loose her at one point, but she did her usual turn around and came back to us." Bill let out a sigh of relief.

"Can I see her now?"

"In a little while. They are taking her to recovery right now. When we get her in a room then you can go in. I will tell you right now that she is awfully weak. In fact, if you hadn't got her here when you did, we would have lost her. Do you feel like going for a coffee and to talk a bit?"

"Sure, I could use a coffee," said Bill as he and Dave headed down the hall to the cafeteria.

"Tell me exactly what happened, Bill?"

"Well, ever since your phone call the other night, we have been taking extra precautions with regards to her safety, just in case. I would pick her up and drive her wherever she was going. Today went the same way with the exception that she got a call from the investigator that she had hired to track down the family's background. She phoned me and told me to pick her up there. She was just opening the car door, with some paper in her hand that she wanted to show me. She had one foot in the car when she must have been shot because she slumped down in the seat. I reached over touching her back and found blood all over my hand. I shut the door and raced over here." Bill had tears in his eyes as he was telling Dave the events.

"Did you ever see what was on the paper the she had?" Dave asked.

"No, the last time I saw the paper, it was in her hand as they rushed her into the emergency room. Why?"

"The bullet I pulled out of her was shot by a professional. Whoever it was had to be watching her in order to know that you would have to pick her up there."

"Would you be able to get that paper the she had Dave?" Bill looked at him with eyes that lit up with the thought that maybe that piece of paper might lead to the shooter.

"I'll check on it and I'll get back to you. Just take it easy now."

Bill went home after finally getting to see me, only to get bombarded with phone calls about how I was. Then the phone rang again. He was starting to think that everybody had called.

"Bill, congratulations!" said a voice from the past, one he didn't figure on hearing from. "I was just in town and heard the good news from Stuart that you and Stephanie are getting married. I thought that you and I could get together to show that there are no hard feelings."

"Tom, thanks but no thanks. I'm not in a celebrating mood. I guess that you were talking to Stuart early today."

"Yes, why is something wrong?"

"Stephanie was shot today." Bill had a lump in his throat as he got the words out.

"Oh my God! You've got to be kidding. Is she okay?" There was concern in his voice.

"She's in serious condition, but she is going to make it."

"Who would want to kill her?"

"We don't know. Now if you don't mind, it's been a long day. It was nice to hear from you though Tom." Bill hung up the phone with the last question lingering on his mind. "Who would want to kill her and why?"

Bill had a couple of drinks to help him sleep that night, but although it let him sleep, it was a restless night. He kept tossing and turning, running things through his mind. Did she get shot for what was on that paper? Was it something to do with the trial that she was working on? And then another thought popped into his mind. Wasn't it strange for Tom to show up on that very day?

When Bill arrived at the hospital the next day, Dave came in to see him.

"You know that paper that she had when she came in here?"

"Yes, did you get it Dave?"

"No, it seems to have vanished. The nurse remembers putting it to the side in the emergency room, but after that nobody seems to remember seeing it." They both had a puzzled look on their faces. This slip of paper may lead them to the person that pulled the trigger, but now it was gone.

"Dave, I don't know if this has anything to do with it, but Tom is in town. I don't know if you ever heard of him. He was Stephanie's old boyfriend."

"The one that left her out on the road that night that she got hit by the drunk driver."

"Yes, that's the one. He phoned last night to congratulate us on our forth coming marriage. He wanted to go out for drinks to show that there were no hard feelings."

"It might be nothing Bill, but did you mention it to the police?"

"No, but I think that maybe I should and I will also mention the missing paper."

Bill left the hospital and headed to the police station with the information hoping that something would lead them into finding whoever it was that wanted Stephanie dead.

On the weekend they had been so happy, looking forward to their wedding. Now, he was looking forward to just getting her out of the hospital. Her room almost looked like a florist shop. Everyone in the family had sent flowers to her. There was a police officer posted outside her room, hoping to keep the assassin out.

Dave would stop in my room every night as he was going off shift and then phone Bill at home with an update.

"You know Dave even with your warnings; we still can't seem to keep her safe, can we?"

"I know what you mean, but she is a fighter. I'm sure that she will soon be able to give us some leads to this mystery. I am also sure that she is not going to take this lying down, so be prepared to tie her down when she starts to recover."

"I don't know if that is possible Dave. When she wants something, she always finds a way. I guess that I will see you at the hospital tomorrow then."

"Yes, we can grab a coffee together."

They say that history repeats itself and I am sure that the thought had crossed Dave's mind more than once while I stayed in the hospital. He would come in at the beginning of his shift, then he would meet Bill for a coffee to tell him whether or not I was improving. Later, he would check in on me on rounds and then one last time before he went home.

"Hey Cat, we've been here before. Remember that day by the pond. Remember you said that you would get even with Deborah-Anne someday. Well, how about showing us the cat instincts that you possess and some of that animal drive that you survive on. You know that you have Bill worried that he's never going to see your wedding day." Dave was giving me one of his old pep talks that he was so good at, holding my hand while he was doing it. "You know that you have quite a guy there. He really loves you. So don't you think that you should wake up from this catnap that you're having so that you can start planning this wedding."

"Don't you know that in order for me to look beautiful for my wedding that I need as much beauty sleep as I can get. What am I doing here, anyway?" I replied showing that I hadn't lost my sense of humour.

"What is the last thing that you can remember, Cat?" Dave started to ask as he check my pulse while jotting things down.

"I remember running to get into the car with Bill, and then everything seems to go blank. How long have I been here, Dave?"

"Tell me whether you feel pain and if so where? As for answering your question, you have been here three days now. You don't remember anything about the shooting?" he asked as he continued to probe me for any other complications.

"What shooting? Is Bill okay?" All of a sudden I was panic stricken. They couldn't take Bill away from me; not when I had decided to live. Dave was checking my blood pressure at the time.

"Calm down getting your blood pressure up isn't going to do you any good. Bill is okay. You are the one that got shot. Somebody out there is trying to kill you. Do you have any idea who would want you dead?"

"Not one, Dave. So your feeling was right again, heh."

"Unfortunately, yes. The police have been waiting to question you. By the results of these preliminary tests, you seem to be strong enough to answer their questions providing that you don't get yourself upset. There is a chance that with them asking questions you memory may come back a little stronger. I will let them in, and then Bill should be in to see you shortly. You know he has been here every minute that we would allow him."

So after Dave left, the police came into the room. As they questioned me, a nurse stood by watching that I didn't get upset.

"We don't want to tire you too much, but there are some standard questions that have to be asked, Miss McConnell. Do you know of anybody that would want you dead?"

"No one in particular. It could have been somebody whose family member I put away, who they thought was innocent. As far as one particular person, there's nobody that comes to mind."

"What about your family members? Is there anyone there that could have done this?" the officer asked calmly.

"No, I can't see that anyone there would ever do this. Sure we have our differences in opinions, but none of them would ever do this?"

"Well, what about Tom Brennan? Could he have done this?"

"Tom? He's in Montreal?" They had caught me by surprise. I would never have given him a thought. Sure I kept track of where he was photographing, but Tom? No, he couldn't possibly have done it.

"He was in Toronto the day that you were shot. He was your boyfriend at one time, wasn't he?"

"Yes, but that was over twenty years ago. What reason would he have? He's married to Monique now. No, that's out of the question." Although this is what I was saying, they had started my brain in motion.

"Well, he did have an alibi when we talked to him."

"You have already questioned him?"

"Yes, we had to investigate everybody that had anything to do with you. I have to admit he did seem to be shook up at the news." The police officer chuckled as if he didn't believe Tom. "Well Miss McConnell if there is anything that you can think of, just give us a call. We'll leave now so that you can get some rest."

They left and I managed to get some rest before my next visitor Bill popped his head around the corner of the door.

"Dave informed me that my wedding was still on, that my bride-to-be has woken up, and was recuperating just fine."

"If you thought that you were getting out of marrying me that easily, well you have another thing coming."

"How are you feeling, sweetheart?" He came over to the bed and gave me a kiss.

"Much better now that you are here. Dave said that I was getting too much beauty sleep and to wake up," I laughed.

"I can see your humour hasn't been hurt," he laughed.

"It only hurts when I laugh, but what's this I hear that because the boss is laid up that the hired hand takes a break from work. How is the construction of the new building going to be done if the boss is in here?"

"Leave it to you to come out with a line like that. The business is okay. After all, Ben is in charge when I'm not there, and if there is any problem he contacts me here. You don't have to worry about the business because it is in good hands."

Although I didn't really do any of the business work that was involved, I had arranged that I had the final say in everything. If I didn't like something or I didn't think something was right, then they didn't start until I was satisfied. It was after all going to be my dynasty, that would hopefully go on after my death through probably Ben's family, since the thought of Bill and I having a family was almost impossible.

"Just because I am down doesn't mean that I am not out. By the way the police were in today. They say that they questioned Tom in regards to my shooting.

Have you been talking to him?"

"Strangely enough, he phoned the night that you were shot, to ask me out for a drink to show that there were no hard feelings between the two of us." He had a strange look on his face.

"You think that he might have done it, don't you?"

"I can't actually say that he did it, but it just seems too coincidental that he calls the night that you are shot."

"You know as well as I that Tom isn't the kind to hold a grudge, not for these many years anyway. Also, you have to remember that he is married now. No, I think that it was just somebody that had a grudge against me for putting somebody that they knew in prison."

Chapter Twenty-Eight

While Bill and I were going over the events that had happened, somewhere else in the city, in an apartment room, another couple was discussing these same events.

"I thought that you said that you had a perfect shot, that we had nothing to worry about?" The woman was screaming as she paced back and forth in the room.

"I have got a perfect shot," he yelled back at her. "I still don't know why we had to shoot her in the first place. She wasn't bothering us anyway," he replied, as he tried to soothe the nervous and tense woman.

"If she continues, she soon will be bothering us. Don't you see that as long as Stephanie McConnell is on the loose, we do have to worry?" she screamed at him.

"I really can't see it. I mean no-one has caught on to us yet. We only meet when our schedules allow it, and at social events."

"Don't you see, she goes to all the social events. She and her lawyer friends go to all those functions with her cat ears perked to see what is happening and with whom. After all, that is how she became the best in her field."

"So are you saying that you don't want to see me anymore?" The man asked with concern in his voice, thinking that this might be the big kiss off in their relationship.

"No, that is why I want her dead. I never want to stop seeing you. You are so much more exciting than that bore of a husband that I have. You have given me the things that he could never even think of." She pulled him closer to her and started to kiss him.

"I have to admit that you are the most exciting thing that ever came into my life. Don't worry about Stephanie, I will take care of her somehow, but right now I have more important things on my mind." He gracefully placed her on the bed, slowly removing her clothes as he had done so many times before. Then as he was making passionate love to her, she whispered in his ear. "I am yours to command, I am your slave as long as you take care of 'The Cat'."

Chapter Twenty-Nine

They finally let me out of the hospital. Bill sent me up to the cottage to recuperate knowing that this was probably the only safe place for me to be. He also sent our housekeeper up with me so that I didn't need to lift a finger. I was just to sit back and enjoy the peace and quietness, and let Mother Nature help me recover. He would come up on weekends and phone me every night to make sure that I was behaving myself and following the doctor's orders. We had set our wedding date and neither one of us wanted anything to happen to spoil that. The time seemed to move so quickly and our day seemed to be just around the corner. The police had sided with my theory in the shooting that somebody had a grudge against me from some case in court.

Although, I loved being at the cottage, I disliked being left out of what was going on in the city, so I made up my mind that we were going back to the city.

"Maria could you get the stuff packed. We are going back to the city tomorrow."

"Excuse me Madam, but are you sure that Mr. MacGregor will approve?"

"I will handle him when we arrive in the city, but I need to be down there."

We left as I planned and when Bill arrived home from work that night, he just about took the roof off.

"I thought that we agreed that you were to stay up there until Dave said that you had recuperated enough," he yelled at me. It was the first time that I had ever seen him this mad.

"I couldn't stand it anymore. I wanted to get

things done for our wedding. I couldn't very well do them up there, now could I?" As I explained to him I went over and gave him a little kiss looking at him with sympathetic eyes. "Besides, didn't you miss me being around here?" I gave him another kiss.

"You know darn well that I miss having you around, but I also want you to be safe." He put his arms around me and gave me a passionate lulling kiss. "Oh how I have missed you." He bent down and picked me up in his arms, kissing me as he did so. "Do you feel well enough that I could show you just how much I have missed you?"

"If you don't show me how much you missed me, then I won't believe that you did." I joked with him and then gave him another kiss. He carried me up the stairs to the bedroom, laying me gently on the bed. "Now how much did you say you missed me?" I pulled him down on to the bed beside me. He started to gently re-examine my body with slow kisses and went into his gentle passionate art of lovemaking. We slowly drifted off to sleep in each other arms where we found each other the next morning.

"Are you sure that I can't play hooky from work today. I'm sure that Ben could handle everything," Bill said as he looked over at me. He kissed me gently as he was asking, hoping that he could tempt me with his gentle persuasion.

"If you keep doing what you are doing I might consider staying where I am, but as far as letting you play hooky, no way. However, you might tempt me into letting you go in late." I smiled back at him, moving my head high enough to give him a gentle kiss.

"Just to go in late, heh?" he said as he blew gently into my ear. Moving down from the ear he started to caress my neck with gentle kisses as he moved toward my lips. "Are you sure that we can't work on that late bit toward the hooky bit, just a little."

"Well, I don't know. You're making it awfully hard for me to think of resisting that last offer," I sighed.

I soon yielded to his request as he proceeded to caress my body, smothering it with kisses from time to time, making such passionate love to me. We spent the rest of the day in bed.

"Now, isn't this nicer having someone to share your bed with while you're recuperating, and isn't it more fun too?" he asked between his kisses.

"I must admit it's a nicer way to recuperate." I smiled back at him. "However, tomorrow it's back to work for you." I pointed at him and touched his nose with my finger.

"Yeah, we'll negotiate that later."

Morning came earlier then either one of us wanted, but now it was time for Bill to go off to work and for me to get things set up for our wedding day. He left for work and I left for the stores, with a minor stop that I hadn't told Bill about. He had made me promise that I would leave the family thing alone for the time being, and that I wouldn't see my investigator with regards to that matter. I know that he would be mad at me if he knew, so I just didn't tell him. I was keeping a low profile for the time being. What else could he ask for? I left the house and headed straight for Ed's office (he was my investigator at the time).

Ed had done some extra investigating since I was shot; he not only followed up on leads in my family, but any lead that would lead him to the person that shot me. His investigations turned up some very interesting leads. It seems that my Aunt Elizabeth had been more than friends with my father according to friends who were still around. Apparently, she had turned up at several locations that my father had to go to and that Mother apparently couldn't make it to. It was also brought up that Deborah-Anne was born nine months after one of these meetings and that my Aunt Elizabeth passed her off as Uncle Pat's. This meant that she was actually my half-sister, something that I sure didn't want to brag about and I am sure that neither one of them did either.

"You see Stephanie, anyone in that family had more than enough reason to want you dead and the truth of the matter is they didn't even have to pull the trigger. To check it out a little further, I have been following Deborah-Anne to see whether or not it was her," Ed said to me as he was showing me documentation that he had gathered on the case.

"Good. If she makes one mistake then I want to know about it. She and I have an old score to settle, and with this information that you have given me so far, I could blow her out of the water right now. You have done an excellent job so far Ed. I'm sure that there will be a bonus in it for you." I packed up the papers and was preparing to leave when I remembered the missing copy of the will. "Ed, do you think that you could get me another copy of the will? The last one vanished at the hospital."

"I managed to get a copy before, I can't see any problems with getting another copy. Now you take care and be careful. Whoever tried to kill you, is still out there," he said as he saw me to the door.

I left there and headed to the Bridal Shop to purchase my wedding outfit. At the shop I tried on several different and beautiful outfits. I settled on a white satin dress just below the knee, with a tailored fitting jacket. The design of the dress showed just enough cleavage to be tasteful and just enough to be enticing to the groom. From there I headed to the florist to order my flowers which would be a bouquet of nicely shaded pink roses. Bridgette, who was to be my maid of honour would have a smaller, but similar bouquet, and of course, there would be carnation boutonnieres for Bill and Ben.

It was hard to believe that in just a few weeks I would be Mrs. Bill MacGregor. Bridgette and her family would be coming up the week before the wedding, and Sandy her family would be in town a few days later. It was a good thing that we had moved from the apartment to a house. At least, there was space to put up everyone. The plans were all made now and all we had to do was sit back and wait for the day to arrive. I went back home and made several calls to the rest of the family making sure that they would be all able to attend. I called Dave to make sure that Sue and he would also be attending, then I told Maria how many there would be for the reception.

Once Bridgette arrived the time would go by quickly. We went shopping to choose her dress for the day. It was just as it should be with us spending time doing sisterly things that we didn't seem to have time for when we were young. I got to show her around the city. Doing all these things with Bridgette and Sandy when she arrived left little time to be with Bill, but he didn't seem to mind as he was off with Ben, and Bridgette's and Sandy's husbands.

The big day finally arrived, and although I am not normally a nervous person this particular day I was a bundle of nerves. I wanted everything to go perfectly so that it would be a day that we would both remember for the rest of our lives; a day that we would hopefully someday tell our children about. That is, if the day ever came that we had some, after all, I was now over forty.

The day was beautiful when I awoke and I looked out the bedroom window to see a beautiful blue sky with immaculate grounds below it. They had groomed the grounds the day before and what made it even more picturesque was the white gazebo where we would be saying our vows. It was decorated with white ribbons and roses with stands containing more white roses at the top and bottom of the stairs to the gazebo. They had set up the chairs that the guests would be sitting on in front of the gazebo.

Bridgette knocked on the bedroom door. "Hey your big day is finally here. Shall we get you ready for the big event?"

"Pinch me Sis, show me that I am not dreaming when I look out this window."

"You're not dreaming, this is your day. Now, how about us getting a look at that wedding outfit that you bought yourself? I bet that you look beautiful in it."

I put on my wedding dress, and then styled my hair before putting on the white hat that looked kind of like the old fashion riding hats that the ladies used to wear. I wore it off to the side of my head with the silk sash that was on the hat flowing down the back of my head, taking the place of a veil. The final touch before picking up my bouquet was putting on my white satin shoes.

"You're just beautiful Stephanie. You look just like one of those models in the bride's magazines and books. Are you sure that you aren't modeling on the side again?" Bridgette asked as she stood back and looked at me. She then rushed over to give me a kiss on the cheek for luck.

"Hey, don't you think that you should be getting ready too?" I asked her as she was still standing there with her housecoat on.

"Don't worry about me; I have been ready for this day for a long time now," she said. As she said this, she took off the housecoat, uncovering the pretty pink dress that she had chosen for the day.

"You look beautiful Bridgette, now for the finishing touch. I got some baby's breath to place in your hair." I took the baby's breath and gently placed it in her hair.

I looked out the window at the people that had

already started to arrive and take their seats down on the grounds. As I saw the last person take their seat, I saw Bill and Ben take their place in the gazebo. I knew then the moment that I had waited for all my life had finally arrived.

"Okay Stephanie, this is it," Bridgette said to me as she handed my bouquet.

"Yes, it is now or never." I smiled back at her. We started to walk down the staircase and out into the yard and as we reached the last chair they started to play the wedding march. I could feel my face glowing as the only person that I could see was Bill in the gazebo. When I reached him, he held out his hand and took mine.

"You look beautiful," he whispered to me with a smile.

The minister started the service.

"Friends we have gathered together today to join this couple in holy matrimony. Is there anybody that can see just cause as to why they cannot be married?" A thought ran swiftly through my mind; no one in their right mind would dare to stand up and say that we couldn't get married. If they did there would be a murder instead of a marriage, because I would kill anybody that would have the nerve to do that.

"William, do you promise to take Stephanie for your wife in sickness and in health, for richer or for poorer, forsaking all others till death do you part."

"I do," Bill replied never taking his eyes off of me.

"Stephanie do you take William as your husband in sickness and in health, for richer or for poorer, forsaking all others till death do you part."

"I do," I replied never letting my eyes move from Bill for even one split second.

"William, will you please take Stephanie's left hand in yours and repeat after me." The minister said as he gave the ring to Bill. "I give this ring as a token of my love and to show all others the vows that we have exchanged today."

Then with the power invested in me I now pronounce you man and wife. What God has joined together, let no man put under. You may kiss your bride." Bill stepped closer to me and gave me a long sensuous kiss. "May I now present Mr. & Mrs. William MacGregor."

We started to walk down the stairs, and people stopped us to congratulate us with handshakes and kisses. After we had our pictures taken in the gardens, the party started. We had one area where there was a canopy over where the food was being served. Another area had been set up for dancing. We had approximately one hour after the food was served to arrive at the airport to catch our flight which would begin our month long honeymoon.

For our honeymoon we were flying first to England, then to Switzerland, France and then back home for a few days alone before reporting back to work. I never could sleep on planes, so although Bill slept, I watched out the window watching the clouds below us. As we got closer to England, I watched the sun rise. We had rented a car so that we could just travel from town to town. One day, we were in the county of Devon driving through the moors to the wild countryside of Wales. Then we followed the coast back along Devon. We were staying at little thatched roof cottages and dining in pubs, enjoying fattening, yet delicious tasting Devon cream on scones with a pot of tea as we watched the waves come in from the ocean. In one little cottage that we stayed at, the ceilings were so low that we had to crouch as we went through the doorways. Yet the fireplaces were so large that Bill could lie completely in them. My camera seemed to be working overtime taking shots like these.

"Come on down here. I'm sure that there is

enough space in the hearth for both of us." As I took his picture in the fireplace, Bill grabbed me by the arm, pulling me into the large hearth and causing me to fall on top of him. When our two bodies met, our lips came together in a long lingering kiss. Bill slowly started to follow the outline of my body with his lips.

"Bill, here!" I exclaimed.

"Why not here Mrs. Bill MacGregor?" he said as he continued to undress my willing body.

I have to admit that when I first saw this large hearth, I pictured a large blazing fire with a large kettle cooking over it, and children huddling close to keep warm. I enjoyed what Bill turned it into much better.

We visited many castles that cover the countryside with their magnificent courtyards. The view that we got as we climbed the small stone staircases to the top of the walls with the turrets along the walls was magnificent. As we looked inside the castle walls we looked down into gardens and benches in the courtyards. Then as we looked outside the walls we viewed the lovely country side, that the castle would have protected in the past. Looking at either of these scenes would not have been recommended for somebody that was afraid of heights as these walls rose far above the roses in the gardens. As we climbed the stairs in the turrets, the staircase slowly narrowed and I wondered how the knights could have climbed these stairs with their suits of armour. When I was at the top of the walls walking about with the camera, I thought that it was a great place for taking pictures, for the view was magnificent no matter what wall you stood on.

As we headed toward the central north area we went through the town of Cambridge with their gentle moving rivers that were edged with flowing willows. As we watched some university rowers skim along the water, I started to picture what it would be like in the past. I pictured Bill doing the rowing. I would be sitting in the back of the boat wearing a long flowing dress that would take up most of the boat. I would have had a parasol to keep the sun out of my eyes. Bill walking beside me pulled me close with his arm that was hugging my waist.

"Which century are you in now?" he whispered in my ear.

"I don't know, but you are just as handsome there as you are here," I replied with a smile and then a gentle kiss to his cheek.

As we continued our journey through the rest of England visiting the countryside and the castles, I felt the past running through my veins. The ballrooms along with the sculptured ceilings and the marbled floor all seemed to bring this feeling home to me, as I dreamed about what the past would have been like.

We left England and headed to Switzerland where we stayed in a little chalet in a small town at the bottom of the Alps. It is a good thing that I always come prepared to take lots of pictures, because the nature scenes that we came across were just magnificent. I couldn't have planned a better trip if I tried. We took the ski lifts to the top of the mountain side, taking with us a picnic lunch so that we could spend the whole day in the mountains. The sky, like a deep blue ocean, was bordered by an emerald blanket with small flowers decorating it. There were spots that the ice from the mountain formed small streams that flowed from the top down to the bottom. When we left this little haven, we proceeded down to Lake Geneva whose beauty I could only slightly capture on film. While here, we took in a tour of the chocolate factory, one of my greatest addictions in life was loving the taste of chocolate. Having this addiction, it is amazing that I never really had a weight problem.

The clock factory was the next thing on the agenda

and we purchased a lovely handmade clock for the mantel back home. It was so lovely. It had a little boy and girl holding hands, slowly going in and out of the house on top of the clock. The little boy and girl would turn and face each other, and then kiss each time that the clock would chime the hour.

Skipping down through France we came to the Eiffel Tower. "Do you think that you can get it all in?" Bill laughed as he stood behind me as I lined up the shot.

"Sure I can, do you forget who you have with you," I said as I kept backing up. Just as I heard the shutter click I started to fall back. Thank God Bill was there.

"You know that I could get into following you when you're shooting pictures. It seems to have fringe benefits," he said as I landed on top of him. He tightened his arms around my waist kissing my ear and then placing a kiss on my lips as I turned to look at him.

"You know everybody is watching?"

"I don't care, this is the country of romance. They just think there goes another couple in love," he said, pulling me back closer to him.

We went to the vineyards to see the French wines being made before stopping off at the French beach to enhance our tans before returning home.

We had spent close to a month away from home. It sure would be a change going back into some kind of routine. I shot enough pictures that would warrant me a stay in the darkroom for at least a week steady. I knew though that Bill would not allow that, so I would have to stretch it out for maybe two weeks.

We arrived home to an empty house as we had given Maria the time off when we were overseas and also for and the last week of the holiday. So we had the house to ourselves. Although we had been living together before we were married, we were still newlyweds and were taking full advantage of the title newlyweds. We started the days off in our usual way by staying in bed in the morning with long sensual periods of lovemaking followed by breakfast in bed. We left the bed to do other things during the day, but made sure we went to bed early to continue where we had left off in the morning. I didn't know what we were going to do next week when we had to go back to work.

Like always when you don't want it, time flies by too damn quickly and in no time it was time to go back to work. Now, we hadn't bothered to look at the mail when we came home, figuring that if we hadn't returned home early from overseas then the mail would still be there. Now we were home officially, which meant that it was time to look at the mail to see what bills and letters we had received. Most of the mail was just bills, but one piece caught my eye. I took it and placed in my briefcase so that I could read it at the office. It was from Ed, and I knew if Bill saw it he would get upset knowing that I hadn't put the investigation to rest.

Once at work I took the envelope out of my briefcase, poured myself a cup of coffee, and proceeded to read Ed's letter.

"Dear Stephanie:

I knew that you would want an update on the investigation when you arrived home, so here it is.

Your cousin has been having an affair with no other than your ex-boyfriend Tom. They have been sharing an apartment that they rendezvous at whenever their schedules can allow it. This mainly happens when there are social events that Tom is covering. Her husband doesn't have a clue about her affair, and that seems to be the way she wants it kept.

I hope that you're sitting down when you read this part Stephanie, because your Aunt wasn't the only one that was fooling around back then. I hate to be the one to tell you this but your Uncle Pat isn't your uncle, he is your father. I'm continuing on the investigation and I will see you when you get back.

Ed."

Well, after reading that, I now know why Uncle Pat had been so kind to me, also why I had a nose for the stock market. Now I had the ammunition that I needed to get the estate back, that should have been mine all along. I would confront Uncle Pat tomorrow with the fact that I wanted the estate to be returned to me upon his death, and that under no circumstances could he sell it. I didn't want to hurt him. After all, I loved him as the father he actually was.

I continued drinking my coffee as I was going over the newspaper when suddenly something caught my eye. "Man dies in fire. Ed Bandrill died as his apartment was engulfed in flames last night. There is an investigation underway as it is believed that arson might be to blame." I sat there in shock unable to comprehend what I had just read. Could this be the same person that tried to kill me? Did they kill him hoping to destroy the evidence before I could get to talk to him on my return? Poor Ed it seemed as though he was killed because they found out that he knew too much, and they couldn't take the chance of him telling me. Now I had double the reason for finding out who had done it.

Chapter Thirty

I called Uncle Pat to arrange a meeting. We decided to meet for lunch at a place where we could talk and not be disturbed. We ordered lunch and a drink to have while we waited. I proceeded to tell Uncle Pat of my plans.

"Uncle Pat I have some startling news for you. I found out about the family's past from my investigator. I found out that the estate and the mansion should have been mine, thanks to a small clause that Grandfather had in his will," I said quietly and calmly as I watched my Uncle.

"So what are you planning to do about it Stephanie? I mean you have no proof," Uncle Pat said, as he became defensive.

"Now Uncle Pat, you should know better then that. I do have a copy of the will that I could show to the courts, but I would hope that it wouldn't come to that. All I want is what rightfully belongs to me, and all that it takes is for you to write a new will leaving it to me," I replied with the coolness of a cat watching a bird before it springs into action. I took a sip of the Brandy Alexander that I had ordered.

"Do you think that your Aunt or your cousins would stand for you inheriting everything that they think belongs to them?" He looked back at me as if to say they would never let me have it without a fight. His face was now stern, the love that seemed to glow when he looked at me before, seemed to be slowly vanishing.

"No, but that will be up to me to handle when the time warrants it. All you have to do is change your will and that would also include the fact that you couldn't sell the estate either." I didn't like what I was doing to him, after all he was my father and I loved him so very much. I knew though that if I didn't force the issue, then I would lose everything.

"You seem to have everything figured out, don't you?" I could hear the anger in his voice, yet at the same time I could detect that he was sorry.

"I don't mean to hurt you Uncle Pat. I love you as if you were my father, but I also want what is rightfully mine."

"I suppose that the way you have put it I have no choice in the matter, do I?" Our meals had arrived but the way the conversation was going we weren't too hungry.

"I wish that there was another way because I really don't like to do it this way, but I don't see any other way. The only way that I will know that you have done as I ask is to see the new will."

"Don't you trust me, Stephanie?" he said with shock ringing in his voice. "Do you trust anybody?" he asked as he stood up to leave the table.

"I trust people until they show me that I can't trust them, and Uncle Pat I am afraid that is what you did here," I replied calmly as I looked up at him.

Knowing that I had lost the love that my Uncle once showed me, I picked at my plate and then slowly drank the coffee that the waitress had brought. Poor Uncle Pat had lost his appetite completely and never touched a bite. I know that I won't be hearing from him for a while, and now I would have to be extra careful. After all, who was to say that Uncle Pat wouldn't side with the people that wanted me dead?

I had a doctor's appointment with Dave just to make sure that everything was okay, and that I had recovered well from the shooting. God, he ran every test that they ever made, and then I think he made up a few new ones. I was starting to feel like a guinea pig when he finally let me go home.

"I'll call you later with the results of the tests, so you can go home and rest now," he said to me in his calm voice.

"Are you sure that you can check all those tests by then?" I said back to him in a tired and sarcastic voice.

"Come on now Cat, there weren't that many. Now go home and I will talk to you later."

I drove straight home from his office and I made it home in time to meet Bill for supper.

"How did things go today?" Bill asked as he gave me a kiss.

"I don't know. Dave ran so many tests at the office today. He said that he would call later with the results," I replied as I returned his kiss. We were watching television when the phone rang.

"Cat, I just got the results back from the tests and want to see you in my office tomorrow morning at nine sharp."

"What on earth for, Dave?" I thought for sure that everything was okay.

"Just be in my office tomorrow morning, Cat. Now good night," he said, then just hung up the phone on me. He knew that by doing it this way, I would be sure to be at his office.

I hardly got a moment of sleep which made me as grouchy as a bear in the morning. Bill came over to me trying to give me a good morning kiss, and I just about took his head off. Poor Bill. He always gets the worse of my bad moods. He didn't even attempt it any further. He just put on his coat and left. He hoped that maybe I would be in a different frame of mind when he came home.

I drove over to Dave's office and arrived there just

before nine so that I was waiting for him when he got there.

"Come in Cat, and how are we this morning?" Dave greeted me with a happy smile and cheerful voice.

"I could have been a lot better if I had some sleep last night, which I failed to get due to some doctor phoning and telling me to be here by nine," I snapped at him.

He ushered me to my chair and then sat down himself. "Tell me what you think of children?" He started to chuckle to himself.

"You know what I think of children, they're great. Remember I do have nieces and nephews." I was getting just a little annoyed with his questions.

"Well, wouldn't you like some of your own?"

"Dave, I thought we covered this a long time ago, and we came to the conclusion that I was too old to have any." Slowly I was becoming curious as to his line of questioning.

"Is that what you would like me to tell this little one in about eight months? That there was a mistake and that its mother was too old to have it." He started to beam.

"Are you trying to tell me that I am pregnant?" I said in a shocked voice and with a look of shock on my face.

"You and Bill must have had some honeymoon." He laughed out loud.

"Why didn't you tell me on the phone last night?"

"What and miss seeing that expression on your face. No way! And besides that, I wanted to be the first to congratulate you."

"When is it going to happen?" I was so happy that I was just glowing and I could feel my face getting hotter.

"Oh, in just about eight months, but because you are over forty years of age, we will do some more tests just to make sure that everything is okay with the baby. You will of course, have to start to take it easier than before and no more getting yourself upset."

I got up to leave, and as I did Dave put his arms around me and gave me a hug. I left his office on cloud nine and I don't really know how I made it home. All I know is that I did. Yes, it seems like my dreams were finally coming true. I had a husband who loved me and whom I loved, and now we were going to have a baby.

Maria prepared a lovely dinner for the two of us with candlelight and flowers on the table. There was a bottle of champagne chilling in the wine cooler beside the table. The lights were dimmed as I waited for Bill to come home. Everything just had to be right. I lay waiting on the sofa for him in the family room when I heard him coming through the doorway.

"What is this in honour of?" he asked with curiosity as he came into the room.

"I thought that it would be nice," I replied giving him a gentle kiss to welcome him home.

"I don't know what Dave did to you, but I'm sure glad that he tamed the wild beast that was in you this morning." He came closer taking me into his arms and returning the kiss that I had given him.

As he held me in his arms, I whispered in his ear. "Darling what do you think of us having children?"

"You know that I have always wanted children, but I thought that you said that you were passed the stage of having any. Are you planning that we should adopt?" he asked as he looked down at me.

"No, but apparently our honeymoon didn't think that I was passed the stage."

"Stephanie, are you saying that we are having a baby?" He looked at me with a shocked and questioning look.

"In about eight months we're going to have a

baby," I cried out in delight.

Picking me up in the air he swung me about. "You aren't kidding me. We are going to have a baby?"

"I'm not kidding you, but soon you won't have a slender wife. In fact, you might not even be able to put your arms around her." I laughed at him.

"I would love you if you were ten tons. Your age though, is it safe for you?" All of a sudden there was concern where there had been happiness.

"Dave is going to run more tests to make sure that there isn't anything wrong with the baby or myself, but he doesn't see that there would be any problems."

We were so happy that night that if we could have harnessed the power from the glow coming from us, we would have been able to light the whole city that night.

Chapter Thirty-One

"Look at me, look at this body. It doesn't seem like it's been six months since Dave told me that I was pregnant." I said to myself as I looked at myself in the mirror. My perfect body now had taken on this deformed shape, like having a beach ball attached to the front of my body. Looking in the mirror usually made me feel unattractive and stupid for ever letting my perfect body go. Then, I would gently ran my hand over my stomach and start to think of the little one that was growing inside me, and a smile would creep up on my face.

"It doesn't seem that long gorgeous, does it?" Bill said as he put his arms around me from the back, gently sliding his hand over my tummy area. As he did this, the baby started to move about. "He's active today, isn't he?"

"Yeah, he has enough of his mother in him to not like being penned in." I turned and looked at Bill.

"You mean that I'm going to have two of you to watch and keep out of trouble?" He laughed as he gave me a kiss.

"You've got it," I answered, gently kissing him back.

Since learning that I was pregnant I had to pick and choose my cases. That meant that I had less court time and more investigations and preparations for cases for the other partners. I seemed to be getting babied wherever I went. At the law offices they watched everything I did. When I got home, Maria had been given strict orders from Bill. She was to watch that I didn't overdo it, that I drank my milk, and ate properly. That I didn't sit in drafts, and got enough sunshine and exercise.

I didn't know that my pregnancy would cause such excitement or concern. Even with all this care and concern, I still got my way in decorating the nursery. After all, this would be the only time that I would have this pleasure. Dave had already told me that this would be the only child that I would have, providing that I followed instructions to a tee. That is why it was so important that everything went right and that I was careful.

Bill was off to work and I was going to work on the nursery. I had this feeling that the baby was going to be a little boy. I had a painter come in and paint the spare room that we turned into a nursery a pretty blue. We hired the painter due to the fact that the fumes of the paint just made my stomach do somersaults. While he did the painting, I spent my time out in the yard enjoying the sunlight and imagining what it would be like to have a baby around the house.

Now that we had the room painted it was time to decorate it. I had purchased these lovely drapes with little blue trains on them, and on the sashes that held them open were little building blocks with the alphabet on them. I had a crib, dresser and nightstand delivered. They were done in white with lovely scrolled handles on them. I got a gorgeous brass cradle for him. When I saw it at the store, I just couldn't resist it and knew that it would be just perfect for him. The carpeting arrived and they laid it down for me. It was a pretty pale blue soft plush shag carpet that was so soft on my bare feet. Since putting on the weight I enjoyed going around barefoot in the house. Bill kept saying that my shopping for the baby, and getting myself new outfits so that I didn't look so fat would put us in the poor house, but I didn't care. People always told me about how I would feel if I ever became pregnant, but I never believed them. Ever since I found out, I've been exuberant. Sure, I have my low times like I had this morning, but then I think about the great gift God has given us, the gift that we gave each other when we thought that we could never have children.

I thought that before I started to decorate, I would go to the stores first just to see if there is anything that I might have forgotten. This is one of the things that I like when you are pregnant, going through the stores picking up those small outfits that are so soft and cuddly. Bill and I both have a soft spot for the toy section, so that when we are shopping that is the last place that we go to. Today would be no different. The toy department just brings out the child in me. By the time that I was ready to leave the store, I had picked up a little light for the top of the dresser that had a little train at the base. I also had a couple of little sleepers with little bears on them, and a little rubber hammer for him to play with.

When I arrived home Maria prepared me a snack and poured me a glass of milk to go with it. We sat at the table while I had the snack, and I showed her the things that I bought. I always did this when I went shopping for the baby, and when Bill got home I would show them to him as well. Maria, not taking no for an answer, made sure that I went to lie down for a while after my snack, so that I wouldn't over exert myself when I started to decorate the nursery. She took all the packages up to the nursery so that they would be in the room when I got up from my rest.

I had a nice long rest, and then headed to the nursery trying to figure out what I wanted to do first as I walked along the hall. I had those cute pictures of the nursery rhymes, The Three Man In A Tub and Jack Be Nimble to hang. Then there were toys to arrange in the room. Also the changing table had to set up, and last but not the least, the drapes had to be hung. I thought I would leave the drapes for Bill to put up under my direction, of course. I decided to hang the pictures first. I would hang them one on either side of the crib. Then I took a fancy doily placing it on top of the dresser after which I placed the new light that I had just bought on top of it. The sleepers I put in the dresser drawers. Bill was worse than I was with the toys. He couldn't pass a toy shop without buying something. I picked up the purple dinosaur that he bought the baby just last week, squeezing it close to my chest, and feeling how soft it was.

    Putting the dinosaur back down, I looked over to the window. It looked so bare. Maybe I could just put the drapes over the rods and then Bill could hang them when he got home. I started to place the drapes on the rod one drape at a time, when I had them both on, I held them up in front of me to see what they would look like.

    "This is ridiculous. You know that you can try to picture what they look like, but until they are actually up there you don't really know what they will look like," I said to myself as I stood there with the drapes in my hands. I started to look around the room and there in the corner was a step stool that would do just perfectly. After placing the step stool just below the window and with the drapes in my hand I took a step up. "It will only take a second to put these up," I said to myself as I continued to the top of the step stool. The first end went in with no problem now I knew that I had to finish before Bill came home, otherwise all hell would break loose. Things like this I was supposed to leave for him to do, and he was expected home anytime now. Just as I was thinking this, Bill was on his way up the stairs with his latest gift for the baby.

    He had the large teddy bear that he had just bought in front of him as he came through the doorway. "How's my baby today?" he asked from behind the bear. Just as he did that I lost my balance, as I struggled with the stubborn end of the drapes. Bill looked around from the bear just as I was falling from the stepstool. "Stephanieeee!" Bill yelled as he dropped the bear and ran to my side.

"Maria, Maria call an ambulance quick," he yelled at the top of his lungs. Looking down at me he asked, "Where does it hurt? Are you okay? Don't move. What the bloody hell were you doing up there anyway? I told you that I would do that when I got home." I had him so worried that he was running off at the mouth.

All I was worried about was the baby. Had I hurt him? He seemed to be moving an awful lot. I was afraid to move in case I hurt him more. How could I have been so impatient that I didn't think of the baby first?

Finally, after what seemed forever, the ambulance made it to the house. They placed me on the stretcher and rushed me to the hospital where they had already contacted Dave to meet us.

"Dave, don't let me lose this baby. I don't want to lose this baby," I cried as he met us at the emergency door.

"Cat, we will see what we can do. Now, just relax. You're not doing the baby any good by worrying," he said, trying to comfort me as he turned to the paramedics that brought me in. After they told Dave my statistics I heard him yell, "Take her up to the operating room. I think that we may have somebody that doesn't like his mother's rough housing anymore."

They rushed me into the elevator. The last thing that I remember Dave saying was, "Cat this is going to help you relax don't fight it, and I'll see you later."

When I came to, Bill was sitting in the room with his head in his hands. "Bill is the baby okay?" I asked in a low voice. He got up and walked over to me, and holding my hand he kissed my forehead.

"Stephanie we were lucky. We have a son. They

say that he'll have to stay in the hospital in an incubator, but otherwise, he'll be okay."

"A son!" I said as I started to cry.

"Yes, we have a son. He has black hair with a little cleft in his chin, but he's a fighter just like his mother," he laughed. "But what the hell were you doing up there?"

"I got impatient, and I forgot that my balance wasn't as good as it used to be. I almost lost my son because I was so damn impatient." I started to cry again as he held me in his arms.

"I hate to break up this little family get together, but I need to see the patient for a minute, and then maybe I will allow for a real family get together." Dave came into the room with a crossed look on his face. Bill gave me a kiss and left the room.

"Cat, I should turn you over my knee right now. I thought that having that baby was the most important thing in the world to you. Yet, you go out and do something that stupid and irresponsible," he scolded as he checked me out.

"Is he okay though, Dave? I mean I didn't hurt him, did I?" There was panic in my voice.

"He's okay. He will just have to do the rest of his growing in the incubator. You're darn lucky you know. You could have lost him and we could have lost you as well. As it is you're going to be stiff and sore for the next couple of weeks. You managed to strain yourself pretty well."

"When can I see him, Dave?" I said with begging eyes.

"How does right now sound?" He had a smile on his face that covered his entire face.

"Right now, where is he?" I started to glow.

"Bill is getting a wheel chair to take you over to the nursery right now."

They helped me into the wheel chair and wheeled me over to the glass of the nursery. Dave left us and went inside to get our son. He appeared on the other side of the glass with an incubator, and inside was our tiny son with wires going into him. My God what have I done to my son? Dave said that he was going to be okay, but he doesn't deserve to come into this world and then be put on wires to keep him alive. Dave came out of the nursery and walked over to us.

"Well, what do you think? Isn't he his mother's son?" he joked.

"Dave those wires in him, does he have to have them?" There was concern not only in my voice but also on my face.

"He only needs them for a little time. He is a healthy boy, he just came into the world a little sooner then he was supposed to."

"When can I hold him Dave?" I had to ask him the question.

"Maybe in a few days, but you can touch him tomorrow and check him out. Right now, I want you back in bed."

They wheeled me back to my room and Dave left us alone for a few minutes. "Bill can you tell the family that we have a son?" I said to him.

"I thought that we could put an announcement in the newspaper, but what are we going to name him?" he asked.

"How does Kyle Alexander MacGregor sound?" I looked at him waiting for his approval.

"Kyle Alexander MacGregor, Kyle Alexander MacGregor," he repeated it again. "Yes, that has a good sound to it, so that is what he will be known as."

"Now, do you know everybody that you have to call?" I asked. I didn't want anybody to be left out.

"Yes, the list is by the phone. Is there anything

that you want me to bring back with me when I come?"

"Just a nightie and a housecoat. Maria can help you with that."

"Okay, get some rest while I am away." He bent over and gave me a kiss. "Thank you for such a beautiful son."

He left and went home for the night, while I lay there in the hospital bed thinking about how I almost lost my son before I had even had him.

The next few days, visitors came and went as if there was no door to my room. Whenever it was visiting hours, my room had a steady stream of visitors coming through and going to the nursery as well.

Chapter Thirty-Two

Finally, we were allowed to take Kyle home from the hospital. We planned to have his christening in a couple of weeks. This would also act as our official way of introducing him to the rest of the family. Uncle Pat and Aunt Elizabeth, Stuart and his family, even Deborah-Anne and her husband came. Also present was Ben and his family along with Bridgette and her family. Sandy and her family flew in for the occasion. We all went to church where the minister gave a very lovely sermon. We had Kyle dressed in a very antique looking christening gown; it would be the only time that he would ever be seen in a dress. The minister made the sign of the cross with a rose bud dipped in holy water and said, "I name you Kyle Alexander MacGregor. May God bless and keep you. In the name of the Father, Son and Holy Ghost." It seemed that Kyle had a smile on his face, as the water slowly trickled down his face.

We headed back to our house for tea and a family gathering after the service. We gathered in the family room for pictures; everybody took their turn including Deborah-Anne. After we finished taking the pictures, we opened the gifts that everyone had brought for Kyle. Uncle Pat and Aunt Elizabeth brought him a lovely sterling silver cup with his name and date of birth engraved on it. Stuart and his family brought him an adorable outfit that looked like a miniature riding outfit.

"Is there a meaning behind this Stuart?" I asked as I held out the little outfit to show everyone.

"Well, if he is anything like his mother, then he will be in the saddle early enough to be a champion rider for the Olympics," Stuart said as he laughed.

Ben and his family gave him a lovely silver picture frame that would hold many pictures of him in the future.

Bridgette and her family gave him a lovely set of clothes. Deborah-Anne and Michael's gift was a lovely set of Royal Doulton dishes. Sandy and her family gave him another outfit to wear. Last but not least was Dave and Susan's family gift. They gave him his first horse, a toy one of course, but one that he would be riding soon enough. When we opened that gift, we all had a good laugh.

"It seems pretty obvious that we all think that Kyle should take over where his mother left off in the jumping circle," Stuart said with a laugh.

We all dispersed after that to do our own things on the grounds or in the house. I took Kyle up to the nursery to lay him down for his nap.

"He definitely is your son Stephanie," I heard from behind me as Uncle Pat came into the room.

"Would you like to hold him Uncle Pat?"

"Yes I would, that is if you don't mind." He sat down in the rocking chair. I handed Kyle to him and straightened his gown out on Uncle Pat's lap. I went over to the dresser and grabbing my camera I started to shoot pictures of the two of them.

"I don't know, but I sure can see his Grandfather in him," I said to Uncle Pat as I continued to shoot pictures.

"There's no resemblance to James in this little one."

"Take a good look Uncle Pat, the pitch black hair, the cleft chin. Can't you see the resemblance?" I moved in closer to him.

"James didn't have any of those features." He was looking at Kyle and then at me.

"He didn't but you do, Uncle Pat. I found out that

you are my father, not James. This is your Grandson."

"How did you ever find that out, Stephanie? Your mother and I told no-one." He looked at me with eyes of disbelief.

"You should know that when I start to look into things that I don't leave a stone unturned. The only thing that I don't understand is why you took the estate away from me when you knew that it was mine. You actually stole it from your daughter. Now you know what I am going to say, don't you?"

"Stephanie I did what I had to do and if it had been left in James hands do you think that it would have done so well? Does anybody else know?"

"Nobody else knows, but now of course I want the estate back, not just for me but for your Grandson."

"Just how do you propose that I do that without causing suspicion?"

"It's very simple. You just write a new will leaving it to me as we discussed before," I said as I reached for Kyle.

"What about your Aunt Elizabeth, Deborah-Anne and Stuart? What do I say to them?"

"You don't have to say anything. I will handle that when the time comes. I don't want to hurt anybody; I just want what is mine. You know I couldn't believe it, when I first found out that you were my father, but then I started to understand because of how you cared for me when I stayed at your house, and how I caught on to the stock market so well."

"When you were growing up with us, it was as if the Lord was giving me a chance to watch my daughter grow. There were so many times that I wanted to tell you but I couldn't." As he was talking there were tears forming in his eyes.

"You don't know how much those years meant to me or how happy you and Stuart made me." I walked over to him and gently kissed him on the cheek. "Don't worry our secret is our secret." A gentle smile crossed his face.

I laid Kyle down in his cradle, tucking him gently in. Then Uncle Pat and I went down the stairs to the family room where the rest of the guests were. The food and refreshments had been served and everybody was enjoying themselves. Bill spotted us coming down the stairs and came over to meet us.

"Isn't he a perfect kid, Uncle Pat?" Bill asked as he met us.

"He sure is, he is just like his mother," Uncle Pat said as he looked over at me.

"I hope that he is like his mother in some respects, but not in others. I couldn't handle it if I had two of the same." Bill laughed as he put his hands to his head.

After they all left, I went upstairs to rest stopping in Kyle's room first. I sat down in the rocking chair and as I rocked in the chair, Kyle woke up. I picked him up and began to rock again with him in my arms his head tucked in under my chin. As I rocked, I hummed a tune and we drifted off to a world of just Kyle and me. I felt the flash of my camera going off, I snapped out of my dream world to see Bill taking a picture of us with my camera, something that he doesn't do too often.

That was my most prized shot when I developed the pictures. I eventually enlarged it to a sixteen by twenty picture along with the portrait of the three of us. I had these two framed and hung them on the walls. The one of the three of us hangs over the fireplace, and the one with Kyle and me in the hallway.

Chapter Thirty-Three

Time was moving faster than before; the business was now international as I always knew that it would be. The advancement of the business meant that either Bill or Ben had to be constantly flying overseas. Kyle was now enrolled in a private boy's school that offered an equestrian riding program. If he was going to follow after me, then he better have the best teachers that were available. He was confirming what everyone thought by winning competition after competition.

I had now returned to work to full time and was now a senior partner. I had put the family investigation to rest for now, since I have all the information that I need to know for the moment. As far as Deborah-Anne goes, I never let her out of my sight at any of the social functions that we attended. Although this was driving her nearly insane, she still managed to rendezvous with Tom.

"I don't know how much more I can take. Wherever I go at one of these functions, there she is. She's like my shadow," she said to him as they lay in bed.

"Don't worry. Maybe I can change the tables a bit. I was asked if I would like to do an article on the life of 'The Cat'. Maybe I can catch her off guard."

"You have to remember who you are dealing with. She just might get you."

"Don't worry I know her better than she knows herself," he said with a devilish laugh.

About three days later he started to put his plan into operation. I received a phone message from him during a recess in the case that I was handling. As I read the message that had been left for me, I started to wonder what he could possibly want. At the same time my cat instincts were starting to run in two different directions, first curiosity and the other caution. I called him back only to get his answering machine, so I left the following message for him. "Received you message, I will meet you at the Skipper at six o'clock for drinks." I phoned Maria to tell her that I would be late coming home for dinner. I told her that if Bill called to get a number where I could reach him later, and to tell him that I had a business meeting. It was Bill's turn to be overseas for the business, and we made it a practice to talk to each other every night that he was away.

At five thirty I headed to The Skipper down on the waterfront. The Skipper was a quaint, fishing shack like building on the outside, while on the inside it was decorated with everything that was connected with the sea. There was an area in which you could sit and eat, then there was an area that you could meet friends to have a social drink. I enjoyed coming here because no matter who you were, you could blend into the woodwork. I sat down at the bar, ordering myself a Brandy Alexander and asked if there might be a table for two becoming available in that area. They said that they would check on it and let me know. Meanwhile, I sat at the bar enjoying my drink by myself.

"Well I see that 'The Cat' still enjoys her cream. Could I have a scotch on the rocks please?" Tom said to the bartender as he came up behind me. Giving me a peck on the cheek, he sat down on the stool beside me.

"And I see that you still enjoy your scotch. I've asked for a table so that we can sit and talk freely. They said that they would call us when one becomes available."

"You are looking just great Stephanie. Looking at you I would never guess that you are fifty-six and the mother of that strapping boy Kyle. The fact of it is that if I didn't know better I would swear that you're still one of my models," he said with flirting eyes.

"Now Tom, I know that you didn't call me up to flirt or to boost my ego. What is the real reason for this meeting?" I replied with eyes that sparkled with curiosity.

By this time they had shown us to our table and we ordered another round of drinks.

"Okay Stephanie, because of our past history..." he started to say.

"That's right our past history." I stepped in.

"I have been asked by the Business Woman magazine to do an article and layout of the life of 'The Cat'. What do you say to it?"

"I say who would be interested in this person. The days of people being interested in me have long passed." The cat was back in my eyes as I replied, playing with the glass in my hand.

"Believe it or not, they want to use it as a story that focuses on a girl who wants something bad enough to go out after it. After all, hasn't there been a rumor going around that you could possibly be headed for the Supreme Court?"

"Only rumors. There are also rumors that I may decide to take it easy and go back to photography." I tipped my glass toward him as if to say touché. As I did this, I looked at him from the top of my eyes.

"See there is a story worth telling. What do you say, will you go for it?" He asked.

"What is in it for me?" I questioned.

"That sounds like the old Stephanie, always finding out the bottom line before committing herself," he chuckled "How does twenty thousand sound?"

"They must want the story pretty badly, but I can't commit myself just the same until I have time to talk to Bill. After all, this will affect him and Kyle too. I will give it some thought and then I will let you know, but now I must be going." I said as I rose to leave.

"You will think about it then?" he asked as I got up from my chair. I just looked back at him and flashed my cat eyes at him.

When I arrived home the phone was ringing, hearing this I ran through the doorway yelling at Maria that I had the phone. Catching my breath I answered the phone. "Hello."

"Stephanie you sound like your out of breath, were you running again?"

"Bill, is this the first time that you called, I just got in."

"Yes, we had some complications but everything is okay now. How is everything there? Kyle okay? Better yet are you behaving?" He chuckled with the last remark.

"Yes Kyle's okay. The way you talk it seems like I am the child," I said laughingly. I was gradually getting my breath back. "When will you be back?"

"Not for another week, I'm afraid. I want to confirm that everything is going okay before I leave here. Was there anything that you wanted to talk about?"

"Only that I had drinks with Tom today."

"What did you do that for?" I could hear his voice hardening.

"Some magazine wants him to do an article on 'The Cat' from the point of view of a girl that accomplishes her dreams. I said that I would have to talk it over with you since my life now involves you and Kyle. He says that they want to pay twenty thousand for the story. I thought that I would verify the story with the magazine tomorrow. So what do you think, do you want me back in the lime light again?"

"Stephanie if you want to do it, then do it because even if I was to say no, you would still do what you want. As far as being back in the limelight, you always seem to end up there, regardless of whether you want to or not."

"Thanks Bill that is why I love you so much. Do

you think that you could speed things up a bit over there? I really miss having you around the house?"

"I will do everything that is possible to hurry home. You don't realize how lonely it is here at night without you."

"Don't bet on that one, I love you."

"I love you too."

I heard the phone disengaging at the other end and I slowly placed the receiver down. Going through the mail, I walked to the kitchen. Maria had prepared me a cold plate to have when I got home.

"Maria, were there any messages tonight?" I asked as I entered the room.

"You had calls from your brother Ben, Dave and Stuart," Maria replied.

"I guess that I will call them back in that order. I then sat down to eat my meal, after which I went into the family room, lay down on the sofa with the phone beside me and started to return their calls.

"Ben, Maria said that you called."

"Yes, have you heard from Bill as to when we can expect him back?"

"I just got off the phone with him. It seems that he ran into some complications that he has taken care of, but he won't be back for another week. Why do we have a problem here?" I asked concerned.

"Nothing that I can't take care of. It was just a new project that we were landing. You know how I like the two of us to be there, but I guess I will just have to solo this one." There was a slight pause in his voice.

"I could fill in for him if you wanted."

"I thought that you wanted to be out of the picture as far as the company went?"

"I do, but I could just say that I was filling in for my husband. Anyway, I know everything that is going on in this company. I may not have studied these fields, but

I have learned first hand from the two of you everything that I need to know. If you want me there just say the word and I can rearrange my schedule."

"Okay then, rearrange your schedule. We meet the client at twelve o'clock at The Red Baron."

I hung up the phone and dialed Dave's number.

"Could I speak to Dave, please?" I waited for a few seconds.

"Cat, I just phoned to check up on you."

"Dave it is a good thing that you married a good person like Sue who isn't jealous."

"She has great trust in me and besides she knows how much you love Bill."

"While I have you on the phone though, I do have a question for you."

"Ask away, I will help if I can."

"Tom approached me today. He wants to do an article for a magazine about me. The storyline being of a girl that goes after her dreams and gets them. What do you think, should I do it or not?"

"Sounds pretty good, after all that is what you did, isn't it?"

"It sounds like you are for it then?"

"Let's put it this way, I'm not getting any bad vibes from it."

"That's as good as a go for it that I could get from you, thanks. I'll talk to you later then."

"Okay Cat."

Now for Stuart, I dialed the phone and waited.

"Hello."

"Hello Stuart. You called earlier?"

"Yes, we just wanted to confirm what time Kyle was competing on the weekend?" Uncle Pat, Stuart, Dave and their families stood by Kyle just as they had done for me when I was competing.

"It is starting at one o'clock on Saturday after the

compulsories. They will resume for the final competition on Sunday at twelve. It looks like Bill won't be able to make this one; he's tied up overseas on business.

"Well, that's the trouble when your husband has such a well known business." Stuart started to laugh at me.

"Yes, that's true, but it hurts Kyle when we both can't make it."

"Well, maybe he'll make it for Sunday and see Kyle take the Championship."

"That would be nice. I guess that I will see you on the weekend then."

"Yes, goodnight Stephanie."

I hung up the phone and headed upstairs to my bed, a place that I was long overdue for.

Chapter Thirty-Four

I gave my consent for the magazine article, and Tom began to work on it. We would meet over dinner several nights going back to my early days pulling out our old pictures, bringing back old memories for the two of us. Wherever I went, he seemed to be around even when I went into court. He managed to sit in on a few cases. He carried a note book along with his camera and a tape recorder. It was almost as if the hands of time had turned back the clocks forty years. Here we were working together again, his camera capturing shots showing the hidden cat inside of me.

Since he was my trusty shadow for the time being, it meant that he would accompany me to Kyle's equestrian competition. When we arrived there, Stuart came over to greet us with one of his smart remarks.

"What's this? I see that while the watchdog is away the cat will play," he said laughingly.

"Watch it counselor or I'll see you in court," I snapped back.

"Hi Tom, I see that today is not the day to ruffle Stephanie's feathers. I didn't know that you covered equestrian events?" he said to Tom.

"Good to see you Stuart. I don't normally but if it involves Stephanie then I have to. I am doing a magazine story on her from her early days until now, about a girl who had a dream and fought to make it come true."

"Well, you have her pegged there," Stuart chuckled.

"The truth of the matter is they want to see whether or not he can keep up to me or if that is just a line that he uses," I piped up flashing my eyes in their direction.

"I don't envy your job Tom. In all the time that has gone by she hasn't lost her touch or her speed." Stuart flashed his eyes back in my direction.

"Well, are we going to watch my son compete or not?" I snapped as I grabbed my camera out of the car and headed to the arena where the competition was being held.

As we watched each competitor do their jumps, the crowd was perfectly quiet. I followed Kyle with the camera over each jump as he performed. Through the lens I could see where he needed help and coaching. He wasn't as light as I was when I was in competition, but he was smooth going over the jumps. He had the same style of riding that I had. We both put our bodies close to the horse when we jumped and sat tall in the saddle when we rode. He had almost finished his ride and was coming to the last jump that was the triple. As I watched him go over the first two jumps in the triple I held my breath. He and his mount left the ground to go over the last part of the jump. As the front hooves of the horse touched the ground, the back ones gently tapped the last bar. We watched as the bar slowly fell to the ground. With him having just one fault I knew that in the competition on Sunday that Kyle would need clean rounds in order to win the championship. We went back to where he was dismounting so that I could give him some helpful tips.

"Kyle you did good out there," I said as I planted a kiss on his cheek.

"It wasn't a clean round though, Mother. Where is Father, isn't he coming?"

"He's overseas, but he is going to try to make it back for tomorrow's competition. You know how he hates to miss your competitions," I said as I put my arm around his shoulder. "By the way, I want you to meet Tom. He's an old friend of the family. He's doing a story on me so you will be seeing a lot of him."

"Nice to meet you Tom," Kyle said extending his hand to Tom.

"Nice to meet you Kyle. I've heard a lot about you," Tom said shaking Kyle's hand. "That was pretty nice riding that you did out there. It looks like someday in the future that you will be holding the championship just like your mother."

"Not if I keep making errors. You knew my mother when she was in competition?"

"No, shortly afterwards, but I understand she had a certain way about her when she jumped. They say it was as if she became part of the horse." Tom looked back at me with a glare in his eyes. I was patting Kyle's horse, saying things to it just as I used to with Stephanie's Fury. "I did manage to see her ride though, a sight that I will never forget," he continued.

"So, I guess you will be here again tomorrow then, because Mother wouldn't miss the championship. Now would you Mother?" He turned to me looking for an answer.

"No way! I want to be here more than any other place in the world." I went over and gave him another big hug.

"Stuart don't you think that he has the championship wrapped up?" Dave was saying to Stuart and Uncle Pat.

"Brings back happy memories, doesn't it?" Uncle Pat said.

"Yes, I will never forget her face when they presented her with the cup that year. Kyle has enough of her style and drive to be a winner. He'll make it," Stuart responded.

"I'm so glad that you guys are in my rooting section. I would hate to think that somebody else had this team behind them," Kyle said to them as he put his arms around Dave and Stuart.

Later, when it was time to leave I went to find Kyle. I found him with his friends.

"Look, we will see you tomorrow. Don't worry about the outcome tomorrow as long as you do your best." I had my arm around his shoulder as we walked back to the car. When we reached the car I gave him a kiss on the cheek and said good night.

In the car on the way home Tom kept watching me as I drove. "You really love that boy of yours, don't you?"

"I love him and Bill more than life itself, and I would die if anything happened to either one of them." I was straight and to the point. These two guys were my world. Sure if something happened to them I had my wealth and I had the business, but that was all meaningless unless I had them to share it with.

The next day I waited to see if I would hear from Bill and when I didn't I went to pick up Tom. We drove to the competition and everything went basically the same as Saturday. I was following Kyle over the jumps with the camera.

"How is our guy doing?" I heard and then felt a gentle kiss on the cheek.

"He's down a bit in his time, but if he can make it through with no faults then he has a chance. He'll be so glad that you made it back in time." Bill was used to the fact that my eyes never left Kyle when he was in the ring. I put down my camera as soon as he finished, and turned my head in Bill's direction. I pulled him close to me so that I could give him a proper welcome home kiss. Tom of course, was sitting up higher from us where he was catching everything on film. "Now let's go see our boy before the finals. Knowing that you are here might make the difference in his performance."

Kyle was watching for us to come and give him his pointers as to what to do to improve his performance in the finals. When he saw his father, he came running to meet him.

"Father you made it, Mother said that you would."

"You know that it would take something for me to miss you in competition."

"How was your flight Bill?" Tom came up behind us.

"The flight was fine and the day was fine until you appeared."

"Bill, that wasn't called for. You know that Tom is doing the article on me. I think that you owe him an apology," I demanded.

By this time Dave and Stuart thought that Bill was going to punch Tom. The look on his face was tightening as if a spring inside was being wound too much.

"Okay, I will apologize, but it seems that whenever he is around something happens to you. Sorry Tom." Bill walked off with Stuart and Dave close behind. Kyle stayed with me. He had never seen his father act this way.

"I am sorry Tom. I guess I should have expected something like this."

"No need to worry Stephanie. I thought that old wounds between us would have healed by now. I guess that I was wrong. If you want I can leave."

"That might be a good idea at this time. I will try and calm him down," I said as I looked in Bill's direction.

Tom left as Kyle and I walked toward Bill and the

guys.

"Are you sure that Tom has something to do with Stephanie's accidents?" Stuart was saying to Bill.

"I have no proof, just a gut feeling and the coincidence that he is always around when they happen."

"Have you calmed down now, or do I have to send you home like a child?" I had a voice that wasn't loud but it was demanding and very reprimanding. My eyes were flaring as I was putting the questions forth.

"Where did Tom go?" he said trying to dodge the question.

"Bill, don't you try and dodge my question. Tom left. He figured that he was in the way and that he was becoming a problem. Now answer my question have you calmed down enough so that we can enjoy ourselves?"

Stuart, Dave and Kyle had their eyes fixed upon us.

"Okay, I've calmed down."

"Good. Now let's enjoy the rest of the day." I put my arms around Kyle and Bill. I gave Kyle a pep talk before his final round, but alas he failed to make a clear round and placed second.

We said our good-byes and got into my car. It was a quiet ride home. I parked the car and walked a mile ahead of him. Up the stairs I went, getting into the sexiest negligee that I had, quickly putting it on and waited for Bill and his wounded ego. I turned the lights down low and waited and finally the door opened.

"Come in here you wounded beast," I purred beckoning to him with a curled finger. He slowly came over to the bed. I started to undress him. "Now what on earth set you off today?" I started to bathe him with kisses. "Was it the fact that an old boyfriend is spending time with me while you were away?" I continued to caress his body with kisses. He responded to the caressing by smothering me with kisses. "Can't you see that I can handle myself. There is only one man who is man enough for me, and he's right here." Now nibbling on his ear I whispered, "I don't want to see another outburst like that ever again, understood?"

He moved up to my ear and whispered. "Never again, I promise. Now let's drop this subject we have some catching up to do." He slowly slid in under the covers. We started to put the pieces of our lovemaking puzzle together. Slowly and carefully placing the final part of our puzzle in place, my body arched as it accepted his part of the puzzle.

Chapter Thirty-Five

The article was almost finished. Bill had calmed down in his jealous nature toward Tom. However, Tom was hoping that he could rekindle old flames of passion by going over the old memories and with hopes that he could use this to destroy my happy home.

The group of us were headed to the cottage for the weekend. Bill was picking up Kyle from school and driving up earlier in the day with Stuart and his family. Ben would be leaving after work with his family and Dave's family. Dave and I would leave later after his shift as I had one last meeting with Tom about the article, then I could let him fade out of my life again. He was to be at my house by six so that we could have a nice meal and then finish the article.

We sat down to the meal that Maria had prepared. She cleared away the dishes as we finished the meal and then she informed us that she would be going out when she had finished the dishes. I poured us an after dinner drink and we headed into the family room where we had all the work laid out. Examining the information that he had collected starting from when I was an equestrian rider, to being a model, then a lawyer, a mother and a wife. The final part was what was in store for The Cat. The pictures that he laid out in front of me brought the memories to me and to him. He reached over me to retrieve a picture. As he sat back down his arm slowly dropped onto my shoulder. Gently he pulled me close and looking into my eyes he began to kiss me. I didn't resist, but instead let him continue. I wanted to see just where he was headed.

"Just like old times. You seemed to have enjoyed that as much as I did," he said with a smile on his face, his arm still around my shoulder.

"That was just for old time's sake, just for the memories not for the present. I don't go behind Bill's back and I am not Deborah-Anne."

"You loved to make love to me before, and I am sure that you want to do it again. Your kiss said so. You can't say you didn't enjoy it." His eyes were flaring as his arm tightened around me. "Maybe you would like a second taste in order to reconsider." He moved in closer to me as he started to force his kisses upon me.

"Tom, I am giving you one more warning, back off. It's time for you to leave. Maybe if you are lucky Deborah-Anne will be in the mood for your pleasures tonight, but as for me you have worn out your welcome, now leave." With that I started to get up from my chair, as I rose from the chair I heard a rip and the cold air over my breasts. Looking down at myself I could see that my blouse had been torn off my back. I looked back at Tom, my blouse in his hand and this glare in his eyes.

"I told you that you would reconsider. Now, you have told me that you have changed your mind." He started to rise from his chair, moving toward me. "Come on Stephanie. Why do you always have to fight?" He was almost next to me by now.

"I'm warning you. You can leave now, but if you try to touch me, you will wish to God that you had never set eyes on me."

I started to flash my eyes at him, my body started to feel like a cat, my back felt arched, my manicured fingers felt like cat claws. I started to move around out of his way over to where my torn blouse was. I reached for my blouse and just as I did he made a lunge for me. I just caught a glimpse of him, seconds from me. I turned around catching him in the neck with my claws, drawing blood as they sank into his neck. As they found their destination the doorbell rang. I ran with my torn blouse in my hand to the door. As I opened the door I found Dave standing in shock as he viewed my partially clad body.

"What the hell happened here?" he yelled as he barged in.

"Tom was just leaving," I said catching my breath. Tom was making his way toward the door.

"You bitch. You can't reject me twice," he said as he grasped my chin between his fingertips pushing me a bit as he passed by. That was all that Dave needed to hear and see. He brought back his fist and in one quick motion sent Tom flying the rest of the way out of the door. He yelled at Tom as he went flying through the door.

"Don't you ever let me catch you around 'The Cat' again." He slammed the door after him. Turning to me he put his arms around me and comforted me. "Cat what the hell happened?"

"Tom got taken up in the memories, tried kissing me and when I refused to let him go any further, he tore my blouse off me. He believed that I still loved him, and that I wanted to make love to him," I cried in Dave's arms.

"You just cry it out," he said putting my head on his chest. "Bill was right, we do have to watch him. Let me call the police and have him picked up."

"On what charge? He was at a friend's house and things got a little out of hand on memory lane. They wouldn't even hold him. No Dave, it's better to let it rest.

You can't tell Bill either. If he found out, he would kill Tom. Promise me Dave, please." Panic was running through me.

"But Cat, I think he should know." He was pleading with me.

"No, you saw him that day of Kyle's competition. Well if he found out about this, he would definitely kill him. Christ look you even hit him." That was the first time that Dave had ever heard the slightest bit of swearing from me.

"Okay, you have a point, but I don't like letting scum like that get away." He looked at me with sad eyes.

"Don't worry he'll get his when Deborah-Anne gets hers."

"What do you mean Cat?"

"You know how they say that scum like that has strange bedfellows. Well guess who's his is?"

"Deborah-Anne?"

"You've got it. Now, let me get changed and we'll be off."

When we arrived they all wanted to know what had kept us.

"You know women," Dave started nodding his head toward me. "They're never ready, when you get there."

"What seemed to be the problem?" Bill asked as he gave me a kiss.

"Oh you know Stephanie, she wasn't quite finished with her meeting with Tom and then she had to change." Susan put her arms around Dave's waist. I have to admit that I couldn't have handled the situation as well as he did.

While we were starting to enjoy our weekend, Tom was recuperating from our little entanglement. Where I had connected with my nails there were now four deep claw marks. Tom looks in the mirror at the scar.

"Just you wait, you'll wish I had killed you the first time." He held a roll of film in his hand.

Chapter Thirty-Six

Tom hadn't realized what a favour he had done for me by writing the article. I couldn't have asked for a better press coverage than what the magazine gave me. I received invitations to give lectures encouraging girls to follow their dreams, no matter how impossible they seemed and no matter what the obstacles were. I also engaged another investigator to investigate Deborah-Anne and Tom more thoroughly then Ed had. I wanted to know if Deborah-Anne was indeed my half sister or not. I wanted to find out if Tom ever possessed a gun and I wanted to know everything there was to know about these two.

Tom had chosen to go against 'The Cat' and now we were at war. If he had anything to do with my shooting, then I was going to nail him to the board.

The phone interrupted my line of thought. "Stephanie meet us at the hospital. It's Father," Stuart was saying frantically.

"Go on. I'll meet you there," I replied.

I put the phone down and ran to my car. I knew that Uncle Pat was getting old, but I never really thought of anything ever happening to him. I sped all the way over to the hospital; thank God that they didn't have the radar traps out today. There in the emergency room were

Stuart with his wife Michelle comforting each other. Aunt Elizabeth was sitting in the corner of the room crying. Then there was Deborah-Anne with Michael trying to console her. When she saw me coming into the room she rose from her chair.

"What is she doing here?" she demanded.

"Father wanted her to be here," Stuart snapped back at her.

"What's wrong? What happened to Uncle Pat?" I asked Stuart almost not wanting to hear the answer.

"Father had a heart attack, but before they took him in the ambulance he told me to have you meet us here," Stuart explained as he tried to control his emotions.

"Who's working on him?" I asked.

"Dr. Yu, he's the top heart specialist, but Dave's in there keeping an eye on things."

"Let's not think the worse then. Let's look to when we can see him again," I said as I put my arm around him and headed over to Michelle.

Time seems to go by slowly when you're in the waiting room, something that I hadn't done before as I had always been the one they were waiting on. I phoned Bill and Ben to tell them where they could reach me. Then I picked up some coffee and took it all back in with me. We sat and waited some more, finally the doctor came in. Uncle Pat was in critical condition and his time with us was limited. The family asked whether they could see him.

"He's conscious but very weak. He wants to see Stephanie and Stuart together. I am allowing it, but only because Dr. Thompson will be in the room with you to assure that he isn't over extending himself. After they come out the rest of you can go in one at a time," Dr. Yu said sternly.

"Thank you doctor," Stuart said as he put his arm

around my shoulder to lead me into his room.

"Why should she go in first? It should be Mother," Deborah-Anne said.

"It's your father's wish, now we must wait," Aunt Elizabeth said. "Now go ahead Stuart, just don't be too long."

We went slowly into the room; there were machines everywhere connected to Uncle Pat. He slowly motioned for us to come closer.

"Stephanie I'm glad Stuart was able to get you. I hope that you don't mind, but I wanted Stuart in on our secret. I (cough, cough) did as you asked that day with a few exceptions (cough, cough) that I'm sure that you'll allow."

"Uncle Pat have a little drink of water, please. Don't exert yourself too much," I said as I gave him a drink of water.

"Stuart you must stand by Stephanie no matter what the others say, but you must keep what I am saying to you as our secret till the day that you die. Promise me Stuart." (cough, cough.)

"I promise Father till the day I die," Stuart replied with tears in his eyes.

"Stephanie call me by my name just once before I die, let me hear it just once," Uncle Pat said to me with tears in his eyes.

"Father please don't leave me," I cried.

"Father?" Stuart repeated in a shocked voice. "Yes Stuart. Now it's your secret to keep. You must never say that she is your sister. Do we have your word on that (cough, cough) Stuart?" Uncle Pat was struggling with his words.

"I'll keep it Father; I'll stick by her side no matter what." There were tears in his eyes as he answered his father, grasping his hand.

"Now send your mother in and remember no-one

is to know." He gasped as he spoke.

Stuart helped me out of the room. Both of us were crying now.

"Mother he wants to see you now," Stuart said to his mother as he helped her out of her chair. "He hasn't got much time." We all started to cry again when he said that.

Aunt Elizabeth had been in there a short time when they announced code blue in Uncle Pat's room. People seemed to be coming out of the woodwork rushing into his room.

We all seemed to know that this was it that Uncle Pat wasn't with us anymore. The tears started to flow. Stuart, Michelle and I were holding onto one another trying to stop the pain rushing through us. Aunt Elizabeth just sat there stunned with tears flowing down her cheeks. Deborah-Anne with tears in her eyes came across and pulled me from Michelle and Stuart.

"I don't understand why you're here, but he was my father not yours. Couldn't you let me at least say good-bye to him?" Michael tried to pull her off me and to comfort her.

"Deborah-Anne, this isn't the place," Stuart said to his sister.

Dave came out of the room. "I'm sorry Stuart but he's gone." He said as he put his arm around his friend's shoulder.

"Thanks Dave, but we knew once they called that code blue. I guess we better take Mother home."

"I'll stop by later and see if she is okay and if there is anything that I can do."

"Do me a favour see that Stephanie gets home safely," Stuart directed with his head back toward me. I was huddled crying with Michelle.

"No problem. I'll take her home myself. Dave said and started to walk over to me. "Come on Cat, I'll take you home." He put his arm around my shoulder and started to lead me out.

"Wait, what about my car?" I suddenly remembered that I drove myself to the hospital.

"Don't worry we will get it later."

He drove me home and there waiting for us was Bill. "Let's get her upstairs and I'll give her something to calm her down." They put me in bed. "Cat this will help you rest." I felt a pin prick. "She'll sleep through the night."

"How is the rest of the family?" Bill asked.

"Not good. After all, he is really the first one in the family to go. I'm just on my way over to the house to see Stuart's mother and if there is anything that I can do."

"Give Stuart and the rest of the family my regards and we'll see them tomorrow," Bill said with sadness in his voice.

Dave left and headed over to Aunt Elizabeth's there he sedated Aunt Elizabeth as he had with me. He and Stuart then went for a walk.

"How are you doing old buddy?"

"I feel as if my whole world just caved in. I can't believe that he's gone," Stuart said as he started to cry. "It makes me feel so damn helpless."

"You know, there isn't anything that anyone can do when it is your time to go. Your father knew that and accepted it. Now you have to accept it too, because if you don't you'll go crazy."

"I know that, but it's so bloody hard and the one time that I need Stephanie's strength, it looks like the one time that I won't get it."

"I wouldn't count 'The Cat' out yet. I gave her a sedative so that she could sleep through the night and then she should be strong tomorrow."

Stuart arranged for Uncle Pat's funeral to be on

Wednesday. I stood back from the graveside with my family so as not to set Deborah-Anne off again. Bill held on to me tightly as they lowered the coffin into the ground. I now released all my pent up grief at the loss of my father. This was the last time that I would see him.

Chapter Thirty-Seven

The day came when we were summoned by Uncle Pat's lawyer to hear the reading of his will. We gathered in Mr. Archibald's office. There was Stuart and Michelle, Deborah-Anne and Michael, Aunt Elizabeth and I. Once Deborah-Anne saw me her eyes started to throw daggers and if looks could kill, I would have been dead. For most of us it was a somber occasion and I in no way wanted to do anything that would create an incident.

"I see that we are all here," Mr. Archibald started. "If you take a seat then we shall get started." With that we all took our seats. I sat over by Stuart and Michelle far away from Deborah-Anne.

"Okay if we are settled then I will begin." Mr. Archibald then began to read Uncle Pat's will.

"Being of sound mind I Patrick Alexander McConnell hereby bequeath my earthy possessions as such. To my daughter Deborah-Anne I leave the sum of fifty thousand dollars. To my son Stuart I leave the sum of seventy-five thousand dollars and to my wife Elizabeth I leave the sum of one hundred thousand dollars. The remainder of the estate, the house, horses and stocks will go to my niece Stephanie MacGregor, who it was to go to originally from my father's will with one request to Stephanie, that although she will own the estate, that she allow her Aunt Elizabeth to live out her remaining days in the mansion.

                              Signed   Patrick Alexander McConnell"

"Now are there any questions about the terms?" Mr. Archibald asked.

"Why should she get the estate?" Deborah-Anne said with a smirk.

"These were the wishes of your father, he did mention that it was in fact your Grandfather who left it for her in his will. If you wish to contest the will it is your privilege," he said to her.

"For God's sake Deborah-Anne, can't you accept anything? It's what Father wanted. If you looked at the date of the will you will see that he's wanted it for a long time," Stuart yelled at her.

"Now if you sign here accepting the conditions of the will we can conclude this meeting," Mr. Archibald said as he handed the pen first to Aunt Elizabeth, who signed without hesitation. Stuart after signing turned to his sister. She took the pen reluctantly but signed anyway. Mr. Archibald took the pen from her and gave it to me to place the final signature on the document.

"Everything is done here. I will be in touch with each one of you later," Mr. Archibald, said motioning with his hand that we were free to go.

"Stephanie, can we give you a lift somewhere?" Stuart asked as he and Michelle came out of the office.

"Thanks, but I have my car. How about going to the Skipper for a coffee or a drink?" I replied

"Okay, we will meet you there." We went our own separate ways only to meet later.

Michelle looked at her husband as he drove the car with a look of wonder on her face.

"A penny for your thoughts," he said to her as he glanced at her.

"Why didn't you object to your father's will like Deborah-Anne did?"

"I promised my father that I would stick by Stephanie no matter what and that is what I have done. He had his reasons for doing what he did and we will abide by his wishes." His voice told Michelle that his mind was made up and there wasn't anything that she could do to change it.

They slowly pulled into the parking lot of the Skipper. There beside their car was parked a jaguar with the license THE CAT. I arrived there first and got a table. When they came into the room I motioned for them to join me. I was already enjoying a Brandy Alexander. After the reading of the will, I needed something to calm me down. My dreams were coming true. The estate that was owed to me from my birth was now mine. Thanks to Tom's article I was back in the limelight. I had money, a husband and a son who I loved and who loved me. Oh! What a perfect world.

"I see you did well back there. I guess that is why father asked me to stand by you," Stuart commented to me.

"Yes, I'm still in shock, thanks for siding with me," I said with a smile.

"I told Father that I would and I stand by my word. Now that you're a richer lady than you were before, and now that you have a business to control, does this mean that you will be leaving the courtroom?" he questioned.

"I hadn't really given it very much thought, but let's change the subject. We seem to be leaving Michelle out in the dark," I said.

"Don't worry about me I'm used to it with Stuart," Michelle said politely.

It didn't take Deborah-Anne long before she went crying to Tom.

"That bitch! I don't know how she did it but Father left practically the whole estate to her."

"Would you calm down," Tom said to her as he tried to hold her in his arms.

"All that I got was a measly fifty thousand and she got the mansion, the horses, everything." Finally Tom got a hold on her and to stop her from complaining he planted his lips on hers.

"Don't worry we'll get her. We'll get her good," he said with fire in his eyes as he proceeded to kiss her. Then he slowly removed her clothes. They took all the hate and anger that they had for Stephanie and turned it into intense lovemaking.

Chapter Thirty-Eight

Over the next few years I kept my word to Uncle Pat allowing Aunt Elizabeth to stay in the mansion. I even grew close to her over the years. When I went over to check the grounds or to ride, I would have Anna make a pot of tea for the two of us to be served in the garden. Stuart was amazed at how we got along. Now we seemed to be more like mother and daughter instead of Aunt and niece. I went over to check on the place today because Bill and I were leaving on a business trip. The trip would keep us out of the country for at least a week maybe two. Since receiving my inheritance I had given up working at the law firm. I kept my connections with firm, but the size of our business was growing in all directions and didn't give me much time for my law practice. We were slowly breaking Kyle into the business, even though he was still in university and was still in the equestrian sport.

I sat and talked with Aunt Elizabeth while we had our tea and then I left for home. My bags were packed and waiting for me so that when I arrived home Bill and I could leave for the airport. We were just waiting for the call to board the plane when we heard an announcement. "Would Mr. or Mrs. Bill MacGregor come to the information booth?" The call was repeated a second time. We proceeded to the booth and inquired as to why we were being paged.

"There's a phone call for you," the girl behind the booth said as she pointed to a phone that we could use.

"Hello, this is Mrs. Bill MacGregor."

"Mrs. MacGregor this is the University calling. We just wanted to let you know that there was an accident in the riding ring. We don't think that Kyle was hurt too badly, but we are taking him to the Aurora Memorial Hospital to be checked out all the same." My heart stopped when I heard the voice on the other end of the phone.

"Look, tell Kyle that I will meet him there and not to worry." I hung up the phone and turned to Bill who could already tell by the look on my face that something was wrong.

"Kyle has been in a accident, they've taken him to the hospital. I'm going to have to go to the hospital." As I said it you could hear the apprehension in my voice. "You will continue without me. If Kyle is okay, I will follow on the next plane out."

"Don't worry though, remember he's got an awful lot of you in him. Call me when you find out how he is. Are you sure that you don't want me to stay behind too? Then we could fly together," he said with concern in his voice.

"No, I will phone you before I leave here and you can have a pot of tea waiting for me. I have to go now." I kissed him good-bye and ran off to the car.

I rushed all the way over to the hospital and when I got there, Kyle was sitting in the waiting room with a cast on his arm. As I got close to him he said, "You know that you didn't have to come, Mother. All I have is a broken arm and a slight concussion. You should have gone on your trip with Father."

"Don't worry about me missing the flight. When it comes to your health, I would cancel everything. Besides, your father and I wouldn't have it any other way. How are you feeling now anyway?"

"Other than a terrific headache, not too bad," he chuckled.

"Good, then once I get you settled at home with Maria, I'll catch the next flight out," I said as I led him out to the car. We drove home and I told Maria to take care of him. I then headed back toward the airport. Halfway there, there was a sudden pain in my chest. It started to grow and continued till I couldn't stand it anymore. I had to get off the road, everything was going black.

"Lady can you hear me?" somebody was yelling.

"Her pulse is low. We better beat it to the hospital. Call it in that we have a possible cardiac arrest."

"I can't believe that she didn't smack that car up, it's totally a miracle. Better phone it in." The police were saying to each other. We have a green jaguar license plate reads Thomas Henry Edward Catherine Adam Thomas, that's right THE CAT. The driver named Stephanie MacGregor has been taken to the Metropolitan Hospital."

The red and white lights flashed in the dark of the night as I was rushed to the hospital. I was feeling lighter, the pains seem to be subsiding, yet they were still working on me.

"Better beat it Joe, we're loosing this one. She seems to be slipping, her pulse is getting weaker. Come on lady fight, don't give in," he said as he was injecting something into my arm.

"We're coming into the hospital now. Are we going to make it?" the driver yelled back.

They pulled the ambulance into the emergency area of the hospital. They removed the stretcher from the ambulance and ran through the doors with me. "Quick we've got a code blue, the pulse just stopped."

"Get the paddles ready, doctor." The doctor put the paddles on my chest; a bolt of energy hit my body, as the body on the table jumped with the shock going through it. "Damn it lady, fight. You're too young to die."

"Doctor, we're getting a pulse, weak but it is a pulse." Somebody was saying. "Hook her up on the monitor quickly. We have to stabilize her."

The pain was slowly returning to my body.

"Take her to the ICU. Has her family been notified?" the doctor was saying to the attendants.

"Yes, doctor her son has been notified. In fact, he is in the waiting room with a Dr. Thompson."

The doctor went out into the waiting room to find Kyle waiting with Dave.

"MacGregor?" he said in the direction of Kyle.

"Yes doctor. How is my mother doing?" Kyle asked as he stood to meet the doctor.

"She's going to be all right. However, it was touch and go there for a while. She has suffered a heart attack. Do you know whether she has had any heart problems in the past?" he asked Kyle was relieved to hear that his mother would be all right.

"Not that I know of, but this is Dr. Thompson. He is her doctor and he could fill you in better than I could. When can I see her?"

"Not right now son. We are monitoring her and then she will be put in the ICU. When they get her settled in there, you will be allowed to see her." The doctor then turned to Dave. "Dr. Thompson is there anything that we need to know about her?"

"She had a bad case of pneumonia when she was young, she was shot in the chest about eighteen years ago, but basically she has been in good health. By the way how did this happen?" Dave asked after giving a brief medical history to the doctor.

"They say that it was amazing that she didn't cause an accident. When she had the heart attack somehow the car slowly went off the side of the highway. A motorist seeing this car going off the road pulled over to check it out. When he got over to it he found her in the seat unconscious. Somebody up above was looking after her, that's for sure. When they brought her in, her heart had just stopped and we had to use the paddles to bring her back."

"I would like to talk to you later about having her transferred to the hospital that I work at once she is strong enough to be moved."

"I wouldn't advise it until we have her stabilized. I'll have somebody tell you when she is in her bed in ICU," the doctor said to Dave just before leaving the waiting room.

"Don't worry about your mother Kyle she will be okay. She just has the tendency to over dramatize situations a bit. After all, she couldn't have you getting all the attention with that broken arm." Dave joked with Kyle but it wasn't working.

"She was going to join Father in England. She would have been there if it wasn't for me. Damn it. Why did I have to get hurt in the first place," Kyle said as he was putting the blame on himself.

"She would have had the heart attack all the same. You couldn't have prevented it. You know all this isn't going to help your head any," Dave told him as he put his arm around him.

They waited around till finally a nurse came toward them. "Kyle MacGregor, if you would like to follow me I will take you to see your mother now," she said with a very pleasant smile. They followed her to a glassed in room. Inside the room there was a nurse sitting beside me. There were wires going from me to the machines that were monitoring my heart beat, blood pressure and all my vital signs. "You can only stay a few minutes and one at a time." As the nurse left, Kyle entered the room there was fear written all over his face.

"Mother would you please wake up? What am I supposed to tell Father?" I just lay there motionless. The quiet in the room was only disturbed by the monitors. Kyle came out of the room crying his heart out. Dave put his arms around him and tried to comfort him. "Dave she's not awake, she just lies there. Why doesn't she open her eyes?" he cried.

"You've have to give it time. Let me go in and then we will get you home. She'd have my head if she knew that you weren't resting," he said to Kyle and then left him to watch through the window. Nodding to the nurse that was sitting watching the monitors he turned to me. "Cat, I know that you can hear me. You've scared your son half to death. I'm telling the nurses to take no monkey business from you, and by the time we come back tomorrow we expect to see you awake." He bent over and kissed me on the forehead.

He walked out and putting his arm around Kyle took him out of the hospital and headed for home. As they were driving home Kyle asked Dave to come in for a cup of coffee while he made some phone calls. As they approached the driveway they noticed Ben's car was in the driveway.

"What's Uncle Ben's car doing here? Did you call him from the hospital?" Kyle asked as he looked at Dave.

"No, maybe he called and Maria told him," Dave suggested.

As they walked into the house they heard voices coming from the family room. They followed the voices into the family room. There were Ben and Louise sitting having a drink, their faces were red from crying.

"Uncle Ben, I'm glad that you're here than I don't have to call you. Maybe I could get you to call Father about Mother." Ben started to cry again. "You don't have to cry, they say that Mother will be just fine," Kyle said with a slight smile.

Through his tears Ben put his arm around his nephew directing him to a chair that was close by. "Kyle there's been more bad news. I think that you better sit down." He assisted him to a chair he was standing in front of. Dave's face had taken a concerned, but curious look.

"They didn't phone to say that she was worse, did they?" Kyle said in a frightened voice, grasping his uncle's arm.

"No, this has nothing to do with your mother. It's your father."

"What about my father? Couldn't you reach him?"

"Kyle, your father didn't make it to England. The plane went down just before touching down on the runway."

"Was he hurt badly?" Kyle was saying as he jumped out of his chair grabbing his uncle.

"Kyle, I'm sorry but your father didn't survive the crash. I'm sorry." He hugged his nephew; both were crying openly.

"No, there has to be some mistake, they must be wrong." Kyle was going crazy with the news.

"Kyle, I wish that they were wrong, but your father's seat was in the lounge. They said that all the passengers in the front of the plane didn't have a chance. I'm going over with Bill's sister Sandy to bring Bill's body back. We just wanted to wait until we told you and to find out how Stephanie is doing."

"What time did this all happen, Ben?" Dave asked with a queer look on his face.

"They say it was about seven in the evening," Ben replied.

"Kyle, what time did your mother leave for the

airport?"

"She would have left here about six-thirty," Kyle replied through his sobs.

My God that would mean that when Bill's plane was crashing, Stephanie was having her heart attack, Dave thought to himself.

"Dave, I'm going to have to ask you to tell Stephanie since between you and the doctor you should be able to tell when and how to tell her. I don't think that Kyle is capable of it. Could you also call my sister Bridgette and the rest of the family?" Ben said between sobs.

"Sure, I'll do that," Dave replied still not believing that Bill was gone.

"We have to leave now, but we will call you later with anything that we find out."

"I'm sorry Kyle," Ben said as he tried to console his nephew one last time. Louise and Ben left for the airport to do a task that no-one wanted to do. Nobody wanted any of the tasks that were being passed out tonight. Dave's first task was taking care of Kyle, who had become completely bewildered by the happenings of the day. First, he had been thrown from his mount, suffering a slight concussion and a broken arm. Then his mother nearly dies from a heart attack and now his father dies in a plane crash. How could this possibly be happening? He stood by the mantle of the fireplace looking at the picture of the three of them. Picking it up he smashed it against the wall. Dave went to try to calm him down, but even with one arm he packed a good punch, striking at Dave with his one free arm, he made contact with Dave's face. He showed the power that his mother had given him. He was like a wounded animal striking at anything that was near him. Dave knew that he had to contact Stuart and the rest of the family, but right now he needed Stuart. Backing away from Kyle he moved toward the phone, not letting his eyes leave Kyle. Picking up the phone he called Stuart.

"Stuart, I need you at Stephanie's immediately," Dave said quickly to Stuart as he answered the phone.

"What's the problem?" Stuart asked.

"I need you to help me with Kyle. I'll explain when you get here," Dave said and hung up the phone.

He would have to try and calm Kyle down so that he could sedate him. He approached him with a glass that he had mixed some tranquilizer in. Kyle was staring at the wedding picture of his mother and father. "Why Father, why did you have to die? How could you do this to me?"

"Here, drink this Kyle it will help. You know you could have lost both of them. Now you have to be strong for your mother."

He slowly drank the sedative. "You may have saved your mother by having your accident. It stopped your mother from being on that plane." Dave was trying his best to get Kyle's mind from his father to his mother.

"But why did he have to die?" Kyle screamed out as he put pressure on the glass in his hand. Even though the sedative had started to work, he still had enough pressure in his hand to break the glass. Dave ran quickly grabbing materials close at hand to bandage Kyle's hand that was now dripping blood. "Christ Kyle be careful," Dave snapped at him but Kyle didn't even realize what he was doing. "Kyle I want you to lie down on this couch and calm down. I don't think that I could handle giving your mother any more bad news."

Stuart finally arrived as Dave was picking up the pieces of the shattered glass with Maria.

"What the hell happened here?" Stuart blurted out as he saw the mess in the family room.

"Stuart, come into the other room with me," Dave said pouring them a drink. He followed Stuart out of the room and instructed Maria to keep an eye on Kyle, who was slowly calming down. When they got in the other room Dave motioned to Stuart to have a seat.

"Stuart, I've got some bad news to tell you. I guess there is no easy way to say it but to say it." Stuart took a sip of his drink. "There have been some accidents today."

"Stephanie and Bill were headed for England," Stuart said in a shocked voice. "What happened, Dave?"

"They were at the airport waiting to board the plane when they were paged that Kyle had been taken to the hospital. Stephanie left the airport to be with Kyle and Bill continued on to England. Finding out that Kyle would be okay, Stephanie headed back to the airport to catch the next flight to England, but she never made it. Halfway there, she had a heart attack."

"Oh my God! She isn't dead, is she?" Stuart asked almost in tears.

"No, they almost lost her, but she is in ICU at the hospital out by the airport. They say that it was amazing that she didn't cause an accident when her car went off the highway. The same time that she had her heart attack, Bill was landing in England but he wasn't so lucky." Dave paused as he took a drink from his glass. "The plane crashed as it was approaching the runway. Bill was killed."

"Oh my God, no!" Stuart cried out as he took a large mouthful of his drink in order to absorb what he had just heard. "Kyle knows then?"

"Ben was waiting for us when we got home from the hospital. He was on his way to pick up Bill's sister Sandy, and then they are flying to England to bring Bill's body back," Dave said as he took another sip.

"My God how is Kyle taking it?" Stuart had risen from his chair and was motioning to the other room where Kyle was.

"That is why I called you. He has enough of Stephanie in him that he turned into a wounded animal. As soon as Ben left he went berserk, I finally got him to take a sedative."

"Is that what happened to your face?" Stuart pointed at Dave with the glass in his hand.

"Yeah, he got me good when I tried to get him to calm down. Then he smashed a glass in his hand. I can't leave him alone, and we still have to notify Bridgette."

"What about Stephanie, she doesn't know yet, does she?"

"No, that's going to be my job too. I will have to do it with the doctor involved in her case. I'm phoning Sue to let her know what's going on and that I won't be home for a while."

Stuart got up and went into the family room where Kyle lay on the sofa. He was still awake although he was starting to get a little groggy with the sedative. He was at least calmer. Stuart bent over him and gave him a hug.

"Don't worry everything will be okay." Kyle started to cry. When Dave finished making the calls, he joined them and with Stuart's assistance helped Kyle to his room. Stuart and Dave came back downstairs and poured themselves another drink, still not believing what had happened.

"Dave how are you?" Stuart put his arm around his friend.

"I'll be okay, but I was never so scared in my life. I thought that we had lost her this time. We still might when I tell her that Bill's dead."

"It was that close this time?"

"Yeah, her heart actually stopped. They had to use the paddles on her. You know that she had the attack at the exactly the same time Bill crashed. She's never had heart problems before," Dave said shaking his head.

"Don't worry. I don't think that she is ready to

leave us yet." Stuart patted Dave on the shoulder as he looked out the window.

The doctor put Dave off from telling me about Bill for three days which was very hard on him and Kyle. Every day they came into my room putting on a show. They had to lie so well that I wouldn't know what was going on. Finally, the day came and the doctor thought that it would be better to get it over with while I was still on the monitors. Dave thought that it was best if Kyle wasn't there. He didn't want to risk anything else happening. It would be bad enough when they brought the body back.

The doctor and Dave came into the room together which I found just a little bit strange since Kyle wasn't with Dave. He was always with Dave when he came to visit. Dave came over to the side of my bed, kissed me on the forehead and then he took my hand in his.

"Cat, I've been putting off telling you something. We've been waiting until you got a little stronger." Dave eyes never left mine as he was talking. If he hadn't said another word I still would have known what he had to say, I could see that it was tearing him apart. "The day that you were brought here, Bill had already left for England."

"Yes Dave, you were going to call him for me. Nothing has happened to him, has it?" My eyes started to flash like lightning, his eyes were filling with tears, the monitors started to show erratic movement.

"Better do it quick, Dr. Thompson" the other doctor said.

"Cat, there was a plane crash that day. Bill didn't make it. I'm sorry Cat, but you have to fight through. You still have Kyle." First his voice was saddened then it became an urging voice as the monitors were showing that they were losing me. The doctor was getting ready to jab me with another needle before they had to use the paddles again. Dave didn't give up.

"Cat, think of Kyle. He couldn't stand to lose both of you. I couldn't stand to lose you, fight Cat, damn you Cat fight. Get that wildcat blood going. You'll destroy Kyle if you give in. Think of all we've been through. Think. There's a reason for you not to be on the plane. For Christ sake Cat, come back."

"Her vital signs are improving, she's stabilizing," the nurse said as she read the monitors.

"Doctor, I've heard of bedside manner, but that was something else. She's not out of the woods yet."

"I know that and I also know that when she wakes up again she is going to have questions and she is going to want to go for the funeral," Dave said, looking down at me as I lay there sleeping from the exhaustion that the shock had caused.

"I'd have to say no to that. God we almost lost her again. We might not be so lucky the next time," the doctor was saying to Dave.

"I would have to agree with you on any other patient, but not with 'The Cat'. When she wakes up I will have to answer her questions including that one." Dave looked at me with a worried look.

"Where will you be until she wakes up?"

"I'll be down at the cafeteria, having a coffee. I think that you agree that the sooner I answer her questions, the sooner we can get her to relax."

"I agree with you there, but if she is the fighter that you say that she is, then let's hope that this is the end of our troubles."

Dave came back when the doctor informed him that I was awake.

"Now Cat, the doctor's have given you a sedative to calm you down. I will answer your questions, but you have to try to remain calm. I realize that it is a shock to you to lose Bill, but I am sure that he wouldn't want Kyle to lose both of you."

"Dave, when and how did it happen?" I asked with tears slowly forming as I spoke.

"Being a doctor I am not supposed to say this, but when you had your heart attack, it was exactly the same time that Bill's plane crashed. It was as though you knew that he was dead, and that you couldn't stand to live without him."

"Then how do you explain that I am alive and he's dead?" I asked with anger in my voice and tears in my eyes.

"Maybe it is because you are still needed here. Maybe you have to finish what you came to do in the first place," Dave answered with a caring smile on his face. "All I know is that you weren't meant to die, at least not yet anyway."

"Kyle does know then?"

"Yes, he found out that night. The doctors wouldn't let us tell you until now for fear that we would lose you. If you want I will have Stuart bring Kyle to the hospital."

"Maybe tomorrow. Right now, I just want to be alone. You understand, don't you?" I said softly with tears still slowly running from my eyes.

"I understand Cat. If you need me just have them call me. If you need anything just ask this lady, and I am sure that she will see that you get it." He smiled toward the nurse who smiled back at him.

He went home stopping off to see Kyle, to inform him about how his mother was. He had been filling in for both his parents at the office with the help from his Uncle Ben who phoned him every day with instructions. It was a big job for someone who had just been broken into the business, but he was his parent's child, and he would meet the challenge.

They were still going through the formalities required

to enable them bring Bill's body back home. With the ongoing investigation into the crash, it was taking them a bit longer to get clearance to bring the body back home. The main question seemed to be why would a plane that was coming down with no problems, all of a sudden crash. It was as if the plane was sabotaged.

The funeral was arranged for the following week. The doctor had started to bend toward my ways. He promised that he would allow me out on a day pass on the day of the funeral providing that I kept improving. I had been moved out of ICU to a private room and was now allowed off the monitors. There was no way that I wasn't going to be allowed to say good-bye to the man that I loved.

They had made arrangements for a private funeral. If I was allowed out of the hospital then they didn't want it to be anymore traumatic then it already was. Stuart and Louise met Ben and Sandy at the airport the day before the funeral. At the same time the funeral parlour sent its hearse to take Bill's body to the funeral parlour.

Today was the day the doctor would either say yes to my day pass or confine me to my bed. If he was to do that, then he would have to knock me out with the strongest sedative that he had. After he finished checking me out I asked him, "Well doctor?"

"I'm going to let you go on the following conditions. If you start to feel sick you must leave immediately. Dr. Thompson will be watching you at all times, and after the service you are to come back here to the hospital no later then three o'clock."

I had them bring my black outfit yesterday because I had full intentions of walking out of this hospital today. They sent Dave and Sue with Kyle in the funeral limousine to pick me up from the hospital, since Dave was the doctor in charge of me while I was out of the hospital. Sue and I had become great friends over the years and it was now coming in handy since this was the time that I could use all my friends. The rest of the family would meet us at the funeral parlour. They escorted me to the limousine in a wheelchair; I never felt so helpless and old. This seemed to be the longest day of my life. I had given instructions that before the service I wanted one last look at Bill. I had to be sure that it was in fact him and not somebody's idea of a sick joke.

When we arrived at the funeral parlour we went into a room just off from where the service was going to be held. Sue left us and went into the other room where the service would be held. Kyle held me on the one side and Dave held me on the other side as we went up to the casket.

"Are you sure that you're ready for this?" Dave asked before we got to close to the casket.

"Yes, I have to see that it is him. I have to say my own good-byes to him," I replied looking at him.

As we stood next to the casket I saw the man that I loved, the man that had stood by me and who had believed in me and understood me. I started to cry aloud, finally the reality set in. Poor Kyle was crying at the sight of seeing his father in the casket, yet still trying to be strong for me. Dave took us into the other room while they closed the casket.

After the service we headed to the cemetery where we laid my poor Bill to rest. As we stood around the graveside, the wind blew briskly in our faces as though to dry our tears. The minister said his last words over Bill as they slowly lowered him into the ground. Under my breath I spoke my last words to him. "Farewell my love. Life will never be the same without you."

I did as the doctor ordered and headed back to the hospital to continue my recuperation.

Chapter Thirty-Nine

The road to recovery was a long one. They said that one day I would be fully recovered and that I should be patient since after all I had almost died twice in that one week. The truth of the matter was that half of me had died the first time. The love that Bill and I shared had joined us in so many ways that even in death we were still joined. I knew that maybe that is why I started to age. It seemed now that my appearance though it still mattered to me, didn't seem to be as important as it once had. When they finally allowed me out of the hospital I was confined to the grounds around my house. Eventually, they sent me to the island hoping that being close to nature would help me relax and in doing so my recuperation would be easier. Kyle was taking on more and more responsibility with the business which put my mind at ease, since I knew that he would be the person to carry on in the future. Though they would still consult me in major decisions affecting the business, Ben and Kyle now ran the business.

I had started to accept the fact that my life would never be the quick pace that I had been used to. My activities had to be chosen with my health in mind. My photography was the only thing that they weren't restricting me on. While up in the serenity of the north; the hustle of the city continued without me.

"Well, I guess that we don't have to worry about Stephanie anymore. It seems that episode with the plane did a pretty good job on her," he laughed as they lay in bed together.

"It's just too bad that she wasn't on the plane too," she replied with a look of disgust on her face.

"That was something that couldn't be helped. I don't think we will have to worry about her too much now."

"I wouldn't count her out yet. Remember she came back twice as strong the last time."

"But she never figured out who shot her either, just the way she won't find out what happened with that flight," he smiled and went back to their favorite pastime, slowly moving along her naked body with slow lingering kisses. "Let's drop this conversation." With that she responded by kissing him back as they slowly slid under the covers.

Maybe they were counting 'The Cat' out a little too soon. Although I had to be careful as to what I could do, I was still very much in the real world. I still had my investigator working for me and I was waiting on the report of the plane crash. When someone or something takes someone that I love away from me, you can count on it that I won't rest until they are found. I must also know all the facts, so that whoever did it pays dearly for crossing 'The Cat'. After all, I didn't get where I was in the legal circles without getting all the facts. I also learned never to leave a space open for error.

They might be enjoying their victory for the moment, but they should be making sure that the snow had covered their tracks.

I was beginning to work half days at the office as my strength was slowly returning to as close as it could be to being fully recuperated. Every day at the office when I looked at Kyle I saw Bill. He was becoming the spitting image of his father. In fact many times when I looked up, I almost called him Bill. His physique was better than his father's but his hair was his father's. Although he was born with my dark hair, as he grew his hair changed to the dirty blondish colouring just like his father's. He also had his high cheek bones, but most of all he had his father's eyes. Every time that he passed the girls in the office, their eyes would follow him until he was out of sight. I don't blame them since he was a great catch. He had good looks, a great personality and was next in line to take over this business empire. I wonder which lucky girl would catch his eye though. He was in the eyes of all the socially accepted young ladies, mingling with the lower class to royalty. He was accepted wherever he went. When I look at him I think what an excellent job that Bill and I did in raising him.

The report finally came from the airline's insurance investigation. I called Ben, Kyle and Sandy to join me in the office while we found out what they had discovered. I arranged that we were not to be disturbed and had coffee served. The head of our legal department was present so that if there was any foul play, I could find out our legal position and act upon it immediately.

Mr. Axley read the report as follows:

"After the black box of the plane was retrieved it was uncovered that minutes before the plane crashed, the crew in the cockpit was following normal procedures for the landing. However, in the autopsy it was found that the crew suffered from carbon dioxide poisoning which would account for the front end plane crashing into the cliff as it approached the runway."

"Mr. Axley, wouldn't the crew be able to put on oxygen masks in time to prevent the crash?" My lawyer mind was starting to work.

"They mentioned that just before the crash, the pilot radioed in that the crew was starting to feel tired, and that they were putting on the oxygen masks. We can only assume that the way that the carbon dioxide was dispersed into the cockpit, it must have been done so that it took effect before they could get the oxygen masks on. They mentioned on the last radio message that they thought that they could still land the plane."

"In other words Mr. Axley that plane was sabotaged. Somebody wanted it to crash," I replied to him as though I was back in the courtroom.

"Yes, that is what it looks like," he replied.

"Did they ever find out where the carbon dioxide came from? Was there anybody of great importance on that plane that somebody might have wanted dead?" I asked tapping a pen on my desk.

"They are still investigating that aspect of it. As far as anybody of great importance being on the plane, there was nobody of too much importance. The insurance company will be making settlements soon. I am sorry that I couldn't be of any more help."

"You were of a great help Mr. Axley. Please let us know as soon as they hear how that carbon dioxide was released into the cockpit. I'll be in touch with you." I stood up shaking his hand as I saw him out of the office and then went back to my desk.

"Mother what are you thinking about?" Kyle said with a look that Bill used to get so many times when I was about to do something dangerous.

"I'm thinking that the crash was not an accident. Ben, who knew that Bill and I were going away?" I asked with a suspicious look.

"Everybody in the firm and then if anybody called in they would be told that the two of you were leaving the country, but nobody knew your seats," Ben replied with a look as if he was trying to figure out where I was headed with my questioning.

"They could find out though if they checked with the airlines after we checked in." The lights were starting to go on in my head.

Everybody in the room thought that I was losing it. They thought that I had become preoccupied with the thought that somebody was out there to get me. I picked up the phone. "Teresa, could you get me Mr. Sam Batch on the phone?"

"Why do you think that someone did this to kill you and Bill?" Ben asked wondering if there was anything else he should know.

"Mrs. MacGregor, I have Mr. Sam Batch on line one," Teresa said over the intercom. "Thanks Teresa," I replied before I picked up the phone.

"Hi Sam. This is Stephanie MacGregor."

"How are you feeling? I'm sorry about your husband."

"I'm feeling much better, thanks for asking. Look I was wondering how your investigation was coming along?"

"It's coming together quite well. I think that you will be quite impressed when I see you."

"Well I've got some new information that I want you to check out. The plane that Bill was on was sabotaged. I want you to check and see if there is a link."

"Okay, I will check it out and get back to you later this week."

I hung up the phone and turned back to the three people in the room. "I guess that maybe Bill and I should have told you, but we figured out that we could handle things. Up to this point the attempts were just against me, though Bill tried to protect me, it didn't always work. He thought that I had put the investigation to rest, but I couldn't and we didn't have enough evidence to go to the police. We believe that if we kept it to ourselves that we could protect the others in our lives. I don't want any of this conversation repeated to anyone for it may put you in jeopardy."

"Can't you go to the police with your beliefs,

Stephanie?" Sandy was speaking up. "I mean if you had gone to them, then Bill might be alive today."

"No, even if we had gone to the police the people that we had in mind would still be out there, and they would still have killed Bill. We didn't have enough evidence to hold them."

"Then, there was more than one person involved," Kyle spoke up.

"Yes, that much we do know."

"But why?" Kyle asked.

"Your father was killed because he was the most important thing in my life. Getting to where I am today I have stepped on a few people's feet and those people want to hurt me." I stood up and walked over to the window. "Now you can see why none of you can seem to know what is going on. If they catch on that you know anything, your lives will be over."

They all left except for Kyle. He walked over to me. "Mother, are you okay?"

"Yes, I'll be okay, once I do what has to be done."

"They might try for me next, won't they?" he looked down at me with a worried look on his face.

"Yes, they might but you will just have to be careful. I am not as worried about you though son. You seem to have my knack for fouling their plans," I said as I held him in my arms, but I still had a worried look on my face.

"Then what are you worried about?" He stepped back looking at me with his father's eyes.

"I can't figure out where or how they are going to strike, but I will." I looked up at him with my cat eyes flashing.

"I don't know what you are up to, but I wouldn't want to be on the receiving end of it."

Chapter Forty

As Kyle had now joined the business, positions were also offered to Sandy's, Ben's and Bridgette's children as they came out of school, so that no matter what happened this would always be a family business. The highest positions were reserved for Kyle and Ben's son Jason. The others would be offered positions of equal importance. With our offspring taking over in the offices, Ben and I were allowed more recreational time and we reserved the right to wine and dine the customers, allowing Kyle and Jason to join us occasionally.

Sam arranged a meeting so that we could discuss the investigation. Kyle found out about my meeting with him and requested to be there with me. I felt it would be better if I went to meeting alone.

"If you won't let me be there, then at least be careful this time."

"Don't worry. You're getting more and more like your father everyday." I kissed him on the cheek and left the office for home where I was to meet Sam.

As Sam and I sat over some tea, we discussed the information that he had for me. He opened his briefcase in which there were documents galore. He removed the first two file folders, one was headed up Tom Brennan and the other one was Deborah-Anne Burnaby. As he handed them to me he said, "We've got them."

I opened Deborah-Anne's folder first. He had started the investigation from her parents, but there he disagreed with Ed. Sam had found out that her father wasn't Uncle Pat or even my father, but a banker friend of theirs.

"Are you sure about this part about Deborah-Anne's father?" I asked him in alarm as I held the documents out in front of me.

"Positive, her blood type doesn't even match. She couldn't be Patrick's or James's. It was well known that Elizabeth was in love with Gerald O'Brien before she married Patrick. The only reason that the marriage never came to be, was because her family wanted her to marry into a well to do family and that happened to be Patrick's."

"But after she married Patrick didn't she forget about Gerald?"

"She led everyone to think that she had. Actually, that's when her affair with James came in. She knew that James and your mother were having problems and she took full advantage of it. She used to use James as her cover when she was seeing Gerald. Oh she was smart, she still slept with Patrick and when she told James that she was pregnant he smartened up and went back to your mother. Elizabeth had to make it look good, so she passed Deborah-Anne off as Patrick's. The fact that she hadn't stopped sleeping with him meant that there would be no reason for anybody to doubt that the child was his."

"What about Gerald?"

"He accepted the fact that Deborah-Anne was Patrick's. She was still seeing Gerald when you moved into the mansion."

I continued to read the information. "She married Dr. Michael Burnaby. She also shares an apartment with one Tom Brennan. They meet routinely on a different day each week and for longer periods when her husband Michael is away at conventions. Her husband only knows

Tom as a social friend from the functions that they attend. It has been long known by friends that she didn't like anybody that would interfere with her standing in the social world. Finally, it was well known around the mansion that she had a grudge against her cousin Stephanie McConnell."

Then I opened Tom's file, starting with his parent's Tom and Brenda Brennan, boyfriend of Stephanie McConnell through High school until their early twenties during which time he was also her photographer while she modeled. The night she broke off with him he left her at Look Out Point where she would later be hit by a hit and run driver. He left for Montreal to do photography where he met his present wife Monique. His photography became world known and he started to cover social affairs. He became known as one of the jet set photographers and very seldom did his wife accompany him. He owns an apartment jointly with Deborah-Anne, which his wife has no idea of. He stays there when he is in town and is joined there by Deborah-Anne at least once a week, sometimes more. He owns a very high powered rifle and to this day still possesses it. When Ed's apartment was torched Tom was in town, although he was supposed to be in Chicago. The day of the plane crash both Deborah-Anne and Tom were seen at the airport. She was identified by the ticket clerk that had booked you in.

I finished reading the file and started to look through the pictures that he had taken. Now I know why so many lawyers and even the police use this guy. God he was thorough. His photography wasn't the quality that Tom or I shot, but they served the purpose. The first couple pictures were of Tom and Deborah-Anne getting into some pretty heavy lovemaking. He made sure to get their faces in the pictures. There was one of Deborah-Anne holding some sort of papers in her hands. The papers had red spots on them. I held that in my hand while I looked at another picture that was of Tom apparently holding a picture that he had just developed. In the picture Tom had fresh nail marks on his neck.

Holding the two pictures in my hand I looked up at Sam. "I need these enlarged can I get the negatives from you tonight?"

"Sure, no problem with that."

"You did a great job Sam. You were right we have enough to make them wish they'd never met me." There was a gleam in my eye.

"I'll be back with the negatives," Sam said as he went toward the door.

If that one picture that showed Tom had taken pictures of Dave comforting me that night, then I might be a step ahead of them. Calling Dave up on the phone I asked him and Sue over for dinner. If what I thought Tom was up to was showing the pictures to Sue then I would have to tell Sue first. I would also have to explain my beliefs that I was going to present to the police. The repercussions of what was forming could destroy a lot of lives that I cared for.

Sam dropped off the negatives on his way home. I took them down to my darkroom in the basement where I started to enlarge them, first into an eight by ten and then a sixteen by twenty-four. I must have what they are holding large enough to see what it was. Dave and Sue came while I was still developing the enlargements and Kyle came in shortly after.

"Where's Mother?" Kyle posed the question to Dave.

"Maria says that she is down in the darkroom," he replied.

"And she left you here. I must have a word with her about proper etiquette," Kyle said as he laughed. "Would you like a drink while we are waiting or shall we intrude on her private domain?" he joked.

"Maria seemed to think that she wouldn't be too long," Dave replied.

"You have to be kidding. When she gets into that room, she forgets that the rest of the world exists. I better go knock on her door," Kyle said as he turned to head for the stairs that led to the basement. Just as he approached the doorway I came through the door.

"Dave and Sue I'm so glad that you could make it. I see that Kyle took care of you while you waited," I said as I came through the doorway with the pictures in one hand. "I'm sorry that I've kept you waiting."

"Kyle has been the perfect host," Dave said with a smile on his face.

"Yes, someday he will make some girl a wonderful husband." Sue added, looking toward Kyle with a large smile.

We sat and talked till Maria announced that dinner was ready. Into the dinning room we went and enjoyed the lovely meal that was set on the table. When we finished the main meal, Maria brought in a chocolate mousse for dessert. We then took our tea into the family room to talk and relax after dinner.

As we sat down I started to talk, "Sue you and I have become close friends over the years. I trust you the way that I would trust a sister. For that reason, I have something to tell you and I pray that trust will keep us friends." Everybody was trying to figure out what was going on. "You know that I loved Bill more than life itself. We had a marriage like yours with Dave. We had such a strong relationship that when he died part of me died too. I also know that because of the trust that the four of us shared..." I stopped I looked at Sue and then to Dave and then back to Sue again.

"Stephanie what is this all about?" Dave said in a worried tone of voice.

"Remember the weekend that we all were meeting up at the cottage. Dave was picking me up after Tom had finished the article for the magazine and we were late arriving at the cottage. When Dave arrived I was fighting Tom off. He thought that things hadn't changed between him and I. He tore my blouse off me and when Dave arrived I had managed to break free. As Tom left he called me some pretty strong names. Dave, being the gentleman that he is, made sure that he left by throwing him out using his fist. He wanted me to call the police. I refused because I knew that Bill would kill Tom. Afterwards, Dave held me in his arms to comfort me. What we didn't realize was that Tom ran to his car for his camera. He shot some pretty good shots, and although everything was quite innocent the shots may look otherwise."

"Why are you bringing this up now Stephanie? Sue asked. "You were right I do trust you and Dave together because of the love that each of us has for our spouses. But I don't understand why you're bring up the past now."

"The reason is these pictures may surface soon either by being sent to you or to somebody else. After that incident, I hired a private investigator to investigate Tom. Bill had always thought that he had something to do with my accidents, but it couldn't be proven. After this happened I needed to know whether or not he was capable of it. The private investigator turned in a very interesting file on Tom with some interesting pictures. I'm going to request that police re-open the file on my shooting and on Bill's death."

"Could we see the pictures that you have here?" Dave requested.

"Sure." I went over to the table where I had placed the pictures that I had just enlarged, picking them up I handed them to Dave.

"Stephanie, this one is of Deborah-Anne," he exclaimed with a shocked look even though he knew that they were sleeping together.

"That's right. Do you see what she's holding in her hand?" I looked at him directly.

"The copy of your Grandfather's will. That is what went missing from the hospital when you were shot," he exclaimed as Sue looked stunned. "Do you mean that she's been in on it all this time?"

"It sure appears that way. Now do the two of you understand why I had to tell you and to show you these things before I go to the police?" Dave had given the pictures to Sue. "You see if Tom doesn't use them, they might just come out in court."

"I'm glad that you showed them to us. Now we can be prepared and after what you have just told me, you can count on the two of us to be by your side," Sue said as she got up and handed the pictures back to me. As I stood up to take them back to the table Sue gave me a hug. "It's just too bad we couldn't have done this before Bill got killed."

"Hopefully, this will save somebody else from getting hurt or even killed," I said.

"What about Stuart and your Aunt Elizabeth. You know it's going to devastate them when they hear about it," Dave questioned.

"I hope that the love Stuart and I share will help him understand why I have to do this once I show him the facts. Aunt Elizabeth, well I'm not sure about her," I said with doubt in my voice.

"When are you going to the police?" Kyle spoke up.

"I'll be going tomorrow. The sooner we get it over with the better."

"Then I'm going with you," Kyle spoke up in a demanding voice.

"No, I can do this myself," I said.

Sue and Dave both spoke up. "I think that you should have Kyle with you," they both said at the same time.

It was settled that Kyle would join me at the police station.

Chapter Forty-One

We went to the police station requesting to speak with Officer Brooks who was in charge of my case when I got shot. After viewing the files that I presented him, he agreed that we had enough information to reopen the files. He would have to show the files to the crown attorney's office showing that they had just cause to reopen the case, and then to have a search warrant issued to check out Tom's apartment. Though we had given the original files to Officer Brooks, I ran a copy of them so that I could show them to Stuart after we left the police.

Maybe I should have gone to him first, I don't know. I did know that no matter what he thought, the files were going to the police. I dropped Kyle off at the office and headed over to Stuart's office to show him the files. As I walked into his office, I hoped that I was as sure of myself now as I was earlier in the police station.

"Stephanie, to what do I owe to have this visit?" he said as he came over and greeted me with a kiss on the cheek.

"I hope that you will still be in this good of a mood toward me by the time that I am through here."

"It sounds serious." He made a motion of his hand directing me to the chair in front of his desk.

"Stuart, I have just come from the police station. I am asking them to reopen the case of my shooting," I said cautiously.

"Why? I thought that they closed it saying that it was some crackpot shooting at you." He gave a little chuckle.

"That's right. However, I have reason to believe that the crackpot was Tom Brennan," I said not changing my facial expression.

"What would make you think that?" he asked as he massaged his hands. I proceeded to tell him about the night that Tom tried to attack me. I then pulled out my briefcase with the two files in it.

"After that night I hired Sam Batch, I'm sure that you know him."

"Yes, I've used him on several cases. He's one of the best, he's very thorough in his work."

"That is why I hired him to check Tom out," I said hesitantly.

"He must have come up with something or you wouldn't have gone to the police."

"That is why I am here. It wasn't just him that's involved." I hesitated again.

"What do you mean? He had help?" He sat up in his chair. "Who is the other person or should I say persons?"

"Deborah-Anne," I replied.

"Deborah-Anne, you have to be kidding. I know that she's always had it in for you but to have you shot." He was shocked at the thought and the accusation that his sister was involved.

"I knew that you would have a hard time accepting that what I say is true so I brought you a copy of the files that I turned over to the police. You know Stuart, that before I go into a courtroom that I make damn sure that I have a case that is going to stick, and that I have left no stone unturned. I hope that you will read these files before you pass judgment on me."

"You aren't kidding are you?" He took the files from me.

"I wish I were especially when it comes to Deborah-Anne. We may not have got along but I never wanted this to happen. This could tear apart the family that I grew up with and that I love." I had a sad look on my face as I looked down at the files that were in his hands.

"You know that if this comes out that it might kill Mother?" He was getting angry from the shock and the thought of the repercussions.

"I pray to God that it doesn't come to that. That is why I've given you the files so that at least you will know what might become public knowledge. Stuart please read the files first then let me know where you stand," I said almost with a plea in my voice.

"You know Stephanie that although I don't like what you are saying, I am a good enough lawyer to view the facts before judging the situation," he said with a disappointed look on his face.

"That's all that I can ask. I just hope that you understand and agree with me after you have read the facts."

"I will give you a call once I finish reading the files," he said looking sadly at the files.

"Thanks Stuart." I stood up from my chair. "I really am sorry that this had to happen."

"That much I know; you would never do anything to purposely hurt my family."

I left his office and headed for home. Now I would have to wait for Tom to make his next move, or for the police to make theirs.

Chapter Forty-Two

Stuart though he didn't want to admit it had to agree that the facts that were presented did in fact implicate his sister or half-sister as the files had put it. He wanted to tell his mother so that he could prepare her for the ultimate outcome, but I had to advise him not to.

"If you tell your mother, she in turn will tip off Deborah-Anne, who in turn will tip off Tom. I am sorry I know that you are trying to protect your mother, but you can see that I am right," I said to him as I put my hands on his shoulders.

"As a lawyer I know that you are right, but if I don't tell her when she hears it then she'll die for sure," he said raising his voice.

"I know that if there were any other way that I would take it." I pleaded with him.

He had been in the courts long enough to know that I was right. Though it seemed cruel, that was just the way it had to be. We would just have to wait until something happened.

The police proceeded to Tom's apartment with a search warrant in hand. They couldn't have had better timing if they had tried. They knocked at the door, nobody seemed to answer so they banged on the door again. Finally, they heard movement from inside the apartment. Tom opened the door just a crack keeping the safety catch on.

"Yeah, what do you want?" he asked in a not so

polite tone.

"Police, Mr. Brennan we have a search warrant. Would you please open the door?" Officer Brooks replied.

Tom clothed in a housecoat fumbled with the safety catch as he opened the door. "What's this about officer?" he inquired.

"Just a routine check. We had a tip that we didn't believe, but you know how it is we have to check things out. You don't mind if we look around do you?"

"No, I don't mind, I have nothing to hide. Look around but you did catch me at an inopportune time, I was busy if you know what I mean." He nodded to the bedroom door.

"We'll only be a moment, we are sorry to disturb you," Officer Brook said with a smile on his face. He directed the officers with his hands. "Do be careful after all Mr. Brennan's cameras are very expensive."

The officers went slowly through the closets and through the drawers of the dressers. Then two officers headed toward the bedroom. Tom turned to officer Brooks. "I told you that I wasn't alone. You can't let them go barging in there," he shouted at Officer Brooks.

"Oh, I can but if you want you can go in with them and watch what they touch."

Tom ran to open the door before the police. "Tom what's going on?" Deborah-Anne asked partially clad by the blankets.

"The police are searching for something. I don't know what though. Just stay where you are, I'm sure that they will be gone momentarily," Tom said to Deborah-Anne, trying to reassure her as he sat on the bed that everything was okay.

As the officer that went through the closet pulled down a box, Tom sat on the bed trying to look quite calm. The officer opened the box and inside there were photographs that he sifted through. Then putting the lid back on the box he took it out to Officer Brooks. The other officer continued to search the bedroom. He opened a cedar chest that was in the corner of the room. He removed the blankets that were in the chest, so that he could take a closer look at the bottom of the chest. Tom watched him carefully.

"Officer Brooks, could you come here for a minute please?" the officer called out. Deborah-Anne's face was turning white.

"What have you found?" Officer Brooks answered.

"Take a look at this." The officer was pointing to the bottom of the chest.

Deborah-Anne turned to look at Tom, but his eyes weren't moving from the officers.

"Can you open it?"

"I'm trying. Bingo, look what we have here," the officer said as he removed a high powered rifle from out of the chest.

Officer Brooks turned to Tom. "Mr. Brennan we are charging you with the attempted murder of Stephanie MacGregor. You have the right to retain legal council. You have the right to remain silent. Anything you say will be used in a court of law against you. Do you understand the charges that you have been charged with Mr. Brennan?"

"Yes, I understand." said Tom gruffly.

As the officer put the handcuffs on Tom he asked, "Do you wish to waive the right to council?"

"No, I'm not saying another word until I see my lawyer," he replied as he looked at Deborah-Anne who sat in a state of shock.

"Miss, I would advise you to get dressed, the party's over."

They took Tom down to the police station dressed only in his housecoat and booked him on attempted murder. His lawyer did a great job of getting him off on bail. However, not as quickly as the newspapers that had headlines like "World Wide Photographer charged in Attempted Murder of The Cat." They showed pictures of the police escorting Tom clad in his housecoat with a shocked Deborah-Anne in the background. The other headlines read, "Police Reopen the Case of the Shooting of The Cat With the Arrest of Ex-boyfriend."

Well, it finally broke. Kyle rushed home from the office to confirm that I was okay. I assured him that I was and that I knew that this was only the beginning. The next few days there were new headlines like "Photographer and Girlfriend Questioned in Plane Crash" underneath was a picture of Tom and one of Deborah-Anne. I was sitting over my morning tea as I read the headlines. Putting my cup down I sighed to myself that this was just the beginning of what could turn out to be a very messy court case. As I was deep in thought about the article the phone rang and Kyle came into the room. "It's Stuart on the phone for you."

I took the call in the family room. It was a call that I had half expected.

"Hi Stuart, I take it that you have seen the morning newspaper," I said in a bland voice.

"Yes, I have seen it. You know of course when this goes to trial that it's going to get messy. The newspapers are going to have a field day with it."

"Yes, I know that. How is your mother holding out?"

"Not too bad, yet," he replied, but there was doubt in his voice.

"I was going over there to see her this morning, maybe I can smooth things over."

"Maybe, but maybe it will make matters worse. I know that you two have become close, but you have to remember that Deborah-Anne is her daughter," he said with caution.

"I know but I still want to try. What about the rest of your family? How are Michelle and the children taking the news?"

"They are completely flabbergasted. The girls are shocked (he now had two daughters, Erica and Shauna and a son Craig) they can't believe that their Aunt is capable of such things. Craig says that he can understand it although he never was close to his Aunt. Hey, the question is, are you going to be able to stand up to the questioning counselor?"

"Remember counselor that the courtroom is like a second home to me. I will be okay. Look if you would like I can call you after I'm through seeing your mother."

"Yes do that. I would like to know how you make out."

I went over to see Aunt Elizabeth. I knew that she had the right to be prepared for what was soon to be public knowledge through the trial of her daughter. This part was going to be hard, for I didn't want to hurt her. I figured that she had paid enough for her past. We had posted security around our homes so that at least we could have some privacy from the press. I had just checked through the gates at the end of the long driveway. It didn't seem to matter how many times you made the trip, it never seemed to get shorter. Parking my car I went into the house calling out to Anna. As she approached I asked her, "Anna where is my Aunt?"

"She is in the family room." she said with a smile.

"Could you prepare a pot of tea for the two of us and serve it to us in there, please." I requested as I headed toward the family room.

When I came through the doorway I found Aunt Elizabeth. She was now a feeble old woman; her looks had long gone from her. She was sitting in her chair with the morning newspaper in her lap. She had to wear thick glasses and I often wondered whether she could actually see. As I approached she looked up to see who was coming into the room.

"Aunt Elizabeth, how are you feeling today?" I said trying to ignore the newspaper on her lap. "I've asked Anna to make us a pot of tea."

"Stephanie, I take it that you have read the newspaper?" she asked in a scratchy sad voice and as she spoke she motioned to the newspaper.

"I have and I am very sorry if it hurts you. Deborah-Anne is a big girl and knew what she was getting into. I am sorry that her actions and the fact that her actions will be publicized are going to embarrass the family," I said with compassion in my voice. As I said it, I took her hand in mine and looked into her eyes. "You do believe me don't you?"

"Stephanie when you first came into our house, I knew then that you wouldn't rest until you found out about your background. I knew that people would get hurt. Yet over the years, since Patrick died, you have become like a daughter to me. You and Stuart visit and check up on me. Deborah-Anne, although we gave her the best in the world, has never cared for me the way that the two of you have." She was slow about her words now. Anna had just served tea.

"However, Stephanie you being a mother know that no matter what your child has done, as a mother you will stand by them."

"I know that and I wouldn't have thought that it could be any other way. Though there are some things that I think that you should know."

"What's that Stephanie?" she said with saddened eyes.

"Stuart and I both wanted to spare you the shock of the news. However, because of the fact that you would have tipped Tom and Deborah-Anne off to the police, we couldn't. Aunt Elizabeth I want you to know that during the investigation it was found out that Deborah-Anne's father wasn't Uncle Pat. I'm afraid that it may come out in court. I'm going to try to have it omitted, but the fact that it gave Deborah-Anne motive I doubt that they will go for it. I really am sorry."

"Oh my God! Does Stuart know about this?" she asked with a shocked face.

"I'm afraid that he does."

"All my errors in life are coming back to haunt me. If they do bring it out in the trial do they have to say who the father was?" she said as she held her head in the palm of her hands.

"That much I think I can arrange to have kept out of the trial." I tried to give her some hope. "I know that it's hard but maybe we should change the subject, it might help."

I spent the rest of the day with Aunt Elizabeth. We talked about anything but what happened in the news. When I left she seemed to be in a better frame of mind. Upon arriving home I called Stuart and advised him on how his mother was taking the news.

On the Sunday after my visit I received a phone call about six in the morning. I knew that it couldn't be good news because nobody in their right mind would ever phone me at that time in the morning on a Sunday. I reached for the phone and slowly answered. There was a tearful voice on the other end.

"Stephanie, Mother just died." Stuart was sobbing on the phone.

"When did it happen? Where are you?" The questions came quick.

"She just died about an hour ago, the doctor just left. I'm at the mansion right now."

"I'll be right over Stuart." I hung up the phone and woke Kyle up. "I'm on my way to the mansion. Aunt Elizabeth has just died."

Kyle still groggy from being woken up from a deep sleep, called to me. "Wait Mother I'll get dressed and come with you," but by the time that he got out of the bed he heard the engine of my car pulling out of the garage. "Damn it Mother you're headed right into a battlefield with Deborah-Anne," he yelled at me.

When I pulled into the parking spot there were Stuart's, Deborah-Anne's and Craig's cars in the spaces. Finally, it struck me what might happen. I walked in just the same since this was my house. Anna greeted me as I came through the doorway.

"Would you like some tea, Stephanie?" she asked.

"Yes, thank you Anna."

I proceeded through the hallways to the family room. There was Michelle, Stuart and his family in one area and then there was Deborah-Anne at the other end of the room all by herself. Heading directly over to Stuart I put my arms around him, giving him a kiss on the cheek and then I proceeded to Michelle following the same routine with her.

"Is there anything that I can do for you?" I posed the question to Stuart.

The sound of my voice seemed to travel directly to Deborah-Anne's ears and in a matter of minutes I felt my shoulder being pulled back. "What the hell are you doing here, haven't you done enough, or did you come to reclaim the mansion since the old lady is dead."

"Deborah-Anne," Stuart started to shout.

"Stuart let her be. I'll handle Deborah-Anne," I said with sternness coming into my voice. "Deborah-Anne it is out of respect and love for your mother who you referred to as the 'old lady' that I am here. You may not like it, but I am here to help. As far as the mansion goes, it will be here for a long time to come. As far as gloating goes, I have nothing to gloat about. What happened to you is your own doing. Now if you don't mind, there are things to be done." After I finished I just walked away, taking a cup of tea from Anna. I walked out of the room just as Deborah-Anne's husband Michael walked in.

He went into the family room, straight past his wife and over to Stuart. They hugged and consoled each other. With an angry look on her face Deborah-Anne just watched. Then came Dave and Sue, with their oldest daughter Monica. Once again they went over to Stuart's family; Deborah-Anne was being totally isolated. Michael took his cup and walked out of the room and into the dining area where I was sitting.

"Stephanie, how are you holding up?" he said to me.

"I'm not too bad. I'm sorry about how things are happening right now. I didn't think that you would want to talk to me."

"I should actually be thanking you. You opened my eyes with regards to a lot of things. I'm filing for divorce and if Deborah-Anne is smart she won't contest it."

"I'm sorry to hear that."

"Don't be, we haven't been man and wife in I don't know how many years. Now with her affair out in the open, I can't see putting the charade on any longer."

"I guess I should go back in the other room and see if I can do anything. Keep in touch Michael."

"Yes, I don't know whether you will stay in there for long, Deborah-Anne's still in there."

"She doesn't bother me," I said and then I proceeded to go into the other room.

Sue came over and greeted me with her daughter. Dave who had been talking to Stuart came over and joined us a little later.

"Has anybody even talked to Deborah-Anne?" Sue asked as she looked over in Deborah-Anne's direction.

"You might say that I talked to her, but it was only after she verbally attacked me."

"You two didn't have a cat fight now did you?" Dave asked.

"No, I just pointed out why we were here," I said flashing my eyes. "You can ask Stuart, I was a perfect lady." I looked over at Deborah-Anne. She was sitting and sobbing by herself. "You know I really do feel sorry for her. You know that Michael won't even talk to her. He just told me that he's filing for divorce."

"You're kidding, aren't you." Sue piped in as she also looked over in Deborah-Anne's direction.

"If you excuse me, I am going over to Stuart for just a moment."

I walked across the room to where he was standing with his family. "Stuart don't you think that maybe you should try to console Deborah-Anne. I would, but I don't think that she would let me near her," I said motioning in her direction.

"How can you think of her right now after what she has done?"

"It doesn't matter right now. She is part of the family and she is hurting. She is the only one that has nobody, even Michael won't talk to her. Please Stuart won't you please go over to her?"

"Yes, I guess I should. I really don't understand you." I gave him a reassuring look that he was doing the right thing. He left us and went over to try and console his sister.

Chapter Forty-Three

Timing is a marvelous thing if one can master it or if it is handed to you on a silver tray. The trial date was set for several months down the road from Aunt Elizabeth's funeral giving us time to mourn her death and get on with things. Kyle's twenty-fifth birthday was coming up and with that I planned a surprise party out at the mansion for him. No one lived at the mansion at present, although I did keep Anna on to manage the house. The stables were still stocked with horses so that meant that the grooms and stable hands were also still employed.

I planned it for a Friday night with all his friends from school and the office. I also invited Stuart, Michelle and their three children who of course brought their dates and spouses along. Sue and Dave came along with their children (they had three girls and one son). Their oldest Monica who was starting to show that she was pregnant was here with her husband Robert. The second daughter Shelly came with her new husband Richard, and then there was their son Mark and their other daughter Sabrina. Ben, Andrea and their son Jason along with his wife Jillian were amongst the crowd that had gathered. Now it was a matter of getting the birthday boy there. I sent Jason out to the stables to retrieve his cousin from his favorite spot.

Jason left and in a short time returned with his cousin. As they came through the doorway, the crowd yelled out "Surprise" and from that moment on the party rocked. Dave walked over to where I was standing.

"You did a great job as usual Cat."

"Dave I hadn't realized that your daughter Sabrina had turned into such an attractive lady. It seemed like every time we ever visited your place that she was always somewhere else." I looked over toward Dave's daughter. She was very attractive with a lovely shaped body, long blonde hair and with eyes that sparkled.

"You might say that we did a pretty good job with our children. Your son has great looks, great personality and if I'm not mistaken, he is one of the most eligible bachelors around." Dave laughed.

Kyle was mingling with the guests, and for some this was a great way of getting to know the boss. Jesse was a striking brunette from the office, a nice catch for any of the guys, but the only one that she was attracted to was Kyle. She was on her way over to Kyle to ask him for a dance when Sabrina appeared before Kyle.

"Happy Birthday, Kyle," Sabrina said to him.

"Thanks," he replied but you could see from his expression that he didn't recognize the girl. "Excuse me, but you do seem to have me at a disadvantage."

"That's amazing Kyle is at a disadvantage with a girl," Jason remarked as he slapped Kyle on the back.

"Now, it has been along time since we met, but has it really been that long that you don't remember me. I used to go to all of your equestrian meets." She was playing with him, enticing with those eyes.

"You've still got me. I'm sure that if I saw you there that I would remember you."

"Of course, that was such a long time ago," she yawned. "Oh there's Monica and Robert, I'll catch you later," she said and then turned away to join her sister.

"Kyle, could I have this dance?" Jesse was saying. She had moved up beside him while Sabrina was playing her game.

"Of course Jesse," he replied, but as they danced his eyes caught those of Sabrina's at the other end of the room. Sabrina left the room to go outside and catch a bit of fresh air. Tim one of Kyle's friends followed her out.

"You know you really had Kyle going in there," he said coming up behind her.

"That's good, they say that girls should keep guys guessing," she said as she flashed her eyes that sparkled in the moonlight.

"My name is Tim O'Brien. Do you think that I might have the honour of knowing you name? Or is it to be a secret to all men at this party?" He tried to coax an answer out of her.

"My name isn't a secret and if Kyle thinks of it long enough, he will remember it." She shook her head making her blonde hair move like a river of gold in the moonlight.

"Her name is Sabrina, Tim." Kyle stood behind him. "You haven't lost your touch for being a tease, have you?" He walked over to her.

"No, in fact I think I got a little better with age, don't you think?" She tilted her head back and looking up at him she blinked her eyes at him.

"I must admit you have grown more beautiful with time. Where have you been these last few years anyway?"

"Oh, I was traveling. Father said that I should do it now so that I can get that restlessness out of me," she laughed.

"And did it work or have you still got some of the restlessness left?" He stood beside her with his hands on the cement wall of the flower pot; his head tilted looking down at her.

"Why don't we take a moonlit stroll and see," her eyes lit up as she looked back at him.

"What about the party?" he inquired as they started to walk.

"They will be there when we get back."

They left for their walk leaving the party going full tilt. Tim watched as they vanished behind the hedges. He was by himself but it didn't take him long before he and Jesse struck up an interesting conversation. Soon they were dancing and having a great time and in a little time they found that they were better suited to each other and soon forgot all about Kyle and Sabrina.

Meanwhile, Kyle was walking with Sabrina, his arms around her shoulder catching up on all the time that had passed.

"I wondered what happened to you. It seemed like you just vanished in thin air."

"I thought that I would just take advantage of my father's offer while it was still being offered. I'm sorry to hear about you father. I heard that you were hurt too." She had stopped walking and was looking at Kyle.

"Yes, and you weren't there to make it better." He looked down at her.

"I'm here now." She looked at him as he bent down and kissed her lips.

"You don't know how much I missed you. They couldn't have given me a nicer birthday gift than to have you come back to me." He looked down into her eyes.

"This isn't your birthday gift, this is." She held a small package in her hand. "I've had it for years wondering what to do with it." He opened the small package. Inside he found a shiny horseshoe with the inscription 'to KMcG h.25TH B Luv S.T.' "Do you remember this?"

"How could I forget it? My horse threw his shoe; you picked it up and tried to make a ringer around my leg, by throwing it from behind the bush. You had such a terrible shot that you got me in the head. Seeing what you had done you ran over and tried to kiss it better. That was the first time that we ever kissed." Holding the horseshoe in his hand he smiled at her and then gave her a long kiss. "Thanks for the gift and thanks for coming back," he whispered in her ear.

"Shall we go back to your party now?" she asked looking him in the eye.

"I don't want to but I know that we should." He took her by the hand and they headed back to the house. When they arrived back the lights went out. "Somebody has the right thing in mind." As he looked up from Sabrina he saw Anna coming through the doorway with a cake blazing with candles, everybody in the room was singing Happy Birthday to him. He went over and blew out the candles.

"I hope that you made a good wish son," I said to him.

"I'll let you know next year Mother," he said with a smile on his face and then he turned to look at Sabrina.

The party continued till way after four in the morning with some of the people still being there the next morning. Kyle was up early and gone before anybody seem to know that he was gone. This seemed to be his pattern for the future, up early in the morning and off to the office and back late in the evening. Dave and Sue said the same thing about their daughter Sabrina. On weekends you would be lucky if you caught sight of either one of them.

Chapter Forty-Four

Tom had been charged with the attempted murder on me, the murder of Bill and the sabotage of the flight that he had been on. Deborah-Anne was charged with being an accessory in both cases. Through the whole mess they both lost their spouses in divorce. Tom although he was still a great photographer, had his reputation tarnished and nobody would hire him again even if he did manage to beat the case against him.

It was a dragged out situation with people being put on the stand examined for hours and then cross examined for several more hours. After each week of the trial, I would head to the island either alone or with Stuart or Dave and their families. We all looked for some peace and quietness from the dragged out affairs of the week, and we could always find that up there.

Mondays always found us back in court. This Monday they had called Deborah-Anne to the stand. Mr. Lamonde was the lawyer for the crown and was now in the process of cross-examining her.

"Do you know Mrs. Stephanie MacGregor?"

"Yes," Deborah-Anne replied.

"What is your relationship to her?"

"She is my cousin."

"Would you tell the court what kind of relationship that the two of you have?"

"It was like any cousin relationship."

"Is it not true that you despised your cousin? That you actually hated her?"

"I object your honour the crown's questioning is

based purely on hearsay," the defense lawyer spoke up.

"Let me rephrase the question. Were the two of you close?"

"We were family but I didn't love her."

"What about Tom Brennan, did you know him?"

"Yes, I know him as a photographer. He used to go out with Stephanie."

"Wasn't he more than that to you?"

"No."

"Wasn't he in fact your lover?"

"No."

"I'll remind you that you are under oath. Were you not in his apartment when they arrested Mr. Tom Brennan?"

"Yes."

"Then I will repeat my question. Was he not your lover?"

"Okay, yes he was my lover," Deborah-Anne replied starting to get a little bit flustered under the questioning.

"Isn't it also true that the two of you conspired to kill Stephanie MacGregor, because she was investigating your family's past and she would uncover the fact that you were having an affair?"

"No."

"And the fact that she also had full claim to the mansion that you lived in all of your life?"

"No."

"And the last fact that you didn't want her to find out was that Patrick McConnell wasn't really your father, and for that you convinced Tom to kill Stephanie MacGregor."

"I told her that her curiosity would get her killed. She had no right snooping where she didn't belong."

"How did you plan on having her killed?"

"I didn't."

"Isn't it true that you were going to have Mr. Brennan shoot her?"

"No, he was going to do that anyway, just as long as he got rid of her." Deborah-Anne didn't realize what she had just said, but she had now given the court enough information for a conviction.

"What about on the day that Stephanie and Bill MacGregor were leaving for England, were you not also at the airport?"

"Yes."

"What was the reason for you being there at the same time that they were? Wasn't it in fact to check out where they were going to sit on the plane?"

"So what if it was?"

"Why was it so important to know where they would be sitting?"

"Tom needed to know if they would be at the front or not."

"Why was that so important to Tom?"

"He needed to be sure that they would die in the crash." They allowed her to sit down and then they brought Tom up on the stand. Their lawyers had tried for separate trials, but the crown had stood their ground saying that both cases could not be separated and therefore should be heard together.

"Mr. Tom Brennan, could you tell us about your relationship with Mrs. Stephanie MacGregor?"

"We were high school lovers and later I was her photographer when she was a model."

"When she broke off your relationship, how did you feel then?"

"I felt crushed, I couldn't understand why."

"Isn't it true that you never really forgave her? That you always thought that the two of you would get back together."

"No."

"Are you sure Mr. Brennan? Wasn't your marriage to your wife just a cover up?"

"No."

"Wasn't your affair with her cousin Deborah-Anne to keep in touch with Stephanie?"

"No."

"When Deborah-Anne asked you to kill her, you purposely missed so that you still could have Deborah-Anne and be close to Stephanie, isn't that the way it was?"

"No."

"Isn't it true that you are a perfect marksman?"

"Yes."

"Then why else would you miss on that day other than the fact that you didn't want her dead?"

"Of course I didn't want her dead. I loved her," Tom said as he raised his voice.

"Bastard!" Deborah-Anne yelled as she stood up and tried to get at Tom. "You're nothing but a bastard." The guards came in to restrain her.

"Order, Order, there will be no further outbursts in this court," the judge commanded.

"Then why did you want to kill her on the plane?"

"I didn't. I knew that she wouldn't get on the plane, her son was injured."

"How did you know that?"

"I made sure that he was."

"Then in fact you were trying to kill her husband Bill."

"Yes, if I could get rid of him then maybe I could get her back."

The court was adjourned after the judge finally calmed the court room down from the evidence that had just been heard. With this evidence a verdict wouldn't take too long. Out in the hallway everyone was talking about what had just happened in the courtroom. Just how far was Tom willing to go to get me back? Would he have killed everyone that was close to me? I sat devastated that I hadn't perceived him as a threat before now. Kyle came over to me, putting his arm around me. "Are you okay, Mother?"

"Yes, I will be okay. I just can't believe that he went that far thinking that he could get me back." I looked at him with a shocked expression. "The next time it could have been you that he killed." I started to cry and he put his arm around me and tried to comfort me.

"Dave is there something that you can give her to calm her down. I think that this trial is taking its toll on her." Kyle turned to Dave and Sue who were standing close by.

"Maybe we ought to take her home," Dave suggested.

"No, I want to stay," I demanded.

"But it's taking its toll on you. Stuart can tell you what happens," Dave said to me.

"No, I need to know that justice is being done. I need to hear that they aren't going to hurt anyone that I love anymore," I said gaining control of myself.

"Okay, but if we see that it's really getting you down then we will take you out of the courtroom, Mother," Kyle said with authority in his voice, much like his father.

The jury came back from deliberation finding Deborah-Anne guilty on both charges as an accessory. She was sentenced to thirty years in total. They found Tom guilty of murdering Bill, of attempting to injure me, and guilty of sabotaging the flight. He was sentenced to a total of seventy-five. I bent my head with a sigh or relief. My family was now safe. They took me home and gave me a mild sedative so that I could rest, and as I drifted off to sleep I heard Dave and Stuart talking.

"I always knew that Deborah-Anne disliked

Stephanie; I just never knew how much until today."

"But Stephanie sure got her justice didn't she?" Dave replied.

Chapter Forty-Five

The trial was long behind us and we were now able to look forward to happier times. A group of us went to the island to put it all behind us. I claimed the island for the older generation, telling the younger generation not to even venture near it and they could have it at some later date.

We left the business totally in Kyle's and Jason's hands. They had instructions that Ben or I were only to be contacted if it was a matter of life and death or the business had fallen off the edge of the world. They kidded us that were too old for this kind of time off, and that we wouldn't know what to do with ourselves. We informed them that we might be getting old but we weren't about ready to give up the fun things in life.

The men spent their time fishing while we took the time to swim, read books and just relax. In the evening it was a toss between moonlight cruises and a good old game of cards in front of a roaring fire. Although I still carry a camera with me I now prefer just to take in nature instead of trying to capture it on film. Just to sit on the rocks taking in the sun on my face was so nice now. It doesn't take long for the time to roll around and we soon found that it was time to return to city life.

All of the women got to talking as we packed to go back. We decided that there was no need for us to rush back, and that if the men wanted to go back they could but we would stay for a few more days. Sue suggested that Dave leave their car and drive back with Stuart or Ben. I didn't have to worry about my car since I drove up with Ben and Andrea. Although I could still handle highway driving Kyle preferred that I didn't. The men agreed that they wouldn't mind a little bachelorhood in the city, so we chased them off saying that the next boat load of men was on its way in. I went for a walk with Sue after the men had left.

"You know Stephanie it looks like Kyle and Sabrina might be heading toward marriage," Sue said.

"It looks that way, doesn't it. It's hard to think that he's been going steady with one particular girl," I said with a slight laugh.

"I know we find it hard to believe that about Sabrina."

"Bill would have been happy to see it though. He really liked Sabrina. He always said that she had the spirit in her that would keep a relationship alive."

"That I would have to agree with him, she sure has a spirit. You and Bill had that kind of a relationship, didn't you?"

"Yes, you might say that I always found that the more danger or excitement there was in something, the better I liked it. Bill kept trying to keep me out of the danger." I smiled as I spoke of Bill.

"You miss him a lot don't you?" she said as she looked at me.

"We used to share everything. Even when I came out to shoot pictures of the ducks or the sunsets, he would always come out and join me. It's sometime hard to believe that he is gone. If Kyle and Sabrina have found the same kind of love that we found and that you found with Dave, then they will have a marriage made in heaven." I smiled at her and she smiled back.

We spent the next few days talking, resting and enjoying the fact that it was just the women here. The men went back telling our sons that they were kicked off the island, because they were not satisfactory and that they were being replaced by the next boatload. Kyle and Jason almost killed themselves laughing when they heard that line. We were sitting there in front of the fire when Andrea remarked, "Well, do you think that we have left them on their own for long enough?"

"Starting to miss Ben, are you?" Sue said.

"Well, I don't know about the rest of you but I miss not having Ben in the bed beside me," Andrea responded.

"I don't blame you. It's a heck of a feeling going to bed and realizing that he's not there beside you," I replied.

"Sorry Stephanie," Andrea said in a sad voice.

"Don't worry I'm used to it now," I replied. "Then does everybody agree that we head back to the city tomorrow?"

With everybody in agreement we packed the car and headed back to the city. It was a nice sunny day with a gorgeous blue sky, just a perfect day for driving.

Sue's car was a nice spacious family car which was great. No-one seemed to be cramped for space. We turned onto highway 69. Sue kept to the speed limit since she didn't really like the curves in this road.

"I'm glad that we're coming back in the daylight, I just hate driving on this highway at nighttime. At least in the daytime the rest of you can enjoy the scenery and I can see the traffic better," Sue was saying as she drove.

"I tend to agree with you, there's nothing worse than having a pair of high beam headlights jump out at you in the night or a pair of high beams hitting your mirror from behind," I replied.

I was sitting in the front seat beside her and Andrea and Michelle shared the back seat of the car. We had some fruit and candies in the back seat to munch on as we drove.

"Would you like something up front?" Michelle

asked from the back seat.

"I'll have some candies, thanks," Sue called back.

"If there is an apple left, I will have one of those," I said as I turned to take the things from Michelle. You could feel the car taking the curve in the road. Turning back to my sitting position in my seat, I started to remove the paper off the candy for Sue. I was about to hand the candy over to her, as the car rapidly moved to the left. Sue was desperately trying to avoid a collision with a truck that was headed straight for us. The driver was apparently blinded by the sun as he took a curve. Finally, with the sun out his eyes he gained control of his rig just as Sue was maneuvering behind it. The car caught the edge of the road, the soft shoulder making her lose control. I braced myself for the possible impact by pushing against the dashboard. Andrea and Michelle grabbed the pillows that were in the back seat with them, as the car came to an abrupt stop as it made contact with the granite rocks that border the highway. When the car finally stopped moving, I looked over at Sue. Her head was resting on the steering wheel, there was blood coming from it.

"Sue can you hear me?" I called to her. There was no answer.

"Michelle, Andrea are you okay?" I called back to them.

"Yes I think I'm okay, just a little shaken," Andrea replied.

"Me too," said Michelle..

"Sue's badly hurt." By this time the transport driver had come back to see how we were.

"I've radioed into the police. Is anybody hurt?" "I'll be right back, I'll get an ambulance here too." He left and went back to his rig.

Soon the place was crawling with police; the ambulance took us to the hospital. There, the three of us were checked out for minor injuries from bruises to pulled tendons (from trying to brace ourselves) and a fractured arm that I received from bracing myself on the dashboard. We waited and waited to hear news concerning Sue. We had contacted Dave and he was on his way up with Stuart and Ben. The thought kept running through my head that if only we had left with the men, that we wouldn't be here now.

By the time that Dave arrived with Stuart and Ben they were wheeling Sue out of the emergency. Dave rushed over to her side, as he did the doctor grabbed him by the arm. "What is it? What happened in there? I'm a doctor; I can tell that it's a head injury. What are her chances?" Dave was shooting the questions at the doctor. The doctor put his arm around Dave and led him to the other side of the room. All of a sudden Dave screamed in pain. "No, not her."

Stuart headed over to his friend and put his arms around him. Dave was crying continuously, "Stuart, Sue's slipped into a coma. They say it's only a matter of time. There's nothing that they can do." Stuart helped him into Sue's room and then came back to us.

"Sue's not going to make it, apparently when she hit her head she did quite a bit of damage. She has just slipped into a coma. They say it's just a matter of time." First our faces went into shock and then the tears started to flow. Stuart took both Michelle and I in his arms to comfort us. when we started to calm down a bit, Stuart excused himself to make a phone call.

"Kyle, Stuart here."

"How is everybody, are they okay?" came his reply.

"Your mother, Michelle and Andrea are okay except for some cuts and scrapes."

"What about Sue?"

"Kyle I need you to go to Dave's to inform the

family that Sue hit her head on the steering wheel pretty hard. She's gone into a coma and they don't expect her to live."

"Oh my God, no!"

"We will be staying here and we'll call you later at Dave's."

When we phoned that night, there was still no change in Sue's condition. Their children decided to head up to the hospital and they would be there tomorrow. Kyle brought Sabrina up with him; her eyes were all red from crying. Each one of the children went in to see their mother and as each one came out, they were sobbing loudly. After the last one came out of the room, we heard the call that we didn't want to hear and that was. "Code Blue in Room 314. Code Blue in Room 314."

Our faces all went solemn as we sat and waited till the doctor came back out. Kyle had Sabrina in his arms trying to comfort her as I went to Dave placing my arm around him, I said. "All we can do is pray." When the doctor came out it wasn't the news that we wanted to hear, but then again maybe our prayers had been answered. For had Sue lived, she would have been a vegetable in a coma till it was her turn to go. This way at least her family was saved from long suffering.

Chapter Forty-Six

They say that time has a way of making the hurt go away and that God sends different things into our lives to make the sad times not hurt so much. I found that out the hard way when Bill died and now Dave would have to do the same. Sabrina had Kyle to soften the loss of her mother as did her brother and sisters who had their spouses, but Dave had lost his wife. My door was always opened and he always knew where to find me when the times got too hard.

It had been two years since that fateful day and we were slowly getting on with our lives. I had moved into the mansion and Kyle lived in our house. Kyle phoned me to say that he was coming over for dinner and there would be other guests. I was to tell Anna to set the table for four people and to make something that was special. I don't know what that boy of mine was up to; maybe he was finally going to announce that he and Sabrina were going to get married. No, it couldn't be that, the subject never comes up anymore. Oh well, I guess that I will just have to wait until they arrive then.

As I went downstairs I told Anna to prepare something special for dinner since Kyle was coming and bringing guests along with him. I went into the sitting room and looked out the window at the birds in the trees. When Anna came back from shopping, she set the table with fresh cut flowers and then she went to prepare the meal, singing as she worked. I headed up to my room to get dressed as the time neared that my guests would be arriving. I picked out a lovely lime green outfit to wear along with my white earrings and necklace. Then I headed back downstairs to the family room to wait. Just as I reached the bottom of the stairs, the door bell rang. Opening the door, I found Dave holding a single rose.

"They told me that I was to be here for dinner and that I wasn't to be late," he said as he presented me with the rose and kissed me on the cheek.

"You know that I still have the first rose that you gave me." I blushed. I didn't think that I could still blush. "Do you know what this is about?"

"I have no idea, I haven't been told anything," he replied, as he followed me into the family room.

"I guess then we will have to wait." We sat and chatted about things that were happening and just about things in general. Time was passing and the two of us looked at the clock.

"They're late again," Dave said and with that the front door opened. They were laughing in the other room as they were saying things to each other. Finally, they came through the doorway, the laughter was gone and they were now serious. Kyle came over to where we were sitting. He looked serious.

"I wanted the two of you present so that I didn't have to say what I am about to say twice." He still had a stern look about him. Sabrina was still standing over at the doorway. He had us stumped, if they were going to announce their engagement then why the stern look.

"There has been some speculating in regards to Sabrina and I. Although I thought that with Mother being a lawyer that speculation wasn't allowed in here. We want the speculating to end so that we can get on with our lives." He looked at both of us still with this stern look. "Dave if you would be so kind as to give us your blessing we will be married on June Twenty-Fifth providing that Mother will allow us to have our wedding here in the mansion." He looked from Dave to me and back again to see our reaction. From the smiles on our faces he could only guess what our reaction was.

"Kyle you had us going there for a minute, and yes you have my blessing. I couldn't be happier." Dave stood up and hugged him. Sabrina had now moved over to stand behind Kyle.

"The mansion is yours for that day; you've made me so happy that I could cry." I hugged and kissed Kyle. "Well where is my future daughter-in-law." I called over to Sabrina. She came over. I gave her a big hug and a kiss.

She flashed her hand in front of me, showing off a lovely diamond ring. The diamond heart that was in the center of it sparkled in the light.

"I see that my son has good taste in women and in diamonds. That ring is gorgeous." I looked over toward Kyle with a smile.

"I think this warrants a toast, don't you think so," Dave exclaimed.

"I thought so too, so we stopped on the way and got something just for the occasion." He pulled out a bottle of champagne, and popping the cork he poured the champagne into glasses that Sabrina held out for him.

"To my future wife, the most interesting and beautiful woman in the world." He raised his glass and after taking a sip, kissed Sabrina.

"Hold on there you two, there will be a lot more time for that. Now I have a toast. To the two of you, may you have a marriage like your parents had." Dave raised his glass and touched mine with his.

"To Sabrina for making my son so happy and becoming the daughter that I never had. I couldn't have had one as nice as you," I said.

We finished the bottle of champagne and went into the dining room. Anna served the salad first, then the Cornish hens with young carrots, mashed potatoes, fresh baked rolls and then for dessert, Baked Alaska. We took our tea to the other room. Kyle and Sabrina went for a walk out to the stables. Dave and I sat alone having our tea with a distant look on both of our faces.

"Are you thinking what I am?" I said to him.

"Wouldn't Bill and Sue be happy with this, our two families being joined through our children's marriage?" he replied.

"Uh-huh."

"Who would have thought that when I picked you up for your birthday, that someday we would be here discussing our children's wedding," he chuckled.

"Once we get the two of them back down on earth then we will have to get this wedding organized," I commented.

"I think that they knew they had the best organizer in the world right here in this room when they suggested having it here." He nodded toward me. "I'm sure that you will ensure that it goes off without a hitch."

"I have to admit that it will be nice having it here."

We finally got the two of them to sit down and discuss the wedding plans, finding out their views on different things and making out the guest list. Next, I contacted the caterer, the florists and the minister. We sat for one whole day going over where the actual ceremony was going to happen, what meal would be served, what kind of decorations they wanted. When all was finished Sabrina came over to me, "Stephanie since my mother isn't here to do it, would you come with me while I pick out my wedding dress?" She said quietly.

"If you are sure that you want me to, I would love to," I said with a smile on my face as I embraced her.

I feel that the one thing that women love doing is going shopping for wedding dresses. We went out in the morning and finally left at three after trying on dress after dress. Sabrina chose a beautiful long white dress with a long white veil. They had to do some alteration but would definitely have it ready for the wedding.

    As the day drew closer, time just seemed to fly by. In no time and the caterers were at the door and the flowers had arrived and they started to decorate the house. Down the staircase they were putting white flowers and ribbons along the banister. The chairs were being placed out in the garden area where the actual ceremony would be taking place. The carpet was being laid down from the doorway between the chairs forming the aisle that Sabrina would walk along to a rose covered trellis that they would be married under. Sabrina came to the house early with her bridesmaids and Kyle was staying over at our other house which was actually his house now. Finally, with everything looking perfect, the guests started to arrive and I couldn't believe that my little boy was getting married.

    I wore a turquoise tailored dress, a nice pearl necklace and earrings along with a wide brim hat in a matching colour that I had on at just a slight slant on my head. They led me to my seat and then just as I sat down they started to play here comes the bride. I glanced over at Kyle who was waiting for his bride. Inside the house they had started to come down the staircase, the bridesmaids were dressed in pretty yellow off the shoulders gowns with bouquets of orange and yellow flowers and with baby's breath through their hair. They reached the doorway as Dave dressed in a black tuxedo escorted his princess of a daughter down the stairs. Dressed in a white empire waist joined train that flowed over half the staircase behind her, her neck showed off a simple pearl necklace taking away the openness of the princess style neckline. Her face was covered by a dainty veil that was held on her head with a pearl tiara. In her hand she held a large bouquet of red roses. When they reached the doorway everybody was standing with their eyes on them. Kyle's face lit up as though a light had been turned on inside of his head. Jason whispered to him. "You know there is still time to back out."

"No way! God isn't she beautiful?" he exclaimed.

Finally, they reached the front and the minister started the ceremony. He personalized the ceremony by adding the following; "As long as the two of you continue to enjoy life together, sharing life's ups and downs then you will share a long life together." When he finally announced that they were man and wife and that he could kiss his bride, Kyle took Sabrina in his arms, kissing her with a long passionate kiss. The kiss just seemed to take forever so the minister interrupted them by saying, "Excuse me, but there will be more time for that later."

We started the reception with the meal, starting with a salad and then pheasant under glass was served. The dancing started with Kyle and Sabrina dancing first and then the wedding party and Dave and I joined in later. Dave looked me in the eyes. "Who would ever think that you and I would be dancing together at our children's wedding."

"Yes, who would have ever thought." It was nice to be in his arms again.

We danced several dances together and then Dave said, "It feels nice to have you in my arms again."

"The feeling is mutual," I replied. "Would you like to go for a walk?"

"Okay." We started to go out of the house. It didn't matter that we had decided to go for a walk; since the wedding party wasn't just staying in the house but seemed to be everywhere on the grounds.

"I knew we always had something special, something that kept us close together, but now doesn't it seem ironic that our families are now joined by our children," I said to him.

"I often thought that when we were young that we would end up married to each other," he said softly.

"So did I, but I guess that it wasn't meant to be."

We went back into the house where Kyle and Sabrina were now standing at the top of the stairs. All the eligible girls were standing at the base of the staircase as Sabrina turned around and threw the bouquet. There were fumbling hands as the bouquet emerged in the hands of Sabrina's maid of honour Jean. Now it was Kyle's turn. Slowly taking off the garter off Sabrina's shapely leg, he slung it down at the crowd of eligible bachelors. Suddenly Tim jumped up with it in his hand.

Kyle and Sabrina came down the stairs to say good-bye to everyone before they started their honeymoon in Hawaii. We were the last ones to say good-bye to them as they got into the limousine. We held each one of them with tears in our eyes and we told them to have a great time. As the limousine pulled away, Dave and I held each other as we watched our babies start their new lives together.

Chapter Forty-Seven

Through Kyle and Sabrina's wedding our two families had become quite close. Dave and I now went to the island just to get away from all of them sometimes. We had nothing now that we really needed to tend to in the city. I still had my business, but that was all and those things I could handle when I felt like it.

We seemed to be have been given a second chance to be enjoy a life together that we started so long ago, and we were now taking advantage of it. This was one of those times that we arrived up at the island. Over the time that we had started to share things once again, he taught me to fish and I taught him how to enjoy nature.

"Dave do you think things would have been different had we eventually married?" I asked him as we were out in the boat fishing.

"Sure, we wouldn't be here now. We wouldn't have the pleasure of watching our children and grandchildren grow up," he replied.

"Why do you think that we got separated way back then?"

` "I think that we both needed other people in our lives to grow," he said with a smile. "Now if you don't watch it we won't have any fish for dinner tonight."

"We definitely need to be quiet for this?"

"Pretty quiet."

With that my rod was pulled down into the water. "Dave help."

"Here let me take it." He was killing himself laughing as he looked at me trying to hold onto the rod.

He took the rod and after a nice fight with the fish finally landed a nice five pound bass. "Well I guess that we have dinner after all." He took the fish when we docked the boat and cleaned it and cooked it. He may have got me to catch it, but that is as far as it went. He still cleans and cooks the fish that we catch.

Later as the evening started to set in we headed out for a walk. It was such a beautiful night; everything was so peaceful that you could hear the crickets and the water lapping up against the rocks. The sky was clear with the stars starting to draw their pictures as the sky started to darken. Rising just over the hills was the most gorgeous full moon, the second one for this month, what they called a blue moon. It is so clear that you could see the craters on it and on the water she was laying a train of gold.

Standing with Dave's arms around my shoulder, I said. "Imagine Dave that all this chaos started with a full moon."

"Yes, and if Lady Luck has anything to do with it then maybe history will repeat itself." Dave was referring to the fact that Kyle and Sabrina were expecting their first child this month. It seems like they wasted no time on their honeymoon either.

"You know that they say that I got my strength from the full moon the day that I was born."

"I thought that it was your mysteriousness that you got from it." He laughed and hugged me tighter.

"Just think that we never got to share a child together, but now we are sharing a grandchild."

"If this one happens to be born while this full moon is up, does that mean that it will be as crazy as it's Grandmother?"

"I don't know about crazy, but if it happens while this blue moon is out then it should be stronger then I ever was, not only that but the legacy will continue," I said looking at him.

"That mean's a lot to you doesn't it?" He looked at me with concern.

"It's everything that I have ever worked for. Just think Dave this child will have all my qualities plus Sabrina's ways. Between the two of us that child already has power and strength, the urge to travel, and the will to do what it wants." My eyes flashed in the moonlight.

"Poor Kyle, Bill and I had a hard enough time with you." He laughed, hugged me and then kissed me on the forehead. "Come on let's get back." We sat in front of a roaring fire looking at old photo albums and reminiscing about the past. After a while, we went and settled in bed for the night. We now shared a bed, for although we never would marry we knew that Bill and Sue would understand our actions.

Lying in his arms usually made falling to sleep easy and although Dave had already fallen to sleep, it just didn't seem to be that easy for me tonight. I slowly slipped out from under his arm and walked out to the kitchen to prepare some hot milk with a dash of rye in it to help me sleep. As I walked with my cup I caught sight of the moon, it seemed to be calling to me. I sat out on a chair on the deck just watching it. Off in a distance I heard the phone ring and Dave talking.

"You have a lovely Granddaughter, Kathleen Laura MacGregor just arrived," Kyle exclaimed to Dave.

"Congratulations! I'm sure that your mother and I will be there tomorrow."

Dave came out behind me as I looked at the moon.

"We have a Granddaughter, Kathleen." Dave said as he bent over and gave me a kiss. I smiled back up at the moon. My dreams had been answered. My legacy would continue.

The End

ISBN 1425178936

9 781425 178932